ARRIUS IS FACED WITH THE MOST FATEFUL DECISION OF HIS LIFE WHEN EMPEROR ANTONINUS PIUS PLANS TO EXTEND THE EMPIRE'S BORDER IN BRITANNIA NORTH OF HADRIAN'S WALL.

"On the contrary, Arrius, if you're fortunate enough to see the sun rise tomorrow, it will be you who will be on the way to Eboracum — in chains, I might add. Guards seize him by order of Tribune Quintarius. Marcus Arrius, I place you under arrest for conspiring against the empire of Rome."

At the fort called Banna, one of 14 forts on Hadrian's Wall, Marcus Arrius begins the slow process of turning around a dispirited and ineffective Tungrian Cohort stationed there. His efforts are made more challenging, and dangerous, by the hatred and jealousy of Matius Betto, the centurion he replaced as commander. It does not take long for Betto and Tribune Tiberius Quinterius to combine efforts to discredit Arrius. In time, Arrius gains the respect and loyalty of the officers and legionaries at Banna with the exception of a few disgruntled officers who remain committed to Betto. His malaise caused by the brutality of the Judaean war dissipates as his relationship with Ilya deepens when she becomes pregnant with their child. However, it is Ilya who becomes the unwitting means for Quinterius and Betto to accomplish their objective when her heritage and kinship to Beldorach, High Chieftain of the Selgovae are revealed.

"ARRIUS-Legacy is a fast-paced novel set in the early days of the Roman Wall. Full of action with twists and turns it is an exciting read. It is hard to put down. The detail to the period is remarkable and it is very accurate when dealing with both the Roman Army and the tribes who lived north of the wall. The ending leaves the door wide open for the third in this very enjoyable series."—*Griff Hosker, author of the Anarchy and Dragonheart book series.*

"Preston Holtry's *ARRIUS* Volume 2, *Legacy*, is a smash hit. Disillusioned with how the Roman Empire handled the war in Judaea, Arrius requested a new assignment about as far away from Rome as possible. He's taken to his new duties well, but speaking his mind continues to get him into trouble with his superiors and with the commander he replaced. The bright side to his current posting is Ilya, a Selgovae woman, and her son, Joric."—*Randy Krzak, author of The Kurdish Connection*

"If you enjoyed Volume 1 of the ARRIUS series: *Sacramentum,* you won't be disappointed by the next installment—*Legacy*. The same meticulous research and storytelling will immerse you into the ancient world and have you anxiously anticipating Volume 3."— *William Francis, author of The Katie Dugan Case.*

"Preston Holtry's *Legacy,* the second volume of his *Arrius* Trilogy, is simply excellent historical fiction, marked by memorable and complex characters, strong dialogue, and impeccable research. Preston depicts expertly the period's robust muscle, when Rome sought to maintain its hold of early Britannia."—*John Vance, author of Echoes of November and Awake the Southern Wind*

ARRIUS

VOLUME II

LEGACY

Preston Holtry

Moonshine Cove Publishing, LLC

Abbeville, South Carolina U.S.A.

FIRST MOONSHINE COVE EDITION APRIL 2018

This book is a work of fiction. Names, characters, places and incidents are products of the author's imagination or are used fictitiously. Any resemblance to actual events, locales or persons, living or dead, is entirely coincidental.

ISBN: 978-1-945181-34-4

Library of Congress Control Number: 2017945635

Copyright © 2018 by Preston Holtry

For Lee, my son and my legacy

Acknowledgment

To some extent, any writer of credible historical fiction depends on the historian and their works presenting historical detail and context by which to weave an entertaining tale. There are several authors who helped me draw inspiration and fact for a better understanding of the Romans and Brythonic Tribes. In particular, I want to acknowledge the scholarly works of two authors, whom I found to be especially helpful in understanding the Roman Army and the auxilia. Graham Webster's Roman Imperial Army of the First and Second Centuries A.D. offers detailed insights on every aspect of Roman military life including descriptions of armor, weapons, clothing, food, customs and religious beliefs. Edward N. Luttwak and his book The Grand Strategy of the Roman Empire from the First Century A.D. to the Third provided a much appreciated background regarding Roman organization, imperial strategy, tactics, mobility and so much more. Julius Caesars's The Gallic War, translated by H. J. Edwards, provided additional and near contemporary descriptions of the warfare, appearance and customs of the Britannian tribes that Arrius would have found quite similar. Other scholarly works I found helpful in capturing the second century of the Roman Empire are listed in the bibliography at the end of the novel.

I created the map for Britannia from a terrain map obtained off the internet from maps-for-free.com.

I deeply appreciate the work and toil by my wife, Judy, Bruce and Henry Filer and Don Ayers, D, Ed for the time they spent contributing ideas, needed criticism and trolling for the inevitable typos that often defy discovery before publication but are certain to be found by the reader.

My thanks to Jama Jurabaev who generously allowed the use of his stunning painting of a Roman officer on a horse featured on the jacket cover.

And thank you Moonshine Cove for continuing the saga of Marcus Junius Arrius.

About The Author

Preston Holtry is the author of the Morgan Westphal period mystery  series and the ARRIUS trilogy. He has a BA degree in English from the Virginia Military Institute and a graduate degree from Boston University. A career army officer, he served twice in Vietnam in addition to a variety of other infantry and intelligence-related assignments in Germany, England, and the United States. Retired from the army with the rank of colonel, he lives with his wife, Judith, in Oro Valley, Arizona with much of his time now spent writing the next novel. Holtry is the author of four published mystery novels set in the Southwest during the period 1915-17 featuring the private detective Morgan Westphal.

Read more about his interests and writing approach at his website: http://www.presholtry.webs.com.

Preface

Since the novel's background is focused on the Roman Auxilia (awks ilia) rather than a Roman Legion, it might be helpful to the reader to know something about this extension of the Roman Army and how these units differed from the regular legion in size, organization, use and equipment. The Auxilia refers to the non-Roman forces that frequently manned the frontiers. Comprised of native tribesman representing nearly every province in the Roman Empire, these forces were essential in supplementing the legions along the frontiers with the primary mission of guarding the frontier, conducting patrols and participating in campaigns as necessary. Most often the auxilia were the first echelon of defense with the legions as the secondary and main offensive force. In the early years of the empire, there was no Roman cavalry; consequently, native auxilia provided this capability.

The *auxilia* cavalry *ala* was organized into *turmae* (troops). The term *ala* (wing) was used as the cavalry was used primarily to screen the flanks of the infantry. Cavalrymen wore boots with spurs, a lighter cuirass and carried a longer sword (*spatha*). Their shields were considerably smaller and round instead of the rectangular, curved shield of the foot soldier. In addition to the sword all cavalrymen wore, some were also armed with small javelins or darts carried in a quiver attached to the saddle. Other cavalrymen carried longer spears that were not thrown but were used to jab downward. The saddle during the period had four pommels that helped to maintain a firm seat since there were no stirrups. Stirrups were not used until sometime in the fourth or fifth century.

The mixed cavalry and infantry were called the *cohortes equitata* designated as *quingenaria* (500 strong) or *milaria* (1000 strong). Infantry only cohorts were organized (into centuries) and equipped much like their Roman counterparts in terms of armor, clothing and footgear. Notable differences might be in the different helmets they wore which resembled a medieval conical helmet rather than the larger rimmed helmet with cheekguards common to the Roman Legion. Another difference was in the oval shield they carried in contrast to the square curved shield with the painted thunderbolt design distinctive to the legions.

Auxilia forces were both recruited and conscripted — conscription was common following a local rebellion and allowed native tribesmen to avoid slavery or death by agreeing to serve in the auxilia. It was the policy to relocate indigenous troops to locations along the Roman frontiers in other than their own tribal lands. The latter provided further assurance against continued internal rebellion. In Britannia, legionaries from Tungria (northern Belgium) and Hispania (Spain) and many other Roman provinces garrisoned the forts along Hadrian's Wall. The legions generally remained behind the line of auxiliary forces as reinforcing elements to the frontier lines. This policy also left legionary forces available for vexillations (detachment or century-level) to reinforce other parts of the empire where border incursion or local rebellions threatened or had to be contained. It was common for auxilia tribesmen after serving a long period in another province to remain there as permanent settlers following their military commitment.

While the auxilia was an essential military capability for Rome, it's also true it was generally looked down upon by those serving in a legion in terms of their perceived effectiveness. Roman officers assigned to the auxilia probably felt they were serving in a lesser capacity than the prestige of being assigned to a legion. The potential for serving in the auxilia for native tribesmen was the incentive of becoming a Roman citizen (never guaranteed) after 25 years.

The glossary at the end of the novel can assist the reader in pronunciation and definition of Roman terms used and identification of place names cited in the novel.

PH, Oro Valley, AZ

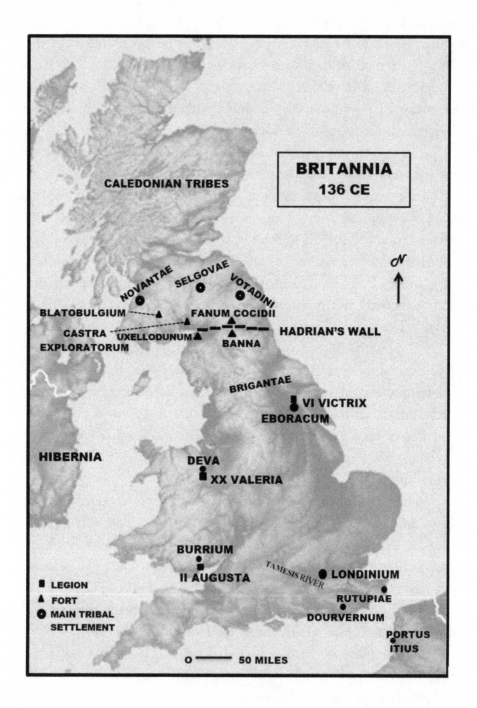

Map of Britannia 136 CE

Summary of *Sacramentum* Volume 1, The ARRIUS Trilogy (PCN 2017945635, ISBN 0781945181160)

The year is 135 CE and Marcus Junius Arrius is a 25-year veteran of the Roman Army and the senior centurion of the XXII Legion, *Deiotariana* engaged in defeating the latest Jewish rebellion in Judaea. Without understanding why, Arrius is troubled by the carnage and brutality of the war. While the savagery on both sides is nothing new in his lifetime serving the legions, this conflict is somehow different. The fanaticism of the Jews in their efforts to win freedom from Rome puzzles him while the raw behavior of the legionaries he commands begins to disgust him as they disembowel Jewish dead looking for gems and gold coins. His precarious relationship with General Gallius, the legion commander, does not help. Gallius is insecure and resents Arrius's leadership abilities even while he feels dependent on the centurion. Arrius believes the General is both inept and detached from the reality of how to fight the war. Tiberias Querinius, the legion's senior tribune, seeking to curry favor with Gallius, plots to have Arrius killed; the plot fails. Arrius is convinced the tribune was behind the attempt.

With the drawn-out Judaean War undermining the will of Rome, Hadrian himself goes to Judaea and appoints General Vitellus Turbo as field commander to bring a quick end to the conflict. Turbo, a close friend of Arrius, develops a plan in which the *Deiotariana* Legion becomes the unknowing bait to lure the Jewish Army into consolidating its forces in a decisive battle to end the rebellion. During the ensuing battle in the Sorek Valley, Gallius proves his worth as a commander but is killed. When Arrius seeks out Querinius to inform him that he is now in command, the tribune is cowering in the medical tent. Soon after, Arrius is badly wounded. By order of the emperor, both Querinius and Arrius are awarded a coveted gold torque in recognition of their heroic actions. Turbo visits Arrius in the hospital and offers him a position anywhere in the empire including command of the prestigious Praetorian Guard in Rome. Disillusioned, Arrius instead chooses an independent command in Britannia as far from Rome as he can go. As he leaves Judaea by ship, he removes the torque and throws it into the sea as a tangible way to put the Jewish war and his own growing malaise behind him.

In Britannia, Arrius visits Eboracum where the VI Legion *Victrix*, responsible for command of Hadrian's Wall, is headquartered. He is shocked to find his command of Banna, one of fourteen wall forts, is subordinate to Tiberias Querinius. Upon his arrival at Banna, he sees two legionaries assaulting a woman and a young boy. He rescues Ilya and her son Joric, but his intervention is met with angry hostility rather than gratitude. His first impression of Banna and the centurions leading the Tungrian garrison is no more promising. Matius Betto, the centurion who has been interim commander, makes clear Arrius has his work cut out for him to earn the loyalty of his centurions and to turn around a command suffering from low morale and prolonged neglect.

Realizing her initial reaction toward Arrius was unfair, Ilya goes to the fort to apologize; this meeting does nothing to abate their mutual antagonism. In time, Arrius has second thoughts about the beautiful native woman and spontaneously visits her. Their third meeting finds them both ready to seek common ground. For the first time since coming to Britannia, Arrius begins to look forward to a future rather than dwelling on a past he has yet to understand.

ARRIUS VOL II

LEGACY

Chapter 1
I36 CE

Arrius was tired. The days had been long, and sleep was a luxury snatched a few hours at a time. From experience, he knew this was the critical period to transform the Tungrian Cohort into some semblance of a fighting unit with the capability of doing more than performing guard duty on the Wall. Fighting formations were practiced on the training field followed by century-size patrols conducted both south and north of the Wall. At first, Decrius and Rufus accompanied all patrols to ensure their recent battle experience was passed on to the legionaries who hadn't gone to Judaea. Arrius planned to accompany each cavalry troop at least once during overnight patrols to better assess their capabilities; the two troops he rode with so far proved their worth, and he was optimistic the remaining one would prove as proficient. In comparison to the infantry, the cavalry contingent at Banna was far more field-ready.

Unfortunately, it was with most of the centurions he felt little change had taken place because of remaining loyalty to Betto, Banna's former commander. Its effects were corrosive and left Arrius feeling uneasy key officers could not be depended upon when put to the test. The indicators were manifested in the way many of the officers responded unenthusiastically to his orders, executing them correctly but with no indication of willingness to extend their efforts beyond what was ordered.

He kept waiting for Betto to say or do something egregious enough to justify transferring him elsewhere, but the centurion never allowed an opportunity to occur when either his competence or loyalty might be legitimately called into question. On the surface, Betto appeared to be the one officer who went out of his way to follow his orders quickly and thoroughly; however, he didn't trust Betto and thought it was unlikely he ever would. He knew eventually something said or done by one of them would precipitate a final resolution essential for maintaining a cohesive, effective unit. Until then, he would keep his senior centurion under close observation.

While Arrius was used to the harsh disciplinary measures and punishment common in the Roman Army, he saw Betto's methods as unnecessarily brutal. Arrius used the most severe measures at his disposal sparingly and selectively. On occasion, he had no choice but to impose a harsh penalty for a serious offense. The day before, he sentenced a legionary found sleeping on guard duty to undergo the *fustuarium,* an almost certain death sentence. Although the offender was paid by another legionary to stand an extra relief, fatigue wasn't an excuse sufficient to mitigate the sentence now about to be carried out.

Arrius waited impatiently for Antius Durio, the cohort's chief administrative officer, to notify him all legionaries not on guard were assembled along the length of the via principalis to witness the punishment. The legionaries from the condemned man's century were assigned to carry out the sentence. The legionary who paid the condemned man to take his shift would be given 50 lashes.

Antius Durio finally arrived. "Praefectus, a signal from Camboglanna has just been received," referring to the fort ten miles to the west and midway between Banna and Uxellodonum. "General Arvinnius arrived there approximately an hour ago. He'll remain a few hours at Camboglanna to inspect the garrison before coming to Banna. He plans to stay the night here before continuing his inspection of the eastern Wall. Do you want to postpone the punishment formation?"

"No, there's yet time, and the two legionaries are reconciled to their fate. Is the cohort assembled?"

"It is, Praefectus."

Arrius followed Durio through the headquarters and considered what needed to be done to prepare for the legion commander's arrival. He estimated they would have an hour after Arvinnius's departure from Camboglanna to assemble the cavalry troop not on patrol and all centuries not on guard duty in parade formation and ready for inspection. Without knowing the general's preferences, he assumed he'd be interested in those things any commander might be concerned with. He would have liked another week to prepare, but at least the changes he considered essential had been made.

Arrius mounted Ferox and walked the horse to the intersection of the fort's two main streets. He reined in the black stallion and waited for the guard detail to bring the two prisoners forward. The legionaries flanking either side of the wide street linking the east and west gates stood silently waiting for the punishment to commence. The centurions were positioned at intervals to ensure only cudgels were used. The legionaries who were to carry out the sentence were cautioned not to hold back out of sympathy or friendship. He knew on a few rare occurrences the condemned legionary survived the gauntlet.

There was a stir in the two facing ranks of legionaries as the guard detail emerged from the doorway of the nearest barracks. The two men to be punished were stripped to their linen underdrawers. The legionary to receive only lashes had his arms tied to a stout pole stretched across his shoulders. He noted with approval both men, ashen-faced, walked toward him without having to be dragged.

Arrius said in a commanding voice, "Officers and legionaries of the Second Cohort, you are assembled here to witness the punishment of two men who failed in their duty to the cohort and to Rome." Then looking at the prisoners, he asked, "Does either of you ask for relief or clemency?"

The legionaries both chorused, "Yes!"

Arrius directed his attention to the ranks of legionaries. "A request for clemency has been requested. Didius is to receive 50 lashes. Should the punishment be reduced?"

A roar of approval echoed throughout the fort along with shouted numbers. "So be it, let the number of lashes be reduced to 25. Sitorix has been condemned to the fustuarium. Should the sentence be reduced to flogging?"

There was an angry uproar, a response he expected. Sleeping on guard was possibly the worst offense known as the lapse potentially jeopardized the entire unit. Even staunch friendships ended when such dereliction occurred.

"Guard detail, give Didius 25 lashes."

An optio stepped forward and uncoiled a whip. Two legionaries forced the prisoner to his knees and grasped each end of the pole to prevent the man from moving. For the first few blows, there was no sound to be heard except the hissing of the whip followed by a sharp smack as it hit bare flesh. By the time the fifth blow landed, Didius was grunting with each successive strike and soon gave way to a continuous moan. Arrius surveyed the faces of the legionaries nearest him. With the widespread inclination for gambling common in the legions and auxilia, he was certain there were wagers placed on how the flogged man would bear up under the punishment. He saw Betto staring with rapt attention at the victim's bleeding back and was disgusted at the obvious enjoyment the centurion seemed to have watching the bloody spectacle.

When the last blow was delivered, the legionary's silence affirmed he was unconscious as the guards carried him to the infirmary. Arrius nodded to the optio, and Sitorix was escorted to the east gate. The ranks of legionaries remained silent as the condemned man walked unaided between his guards. Arrius recalled a few men similarly condemned lost their manhood, soiling themselves with fright and embarrassing all who bore witness. Shameful exhibitions were more often than not met with prolonged suffering. By contrast, the majority who accepted their fate bravely were certain to die mercifully. It appeared Sitorix would meet his gods quickly.

Moments later there was a crescendo of noise as Sitorix started running toward the west gate. He went down first no more than ten paces from where he started. Arrius silently urged the man to regain his feet. Sitorix not only stood up but sprinted vigorously down the street, blood cascading down one side of his face from a glancing blow that left a flap of his scalp hanging down across his forehead. As the legionary approached the mid-point of the gauntlet, he was obviously in great pain. The slower he went, the more blows he received. He fell again nearly opposite where Arrius sat astride Ferox. For a moment, it appeared he wouldn't be able to get up. One legionary administered blow after blow, the dull meaty sound of his cudgel making contact with flesh and bone loud enough to be heard over the shouting of the legionaries. Miraculously, Sitorix managed to regain his feet and stagger a few more steps before falling for the last time. A dozen legionaries encircled the prone man and took turns administering the final blows.

Arrius immediately directed his attention to Antius Durio standing next to Ferox, the drama of the bloody punishment already dismissed from his mind.

"Signal the mile forts General Arvinnius is conducting an inspection of the Wall and to prepare for inspection. I'll meet him at the western mile fort and escort him to Banna. Inform Betto and Durmius Lucillus they have two hours to prepare the fort, legionaries, barracks and stables for the general's inspection. All cavalry and legionaries not on guard will stand formation inside the fort as soon as the western mile fort signals we've departed. Send a messenger to Seugethis to come to Banna with a troop. There's a possibility the general will go to Fanum Cocidii. If so, Seugethis will escort him there and back."

An hour later, Arrius exited the west gate and cantered toward Banna's western most mile fort, stopping briefly at each of the signal towers and mile forts in between long enough to ensure all were in ready in case Arvinnius decided to stop for a quick inspection. By the time he reached his destination, he was satisfied Arvinnius would find nothing amiss at Banna's western garrisons.

Chapter 2

Despite his extreme reluctance to come to Britannia, Tiberius
Querinius thought the impressive ceremonies marking his arrival had
been both appropriate to the occasion and justifiable recognition of his
importance. The presence of Gaius Labinius Arvinnius, general and
commander of VI Legion, *Victrix* was an additional honor. He wore
with great pride the torque Turbo presented him following the battle in
the Sorek Valley; he reveled in the admiration and yes, envy, he
fancied he saw in those who saw it. He was certain even General
Arvinnius cast admiring looks at the neck decoration. After all, a high
valor award bestowed by specific direction of the emperor was
recognition few ever achieved in the Roman Army, even after an
extended military career.

In only a few days, the initial grandeur of the moment was replaced
by the reality of his surroundings and situation. Not only was he on
the extreme edge of the empire under conditions physically
unpleasant, he was once again confronted by the specter of his own
fears. The briefings he received and the discussions with the legion
commander made it clear the question of hostilities with the local
tribes was more a matter of when, not if. At first, he harbored the
thought he would fulfill his command responsibilities mainly in the
comparative comfort and safety of Uxellodonum. The notion was
quickly dispelled when General Arvinnius said he expected his
commanders to spend time north of the Wall and to assess firsthand
rather than relying exclusively on patrol reports. He also realized his
responsibilities included more than Uxellodonum, extending as they
did to the western third of the frontier defense.

General Arvinnius was another matter. Querinius knew little of the
man other than he was a long-serving senator who preferred legionary
duty to the politics of Rome. Initially, the legion commander struck
him as old and long past his prime even though he knew him to be
only ten years his senior. Tall, lean and naturally taciturn, his
prematurely white hair was combed forward over a receding hairline.
His prominent nose was hawk-like. Querinius already surmised his
first impression of Arvinnius as a benign, non-threatening presence

was incorrect. The general's piercing eyes reminded him of a raptor silently waiting for its prey to make a mistake or show weakness. He realized he might be the prey. He was preparing to leave to inspect the forts east of Uxellodonum as far as Banna when Arvinnius sent an orderly requesting his presence. He was caught completely off guard by what the general said to him.

Arvinnius was waiting for him as he entered the large commander's office in the principia, the same office destined to be his when the general departed. Querinius sat down and began to feel increasingly uncomfortable under the general's studied gaze and prolonged silence. He felt he was standing on the edge of an abyss, and Arvinnius was prepared at any moment to push him over the edge.

Without preamble, Arvinnius said, "Querinius, I don't know what to make of you. You're either the soldier Turbo thought you were, or you're very adept at playing the part of one." Querinius forced himself to remain impassive assuming a look of concern. He hoped when he spoke, his voice or expression would not betray his uncertainty.

"General, I don't understand what you mean."

"You have the credentials, and you assure me you're eager to be here. But my impression is you'd rather be back in Rome. That alone does not condemn you. Most of the officers on the frontier think as much, and occasionally when the icy winds blow, I, too, miss a warmer climate. Duty here on this frontier for almost anyone is unpleasant at best; therefore, you need not pretend with me you're happy to be here or conceal ambition as the sole reason you came to Britannia. Querinius, I'm a realist. If it's true you're here because you're ambitious, I approve. I understand ambition. I not only understand it, I applaud it. I want my officers to be selfishly ambitious because I know they'll do their duty to obtain what most of us want — advancement and the power that goes with it. Forget the nonsense about serving for the glory of Rome and the emperor. I prefer a more practical and tangible motivation in my officers. I'm ambitious, and it has served me well. Opportunity and the success following will come to those clever enough and bold enough to go after it. Let it be your challenge, and you'll be successful — if you're willing to do whatever is necessary to achieve it." Arvinnius regarded Querinius silently with a searching look before continuing.

"You seem intelligent enough, and you ask the right questions. I also believe you grasp the essence of why we are here and the military necessities of your position. Then why do I have doubts about you?"

Querinius was riveted to his chair filled with self-righteous indignation. It was outrageous this old man would question his capabilities even if it echoed his own, similar concerns. He reminded himself he was a hero of Rome, and the proof of his heroism encircled his neck. He unconsciously reached up to finger the torque, as he often did, to assure himself the award was not a figment of his own imagination. He realized Arvinnius noticed the gesture. He straightened up, his confidence restored after touching the cold metal.

About the time he thought the lecture was over, Arvinnius said, "What troubles me is I don't know exactly why I have doubts about you."

"General Arvinnius, I've no idea what I've said or done to give you cause for concern. My record should be ample proof of both my character and my capabilities. I don't believe General Turbo had any reservations on either account when he commended me to the emperor for my actions in Judaea. Surely the recognition I received is enough to assure you of my qualifications and abilities."

"I wasn't there when those actions took place, Tribune; consequently, I've no opinion on the worthiness of your recognition in Judaea. I've soldiered enough to know not to place too much importance in such things probably because I happen to have received two such baubles as you wear around your neck, which you seem fond of admiring. Take care, Tribune, you do not fall prey to the delusion you have achieved god-like grandeur because of it. Only the emperor is entitled to such homage."

Querinius felt his face growing red, embarrassed Arvinnius called attention to his vanity. He hated Arvinnius for humiliating him, and he hated Turbo for having placed him in this situation. He began to feel as if he was suffocating, and the chill of the room did nothing to stop the perspiration further betraying his agitation. He groped for the words to persuade Arvinnius he was being misjudged.

"I ask you to seek reassurance from General Turbo who recommended me for this assignment."

"Aye, he did, and his recommendation is all that prevents me from sending you back to Rome. I owe Turbo, and I suppose you as well, the chance to prove my concerns are unfounded. As for verifying your fitness with Turbo in more detail, unfortunately, it's no longer possible. According to the dispatch I received two days ago, Turbo was executed by order of the emperor more than four weeks past."

Querinius was shocked. Had anyone else other than General Arvinnius made such a statement, he would have doubted the truth of it. It was widely known Turbo's friendship was among a select few Hadrian maintained long after he became Caesar. Perhaps the whispered rumor Hadrian's mental health was deteriorating was true, and perhaps Turbo's execution was proof of it. Well, I for one will not mourn Turbo's death, he thought. Possibly if Turbo had been killed sooner, he wouldn't be here and forced to endure Arvinnius's assault on the already crumbling walls of his self-confidence.

"So there you have it, Querinius. I'm forced to give you the benefit of the doubt for the time being. It will be up to you to prove I'm wrong and dispel whatever lingering misgivings I have. I wish you well, Tribune, for I want the assurance of knowing the northwest sector of the frontier is in capable hands." Arvinnius stood up signaling the meeting was over. "Enough of this. Let's be on our way. You'll accompany me as far as Banna. I'm anxious to meet Arrius, the praefectus who is also newly arrived from Judaea. Perhaps you know him?"

Querinius was too stunned at first to realize the general was looking at him strangely. He flushed and stammered an apology blaming his concentration on the points the general made for his inattention.

"I recall Arrius very well. He was the primus pilus of the *Deotariana* Legion." Querinius was working hard to keep his voice casual. "He's a seasoned centurion and well-deserving of promotion to praefectus."

Arvinnius stood. "Come, Querinius, let's be on our way. I'm curious to form my own opinion of how worthy Arrius may be. I'll leave you at Banna to continue my inspection of the middle and eastern sectors before returning to Eboracum."

As the two men joined the escort already assembled, Querinius thought about what Arvinnius said to him. He decided he almost missed the point of the message. Arvinnius was not really questioning whether he was stalwart enough. It was all about doubting whether he was sufficiently ruthless and unprincipled to do whatever was necessary. If that was how Arvinnius equated ambition then he believed the legion commander would in time be exceedingly pleased with Uxellodonum's new commander. The more he thought about it, the more he was convinced he and General Arvinnius may not be so different after all. His main concern still remained the threat of Arrius choosing to tell Arvinnius the truth of his behavior in the Sorek Valley.

Chapter 3

Beldorach's return was not greeted with great enthusiasm. He didn't have any reason to expect a warm reception, and he confirmed it almost as soon as he walked into the tribe's main settlement. The word spread quickly there was to be no agreement with the Briganti, dashing any hope of a major spring offensive against the Romans.

Spurred on by some of the more volatile clan members, the tribal elders were convinced an alliance among the northern tribes alone would be enough to successfully attack the Romans. Beldorach knew differently and so did Bothan, the High Chieftain of the Novanti. He discounted Darach of the Votadini as too weak and indecisive to make a difference one way or the other. No, without the Briganti there was no chance of defeating the Romans, and to attempt to do so without their assistance was folly. He would have to continue the small-scale raids and ambushes on Roman outposts and patrols. Such attacks accomplished nothing more than placing a temporary check on the mindless clamor for battle for the sake of battle. He had seen enough of Rome's capabilities and resolute behavior in combat to understand even with an alliance of all the tribes, it would be difficult to end Roman occupation. He hated the Romans but was compelled to acknowledge their superior fighting ability. He concluded long ago defeating the Romans was no longer a realistic objective, but keeping alive the belief they could be was essential at least to prevent further encroachment. Even more to the point, it would provide the opportunity to achieve his goal of uniting the tribes under one leader, and he was determined unification would be under his leadership. The Romans would be the means to accomplish this objective. United under his banner, the northern tribes would be a serious threat to Rome.

His thoughts were interrupted by a sudden draft stirring the embers of the fire in the center of the circular dwelling causing the narrow column of smoke to swirl as it disappeared through the hole in the thatched roof above. Beldorach looked up and saw Athdara, his principal wife, enter bearing a wooden platter heaped with cuts of meat from the boar he killed a few hours ago. He watched silently as she knelt gracefully and began to thread the meat onto metal rods before carefully positioning the skewers near the glowing coals. Even with strands of grey in her hair and faint wrinkles at the corner of her eyes, she was still a remarkably beautiful woman.

Athdara was many years older than his other two wives, but to him she was still the most favored. There would not have been anyone else but her except for the question of an heir. No matter how often they joined their bodies or the intervention of the priests muttering their incantations and administering noxious potions, it became apparent to both of them Athdara was barren. Instead of casting her off as was his right and as the tribe expected, he kept her at his side unwilling to part with her even though the council of elders more than hinted Athdara was fast becoming a tribal liability.

At the urging of Athdara herself, he took a second wife. Then two years later, he took still another in an effort to get a son or even a daughter. The Selgovi attached no importance to gender in maintaining the royal line. To his dismay, there was still no issue, and he reluctantly concluded no matter how many times he coupled, he would be denied the heir he so desperately wanted and the tribe needed. He already heard oblique comments referring to Ilya and her proven ability to bear a child. The possibility existed the council would ask him and the priests to forgive Ilya and invite her to return. While it didn't necessarily mean he would have to step aside as High Chieftain, if he remained unable to produce an heir, he might be pressured to do so.

Athdara saw he had removed his tunic and heavy sheepskin vest in the warmth of the windowless hut. From the corner of her eye, she covertly watched him and admired the corded muscles of his arms and chest and the elaborate design of the blue tattoos covering his arms and torso. She was pleased when it was her he first took to bed after his return. To be sure, since then he had lain with Cadha and Machara, but she was satisfied he did so in the belief it was duty and obligation not love for the other two women that motivated the coupling. Even though she always assured him otherwise, she secretly resented sharing Beldorach. The familiar sound of lovemaking behind the screen serving as the only privacy for the conjugal bed was hateful to her ears when she wasn't the one in it.

The quiet was interrupted by someone pounding on the door accompanied by a voice demanding entry. Beldorach smiled when he realized it was Tearlach, his oldest friend and staunchest ally within the tribe. The small, wiry man was intensely loyal, a quality Beldorach prized most given the undercurrent of intrigue he dealt with as a natural consequence of his position. Tearlach's one fault was an inability to restrain his impulsiveness, a trait making him an asset on a battlefield but occasionally a liability elsewhere, especially when it came to preserving nominal truces Beldorach periodically arranged with the Novanti and Votadini. Tearlach's fondness for stealing horses from the other tribes was not about the desire to own more horses since he already possessed more than he would ever need. Rather, he was motivated by the challenge of the deed without consideration of any consequences.

Tearlach entered and took a seat on the bearskin opposite his host eyeing the cooking meat as he did so. Beldorach never ceased to be amazed at his friend's voracious appetite. For a man who was a head shorter than most of the other Selgovan men, his capacity for food was legendary and should have made him a giant. From habit, Athdara filled a wooden platter and handed it to Tearlach. Beldorach noticed a fresh bloodstained bandage around one of Tearlach's upper arms. "What happened?"

Tearlach dismissed the query. "It's nothing, a slight mishap."

Beldorach became suspicious at Tearlach's casual attempt to dismiss the wound. "What kind of mishap?"

"A chance encounter with the Novanti."

Without asking further, Beldorach knew exactly what happened. "How many horses did you get?"

"Five," Tearlach replied before realizing he just admitted the circumstances of the wound.

Beldorach slapped his thigh in exasperation. "Before I left, I said there would be no further raids on the other tribes. The alliances I've arranged are precarious enough without you jeopardizing them."

Momentarily, Tearlach looked downcast before he broke into a wide grin. "But they were grazing without anyone around, and I thought perhaps they were strays, possibly even some of mine. I thought to return them to their owner but realized I didn't know who owned them. Unwilling to leave them unattended, and no one there to object, I took them with me. Then an arrow came out of nowhere and struck me in the arm. Wanting no trouble, I left quickly. It wasn't my fault the horses followed me."

"Was that after you killed the Novanti herder?"

"Well, he proved less skillful with a bow than me. Besides he didn't seem in the mood to discuss the matter."

Finally losing the battle to keep a straight face, Beldorach threw his head back and laughed. "I suppose not."

"There, you see, I knew you'd understand."

Beldorach grew serious when he considered the damage Tearlach's action may have done to jeopardize the fragile treaty with the Novanti. Treaties were always tenuous with each tribe as guilty of breaking them as the other.

"Tearlach, I fear you'll never change. If I ignore what you've done, Bothan will send warriors here to even the score at the very time I need to maintain an alliance with the Novanti." Beldorach lapsed into thoughtful silence as Tearlach focused his attention on the platter of meat.

"Here is what must be done. I intended to meet with Bothan eventually, but your encounter makes it necessary to do it sooner than I'd planned. You'll accompany me, and in addition to the five horses you seized, you will select five horses of your own for delivery to Bothan. Perhaps the gesture will be enough to keep the treaty in place a little longer by compensating the grieving widow, if there is one."

Tearlach was relieved and brushed off the loss of the horses without protest in recognition the punishment was lighter than he expected a few minutes ago.

Beldorach stood and began donning his heavy leather shirt and thick sheepskin vest. "We leave as soon as supplies for seven days can be packed and loaded." He began to detail instructions to Tearlach identifying who would comprise the Selgovan delegation. The size of the party was critical. Too large and there would be the risk Bothan would think it was an attack. Too small and it would demean his stature. He didn't like Bothan anymore than the Novanti chief did him, but he was willing to do what was necessary, at least to a point, to achieve a larger purpose.

Late on the second day, Beldorach camped for the night close to Bothan's village. It wasn't long before a large Novanti force arrived and quickly surrounded the camp. Ignoring Beldorach's uplifted sheathed sword to signify peaceful intent, the heavily armed warriors began nocking arrows and brandishing their swords in angry belligerence. The situation deteriorated further when one of the Novanti warriors recognized the stolen horses. From their painted faces and large number, Beldorach knew the Novanti were bent on retaliation for Tearlach's recent escapade. A brief conversation with Neacal, the Novanti clan chief, confirmed his suspicions. Beldorach assumed his most persuasive manner and convinced Neacal to allow them safe passage to meet with Bothan. The Novanti clan chief reluctantly consented to escort the Selgovan party safely to the tribe's principal settlement the next morning.

Although Beldorach slept peacefully, it was not the case for either the Selgovan or Novantean warriors as mutual distrust kept the adjacent camps wakeful throughout the night. The next morning when entering the settlement, the considerably outnumbered Selgovan warriors restrained themselves and ignored the shouted insults focused mainly on the inadequacies of their manhood.

Consisting of circular stone dwellings with thatched roofs, the Novanti settlement was virtually indistinguishable from those of the Selgovi. Bothan, grim-faced with arms folded across his chest, did not conceal his displeasure and dispensed with empty words of welcome. As Beldorach dismounted, Bothan displayed a temper intended more for the benefit of the onlookers than for his unwelcome visitors.

"Beldorach, you try my patience. You are bold to come here when one of my warriors lies under the ground from a Selgovan arrow. Is this the way you think to maintain an alliance? If so, we can drop any further pretense of friendship now and in the future."

Beldorach held up a placating hand. "Bothan, I know of your loss, and I came as soon as I learned of it to make amends. It was an unfortunate mishap, and it cannot be allowed to threaten our alliance. As a gesture of good will, I'm not only returning the stolen horses, but I've also brought more in compensation for your loss."

"Is the worth of a Novanti warrior so little it can be purchased with a few horses?"

Beldorach relaxed inwardly for he knew by Bothan's comparatively mild response it was a signal to begin a negotiated end to the predicament facing both leaders. Accompanied by effusive assertions extolling the worth of the slain warrior by the one and the superb condition of the horses being offered by the other, the haggling continued for some time under the expectant and appreciative eyes of the gathering crowd of onlookers. Second only to a good fight of one sort or another, nothing evoked more pleasure for Novanti and Selgovi alike than participating in or witnessing a closely-matched bartering contest between two skilled opponents. In reality, the outcome of the negotiation was secondary to appreciating the oratorical skills of the participants. Occasionally, spontaneous shouts of approval punctuated a particularly telling argument, and there were as many of those in support of Beldorach as Bothan. Knowing Bothan would be receptive to a negotiated settlement as a practical and less-costly way out of their mutual dilemma, Beldorach came prepared, bringing two extra horses with him certain Bothan would demand more than the initial offer presented. Predictably, the deal was consummated as Beldorach expected, and the twelve horses were surrendered. The tense atmosphere dissipated, and both villagers and Selgovan warriors drifted away content in the outcome and pleased with their respective leaders.

Making a point to walk side-by-side to prevent either one from presenting his back to the other, the two men entered the huge council hall alone. They took seats on opposite sides of a large table and regarded each other with wary interest. Bothan was the first to speak after pouring each a cup of the mildly intoxicating beverage made from fermented grain favored by the local tribes.

"A day later and it would have cost you more than a few horses."

"I came as soon as I heard what happened. I'm grateful you delayed."

"It was no easy matter, Beldorach. The dead man was popular, and his clan wanted blood revenge. I stalled as long as possible before sending Neacal. I'm surprised you talked him out of a fight. The dead man belonged to his clan. You have a silver tongue, Beldorach."

"It was a near thing. For a time, I thought Neacal wouldn't be able to control his warriors."

"Perhaps one day we'll see if your sword is as sharp as your tongue." Bothan leaned forward. "I can't promise next time the outcome will be as peaceful."

"You know such things will happen again no matter what we tell our warriors. There will always be a few who will try to prove themselves without any consideration of the consequences. It wasn't long ago we forestalled a war when some of your warriors raided one of my villages."

"Yes, and it cost me more than a few horses."

"Your warriors killed many."

"As did yours."

Growing irritated at the senseless exchange, Beldorach held up both hands. "Enough of this, what's done is done. What's important is to keep our warriors in check against the day we fight the Romans."

"You're right. We have the same problem controlling the hotheads. I liked the way things were before the Romans built their cursed wall. Then it was possible to fight the Briganti. Now the Romans control our movements south, and it's been years since we've been able to raid their villages."

"You conveniently forget, Bothan, the Roman wall has also prevented the Briganti from raiding north. As I recall, it was the Briganti who did more raiding on our villages than we did on theirs."

There was a pause as each man was momentarily lost in his own thoughts. Bothan broke the silence. "What of your trip south? Will the Briganti fight or not?"

"They insist they will and talk much of it, but it's only words. They say they aren't ready and claim the last attempt cost them dearly. They want more time to prepare."

"How long will it be?"

"I don't know. The Briganti say they are more at risk if we fail. After the last time they fought the Romans, it was bad for them. They haven't forgotten the reprisals that followed. I've the impression when they're ready to fight, they want to be the ones to start it."

Bothan thumped the table. "It will probably be the day when the Romans decide to leave of their own accord."

Beldorach took a long drink. "I couldn't get them to commit. They insist it will be soon but not this year."

"What do we do in the meantime? If we don't fight Romans, we'll end up fighting each other."

Beldorach was quick to respond. "That's exactly what we must not do."

"My warriors won't be content to wait for the Briganti to make up their minds to finish what's long overdue. This news will not go down well when I tell them of your failure."

"This is the reason I came to see you. If we cannot persuade the Briganti to fight, maybe we can force them into it."

Interested, Bothan sat back. "How do you intend to accomplish it?"

"I have a plan, but it will require our combined efforts to make it work. We must first convince the Romans the Briganti are getting ready to rebel again. If we're successful, the Romans will have to fight in both directions." For the next hour, Beldorach described the plan he refined since leaving the Brigantian capitol. At first, Bothan was openly resistant, but the more Beldorach talked, the more the Novanti leader's skepticism turned to approval. Bothan became the proverbial clay in the hands of a master craftsman. By the time the Selgovan finished, Bothan was a willing ally.

"What of the Votadini?" Bothan asked.

"I'll talk to Darach, but his clan chiefs would rather trade with the Romans than fight them."

One of Bothan's wives entered and replaced the empty pitcher with a full one. As he drank deeply, Beldorach was pleased with the results of his visit and satisfied the first essential and critical part of his plan was in place. What he didn't tell Bothan was the final part of the plan when the Romans did come north. Bothan may continue to believe in a Roman defeat, but even with the Briganti, the prospect was unrealistic; however, with or without the Briganti, he wanted the Romans to attack. It was now up to the Roman dogs to play their part. Bothan's actions were critical even though by so doing he would be the agent of his own demise. As Bathar once said, *it's essential for a leader not to let anyone know everything.* It hadn't taken long to understand the wisdom of those words.

Before Bothan understood everything, it would be too late for him.

Chapter 4

After the distant signal flag dipped one last time, Metellus, the centurion commanding the mile fort, saluted Arrius and announced, "Praefectus, General Arvinnius has departed Camboglanna. We'll soon see the escort approaching."

Arrius nodded without comment estimating it would take less than an hour before Arvinnius's arrival. Sensing Arrius was not inclined to engage in small talk, Metellus excused himself and left the parapet to attend to last minute preparations. Arrius turned and leaned against one of the merlons and looked north, observing the trickle of pedestrians and occasional cart traffic passing through the gate beneath him. He noted the progress of a two-wheeled pony cart slowly approaching from the north. He paid little heed to it until it drew close enough for him to see the two individuals sitting side by side. His attention was drawn to the enormous man holding the reins and dwarfing the small figure sitting beside him. The smaller figure wore a hooded cloak and appeared to be a girl, but given the immense size of the driver, it was possible the passenger was a grown woman. A gust of wind pushed the hood back from the passenger's face, and he recognized the woman called Ilya. Impatiently she brushed a stray lock of hair back into place then reached back to pull the hood over her head glancing up as she did. Their eyes met, and he saw hers widen in recognition. He smiled and saw her face brighten. A moment later, the wagon passed from view as it entered the gate below.

He heard the muffled exchange as the tax collector queried the cart's occupants concerning their destination and cargo. He resisted the impulse to go down on the chance it might provoke another spirited outburst. Instead, he walked to the other side of the rampart in time to see the cart exit the gate and proceed south across the vallum then turn east toward Banna. There was no reason to expect she would turn and look his way, but she did and waved before the cart dipped into a swale and disappeared from sight. He wanted to see this beautiful woman again and resolved as soon as his duties permitted, he would. He was still musing over the possibility when Metellus reappeared and informed him General Arvinnius's escort was in sight.

Arrius hurried down the stairway and mounted Ferox. He saw a large body of horsemen at least two hundred strong approaching. The sound of drumming hooves on the crushed stone roadway grew steadily louder as the column drew closer. Arrius identified General Arvinnius by the elaborate bronze cuirass he wore and the ornate magenta-colored sagum flowing behind him. His attention was drawn to the individual immediately to the left of the legion commander. Even at this distance, he recognized Tiberius Querinius. The gods must be against him more than he knew. How else to explain why he was about to meet the one man he hoped never to see again? It occurred to him Querinius probably felt the same.

Arrius saluted. "Salve, General Arvinnius. I am Praefectus Arrius."

General Antinnius returned the salute with a languid wave and fixed Arrius with an unblinking stare. For a long moment, the two men silently took each other's measure. Antinnius appeared older than he'd imagined; however, the hawk-nosed man still looked tough enough to endure the rigors of a long field campaign. Without breaking eye contact, Arvinnius gestured in the direction of Querinius. "This is Tribune Tiberius Querinius, commander of Uxellodonum and the western section of the Wall."

"The Tribune and I have met before." Arrius saw a mix of fear and hate flicker across Querinius's ashen face; the tribune's obvious discomfort had a calming effect on him. He noted the gold torque around the tribune's neck and said in a neutral tone without any change of expression, "Salve, Tribune Querinius, we meet again."

After a brief moment when it appeared he wouldn't respond, Querinius managed to gain control of his emotions and replied in a controlled voice. "It seems we are destined once again to serve the eagle together. Praefectus, I congratulate you on your appointment and rank, and I also want to say how pleased I am to have you as one of my commanders."

"It would seem the gods thought to make it so."

Arvinnius remained silent during the exchange. "I forgot you both served the *Deiotariana* Legion. Since you know each other, let's not waste time here. Arrius, you'll ride with me and tell me what you've accomplished at Banna since your arrival."

As they rode, Arrius related the various things done to improve Banna's defenses including initiating more frequent guard changes and patrols north and south of the Wall. He was frank in admitting his failure to dramatically improve the morale of the legionaries and reckoned it as his most pressing challenge. Throughout, Arvinnius listened without any visible reaction apart from nodding several times. Arrius was unable to tell if it signified approval or mere understanding. When they reached the next mile fort, Arvinnius held up his hand and reined in his mount.

"We'll stop here while I inspect your guard. Querinius, you'll accompany us." After they dismounted, Arrius realized Arvinnius was as tall as he was although more sparely built. As he followed slightly behind, Arrius noticed the general's slightly hunched shoulders and was reminded of an aging eagle.

The centurion in charge of the guard force was unfazed by the number of senior officers approaching him, and when Arvinnius stopped in front of the him, he calmly reported his name and the number of his guard. For the next several minutes, it was if a whirlwind visited the small garrison. Arvinnius seemed to miss nothing as he examined equipment and weapons keeping up a series of rapid-fire questions directed both at Arrius and the legionary guards. The questions were pointed and underscored the general's field experience. Occasionally, he administered a tongue lashing to the centurion when he found something not to his satisfaction, usually having to do with a gladius, pilum or cuirass failing to measure up. Arrius knew the discrepancies were minor even as he was aware it was a performance conducted mainly for their benefit.

By the time Arvinnius was finished with the guard room, armory and small barracks room on the ground floor and ascended the stairs to the parapet above, the leaden sky began to release a light, misty rain. Arvinnius, paying not the slightest heed to the inclement weather, walked toward the nearest legionary who stood frozen at the general's intimidating presence. At the last minute, the legionary had the presence of mind to salute. Arvinnius said something guttural in the Tungrian language, and the legionary beamed. The conversation between the two men far outstripped Arrius's limited command of the Tungrian language. It was apparent from Querinius's face he was completely at a loss to understand the exchange. Arvinnius clapped the legionary on the shoulder and made a final comment that left the sentry guffawing.

Arvinnius was still smiling when he turned to Arrius and Querinius. He noted the quizzical looks on their faces. "I told him to keep his prick down and his pilum up then he'll be certain to keep his mind on his duty and not on the whores. You should learn to speak the languages represented in your commands. Apart from indicating interest in them, it has the practical and more important benefit of understanding what is being said around you. A lesson I learned the hard way when a cohort from Hispania once mutinied on me without any warning. I found out later the bastards talked about it in my presence knowing I didn't understand a word they were saying."

"I agree with the importance of learning the language, General," Arrius responded in Tungrian and received an approving nod from Arvinnius.

Arvinnius wore a thoughtful look as he walked over to one of the merlons and stood gazing north at the sodden countryside. Without turning, he spoke over his shoulder. "Arrius, you're right to increase your patrols. I want you to concentrate as much in the south as the north. Frankly, I've less concern over what the northern tribes may do than if the Briganti decide to take up arms again. The last time they tried it, they came close to pulling it off, and we have one less legion here now."

Querinius frowned. "Are there indications of hostilities?"

"No, apart from the usual and isolated skirmishes. That is precisely what makes me uneasy. It's always when everything seems quiet you must be especially on your guard. The last incident occurred three days before Querinius arrived at Uxellodonum when a patrol from *Blatobulgium* was ambushed and three cavalrymen were killed. I ordered reprisals, and a Novanti village was razed. The only thing these tribes respect is strength. Whenever one of our legionaries is killed, I want ten of them killed in return. And I make no distinction. Warriors, women or brats will do just as well. I hold there's nothing makes the argument better for keeping the peace than witnessing the consequences if they choose not to. We'll take heed of what Hadrian did in Judaea and apply the same stringent measures here. I warrant both of you understand what must be done here from your recent experience there."

Arvinnius noticed the bleak look on Arrius's face. "Arrius, do you not agree with my methods?"

"No, General, I do not. If you said kill ten warriors for every one of ours they slay then so be it. But killing women and children indiscriminately in my opinion serves to stiffen their backs and gives them no alternative but to keep on fighting. I see no glory or purpose in such a policy unless it is to achieve the wasteland we made of Judaea."

Arvinnius's eyes became flinty as he stared at Arrius. Then without looking at Querinius, he said to the tribune, "Do you agree with Praefectus Arrius?"

"No, General Arvinnius, I do not. I believe the emperor was justified in what occurred in Judaea and would expect the same to be applied here should the situation require it."

"Well, I'm glad one of my commanders out here is not squeamish about doing what's necessary. Take care, Arrius, lest the local tribes, and I, think you have no stomach for this business. If the locals behave themselves, possibly there won't be occasion to put you to the test." Arvinnius abruptly brushed past the officers and strode toward the steps leading down to the ground floor. "Come, let us be on our way to Banna."

A legionary cupped his hands to allow Arvinnius to mount and did the same for Arrius while Querinius nimbly vaulted into the saddle. Noting the assistance given to Arrius, Arvinnius was critical. "I'm long in years, Arrius, what's your excuse?"

"A Jewish arrow, General. The cold weather makes it worse."

"I see. I seem to recall you were the primus pilus of the *Deiotariana*. Why is it you managed to survive the battle? Perhaps if you'd been more diligent in your duties, the legion might have fared better."

Arrius felt himself growing angry at the implied criticism of his conduct during the final battle in Judaea and bit back an angry reply. Surprisingly, it was Querinius who commented. "General, if it hadn't been for Arrius, there would have been even fewer survivors." For a brief moment, Arrius's eyes met Querinius's. He gave the tribune a slight nod acknowledging the other man's unsolicited defense.

"Well, there's a tale for another day." Arvinnius kicked his horse into a gallop heading toward Banna.

The remainder of the trip was uneventful. Arvinnius showed neither interest in stopping at any of the other intervening mile forts or towers nor inclination to engage in further discussion. Arrius's impression of Arvinnius was mixed so far. He was impressed with the general's military competence and obvious experience, a welcome change from his opinion of Gallius. He knew the criticism he voiced concerning Arvinnius's proposed methods did not engender any good will, but he didn't regret saying what he did. He questioned if he would still be in command by the time Arvinnius left Banna.

Arrius wondered why Querinius came to his defense. Was it by way of a peace gesture and a means to encourage him to remain quiet about the tribune's behavior in Judaea? If so, Querinius couldn't possibly believe so small a gesture would bridge the gap between them. Aculineous never named the individual who paid him; consequently, it was left to speculation and his conviction it was Querinius who was behind the attempt on his life. He knew trusting the tribune was impossible, but he was willing to leave the past in Judaea if Querinius intended the same.

Chapter 5

Arrius led Arvinnius and Querinius through the gate and toward the ranks of legionaries lined up in parade formation. He was pleased to see Seugethis with a contingent from Fanum Cocidii. If the opportunity presented, Arrius intended to have the Dacians demonstrate their horsemanship for the legion commander.

Arvinnius dismounted and slowly walked the length of the formation stopping occasionally to ask a legionary or an optio a question, generally ignoring the centurions standing to the front of the formation. Arvinnius seemed in no hurry to rush through the ceremony, demonstrating the aging general genuinely relished such opportunities. Most Roman senators who commanded legions, like Gallius, assumed field command out of a sense of obligation or expediency to gain more influence and power. He thought perhaps Arvinnius was commanding the Sixth because he wanted to and because he was good at it.

Arrius was satisfied with the appearance of the legionaries and cavalry. In a relatively short time, the improvement in all aspects of the garrison was finally becoming noticeable. He gave Betto credit. The centurion may not agree with the orders given him, but he did manage to produce results when they were demanded. Betto had so far proven to be a competent, experienced centurion.

Arvinnius signaled he was done with the inspection and wanted to see the rest of the fort. For the next hour accompanied by Querinius and Arrius, Arvinnius prowled the fort looking at everything from latrines to barracks with a critical eye and giving credit to an optio or a centurion when merited. He missed nothing and didn't hesitate to call attention to the least thing out of place or shortcoming requiring corrective action. While Arvinnius seemed to be actively engaged in the mundane details of the inspection, Querinius, by contrast, worked hard to keep from showing how bored he was.

Apart from the occasions when Arrius and Querinius were obliged to exchange comments, they avoided any casual conversation and maintained their distance. In time, Arvinnius noticed the obvious strain between the two men and paused in one of the barracks to comment on it.

"Is it my imagination I sense you two are not exactly on the best of terms?" It was more a statement than a question. He looked back and forth between the two men.

As the junior officer present, Arrius said nothing waiting for the tribune to respond. Smoothly, Querinius replied, "Why, I have every reason to respect Arrius, but our respective duties and the centurion's prolonged field duty provided little opportunity to enjoy one another's company."

Arvinnius fixed Arrius with an unblinking stare waiting silently for his explanation. "It is as the tribune has said. We spent little time together." He avoided looking at Querinius.

When the general realized neither man intended to say more, he said, "It has been my experience men who fought great battles together become comrades. I find it strange the senior tribune and the senior centurion of a legion suffering the fate of the XXII Legion, appear to have so little regard for each other." When neither Querinius nor Arrius responded, Arvinnius shrugged and dropped the subject.

After completing the inspection of the fort and stables, Arrius led the general to the training field where Seugethis was waiting with a troop of mixed archers and lancers lined up behind him.

Seugethis rode up to Arvinnius, reported and took up a position on the general's left. The cavalryman gave the signal for the demonstration and explained the maneuvers and the purpose of each one as they were executed. Arrius observed Arvinnius watching intently with unconcealed delight at the same exercises he saw demonstrated at Fanum Cocidii. The Tungrian cavalry was still a long way from equaling much less surpassing the Dacians — if they ever could.

When the demonstration was over, Arvinnius was visibly impressed. So far Arrius was pleased with how things had gone with the general's visit. He hoped the banquet in his honor would also meet expectations.

The small dining room in the praetorium wasn't large enough to accommodate both General Arvinnius's officers and those assigned to the Banna garrison; therefore, a canvas canopy was stretched over the open courtyard with tables arranged under the colonnaded walkways on three sides. A number of braziers were placed around the tables to ward off the evening chill. As protocol demanded, Arrius was seated on the general's left with Querinius on the right. Betto sat next to Querinius and Seugethis was seated to Arrius's left with Antius Durio sitting next to him. Ordinarily, Publius Gheta would have been sitting next to Betto, but the quaestor breached protocol and took a seat on the other side of Durio. Philos hovered nearby ensuring wine and food were available in ample supply.

The food was good and plentiful if limited in variety. Arrius doubted the banquet, elaborate by local standards, would get an approving nod in Eboracum; however, for a frontier affair, he wasn't embarrassed with the results and grateful for the efforts of Durio and Philos for their time and effort in attending to the least detail. As far as he could tell, Arvinnius seemed relaxed even if he was sparing in the amount of food and drink he consumed. It seemed the officers were also having a good time from the rowdy behavior of the centurions with some, including Betto, already well into their cups. At one point, Arrius glanced past Arvinnius and saw Querinius and Betto in deep conversation with the tribune helping to keep Betto's cup well-filled. He wondered what the senator-designate and the somewhat rough-mannered centurion had in common to risk unduly ignoring their guest of honor. He needn't have been concerned for Arvinnius proved to be quite a raconteur and regaled the assemblage with crude stories featuring mainly brothels and latrine mishaps appealing to coarse legionary humor. Arrius found himself enjoying the evening in a way he hadn't expected given the unfortunate presence of Querinius. Arrius would have enjoyed the banquet considerably less if he knew what Querinius and Betto were talking about.

It didn't take Querinius long to notice the baleful looks Betto occasionally directed toward Arrius throughout the evening. It required only a bit of innocent probing and wine to draw the centurion out. He determined the root cause of Betto's dislike of his commander seemed to revolve around two reasons. He resented Arrius for arriving to take command when he had an expectation, unreasonable as it might have been, of retaining command of Banna. Querinius gathered the unfulfilled expectation also resulted in a financial loss for reasons the centurion did not elaborate. Then there was the matter of Arrius's imperious manner. Betto accused the praefectus of a concerted effort to implement changes he believed were unnecessary in a deliberate attempt to belittle Betto's own previous achievements while in command. It was also obvious the two men differed in their opinion of the worth of the auxilia, an opinion upon which Querinius remained neutral considering his inexperience to date in dealing with foreign legionaries. He gathered from Betto's scathing comments of the Tungrians, Arrius had a different and positive impression of their worth.

It did not escape Betto's attention the relationship between the tribune and Arrius was strained, and he wondered why. He knew both had served in the unfortunate XXII Legion, but that was about all he knew.

Betto turned to Querinius. "Do you have a senior position for me at Uxellodonum? I'd like to get out of this rat-infested hell-hole. Arrius is welcome to it."

Ever mindful of any opportunity to further his own interests, Querinius opted for a cautious reply. "It's possible. I believe there's always a place for an experienced and resourceful individual." Then recalling Arvinnius's lecture before they left for Banna, he added, "I'm always receptive to any man who is talented, ambitious and willing to extend himself." After casting the net, Querinius slowly drank from his cup while watching Betto from the corner of his eye, waiting to see what he may have caught with the comment.

Querinius reflected later if Betto was a fish, he would have jumped in the boat bypassing hook or net. For the next several minutes, Querinius listened attentively to the venom-laced diatribe Betto directed at Arrius. It was clear the centurion was willing to do anything to remove himself from Banna and Arrius with the ultimate objective of regaining a command. Querinius thought it would be better to conceal the improbability the latter would ever happen. He wanted to explore further the extent of the centurion's animus toward Arrius.

"Betto, is your desire to leave Banna based on your dislike of its location, or is it because you esteem your commander so little?"

Betto paused and took another long drink from his cup. "Banna isn't so bad. It's no worse, nor is it any better than the other forts out here. It's Arrius I want to get away from. One way or the other, I will." Betto stopped and thought for a moment. "I wonder if General

Arvinnius would have a place for me in Eboracum. In time, I might even become a *primus pilus*."

Seeing opportunity about to elude him, Querinius said hastily, "Oh, I wouldn't bother the general. He might take such a request the wrong way and suspect you're trying to arrange a transfer to an easier berth than here on the frontier. No, I wouldn't advise seeking Eboracum as a solution to your problem, but I may be able to help you."

Betto's reaction was almost pathetic in his eagerness to respond to the bait dangling in front of him. Before he returned to Uxellodonum, he was certain he and Betto would find an opportunity to explore mutually beneficial possibilities with more privacy than the banquet offered.

There was no time for Arrius and Querinius to speak privately even if they wanted to. It was only by accident when they found themselves alone in the early dawn outside the west gate waiting for the arrival of General Arvinnius. After a minimal civil exchange, an awkward silence ensued. It was Querinius who broke the silence. "I didn't know you would be in Britannia. If I had, I would have turned down Turbo's offer to come here." He paused then reflectively added, "Actually, the truth is, I was given no choice."

"I didn't think you volunteered."

"And I suppose you did?"

"Yes, but I wouldn't have if I'd known you were coming here as well. I thought myself fortunate to come to Britannia and avoid Rome until I reached Eboracum and heard you were going to Uxellodonum. It was bad enough to know you were here on the island, but it got worse when I learned I would serve under your command."

"It appears we've both been mocked by the gods. I never expected to see you again."

"I believe you. My problem is with you here, I have more than the local tribes to be concerned about."

"What do you mean?"

"You know exactly what I mean, Querinius. I didn't realize in Judaea I had as much to be concerned with a Roman gladius or *pugio* in my back than a Jewish arrow. You don't have the courage or the skills to do what you would like, or you would draw your sword here and now and have done with it. I'm certain you've sufficient imagination to explain my death to General Arvinnius should you be singularly fortunate enough to manage it."

"I could have you on charges for threatening me."

"Yes, but you won't because then you'd have to explain the circumstances. I strongly suspect it's the last thing you want. Querinius, you represent everything I detest in a man. I might be able to accept your cowardice in the Sorek Valley, for I've been in battle enough to know every man treads a fine line separating fear and courage. What I cannot accept is you get others to do what you're afraid of doing yourself. For that reason alone, you are contemptible."

"Take care, Arrius, for if I'm as you say, your concern for your safety may be well-founded."

"Tribune, I started becoming cautious when I saw you yesterday."

For the next several minutes, neither man spoke until Querinius cleared his throat and said too casually, "Have you spoken to General Arvinnius about us?"

"You mean have I told Arvinnius you lost your nerve in Judaea or you tried to have me killed or both?"

Arrius heard Querinius breathing hard as the tribune attempted to control himself. "You'll pay for this one day, Arrius. I promise you'll regret those words."

"True enough, but I'll not lie awake at night fearing it as you will do trying to think of another way to kill me. If you do, find someone more capable than Aculineous. But to answer your question, no, I've not spoken to Arvinnius, nor do I intend to. Consider it payment for your comment yesterday to General Arvinnius why the primus pilus was the only centurion to have survived the demise of the *Deiotariana*. The general asked a fair question, and it's one I myself have asked many times since."

Further conversation was curtailed with the arrival of General Arvinnius.

Querinius composed himself while seething inside. When he hired Aculineous in Judea to take care of Arrius, it was only a matter of expedience with no more thought involved than if he had been pissing in the latrine. Now it was different. He never hated or wanted the destruction of anyone the way he desired an end to this man. He vowed if it was the last thing he ever did, he would somehow bring about Arrius's downfall. He hated Arrius for the humiliation he still suffered. Most of all, he hated him for being what he was not.

"What is it you have in mind?" Betto regarded Querinius's bland face with suspicion. At Querinius's invitation, the two officers walked through the east gate out of earshot of the guards following the departure of Arrius and General Arvinnius.

"I believe you made it known last night you want to leave Banna. I want you to clarify your reason; it may have a bearing on how I can assist you in achieving what you want." Querinius carefully ensured his answer left him ambiguously uncommitted.

Betto refused to be drawn out. "I have my reasons."

"I can understand your wish to keep your reasons to yourself, but if I'm to be of any help, I need to better understand your situation and what you mean. How do I know if I bring you to Uxellodonum, you won't find the same reason there for your discontent?"

Betto hesitated as he considered the tribune's practical argument for being more forthcoming. "If Arrius is not at Uxellodonum, I would be content — that is if I was given a senior position."

His suspicion confirmed, Querinius concealed his satisfaction. "So it isn't really Banna you object to, it's your commander."

"Aye, it's close enough to the mark."

"Has it to do with you are no longer commanding Banna and forced to accept changes you do not agree with?"

"I believe you could put it that way."

"Tell me, Matius Betto, in the strictest of confidence, what would give you greater satisfaction, a new posting to Uxellodonum or command of Banna?"

Querinius saw the other man's eyes gleam. "I would choose Banna. But how is it possible? Arrius is newly arrived and will likely remain here for several years. By the time he leaves, he will have found a way to remove me, and I'll be lucky enough to command a signal tower." A crafty look came over his face. "Tribune, are you saying something could happen to Arrius requiring a new commander for Banna?"

"Perhaps. We're in a hostile environment, and there's an enemy on both sides of the Wall representing a capability to solve your problem for you."

With a knowing smile, Betto said, "And your problem as well."

Querinius concealed his delight the centurion concluded there might be other motivations at work other than his own. "My problem? I believe we were addressing your wishes, Centurion, not mine."

"I think there may be more to your interest here than my welfare. Am I right, Tribune?"

Querinius realized he couldn't dodge the centurion's direct question without risk of losing the ground he already gained. "Let's assume for the moment you and I may have a common interest for different reasons. The reasons are not important for achieving a hypothetical objective if accomplishing it will please us both."

"You're right, Tribune, patrols are dangerous. There's always the risk during a close engagement when a gladius instead of a tribal sword takes a Roman life. And more than one man has been found with his neck broken after falling from a parapet at night while inspecting the guard. I can easily arrange such an accident and might even undertake the task myself if I thought it was in my interests."

Querinius held up his hands in protest. "Betto, you misunderstand me. I want nothing of the sort."

Betto's face showed a combination of anger and bewilderment. "I thought the way you were talking you wanted something to happen to Arrius!"

"I do indeed, Betto, but not in the way you infer. On the contrary, I want something a great deal worse. I want Arrius to be publicly humiliated and disgraced. Betto, you are the potential instrument to accomplish this."

Perplexed and intrigued, Betto looked at the Tribune's contorted face with astonishment. "What did Arrius do that death is not sufficient?"

Querinius's face once again assumed a neutral expression. "A fair question, but one I will not give a full answer. It's enough to say Arrius and I have never gotten along well. It is a mockery the gods have thrown us together where we will both have to endure the other's presence. I have reason to believe Arrius wishes no better for me than I him."

"What do you want me to do?"

"For the time being, nothing. I only want you to observe and report to me anything he does or happens at Banna I can use to my advantage. It may take time so we must both be patient."

"Tribune, I'm not a patient man. I'd like to have assurance I'll not be waiting too long, or I'll be taking matters into my own hands,"

"Betto, if you want the reward I alone can give you, then you'll do it my way. I'll take no satisfaction if Arrius dies one dark night. I want to see him humiliated and dishonored before he dies."

"Have it your way for now, but I warn you, reward or no reward, I'll deal with Arrius if you don't. My own preference is to see him dead, and I don't really care how it happens or under what circumstances."

Querinius nodded. "Then we have an understanding." The two men spent the next several minutes discussing the means to communicate privately with each other. They settled on hired couriers from the villages believing them to be more private than the regular couriers routinely carrying dispatches the length of the Wall.

Querinius watched Betto depart and calculated the risk of making use of the impatient and bitter centurion. He realized in the end he may have to settle for Betto's more efficient and cruder methods to deal with Arrius if his preferred objective and the opportunity to fulfill it failed to materialize.

General Arvinnius completed his inspection of the last mile fort before drawing Arrius aside. "I understand you may have been personally acquainted with General Vitellius Turbo."

"I have the honor. We served together on the frontier in *Germania*. I last saw him shortly before I left Judaea when he came to see me as I was recuperating from my wounds."

Arrius was completely unprepared for Arvinnius's next and abrupt statement. "Then you'll wish to make sacrifices in his name, for he's dead. He was executed by order of Hadrian himself."

Arrius went numb, for a moment unable to speak. Arvinnius anticipated the question. "It was for treason."

"Treason? But he was one of the emperor's closest friends and always loyal to him. How can it be?"

"Being close to the emperor is always dangerous. Once I called myself a friend of Hadrian. Now I'm happy to be as far from Rome as I can be. It's been said the emperor is in ill health. They say he's no longer clear-minded and distrusts even those who were once closest to him. Who knows where the truth may lie? I knew Turbo. We weren't friends; we were too busy being rivals. Now I'm glad he was the one who enjoyed the emperor's favor instead of me. Well, I'll speak no more of the matter." Without a word of farewell, Arvinnius strode toward his mount and with not so much as a sideways glance, spurred his horse into a gallop heading south with his escort thundering behind.

Arrius reflected on the fate of Turbo as he watched the last of the general's entourage pass by. It was almost impossible to believe Turbo was dead. He recollected the last time they were together. Despite Turbo's high position, they were friends with a deep, professional regard for each other. For a time, he resented the way Turbo used him and the *Deiotariana*, but in the end, he forgave him, recognizing Turbo did what he might have done if their positions were reversed. If there ever was a man who deserved a place with the gods, it was Turbo. He had his faults, but he was one of Rome's finest. At least Gallius died in battle as Turbo would have wished for himself rather than an undeserved and ignominious execution. He wondered how it was done. Did they at least offer him the opportunity of using his own sword, or did they cut his throat? He tasted the bile in his mouth at the thought.

Chapter 6

The first positive sign the worst of the winter weather was finally over
came with a warm rain marking the initial transition to spring. Only
isolated patches of snow remained on the shaded hillsides. Beldorach
believed the time had come to implement the plan he discussed with
the Novanti High Chieftain — except the part he didn't reveal to
Bothan and key to the outcome he really wanted to achieve. Once the
plans and final coordination for the joint raid south of the Roman wall
were complete, Beldorach ordered the infiltration to begin. Disguised
as farmers and laborers the Selgovan and a pair of Novantean archers
transited several gates one or two at a time. Their weapons were
wrapped in oiled skins and concealed beneath a cartload of manure.
As predicted, the Roman sentries were only too willing to hurry on the
odiferous cargo after Tearlach paid the tax voicing the usual loud
complaints without which the guards' suspicions might have been
aroused enough to conduct a search.

For himself, Beldorach opted for a route he previously used and
planned to keep secret. Two summers earlier, he saw where the river
flowed south beneath the Roman wall through several small arches in
which the builders inserted iron bars designed to prevent anyone
passing through them. One dark night several years before, he found
one of the bars loose. After several attempts at working it back and
forth, he was finally able to remove it. The opening was large enough
to allow a man to squeeze through the duct. He had replaced the bar
by wedging it in with a stick at the top and a large stone at the base to
ensure it wouldn't be dislodged by any debris during a heavy rain.

Although the temperature was comfortable enough, the water
chilled him to the bone in the time it took to remove the iron bar,
wiggle through the opening and replace the bar behind him. When he
emerged on the other side of the wall, his teeth chattered loud enough
he was afraid the sentry pacing the rampart above would hear him. He
lay in the water, his arms wrapped around the oiled-skin bundle
containing his sword, bow and arrow quiver as he waited for the
sentry to reach the farthest point away from the riverbed. By the time
he thought it safe enough to wade to the nearby bridge, he was hardly

able to move. Shaking almost uncontrollably, he pulled himself up on the damp bank underneath the bridge and began vigorously massaging his numbed feet and legs to get feeling back in them. He estimated there were only a few more hours left before daybreak.

Gradually, Beldorach began to get feeling in his legs and feet. He left the concealment of the bridge and began a loping run south down the curving road. There was little risk of meeting anyone at this early hour, and keeping to the road meant gaining time and distance. With daylight, he would be forced to move into the countryside and follow a more circuitous route to take advantage of the cover and concealment afforded by the forest trails and steep hills to reach the location where he would meet the others.

It took two days for the thirteen men, including the Novanti tribesmen and the wagon carrying the weapons, to infiltrate through separate Roman gates and assemble in an uninhabited valley ten miles south of Banna. The forest of birch, pine and sycamore they camped in was dense and provided ample concealment as they prepared for the raid. The weapons were recovered in a nearby clearing leaving the smelly cargo off-loaded until it was time to conceal them again for the eventual withdrawal north. Beldorach took the precaution of testing the capability of the archers himself. Their accuracy was critical to the success of the raid. After confirming Bothan's selection of the two men could not have been better, Beldorach had the men gathered in a semi-circle as he described in detail how the attack on the Roman signal tower would be conducted. When they learned what their objective would be, disappointment appeared on their faces. He quickly explained the importance of the target.

"The tower may be a small target, but the significance of an attack in the south will not be lost on either the Romans or the Briganti. We'll attack tonight. The tower is situated three miles from here on a hill near the road leading to Banna. We will have to pass a farm on the way. If anyone wakes up, they must be prevented from giving an alarm." It was obvious to the listening men what Beldorach meant.

"Why not kill them anyway so we can be certain they won't wake up?" Tearlach said, his words evoking a murmur of agreement. "After all, they're only Briganti."

Beldorach tried to conceal his annoyance knowing under normal circumstances what would happen to the farmer and his family, but it was the last thing he wanted to happen on this raid if it could be prevented. Thinking quickly, he said, "I agree with you; however, the purpose of the raid is to help persuade the Briganti to join the northern tribes in attacking the Romans. If we kill them, we defeat the main purpose of the raid. Another objective is to shake the confidence of the Romans by attacking them in the rear." Beldorach could tell by their silence and expressions the men accepted the logic of his answer even if it was only partly true.

"Surprise and stealth are the keys to our success. I want no battle cries. The only noise I want to hear is the sound of bowstrings and steel entering Roman bodies. When we're done, no Roman must be left alive."

"Once we arrive near the tower, four men will be positioned to secure the road — two south of the tower and two north. I don't want to be compromised by anyone coming along unexpectedly, particularly a Roman patrol. It is critical to silence the sentry at the top of the tower quickly and quietly. For this, I will rely on our two allies from the Novanti and their skill with bow and arrow," pointing to the two tribesmen sitting slightly apart from the rest. He was satisfied to see them smile with self-importance at being chosen for such an important task. Beldorach glanced at Tearlach and saw his face showing disapproval a Selgovan wasn't selected.

Forestalling the possibility of disagreement being voiced by Tearlach or any other Selgovan, Beldorach said, "The most important task of all is to gain access to the top of the tower. Tearlach, you wondered why I asked you to bring the rope, and now I'll tell you. It's for you to climb to the top of the tower after the sentry is killed." Beldorach saw a wide smile break out on the small man's face at being singled out for the assignment. "Once you've gained the rampart, you will assist the rest of the attack force, including me, to climb up and join you. After the guard has been eliminated, the archers will take position by the main entrance in case one or more signalmen are able to escape. Aside from the sentry, we can expect four, possibly five, additional men asleep below. We should have more than enough to deal with those sleeping below. After the Romans are dead, we'll gather their weapons and take them with us."

"But how will we get them back through the Roman gates?"

"The answer is simple, we don't. We'll bury them here in the hole you will take turns digging before we leave here to start the attack." Again Beldorach raised his hands to quell the objections being voiced.

"I may wish to use them in future raids in the south." Although his answer was logical enough, it wasn't the real answer. The Romans would wonder why the weapons were left behind. It was essential to the success of his plan the Romans concluded only what he wanted them to think.

He spent a few more minutes going over the details until he was certain each man knew exactly where he was supposed to be and understood his assigned task. Once they reached the clearing, they would place their weapons back in the cart, cover them with the manure and return through different gates to avoid arousing any suspicions. He then made the assault team practice climbing up the rope Tearlach tied to a high branch of a sycamore tree while the others dug a hole to bury any Roman weapons taken.

It was late that night when Beldorach roused the sleeping men. Silently, they followed him in single file as they traveled the three miles to the signal tower under the dim light of a half-moon. Beldorach was concerned when gathering clouds began to obscure the moon further reducing visibility. There was no question concerning the marksmanship of the two Novanti archers; still, even an expert archer needed to be able to see his target to hit it.

They passed the farmhouse and paused when a dog began barking. Beldorach heard an angry voice and a sharp yelp before the night was silent once again. After a few minutes, he signaled to continue. When they reached the road a short distance from the tower, he motioned for the men assigned to guard the northern approach to take their positions on either side of the road. Those assigned to guard the south were sent in the opposite direction. Beldorach and the remaining men moved toward the tower now a dark shape silhouetted in the pale moonlight. As they approached the stone corral adjacent to the tower, two horses inside began stamping their hooves and whickering nervously. One of the men clambered over the low wall and calmed the horses with handfuls of grain, stroking their necks while the animals happily munched on the unexpected but welcome snack.

When the moon emerged from behind a cloud, he saw why there was no chance of an alarm. The sentry above them was leaning against a merlon snoring, oblivious of any activity in the corral below. Taking advantage of the sleeping guard, Beldorach stood up and motioned for the two Novanti archers to come to him. Standing several feet apart, each archer stuck an arrow into the ground next to him then nocked another arrow in the bowstring as they waited for the moon to emerge from behind a cloud. The moon appeared, and Beldorach heard a nearly simultaneous twang as the two Novanti archers released their arrows. Quickly nocking another arrow, they prepared to launch a second volley, but it wouldn't be necessary. The sentry was facedown between the merlons, one arm hanging lifelessly as if reaching for the ground.

Beldorach whispered a compliment to the two archers and motioned for them to join the other warrior designated to guard the studded tower door. Returning to the corral, he brought Tearlach up to the base of the tower. Tearlach wasted no time in making his first cast which proved both unsuccessful and, to his dismay, noisy. The heavy wooden stave tied to the end of the rope clattered against a merlon before falling back to the ground with a thump. Beldorach held his breath as Tearlach looped the rope readying for another throw. The second attempt was no less noisy, but it held as Tearlach tugged on it to ensure it was secure. Both waited for another moment to see if anyone inside heard the noise. While Beldorach held the rope to keep it from swinging, the smaller man clambered up almost as easily as if he was ascending stairs or climbing a ladder. Tearlach disappeared over the top and after a brief pause, jerked the rope several times indicating it was now securely fastened to one of the merlons.

With somewhat more difficulty than Tearlach demonstrated, Beldorach climbed up as the men behind took turns holding the rope for the man ahead of him. When all were on the rampart, Beldorach moved to the stairway leading to the single room below. Beldorach had once been held briefly in a similar tower near Eboracum and assumed the layout would be as it was there given the Roman habit of adhering to the same design for structures built for the same purpose. There would be two levels; the top level below the parapet would be where the legionaries were sleeping. The ground floor was used for cooking and relaxation. Each floor was accessible by a flight of interior stairs. Beldorach heard loud snoring as he slowly descended the staircase. He wrinkled his nose in disgust at the fetid air rising from below and wondered how it was possible to sleep in such conditions. He saw a faint glow the lower he went and realized there must be a lamp burning for the sentry on guard to find his relief.

Beldorach reached the last step and surveyed the room by the light of the small clay lamp burning on a small table in the center of the room. He counted four men sleeping in double bunks against one wall — the single empty bunk evidently belonged to the dead sentry. A fifth man, presumably the optio, was asleep on a single bunk on the opposite side of the room. Swords, shields and armor hung on a rack on the wall opposite the bunks. The weapons and armor belonging to the optio were slung on a smaller rack next to his cot.

He waited for the other men to enter the room then silently indicated their targets. He pointed to the optio then back to himself. He would deal with him. Beldorach heard the whispering sound of daggers being drawn from sheaths as he moved over next to his designated victim. The legionaries died quickly and soundlessly with only a gurgling noise to disturb the silence of the room. He had a slower death in mind for the optio. The other Selgovi were puzzled when Beldorach grabbed the sleeping man by the front of his woolen tunic and hauled him toward the top of the stairway leading to the upper floor. The wide awake man was mute and paralyzed with shock as he realized what was happening; he managed a low keening sound as Beldorach plunged his dagger first into the optio's lower abdomen then higher into his chest for a final killing blow. Beldorach stepped back and let the man fall on the stairs but not in time to avoid the rush of blood splashing over his arm. Turning to the other members of the team, he said, "I thought to ask him about any signals required before dawn which would reduce the time we need to get away from here. But then I realized the information made no difference." Only Tearlach looked at him quizzically at the unconvincing explanation for not dispatching his victim at the same time the others were.

Beldorach began issuing orders, and the men quickly complied. Tearlach went to retrieve his rope while the others gathered up the weapons. Sheathing his own dagger, Beldorach walked quickly over and took the optio's sword and dagger. He bade the other men go below and open the outside door then wait for him; one of the men he instructed to go down the road to alert the guards to assemble on the road near the tower. They would pick up the other road guards on the way back north to the clearing. When Tearlach finally appeared, the rope minus the stave slung across his shoulder and chest, Beldorach said, "Send up the Novanti archers. I want to show them how well they did their job." Tearlach nodded and disappeared down the stairs. Beldorach withdrew the optio's sword and dagger from their scabbards. In the dim light, he admired the unadorned simplicity of the weapons regretting the necessity of leaving them behind.

He heard the scraping noise of someone coming up the steps and walked over to the head of the stairs. He allowed the first Novanti archer to enter the room before he plunged the optio's dagger into the man's heart. The second man appeared around the curve of the staircase, his head down to avoid stumbling in the dim light. Beldorach saw his eyes widen in shock as he looked up and saw the gladius before the sword entered his throat. He died quickly falling backward down the steps, the weapon still lodged in his throat. Beldorach quickly bent down and retrieved the dagger of the first Novanti warrior and thrust the blade into the optio's chest. A pity, he thought dispassionately, especially after demonstrating such fine shooting. Well, at least the optio will be credited for having done his duty albeit not quite as well as the Romans will assume when they arrive and see the results of his handiwork.

Once outside, he told them the Novanti would remain behind a little longer to watch for any relief or signals before joining them in the clearing. Beldorach looked up at the cloudy sky and smiled with satisfaction. The entire matter had taken less than an hour from the time they arrived at the tower. They would be on their way long before dawn. With any luck at all, they would be passing through the wall gates by the time their night's work was discovered.

Chapter 7

Arrius walked up the steps of the signal tower carefully to avoid the coagulating pools of blood. He stepped over the first body clad in woolen leggings and leather shirt lying in a tumbled heap. The dead man's head was pulled to one side by the weight of the gladius protruding from his throat. At the top of the stairs was another body dressed in similar garb. He slowly scanned the tower room, his gaze taking in the legionaries lying in their blood-soaked bunks across the room; another legionary he surmised was the optio was lying face up on the floor at his feet near the top of the stairs. The cloying, sweetish odor of fresh blood filled the room.

He went up the stairs to the rampart above. The dead sentinel's upper body was wedged between two merlons. The arrow that killed him entered low in the throat and emerged several inches high on the back of the neck; a second arrow inflicted a painful but non-lethal wound when it entered the legionary's cheek lodging in the jawbone. It was obvious from the arrow wounds the legionary wasn't wearing his helmet. Decrius stood to one side with a neutral expression on his face quietly watching Arrius. In the distance, Arrius saw elements of his cavalry escort slowly moving about the countryside searching for any trail the attackers may have left. It had been a courier on his way to Banna from Eboracum who discovered the grisly scene and alerted the Banna fort.

Arrius was caught off guard an assault had taken place without any suggestion of imminent hostilities. He wanted to visit the sight of the raid to make his own assessment and directed Decrius to accompany him. He thought as a Brigantian, Decrius might have additional insights he or the Tungrians would not, the assumption being the Brigantae Tribe was responsible for the attack.

Arrius turned to Decrius. "I don't understand why the Briganti would attack a target such as this rather than ambush one of our patrols. It hardly seems a significant enough objective."

"It may be they were not Briganti at all," Decrius said.

"What do you mean?"

"The two men below are not Briganti. From their tattoos and the markings on their arrow shafts, they are Novanti. I suspect the rest may have been as well."

Arrius frowned. After several months, he was still trying to sort out the cultural and political differences distinguishing one tribe from another. "I don't understand why the Novanti would attack here in the south unless the Novanti and Briganti have put aside their differences and formed an alliance."

"It's possible, Praefectus, but it would be unusual. As you've said, it's even more puzzling the Novanti would come this far from their tribal lands to attack a Roman signal tower here. It's more likely they would attack Blatobulgium or Castra Exploratorum," referring to the two Roman forts north of Uxellodonum. "It wasn't long ago they attacked Blatobulgium."

"Just as strange is what occurred down there." Arrius pointed toward the stairway leading to the floor below. "It's possible someone was careless and left the door unbolted. After killing the sentry first, they came up the stairs and attacked the others. The legionaries were asleep, but the optio woke in time to slay two of the attackers before he was overpowered and died defending the stairway."

Even as he finished conjecturing what may have happened, he didn't require the skepticism plainly evident on Decrius's face to reject the implausible explanation. He threw up his hands in disgust.

"That can't be what happened. It supposes the legionaries killed in their bunks were asleep while the optio was fighting for his life. It makes no sense unless they were killed first. If it's true, why didn't he wake up when the others were slain?"

"Praefectus, I think there's another explanation. It seems unlikely the attackers would allow the optio an opportunity to secure his weapons and slay two of the assailants before they killed him."

"I think you may have the right of it. There are more questions here than answers."

Arrius started toward the steps when his foot struck a wooden stave lying on the stone floor. Thinking it fell out of the cylindrical metal container used to store wood for the signal fire, Arrius picked it up intending to place it back in the container. It was then he noticed the stave was much thicker and longer than the others. On a hunch, Arrius examined the stave more closely and saw abrasions around the center.

"Decrius, they didn't come through the door below; the attack came from here. I believe they used this to secure a rope between the merlons. It explains how they got in even if it doesn't answer the other questions."

The sound of drumming hooves announced the return of one of the cavalry patrols. With Decrius following behind, Arrius descended the steps to hear the report. The two men emerged from the tower as the patrol came to a halt, their mounts steaming in the cool air. The young commander leading the troop dismounted and quickly summarized what they found.

"We picked up a trail leading that way," he said pointing north. "It went past a farmhouse about two miles away. The farmer claims he heard nothing except late last night when the dog started barking. I believe he was telling the truth. We followed the trail to a clearing a few miles farther on. From the signs, I estimate a dozen, perhaps more, in the raiding party. We found where they buried the weapons taken from the tower. They split up and headed generally north taking separate trails. The tracks of a wagon and two mules or horses led in and out of the clearing. We also found evidence the wagon may have been carrying manure; it was unloaded then evidently placed back on the wagon."

Arrius said, "The wagon was probably used to carry the weapons and the manure to conceal them when they came through one of the gates. What else did you find?"

"From the number of trails leading away, only one or two men rode in the wagon. The wagon tracks led to a village four miles from here. We lost them there because of the other cart traffic going in and out of the village."

"Well, they're long gone by now." Arrius noted the mid- afternoon position of the sun. He turned to the cavalry troop leader. "Decrius and I will return to Banna. I want four men to remain here until I can arrange to send a relief detachment to assume responsibility for the tower. I'll send a cart to bring the bodies back to Banna for suitable rites and burial."

As he and Decrius rode toward Banna, Arrius looked at the optio's taught jaw. It occurred to him Decrius would be caught between conflicting loyalties if the Briganti were also involved in the attack on the signal tower. Except for the tattoos on the optio's face and his long hair, it was easy to forget he was by birth a member of the Brigantae

Tribe. He knew Decrius enough not to be concerned over his loyalty, but then he hadn't been put to the test. Arrius thought it was better to address the matter directly rather than allow the thought to lie in the shadows of doubt and speculation. He reined in Ferox to a walk. "Decrius, what will you do if the Briganti rebel? Where will your loyalties lie — with Rome or your tribe?"

Decrius did not answer the question immediately. The optio must have been considering the same thing. Finally, Decrius looked at Arrius.

"You ask a fair question, Praefectus, and for the time being, I don't know the answer. I've worried over the possibility ever since taking the sacramentum particularly since I remained in Britannia rather than seeking a posting away from here where my loyalties would never be questioned. I fear one day I may be in a situation where neither the Romans nor the Briganti will trust me."

Arrius appreciated the honest response and the dilemma requiring a difficult choice for both of them. "I understand, but when you decide, and if you choose to remain with your tribe, I ask only one thing. You must tell me. I will ensure you leave unharmed. However, if hostilities occur and you elect to help the Briganti by remaining with the cohort, I'll kill you myself."

"I will do as you say, and I'll give you my oath on it." Even though both men maintained their silence for the remainder of the ride to Banna, it was evident from their more relaxed expressions the brief conversation had been necessary.

Despite efforts to remain emotionally uninvolved, Ilya realized with every visit Arrius made to the inn she was losing her resolve. A few months earlier, she thought it impossible she would ever feel anything but disgust and hatred for all Romans. On the surface, Arrius epitomized the very image she despised. She accepted the reality long ago she would probably never welcome any man, least of all a Roman, into her life. Now she wasn't so certain. She began to regret when it was time for him to leave and looked forward to his return.

It was also apparent Arrius and Joric had formed a strong attachment to the extent she wondered if the reason for his frequent visits might have less to do with her than it was to spend time with her son. She recalled few times when Joric wasn't present hanging on every word the Roman officer said. She also noticed Joric was unconsciously taking on some of the Roman's mannerisms — Arrius's habit of tilting his head slightly when listening, or the way he stood with his right fist resting on his hip. At first, she resented Joric's worship of Arrius then realized Joric, apart from Attorix, never had an opportunity to be around any man for any length of time. Beldorach's brief and infrequent visits hardly counted. Attorix was tolerant of the young boy's presence but otherwise indicated no special interest in him.

She longed to have a woman friend to talk to, but there was no one. While she was cordial enough with many of the village women, including Decrius's wife, none of the women inspired her to cultivate a relationship where confidences were shared and feminine advice obtained. She was aware of the physical reactions she was beginning to have, the warm, tingling feeling when she saw him accompanied by the involuntary hardening of her nipples. She was embarrassed one morning when she recalled the lurid dream about him and was disappointed when she woke to find it was only a dream. What was more normal for her was the recurring nightmare of her rape so many years before and certain to remain for the rest of her life. To her relief, such dreams were becoming less frequent.

While he hadn't made any physical advances to her, she was beginning to wish he would even if she was still somewhat fearful one day he might. She didn't know how she would react if he did but sensed the time was fast approaching the possibility was likely going to become reality. She was aware his attention was more than casual and wondered why he seemed cautious in pursuing a more intimate relationship. Perhaps he frequented one of the local brothels to satisfy physical urges and was immediately both ashamed and nettled at the thought. Well, it was none of her business, and why should she care if he did? But she hoped he didn't.

She saw and heard verification of the positive effect Arrius was having on Banna from the legionaries who came to the tavern. She noticed their behavior, while still boisterous at times, was less confrontational. The men seemed to complain less and laugh more. Less frequently, Attorix needed to escort an unruly customer out the door. Her business declined somewhat as the number of legionaries coming for wine or beer began to fall off. Eventually, she understood it was due to the increased tempo of training and patrols and not because their commander was often a guest. Occasionally, she overheard snatches of conversation concerning the praefectus, and what was said tended toward praise more than criticism. When there were disparaging comments, they were measured and held grudging admiration for his stern but fair leadership.

The one thing Arrius still seemed disappointed about focused on his officers. She'd been alerted to some potential problem when he made an oblique reference to it during one of their many conversations. He thought good progress was being made in winning over the confidence of the legionaries and hoped to achieve similar results with the officers. She asked what he meant, but he only smiled and changed the subject leaving her to believe there was much more to the remark than he was willing to talk about, at least with her.

Her heart skipped a beat as she heard hoof beats outside and Joric's exuberant welcome. She pictured her son racing up to greet the big black horse. Although Ferox never required grooming beyond the care he received at Banna, it was a ritual for Joric to take the horse to the stable and spend time brushing his sleek flanks and combing imagined tangles from his tail and mane. Ilya was secretly pleased over Joric's attention as it gave her the selfish pleasure of Arrius's full attention for the short time it took to groom the horse.

As was more typical, Arrius walked in bareheaded attired only in tunic and cloak. She greeted him with a warm smile. "Marcus, I didn't think I would see you today. What an unexpected pleasure."

"I'm afraid I cannot stay long. Joric won't be pleased to have so little time with Ferox, but there's much to be done. I'll be leaving in a day or two to patrol in the north. The attack yesterday on one of my signal towers south of here appears to be the work of one of the northern tribes."

Ilya caught her breath secretly hoping the Selgovi had nothing to do with it. "I heard of it. I understand some legionaries were killed."

"Aye, it's true. I lost all six in the detachment. It was a bold move, and at first, I was certain it signaled a possible uprising by the Briganti." She was relieved to hear him add, "However, Decrius says the two tribesmen we found dead in the tower were Novanti; consequently, the commander at Uxellodonum has ordered more patrols north, an action I was planning to do anyway." She was aware he seemed distracted, nervously glancing around the room. "Ilya, I may be gone for a time, and I was wondering if you would be my guest at the fort for a change. I would like you to meet Philos."

He'd often spoken to her of his friend and former slave. She was curious to meet him although she suspected this was not the main reason for the invitation. Nor did she think it had anything to do with an extended absence. She knew she was flushing and hated the way her face always betrayed her feelings. Her immediate reaction was to refuse, citing the need to remain at the tavern with Joric. Then she realized it had less to do with Joric and much more with her fear of her own feelings and the prospect of being away from the security of the tavern. She was concerned she might be alone with him in an environment where she had no control. Even more than that, she was reluctant because she wanted to go. In all his visits here, they were never alone together, or on the few occasions they were, there was always the chance of being interrupted by Joric or one of the slaves. She found herself nodding as she searched his face seeing relief replace the uncertainty in his eyes. His smile was broad as he impulsively reached for her hands. "Good, I hoped you would say yes. Philos is already making the preparations. I'll send a cart for you at dusk."

He was gone before she realized what happened. It was the first time he touched her, spontaneous and innocent as it may have been. The remarkable thing was she didn't recoil as once she would have done. She already regretted her impulsiveness in accepting the invitation. She started thinking of various excuses to avoid going. Before she realized it, her thoughts were overtaken by concerns for the dress she would wear, the perfume she should select and what hairstyle would be suitable. In a daze without being conscious of what she was doing, she walked to her bedroom and began to comb her hair. What would she tell Joric? How should she tell him? Then she admitted to herself she was anticipating more from the evening than sharing a meal

Philos had never seen Arrius in such a state showing an uncharacteristic interest in the preparations for his guest, sampling dishes, making superfluous suggestions and interfering until he was ordered to leave the villa and not return until called. Chastened, Arrius left for the principia where he proceeded to make the staff miserable with unproductive preoccupation in matters best left to the cornicularius and clerks. Finally, in a moment of rare bravado, Antius Durio diplomatically urged the Praefectus to leave the headquarters and inspect the stables, the guard posts or go somewhere, anywhere as long as he wasn't there.

By the time the pony cart Publius Gheta provided for the occasion left the east gate, it was common knowledge the praefectus was entertaining a guest that evening, and speculation was running high. The identity of the commander's guest was hardly a secret given his frequent visits to see the lady who owned the tavern east of the fort. Arrius would've been mortified to know of the bets being placed in the barracks on the outcome.

Ilya was trembling when the cart passed unchallenged through the east gate. The legionary driving the cart was solicitous of her comfort in the short ride but was otherwise silent and concentrated on avoiding the worst of the potholes filled with the spring rains. The driver stopped the cart in front of the spacious villa inside the gate where a household slave was waiting to help her down. Doing her utmost to conceal her nervousness, she followed Linius through the portico leading into a reception room where Arrius was waiting to greet her. As soon as she saw him dressed in a plain, dark red tunic, she realized from his anxious expression he was every bit as nervous as she was; the realization was enough for her to relax.

Arrius helped her out of her cloak and caught the scent of a subtle and immensely pleasing perfume. Except for a trace of coloring on her cheeks, she hadn't resorted to the fashionable paints and oils he privately thought turned the female face into a mask. He took in the simple but elegant gown trimmed in green and belted tightly at the waist. Her hair fell almost to her waist and was loosely gathered at the back of the neck with a gold clasp. He was confident Ilya would grace the richest villa in Rome.

Arrius felt awkward and ill at ease as he took her arm and led her through the reception room into the inner courtyard illuminated by torches. Except for being larger, the courtyard arrangement with its colonnaded veranda on all four sides was similar to her tavern, once a private villa. At the far end of the courtyard was a small bronze statue of a warrior dressed in armor, spear in one hand, the other upraised in supplication on a pedestal. She supposed the statue represented one of the many war-like gods the Romans seemed to favor so much.

She followed him into the *triclinium* where the dining table was set for three. She felt a momentary pang of disappointment she and Arrius were not going to dine alone. As she was wondering who it might be, a slightly-built man entered from an adjoining room. The elderly man had only a fringe of white hair remaining on his head. A broad welcome smile erased some of the deep lines on his face. When she saw he was missing a hand, she knew who he was.

"Ilya, this is Philos, my closest friend."

"I bid you welcome to this house, Lady Ilya. I believe your presence here may be long overdue." His smile became even broader when he saw the look of discomfort on Arrius's face. Ilya was immediately captivated by the lively man whose presence seemed to dispel the awkwardness of the moment. As they seated themselves at the table, another man entered and was introduced as Cito who bobbed his head in acknowledgement of the introduction before filling their cups with wine from the pitcher he carried.

Arrius decided later, and Ilya agreed long after, Philos saved the occasion from becoming a complete disaster. He chattered away on a variety of subjects, asked questions and voiced an opinion to keep the conversation going. Eventually, the combination of good food and an ample supply of wine managed to relax the other two to a point where they began to thoroughly enjoy the evening. At first, Ilya thought Arrius included Philos to dispel any awkwardness that might have prevailed if they dined alone. As the evening wore on, she decided her perception might not be entirely correct. She saw the deep friendship between the two men, and the thought occurred to her she might be on trial. She was certain the older man's approval would be important to Arrius. In a lull in the conversation, she asked with genuine curiosity, "How did you two meet?"

She saw the two men immediately look at each other, and a brief silence descended causing Ilya to believe she may have asked the wrong question. It was Philos who answered.

"I was once a soldier, but as you can see," gesturing to his missing hand, "I was not a very good soldier. When the last battle I fought against the Macedonians was over, those of us on the losing side still alive were sold as slaves. I was fortunate enough to be bought by a learned scholar who, despite not being a particularly kind or good master, provided the opportunity for me to learn many things. When he died, his wife thought to enrich herself by eliminating one more mouth to feed; therefore, one day I found myself once again for sale in the market place. After several weeks, I was finally purchased by a very junior centurion for an absurdly low price — the centurion was

Marcus Arrius. It seems he required improvements in his education, and I soon reached the same conclusion."

"It was the best bargain I ever made." Ilya knew immediately Arrius was not referring to a monetary transaction. "I wouldn't be where I am today without Philos who taught me much more than the finer points of philosophy and mathematics."

"And because of Arrius, I gained not only my freedom but my closest friend as well."

Ilya looked at Arrius and realized how wrong her first impression of him was by focusing on his Roman armor and the superficial brutality of his face from the disfiguring scar. By doing so, she hadn't seen what was so evident now, the humor and compassion in his eyes, the quiet, gentle manner underscoring his preference for exercising reason instead of relying on rank and position.

By the time Philos, pleading his age, excused himself, Arrius and Ilya were entirely comfortable in each other's presence and more than ready to be left alone. Arrius refilled their cups. "Does Joric know where you are?"

"Yes. At first, I intended to tell him I was staying with a sick friend in the village. Then I decided the truth was better than a lie."

"What did he say?"

She laughed. "He wanted to come, too, but I said perhaps next time." Momentarily, she looked embarrassed. "If there is a next time."

"I feel quite confident there will be an invitation, and one it is my sincere hope you will accept."

She smiled, and he was aware her eyes reflected the flickering light of the clay lamps. "You must already know Joric worships you. His secret dream is to become a Roman officer like you." Ilya laughed. "He thinks I don't know and would disapprove if I did."

"And do you disapprove?"

"I suppose at first I did. I think you can understand why; however, since I've come to know you, I no longer feel that way." She thought this was the time to tell him who she really was. For reasons she was unable to explain, she allowed the opportunity to pass without telling him what Joric might one day become. "I want Joric to be what he wants to be."

"If he wishes to be a centurion one day, I can help him. I'm not without influence. His foreign birth does not prevent him from becoming one."

"Why would you want to do that?"

"Because I'm fond of Joric and wish him well. I also have a great regard for his mother whom I'm convinced is the most beautiful and most provocative woman I've ever known."

Ilya heard the simple declaration and knew it was not prompted by empty words designed to flatter. Before she could say anything, he stood up and came to her side. Reaching down he gently pulled her up from the chair enfolding her in his arms. Ilya pressed her face into his neck feeling his strength and the security of his embrace. For several moments, they stood motionless and silent, both knowing words were unnecessary to convey what they were feeling. Instead of resisting as she feared would happen, Ilya began to wish the moment would never pass. When he finally lifted her chin and pressed his lips to hers, she thought her legs would give way. Hungrily she returned his kiss and felt his body stirring in response. A part of her mind waited for her to break away in revulsion for memories still haunting her. Instead, she felt a tide of passion rising she never believed possible until now.

Effortlessly, Arrius swept her up and carried her out of the dining chamber and across the courtyard into a bedroom. Standing in the light of a single flickering lamp, he began to undress her, caressing her naked body slowly at first then with increasing passion. He cupped her upturned breasts, and she felt her knees becoming weak. He traced the small circular tattoo above her breast and looked at her with a silent question about its significance, but she merely placed a finger on his lips signaling this was not the time for words. She wrapped her arms around his neck and returned his kisses with equal abandon. Soon they were locked in ageless passion and the exquisite feeling of two bodies becoming one.

Throughout the night they declared their love for each other as their bodies joined together repeatedly in uninhibited joy. When one of them would fall asleep, the other would soon make demands, and they would begin all over again. Once while Arrius slept, she considered telling him of her father and the significance of the tattoo, but physical desire followed by sleep pushed the thought from her mind. The day would come she would deeply regret her decision to remain silent.

Chapter 8

Matius Betto stood on the rampart of the *porta principalis* and watched with hooded eyes as Arrius led the slow-moving column through the gate and north toward Fanum Cocidii. He smarted over how his authority was undermined since Arrius arrived. He'd even appointed Seugethis in overall command while he was gone leaving Betto in command of only the Banna garrison.

"May the gods and the Selgovi conspire to leave your bones far away from Banna," he swore softly unable to take his eyes off the man he'd come to despise. Mindful of his agreement with Tiberius Querinius, he looked for some opportunity to bring down Arrius, but so far, he waited in vain. He regretted his bargain with Querinius. He should have followed his own instincts and taken care of him in his own way before the praefectus became so popular with the legionaries. Regardless of Querinius's offer for advancement should he achieve what the tribune wanted so desperately, he had no intention of putting up with an indefinite wait. One way or the other before too long, Arrius would be disgraced or dead, and for Betto, dead was preferable.

Even worse, he saw his influence eroding with the centurions. There were only one or two left he could rely upon. He had to give credit to Arrius. The man had a way about him that inspired loyalty with the notable exception of Matius Betto.

The recent pay formation was the latest in a long list of changes where Arrius thwarted his influence. It hadn't taken long for Arrius to figure out the equipment accounts were altered. Betto was positive Publius Gheta was responsible. By the time he was through with the quaestor, even the gods would have difficulty putting him back together again. He bitterly recalled Arrius pointedly telling him what procedures would be followed in the future. During the next pay formation, the bastard stood to one side and silently watched the proceedings. He reckoned Arrius's vigilance cost him several hundred sestercii.

He was incensed Arrius reversed his orders concerning the barley ration, thereby depriving him of still another source of income.

Normally, he didn't care one way or the other whether the stupid Dacians or Tungrians drank beer or wine. He regretted no longer being able to sell some of the barley to the tavern owner in the western vicus. Gone, too, was the extra denarii from the wheat harvested by the cohort. Most of the local wheat crop was destined for Eboracum except for a portion quietly sold to a local merchant for a considerable profit for him and the other centurion also involved in the scheme. Because of Arrius, he was deprived of the extra income making service at Banna halfway bearable. He wanted to put something aside against the day when he would no longer be in this dung heap. Even Uxellodonum would be an improvement over Banna. The only way he could tolerate the fort was if he was in command and able to profit as he did before Arrius came and assumed command.

Adding insult to injury was the report he received an hour ago. The widow who owned the tavern in the east vicus was seen leaving Arrius's quarters before dawn. What was it about Arrius that he succeeded in bedding the cold bitch when no one else had been able to? At one time, nearly everyone at Banna including him tried to get between her legs or at the very least, dreamed about it. It would have served her right if the two drunken legionaries who assaulted her months before had been successful. At other times, the huge servant she kept close by discouraged even the most persistent. Maybe he was the one who was warming her bed? Well, if he was, it looked as if Arrius had his way with her now.

Betto began tapping his vitis against his leg in frustration. What he needed was a woman. He hadn't been to one of the brothels in several days, and he was beginning to feel the need. He was growing tired of the same whores most of whom were past their prime. He started fantasizing what he would like to do to the attractive widow and found he was becoming sexually aroused. He wondered if there was more to Arrius's interest in the woman than physical. The more the thought stayed with him, the more he began to want to know the answer. If it were true, there were possibilities to be explored. He became intrigued at the thought of bringing them both down.

Arrius tried to keep his mind on the two centuries behind him, but the recent image of Ilya's naked body was making it extremely difficult to concentrate. Fortunately, preoccupied as he was with non-military thoughts, the centurions and optiones behind him were automatically attending to the details of the march. His painstaking efforts over the past few months to transform the legionaries and their leaders into something more than guards were clearly evident in the appearance of the men and the way they carried out their orders. He was proud of the transformation taking place at Banna and was becoming more confident every day the Tungrians would hold their own when put to the test.

He was certain the attack on the signal tower was an isolated event. Querinius ordered increased patrolling both north and south of the Wall along the entire sector. The order was based on the recent Novantaean attack at Blatobulgium and the sighting of a large Selgovan patrol ten miles east of Banna. Had he been the senior commander, Arrius would have given the same order.

He did have misgivings concerning Querinius's order to concentrate all efforts on the Novanti that left his own sector more vulnerable than he liked. He also didn't agree with the final part of the orders directing the destruction of any villages they found. He couldn't think of a better way to foster hostile relations with the northern tribes than to undertake actions designed to inflame them. It was evident Querinius was a disciple of General Arvinnius and his belief exercising a heavy hand was key to maintaining peace. When the orders arrived, he thought about questioning them, particularly those concerning the destruction of the villages. But he concluded it would change nothing. It was after all, the traditional Roman way to deal with hostile tribes.

In a moment of sober reflection, he considered the possibility he was the one out of step and not Querinius or Arvinnius. Neither man saw and experienced the carnage in Judaea. The images of laying waste to villages, legionaries cutting open Jewish bellys looking for booty and the piles of burning bodies preyed on his mind. War was one thing, but the kind of wholesale destruction that became the norm in Judaea raised disturbing questions for which he still did not have answers. The battle in the Sorek Valley played no part in such thoughts, nor did the ultimate fate of the *Deiotariana*, profound as it was; it was only an unfortunate outcome of battle. No, the Sorek Valley was what he was trained for, and if he had died there, it would have been no more than what every legionary knew was always the possible outcome of battle.

He estimated they were half way to Fanum Cocidii when he looked to the west and saw one of the flank guards dismounted and leading his horse over the crest of a hill. A moment later, he reappeared, mounted his horse and rode the short distance back to the column and reported to Arrius.

"Praefectus, there's a wagon at the bottom of the hill. It looks to be in very good shape to be abandoned."

Curious, Arrius kicked Ferox into a cantor and followed the cavalryman. Arrius reined in at the top of the slope and looked where the cavalryman pointed. At the bottom of the slope next to a tree-lined stream was an overturned cart typical of those widely used in the region.

Carefully, the two men angled their horses down the steep hill to take a closer look. The odor of manure became stronger the closer they came to the wagon. Arrius was about to turn back to avoid the stench until he noted the comparatively clean cart bed and the oiled cloth lying near a pile of dung. He was confident the dung cart was how the signal tower raiders got their weapons across the border. Nearby, the ground was littered with droppings, and from the considerable amount of them and closely cropped grass, Arrius estimated a dozen or more horses had been there for several days. He followed the streambed and observed a fresh trail away from the cart. The trail led generally north tracing the contour of the narrow valley. Ahead, Arrius saw the stream swinging northwest and surmised the Novanti raiders were using the stream to cover their movements back to their tribal lands. A short distance later, the trail broke abruptly away from the stream and up the slope heading northeast. Arrius followed the trail up the slope and upon gaining the top, saw it proceeded in a straight line northeast toward Fanum Cocidii. He thought if the raiders were Novanti, they certainly took a long way back to their tribal lands.

Soon after arriving at Fanum Cocidii, he told Seugethis about finding the wagon and left it to him to decide whether or not it was worthwhile to pursue the trail any farther. Minutes later, the Dacian was issuing orders for a turma to take up the pursuit. "I'll give you odds Beldorach is involved," Seugethis said thumping the table hard enough to threaten the flagons of beer sitting before them. "You know of the skirmish near here early this morning?"

"No," Arrius leaned forward. "I'd only heard there was a sighting. It must have happened soon after I left Banna."

"A messenger arrived an hour ago with the news. A foot patrol unexpectedly ran into a small party of mounted Selgovi. Evidently, the Selgovi were prepared and although outnumbered, managed to kill two legionaries and wound three more. The legionaries claimed to have hit one or two of them and said a blood trail proved they did some damage. A foot patrol without supporting cavalry against an enemy relying mainly on horses seems a useless waste of legionaries."

"Then you can see why I've asked you for a troop when I leave here to join Querinius on his move against the Novanti."

"Aye, I don't like it, but they're ready to ride when you give the order. Are you sure I can't go as well?"

"I want you here in case things get out of hand while I'm gone. I need to feel I have at least one senior commander I can rely on."

"I take it you refer to Betto."

"Yes, it's my intention to approach Querinius when I see him and request his transfer."

"Do you think Querinius will heed your request?"

"I see no reason why not. Betto's competent enough. My problem is I don't trust him. We haven't gotten along since the day I arrived."

"Well, as you know, I've no regard for Betto, but I also have possibly less for Querinius. Now there's a man not to be trusted. Between Betto and Querinius, I would take Betto since I can expect what he might or might not do. Querinius is a different matter. He's the type who will say one thing and then do the opposite. I suspect you have the same opinion."

Arrius evaded a direct answer to the question. "We've had our differences."

"Very well, have it your own way, but I would take care if I were you. I think Querinius will never have anyone's best interests in mind except his own." Changing the subject, Seugethis asked, "When are you leaving?"

"As soon as the men have rested. We've still a half day to go before nightfall, and my orders are not to delay."

"Too bad, I was looking forward to the company."

Arrius stood up, took a long pull from the flagon and clapped the cavalryman on the shoulder. "I wish it was otherwise, but I'd be neglecting my duty if I remained the night."

Two days later, Arrius led the column to a grassy field near Castra Exploratorum, the main forward outpost for Uxellodonum and the rendezvous point for the diverse units assembled for the campaign. The march was more difficult than Arrius expected as they encountered vast tracts of dense forest where the only alternative was to go through them or spend too much time to go around them. In some areas, the forest was so thick the cavalry was forced to dismount and lead their mounts. Occasionally, the lead elements were obliged to cut down trees to allow the wagons to pass through. Here and there, they chanced upon rude huts tucked away in a forest glade. Even though hearths were still warm, they caught not a single glimpse of any inhabitants or even livestock in these remote enclaves.

Castra Exploratorum was smaller than Fanum Cocidii consisting as it did of an infantry unit from Germania. After ensuring the Banna contingent was suitably camped and fortified, Arrius rode over to the fort and was pleased to find he knew the centurion in command having served with Carbalo years before along the Rhine. While not close friends during their previous service, both drew pleasure in meeting a familiar face so far from civilization. Arrius was shocked to learn the centurion's only contact with Querinius so far was limited to Carbalo's trip to Uxellodonum when the tribune arrived two months before.

By the time Querinius arrived two days late with four cavalry troops and a dozen wagons, Arrius was seething, and Carbalo was completely bewildered. He pushed his legionaries hard for nothing to meet the appointed date specified in his orders. Arrius didn't put it past Querinius to have deliberately shown up late for no other reason than a petty way to assert his authority. Arrius noticed Querinius positioned himself behind the second troop instead of in the traditional lead. Apparently, the tribune was still concerned for his personal safety.

Accompanied by several junior officers, Querinius detached himself from the squadron and rode to where Arrius and Carbalo sat astride their mounts in front of the fort's east gate. Querinius ignored the salutes given by the two officers and focused on Ferox. Addressing Arrius with a humorless smile, he said, "You have a fine horse, Arrius. I recall noticing it during my visit to Banna. I congratulate you on your good fortune in finding such a remarkable beast. I wonder if you would consider selling him to me. I believe he would be quite a suitable mount for the senior commander at Uxellodonum."

Without changing expression, Arrius replied, "I regret the horse is not for sale." He heard an audible gasp from Carbalo at the sharp response bordering on insolence.

Querinius's smile became forced, and his jaw tightened perceptibly. "I can order you to sell the horse. As your superior, I can take the animal, and there is little you have to say much less do about it."

'Tribune, there is much within your authority to do as you like, but this is an issue I think it unlikely you will pursue. Besides, I believe we're assembled here for other reasons than discussing horses. Since you've arrived somewhat late, I assume you'll want to make up for it by getting on with the campaign as quickly as possible — that is after you've told us how the campaign will be conducted."

Querinius's face went white leaving only spots of color high on his cheeks. "Arrius, you're as insolent as ever. How dare you mock me? Take care, Praefectus, you do not go too far with your loose tongue, or one day you may lose it."

Arrius thought he'd pushed Querinius far enough and remained silent. His contempt for the man might be his undoing. He resolved to do better in the future by controlling the spontaneous urge to bait him.

After making a supreme effort to regain his self-control, Querinius said, his lips tightly compressed, "I want all officers in the principia within the hour when it will be *my* pleasure to outline the conduct of the campaign. I trust that will satisfy you?"

Arrius nodded and kept his mouth shut.

By the time the twelve officers were assembled, Tiberius Querinius was composed and his manner brisk.

"The recent attacks on Blatobulgium and the signal tower near Banna are unmistakably the work of the Novanti. Therefore, it is my intention to punish them and make them understand they gain nothing but their own destruction if they continue to attack us. It will also serve as a lesson to the other tribes. If they do not want peace, we will give them war. We leave tomorrow at first light for Blatobulgium. Carbalo, leave sufficient legionaries here at Castra Exploratorum to ensure its security. You will lead the bulk of your command on the left flank of the march with your cavalry screening primarily to your left and front. Arrius, you will take the right flank. Use your cavalry to secure your front and flanks. I want to maintain two to three miles between your columns. We will maintain a wide front to increase the likelihood of locating Novanti villages and strongholds. Any villages we find will be destroyed." Directing his attention to Villaunus, the cavalry squadron commander at Uxellodonum, he said, "Take the center of the formation and maintain contact between the two infantry columns. Be prepared to reinforce either column in the event of a flank attack. The baggage carts will follow the cavalry in the center."

Arrius listened with growing alarm. Superficially, the plan seemed sound enough, and the other officers showed no concern with the exception of Carbalo who appeared preoccupied. Villaunus remained silent and impassive. For someone who had only ventured north of Uxellodonum for the first time, he thought Querinius was making assumptions on terrain conditions to prescribe a formation extremely difficult to maintain even in open country. He recalled the density of the forests encountered the day before and hoped Querinius's information was correct; however, from the look on Carbalo's face, he knew Querinius hadn't consulted with anyone. The tribune's movement formation was based on theory and not on practical reality or consideration of the terrain they were going to encounter. Arrius waited for either Villaunus or Carbalo to comment, but neither man seemed inclined, obliging him to speak up.

"Tribune, the formation you've ordered is a complex one and will be difficult to maintain unless the terrain is relatively open. My concern is if there are dense forests similar to those I encountered on the way here, it will be exceedingly difficult for Villaunus to keep contact with the infantry if we maintain the distances you've prescribed. Perhaps it would be useful to have the opinions of Villaunus and Carbalo on the matter." He hoped his tone of voice sounded neutral.

Looking uneasy, Carbalo said, "I'm familiar with the terrain as far as Blatobulgium, and it is somewhat as the Praefectus has described. Although there is some open country, it will be difficult to maintain contact and advance as you have ordered."

"Difficult but not impossible," Querinius said. "And your opinion, Villaunus?"

"It's as you say, Tribune, difficult but not impossible, and the formation does provide flexibility in the event we make contact with a large force."

Arrius tried another approach. "Have you considered the possibility of keeping the infantry in one column and the cavalry screening the front and on the flanks? Such an approach would facilitate maintaining the integrity of our formation and maximize our capability to deal with any large-scale Novanti attack by focusing our strength quickly and decisively. Cavalry placed far forward and over a wide area would serve to direct the infantry when and where it can be deployed in the most efficient and effective manner."

"I did consider a formation such as you described, but I thought it was too conventional to support my objectives." Dismissing the possibility of further discussion on the subject, Querinius said, "I anticipate we will find villages and homesteads as we advance. If they are small enough, each column will deal with them as they are discovered. In the event a large settlement or force is encountered, I will consolidate our forces and attack in strength. When we do engage the Novanti, I want them completely destroyed. When we leave a village, I want nothing left behind alive — nothing, not so much as a goat, chicken or a child. Do I make myself clear? I realize such measures are harsh, but it is time to make a point, and if it must be accomplished with a sword, so be it."

"Tribune, have you considered the extreme measures you mandate may serve only to inspire the northern tribes to forget their differences and unite in common purpose?"

Querinius gave Arrius a contemptuous look. "Can it be you are squeamish in doing what was typical in Judaea?"

"It is for that very reason I dislike the order." Arrius recalled the hatred inspired by Rome's heavy-handed treatment resulting in the virtual extermination of the Jewish population and destruction of the province. "I wish my disagreement with the order to be included in the campaign record."

"Do you intend to disobey the order?"

"Not at all, I only believe its effectiveness as a policy in dealing with the tribes is potentially dangerous in the long-term for the reason I gave." The other officers shifted uncomfortably in their seats.

The remainder of the consilium was devoted to the more ordinary aspects of readying for the campaign, mainly logistics and the means to maintain contact.

Chapter 9

On a distant hilltop, Beldorach watched the slow progress of the Roman advance with irritation. Although he was pleased his efforts to get the Romans to march on the Novanti had materialized, he was concerned at the rate the Romans were moving, only the weakest and most infirm of the Novanti tribe would be at risk.

For two days, he dodged the cavalry screen to study his enemy looking for weaknesses he could exploit in the future. He was amazed at the clumsy formation see-sawing back and forth when one column or the other slowed down to pass through a forest, obliging the other column to slow its pace as well. What was more surprising was the bulk of the cavalry force was reduced to walking their horses in between the two marching columns. If this was the latest example of the venerable Roman war machine, the reputation was greatly over-stated.

His support of Bothan was nominal, and its only purpose was to serve his own long-term interest. The Selgovan contribution was enough to look convincing without risking the loss of too many warriors. His plan was diabolically simple. Let the Novanti incur the losses. A weakened Novanti tribe would make it easier for the Selgovi to dominate what was left when the Romans were finished. He was due to meet with Bothan that night to discuss how they would deal with the Roman campaign. His plan would feature the Selgovi taking on the prominent role in fighting the Romans in a major battle. He was counting on Bothan's insistence the Novanti should have the honor. Reluctantly, he would give in to Bothan's demand and let the Novanti take the casualties he wanted the Selgovi to avoid.

Arrius was thoroughly disgusted with their slow progress. The formation Querinius mandated was awkward and as slow as he had pointed out. For the third time that day, the cavalry linking the two infantry columns conveyed an order from Querinius to hold while the other column fought its way through a particularly dense forest. It was obvious even to the least experienced legionary something needed to change.

Arrius dismounted and led Ferox slowly along the length of the ranks of legionaries, most of whom were taking advantage of the latest break by catching a quick nap in the warmth of a beautiful spring day. He passed a grim-faced Decrius standing off to one side, his expression and stiff body stance showing his own displeasure at the way things were going. He saw Flavius, his senior centurion, talking to one of the optios and on impulse headed toward him.

"Flavius, I'm placing you in temporary command while I find Tribune Querinius. This has become intolerable. At the rate we're going, another four or five miles and we'll be ready to go into winter quarters. If they are watching our progress, the Novanti must surely be laughing." The centurion smiled and nodded in approval.

Arrius mounted Ferox and urged the horse into a gallop toward the northwest where he presumed Querinius would be found. He kept in open terrain avoiding the thick tree lines. He tried to think of how to get the tribune to listen to reason and change the current plan. The one thing he was positive about was regardless of how well-reasoned and justified his remarks might be, Querinius's first reaction would likely be rejection. Still, he felt compelled to try.

Several miles later, he found the bulk of the cavalry contingent dismounted and walking their horses. He spotted Querinius in animated conversation with Villaunus. The tribune was resplendent in bright armor and greaves more appropriate to the parade field than a campaign. In more practical contrast, Arrius wore his field armor, dull in color and battered from years of service. From the sour expression on the tribune's face, whatever the cavalry officer was saying was not being received well. Arrius cantered toward the two men. As he reined in, both men interrupted their discussion and looked in his direction acknowledging his arrival in different ways; Villaunus appeared relieved to see him while Querinius's expression became darker.

"What are you doing here, Arrius?" Querinius's irritation was evident.

Arrius replied in what he hoped was a neutral tone. "Actually, I was looking for you. I thought perhaps it would be useful to review our current disposition to see if an adjustment might be advisable." Villaunus, facing away from Querinius, gave Arrius a broad smile of encouragement giving him some idea of what the previous conversation may have been about.

"Arrius, when I want your opinion, I'll send for you."

"Since I'm here, Tribune, it would seem reasonable you would want to have a first-hand account of our progress, or should I say our lack thereof."

Querinius flushed. "Have you been talking to Villaunus?"

"Not at all, why do you ask? We haven't spoken since we left Castra Exploratorium."

"Very well, say what you have to say and be off."

"Tribune, at our present rate we may never reach Blatobulgium. We're spending far too much time standing around waiting to be told to move on. And when we do, we lose time trying to sweep through forests that slow us down even more. I believe we're wasting too much time searching every forest tract. If Carbalo were here, I suspect he would say much the same."

"I believe the very point is to find the Novanti, and if we do not search the forests, we stand little chance of finding them."

"A more effective and faster way to find the Novanti is to send out small mounted patrols to locate them then mount an attack. At present, we're wasting time trying to maintain a disposition completely unsuitable for accomplishing the very objective you defined. Meanwhile, the bulk of our cavalry is next to useless or spending time going back and forth between the two columns." Arrius realized he was making little headway with his blunt words and adopted a more conciliatory approach.

"Look, would it not be better to make a few adjustments in the interest of speeding up our advance? I suspect if we're to find any significant Novanti settlements, they will most probably be located far beyond Blatobulgium. I submit the time for a slower and more cautious advance will be more justified farther ahead." Arrius saw a flicker of interest in Querinius's eyes. He thought it possible Querinius may have already determined the formation and movement plan was a mistake and was looking for a face-saving way to change it.

"And what is it you propose we do?"

"Reduce the distance between the two columns." If he recommended consolidating both columns as he would have preferred, it would be too bold a change for serious consideration. "By closing the distance between the columns, more cavalry can be used to screen the flanks and forward of the lead elements. And in the event we do encounter a large enemy force, each column is in a better position to reinforce the other." From the corner of his eye, he saw Villaunus nodding his head vigorously in agreement. He was becoming somewhat encouraged his ideas might be adopted the longer Querinius took to reply. Reason might yet prevail over the reluctance to admit a mistake.

Querinius made a show of deliberating, pursing his lips and assuming a thoughtful expression. "While I appreciate your suggestions, Arrius, I'm not convinced any changes are required yet. I will think of what you've said. Once we reach Blatobulgium, I may consider modifying the formation. In the meantime, we'll continue as we are. Now, if there's nothing else you have to say, you may rejoin your column."

For a moment, Arrius stared in mute disbelief at the tribune's refusal to accept his counsel. Arrius thought it was indeed time to rejoin his column realizing there was nothing at all to be gained in further debate except to risk losing his temper. As he turned Ferox back the way he came, his eyes locked momentarily with Villaunus. The cavalryman shrugged his shoulders in silent resignation.

During the ride back, Arrius reflected on his hostile relationship with the former commander of the *Deiotariana*. At least in the end, Metellus Gallius was willing to seek advice from those more experienced. He was convinced Querinius realized he made a mistake but was too stubborn to admit it in the mistaken belief to change would be viewed as an open admission he was wrong. It seemed he was destined to have trouble getting along with his superiors.

By the time he rejoined the column, the legionaries had progressed barely a mile from where he left them more than an hour ago. He caught a whiff of something burning and noticed smoke rising through the trees ahead. He heard angry voices and kicked Ferox into a gallop to investigate. He was appalled to see the legionaries arrayed in a circle within the tree line, raucously attentive to something he was yet unable to see.

Still astride Ferox, Arrius made his way through the knot of men until he was close enough to look over their heads and see the object of their attention. The noise began to die down as one by one they became aware of his presence and saw his stony face. Beyond the circle of men, he saw the burning remains of a small dwelling. The flames had already consumed most of the building now reduced to little more than ashes. The headless body of a man lay sprawled on the ground; he saw the severed head suspended by his braided hair from a nearby tree limb. In the middle of the circle stood Flavius, gladius drawn attempting to restore order. He saw Decrius standing with his back to Flavius, his optio staff at the ready. On the ground, a woman and a young boy he thought might be about the same age as Joric huddled together. Momentarily images of too many such scenes in Judaea flashed before him including the memory of three Jewish children clutching each other behind a bush. He felt his stomach tighten. He didn't know precisely when he started to consciously distinguish between necessary and unnecessary killing. Death to the enemy on a battlefield, he believed, was a principal objective in achieving a Roman victory. But what constituted a battlefield was becoming blurred. In his mind, summarily executing helpless civilians did not accomplish anything except to stimulate more hatred of the Roman occupation and reduce further any chance for peaceful coexistence.

"Flavius, what's happening here?"

"The men would have their sport with the captives before they're killed. It was my intent to have your orders obeyed to kill only those who resisted." Flavius nodded in the direction of the dead man. "He resisted. What do you want us to do with the woman and boy?"

"Let them go."

"Praefectus, the boy will soon be old enough to use a bow or sword."

Arrius knew what Flavius was saying was true. Now confronted with the consequences of his orders, he was no longer quite as certain whether his or Querinius's position made the most sense. His order calling for restraint created confusion among his own legionaries causing some to believe he might be sympathetic with the enemy when he was not. They wouldn't distinguish the difference between an armed Novanti warrior and an unarmed woman and child. In truth, it wasn't long ago when he would have thought the same.

"Possibly, but release them anyway."

Apart from a split lip and a small cut above her right eye, the woman was unscathed. She was anything but beautiful. Her face was worn beyond her years. She was dressed in a torn and ragged shift that left a pendulous breast partly exposed. He wondered how it was some men were sexually aroused by such an unattractive and pitiful specimen of her sex. It was then the woman looked up at him with naked hate in her eyes. If given the opportunity, she would gut him without a moment's hesitation or word of thanks for saving her and the boy's life. He looked closer at the boy and realized from the vacant look in his eyes he was simple. This was no future warrior, only another mouth to feed for a woman now with nothing left but her freedom. He wondered how they could survive and thought the chance was unlikely they would. For a fleeting moment, he wished he had stayed longer to argue with Querinius then he would not have needed to deal with the problem.

They reached Blatobulgium late the next day. Arrius had to look closely to see any evidence of the recent attack. He suspected, as was usual in such affairs, the report of the enemy force was greatly exaggerated. He learned later in the evening from a disgusted centurion assigned to the fort the so-called attack was nothing more than a relatively harmless fusillade of Novanti arrows launched without any sign a ground attack was ever intended.

In three days, the only encounter with the local population consisted of the one isolated homestead the Tungrian legionaries burned. The few other small farms they found were deserted with the owners taking their livestock and anything else of value as they fled deep into the forests. The failure to encounter any significant Novanti force cast a pall on the morale of cavalrymen and legionaries alike. Discipline was an increasing problem, and optiones wielded their knobbed staffs with regularity.

When Arrius was summoned to the principia, he assumed it was to discuss the next phase of the punitive expedition. Villaunus and Carbalo were already sitting silently waiting while Querinius conferred in low tones with a clerk sitting at a desk to the side and slightly behind the tribune. When he noted Querinius's self-satisfied expression and the strain on the other officer's faces, he began to suspect the meeting might have another purpose.

Querinius wasted no time in preliminaries. "I understand, Arrius, your legionaries captured three of the enemy two days ago, and by your order, allowed two to go free in flagrant disobedience to my explicit orders to leave no prisoners alive. Is this correct, or have I been misinformed?"

"The report is substantially correct if you define anyone living north of the Wall in this sector as the enemy."

Querinius glanced at the clerk. "Record the question and his response." He turned back to Arrius. "Are you quibbling with me, Arrius? I asked you a specific question, and I want a direct answer. I am uninterested in who you believe to be an enemy. Did you or did you not disobey my order?"

"I chose to exercise my own judgment in the matter." Anticipating he would be eventually called to account, he already determined there was no point in denying the incident occurred. In a perverse way, he relished getting the matter over while watching Querinius move farther out on the limb he was about to cut off.

The reply had the predictable effect on the tribune. "You're trifling with me, Arrius, and I'll not tolerate it. You've intentionally and willfully disobeyed my express order to leave no one alive after an engagement."

"The shepherd's wife and son seemed harmless enough to my way of thinking and hardly worth bloodying a sword."

"Did you stop and consider the boy might be the warrior to face you on a battlefield one day? Wolf cubs eventually grow into dangerous beasts."

"I hardly think in this case there's much danger of that occurring. You see, the boy was simple."

"The salient point is you violated my orders. You assured me during the consilium at Castra Exploratorium you would obey them." Querinius shot a glance at the clerk to see if his words were being captured for the record.

"If you put it that way, I suppose I did. I changed my mind. Furthermore, I intend to continue to violate any order you give I cannot agree with including your order for indiscriminate extermination of the local population." Arrius heard sharp gasps from Villaunus and Carbalo. For a moment longer, there was stunned silence. The clerk stared at him with wide-eyed shock at the bold admission, pausing in his transcription of the proceedings. When Querinius spoke, it was hardly above a whisper and directed to the clerk while continuing to stare at Arrius in disbelief.

"Do you realize I can discipline you for what you've done and admitted?"

Arrius leaned forward. "Since these proceedings are being recorded, presumably to satisfy your own purposes, I want to be certain the rest of what I have to say is accurately set down for the record. No, Tribune, you will not have me punished much less executed. For the truth of the matter is you don't have jurisdiction over me. In case you've forgotten or possibly didn't know, you may direct and order me to execute orders involving operational matters, but that is all you are authorized to do."

"Then you condemn yourself by your very words by disobeying my order to execute the local population whenever encountered."

"On the contrary, I did not understand the purpose of the campaign was to exterminate the local population. I logically surmised we are on campaign to reduce or eliminate an operational threat and discourage future tribal aggression. If that is your real intent, then you must clarify your orders now and in the future to ensure the units you lead have no cause for any misunderstanding. The alternative for subordinate commanders is to continue to exercise judgment according to the operational dictates of the situation as it develops. I might add, the Roman Army has always relied on its field commanders to lead their commands with thought first and the sword second."

"By the gods, Arrius, you're not only insolent but treasonous in your words. I could have you summarily tried here in the field for what you've admitted and said in front of these witnesses. These officers would quickly confirm your guilt and oblige me to have you executed."

"Tribune, allow me to tell you what you can and cannot do, since it seems you have little or no understanding of Roman military custom and law, nor do you realize how little jurisdiction you have over me. First, any trial you convene for me would have to involve officers of equal or senior rank; there are no officers present who equal my rank and you are the one senior to me."

"At least you recognize my seniority, and I believe the fact I am gives me the authority to exercise summary judgment including ordering appropriate punishment for disobedience of my orders. Be very careful, Praefectus, or the consequences can be ruinous and possibly fatal."

"I think not. I read very carefully my commission signed by General Arvinnius after I learned you would be commanding at Uxellodonum, and it states I am an independent commander. As such, you may order and make tactical dispositions for my command as operational circumstances warrant, but you have no disciplinary jurisdiction over me or anyone in my command.

"Before I left General Arvinnius, I made a point of defining the extent of my relationship with you and my authority as an independent commander. I found him sympathetic to my concerns. Tribune, I will follow the orders I believe are within your prerogative to give, even those with which I may disagree. For example, I've obeyed your order regarding the formation we've been obliged to follow even though its ineffectiveness surpasses all wonder." Out of the corner of his eye, Arrius saw Villaunus clench his jaw in an effort to keep from smiling. Carbalo was less successful in reining in his emotions and resorted to putting a hand over his mouth to stifle the feigned coughing fit.

Querinius's face was white, his mouth working to speak words he was unable to utter. Arrius almost felt sorry for him. He wondered if the man was as inept and devious as he appeared to be, or was it because he brought out the worst in him for reasons he would probably never fully comprehend. He had no sense of triumph over Querinius. Unfortunately, he succeeded only in creating a public breach serving no one.

"Get out! All of you get out!"

The three officers and clerk stood up without a word and started to file out of the room only to stop momentarily when Querinius yelled, "Arrius, stay!" After the others left, Querinius said, "Damn you, Arrius, one day you'll pay for this."

"Pay for what? Making a fool of you? You seem to manage it well enough by yourself."

"You've always gone out of your way to humiliate me and today is no exception."

Arrius was dumbfounded at the ridiculous and unwarranted accusation. "It wasn't I who ordered this meeting or sought a confrontation. You're responsible for that."

"Even though I'm your superior, you undermine my authority."

"Your own words and actions are responsible for such an outcome. What I don't understand is why you regard me as an adversary."

"Because you are, and you'll live to regret how you've treated me."

Arrius looked closely at Querinius's contorted face and believed the tribune was beyond rational thought or action. There was nothing further to be gained by prolonging the discussion, and he turned to leave only to hear Querinius say through gritted teeth, "Don't you dare leave until I've dismissed you. I'm not through with you."

Arrius turned back to Querinius. "What more is there to say?"

"I'm going to break you if it's the last thing I ever do. You'll make a mistake, and I'll be there to see you reap the consequences."

Arrius was shocked at Querinius's threat. "Querinius, there must be a reason for you to declare yourself so. What have I done to cause you to threaten me? If you feel so strongly, why don't you and I find a quiet place and settle the matter with swords once and for all."

"You'd like that more than anything so you can replace me."

Arrius shook his head bewildered over the accusation that made no sense at all. He wondered if the man's bizarre behavior was the consequence of an unbalanced mind. "You're wrong. I'm neither your rival nor your enemy."

"You are my enemy, and someday I'll see you destroyed. You show contempt for me because of my moment of weakness at Sorek. I know you're only waiting for the day to expose me."

"Your *moment of weakness* was no more than I or anyone else who have seen battle up close and faced certain death has not felt at least once. You have my word, I've never spoken to anyone about the incident, nor will I ever. No, there must be more to it. Aculineous made his attempt on my life long before the *Deiotariana* fought its last battle."

Querinius stood up. "I'll say it again — if it's the last thing I ever do, I'll see you brought down."

Arrius regarded the tribune with undisguised contempt. "So be it. I'll guard my back with unusual vigilance as long as you and I are in Britannia. It's unfortunate for both of us the gods saw fit to put us here. Querinius, hear me well. Do not provoke me too far, or I will deal with you as I did Aculineous."

Chapter 10

To Arrius's dismay two days after leaving Blatobulgium, Querinius still hadn't made any changes to the tactical formation. It was apparent he didn't intend to follow any counsel but his own.

Ever since the incident with the woman and boy, Arrius noticed the subdued mood of the legionaries. The weather was a big factor; it had taken a turn for the worse. They were now more often soaking wet than dry from the daily spring showers. He reckoned the major cause of the dip in morale was also due to the plodding nature of the campaign. So far, it felt more like a leisurely stroll with nothing to show for it but the destruction of isolated homesteads or small villages offering little in the way of booty.

The monotony was beginning to have an effect on him as well, and he felt a growing concern his senses were becoming dulled by the soporific routine. He found himself thinking more and more of Ilya and wishing he was back at Banna. By the third day, Arrius considered trying again to convince Querinius to make better use of the cavalry to locate the Novanti. He resolved he'd wait another day and postpone the unpleasant and most likely vain task.

His thoughts were interrupted when one of the cavalrymen patrolling a mile in advance of the column cantered up to him and reported spotting several mounted men, faces painted blue and openly brandishing weapons before disappearing into a distant tree line to the northeast. Arrius sent the cavalryman back with instructions to continue observing and maintain the current direction and pace. Over the next two hours, similar observations were reported and becoming more frequent. He dispatched a messenger to Querinius to advise him of the sightings with a recommendation it might prove useful to reinforce his forward cavalry screen.

Arrius noted they were entering a long narrow valley generally open but flanked by heavy forest spilling down the steep hillsides. He estimated the tree lines were a bowshot apart. At the far end of the valley, the cavalry advance was about to enter the trees forward and the flanking tree lines. Except for a flock of sheep scattered by the cavalry, there was no other sign of life. Everything about the terrain indicated this would be the ideal place for an ambush. Moments later, a horse without a rider galloped from the eastern tree line confirming his premonition.

Turning to Flavius, he ordered, "Recall the cavalry and prepare for an attack." He rode back and repeated the order to the centurion leading the second century even as the *cornicine* trumpeted the signal for the cavalry to return to the main body. He motioned for one of the mounted messengers representing his link to Villaunus and Querinius to come forward. "Report back to your squadron commander and Tribune Querinius contact with the enemy is imminent. Tell Querinius I request additional cavalry for a thorough reconnaissance of the terrain ahead and on my flanks. Pending the arrival of the cavalry, I will take up a defensive position." He made the messenger repeat the message. As he galloped off, Arrius looked about for a likely place to wait for reinforcements.

He spotted a tree-studded knoll a hundred yards ahead and nearly centered between the tree lines. The knoll represented the best option for repelling an attack if one came. He ordered the column into the *testudo* formation anticipating the possibility a rain of arrows might descend upon them at any time. He wished the auxilia carried the traditional rectangular scutum that gave greater protection than the smaller and rounder shields his legionaries carried.

The order was timely for the scuta had no sooner been positioned overhead when he heard the staccato sound of arrows impacting the raised shields. Thus far, the arrows were launched too far away from inside the trees to find a target except by pure chance. Unfortunately, his returning cavalry section was not so fortunate, and there were now more horses down than still heading toward the column. He resisted the urge to order a faster pace but knew the testudo, while offering the benefit of greater protection, couldn't be maintained effectively except at a walk.

By the time the cavalry closed in, Arrius saw little more than half remained of the twenty-man troop. So far there was only brief sightings of the Novanti warriors, insufficient to gauge their strength or determination to press an assault. As several arrows whizzed harmlessly by, Ferox snorted and laid his ears back. Conscious this was the stallion's first battle experience, he patted the animal's neck and tried to reassure him with soothing words. He regretted his attachment for the horse. Apart from the animal's occasional intractable nature, he would be sorry to lose him.

So far, he was reassured the Tungrians were showing no sign of panic. From an isolated gasp or cry of pain, an arrow found a target. They were a little more than halfway to the knoll when Arrius saw the first enemy warriors emerging from the trees. To increase their stature, the Novanti wore their long hair fastened over tall, elaborately carved wooden frames.

Arrius drew his sword and spurred Ferox toward the Novanti warriors while urging what was left of the cavalry to follow him. Although the Novanti considerably outnumbered the small mounted force, he was counting on the intimidation of a charging horse to even the odds.

He heard a ringing sound and felt his head jerk as an iron-tipped arrow point glanced harmlessly off his helmet. Another shaft lodged in the left saddle horn. He saw the first indication the Novanti line was beginning to waver as several warriors began to slowly back up. Others followed suit triggering the collapse of the Novanti defense as he hoped. The now panic-stricken warriors were running to the safety of the trees. Arrius lowered the long cavalry sword and rode toward the nearest warrior who was running away looking fearfully over his shoulder at the horse and rider bearing down on him. At the last minute, the warrior stopped, turned and raised his sword in a vain effort to defend himself. Arrius felt the jarring impact to his shoulder nearly unseating him as his sword point entered the man's chest. Maintaining a tight grip on the sword hilt, he dropped his arm and allowed the momentum of the horse and the weight of the dying man to free his sword while galloping toward his next target. From the agonized cries behind him, he knew other cavalrymen were wielding their swords with deadly results. His next victim swerved to avoid being spitted only to be knocked to the ground and trampled as Ferox galloped on without breaking stride.

Arrius saw other warriors starting to move in strength from the tree line toward the column and baggage train. He signaled the rest of the cavalry to join him while cursing Querinius for not approving his request for more cavalry several days ago. He pointed to the advancing Novanti and urged Ferox toward them. The Novanti took one look at the charging horses coming toward them and broke ignominiously for the safety of the trees. He guided the horse toward the rear of the advancing column and swept around it yelling encouragement to the legionaries. He was gratified to hear enthusiastic cheers in response. He saw a legionary, an arrow protruding from his leg, being supported by Rufus and another legionary as they attempted to keep up with the column. He rode toward the three men and told the wounded man to grasp the right pommel. Leaning to the left to balance the weight of the legionary, Arrius cantered off to the knoll and deposited the legionary close enough to gain the safety of higher ground.

Arrius estimated the Novanti strength was at least several hundred with possibly many more hidden in the trees. Confirming his worst fears, he heard drums beating a steady rhythm along with the shrill notes of bone whistles adding a strident and discordant accompaniment to the throbbing drumbeat. He looked down the far end of the valley in the direction they had been heading and saw several hundred of the enemy steadily advancing toward the knoll. As bad as their situation was, Arrius knew it could have been much worse. The bulk of the Novanti force were positioned at the far end of the valley where it began to narrow. If the Romans had gone any farther, their present situation would be even more precarious than it was.

Although greatly outnumbered, he felt the situation was far from desperate. He began to weigh alternatives. He estimated it would be several hours yet before relief from Villaunus's cavalry would arrive. What was left of his cavalry contingent was now more a hindrance than a help in the defensive posture they were forced to take.

Arrius beckoned for the cavalry decurion to join him. "Domitius, I want you to take what's left of the cavalry and report back to Villaunus and Querinius. You can do no more good here, and I need you to describe our situation." Arrius impatiently interrupted the cavalryman's protest with a curt wave of his hand. "There's no time to argue." He dismounted and gave the reins to the cavalry officer. "Take Ferox with you." Without further comment, Domitius reluctantly galloped off, a resigned expression on his face.

Arrius joined Flavius standing with Plautus, the red-faced centurion of the second century who was still breathing hard from his exertions. The two centurions were coordinating the construction of the shallow trench and low dirt wall to encircle the knoll.

"Plautus, have the archers concentrate on the flanks and see they make every arrow count. I want to force the Novanti to concentrate their attack where they seem to be intending now — straight down the valley. Flavius, I want your century to move forward with me to engage the enemy forward of our defensive line. The second century will continue to dig while we attack."

Flavius looked startled. Correctly interpreting the expression on the centurion's face, Arrius added, "I think an attack at this point with a well-trained and capable century might give Plautus a little more time to prepare the defenses. And I expect it may temper the tribesmen's eagerness to face Roman swords. If we don't rout them, we'll fall back and defend from here. In the meantime, we'll carry the battle to them." He pointed to the rapidly advancing horde lacking any semblance of organization.

A wide grin appeared on Flavius's face as he regarded the formidable Novanti strength. "Today I may dine with Jupiter himself."

"Jupiter can wait, Flavius, I have more need of you here. Now assemble your legionaries in attack formation in four ranks. We'll blunt their attack with javelins before we give them a taste of the sword. We won't go far forward as I don't wish to risk getting cut-off from Plautus in the event they get past us."

Leaving Flavius to assemble his century, Arrius walked over to the white-faced legionary he brought to the safety of the knoll. He sat with his helmet off, his back against a tree. The arrow projected grotesquely from his upper right leg.

"While you're taking a rest, I'll make use of your shield and pilum."

The legionary smiled. "Does the Praefectus remember how to use them?"

Arrius laughed. "It's been awhile, but I'm sure it will come back to me." He unbuckled his cloak and tossed it to the legionary before picking up the shield and spear. "For the time being, I'll trade you the cloak for the shield and spear. In time, I expect to give you back the shield — the spear I'll give to the Novanti."

Arrius took position on the left front of the formation while Flavius moved to the opposite side and gave the order to advance. If numbers alone became the deciding factor, Arrius knew the odds remained with the Novanti. He was depending on the countless drills and discipline he hammered into the legionaries over the past several months to make the difference. He hoped in the excitement of battle the Tungrians would not resort to the tendency often demonstrated in Judaea of occasionally abandoning disciplined ranks to fight individual battles. He expected the Novanti would do exactly that and erode their advantage in strength. From the look of the approaching mob now close to being within javelin range, his hope was about to be fulfilled. He was relieved to see the Novanti were tightly packed making them even more vulnerable to what was about to happen. Arrius saw the enemy break into a run much sooner than they should have. Good, he thought, they'll be even more tired when the sword work begins.

Moments later, Flavius gave the order for the first rank to begin the short run necessary to build up the momentum to effectively launch their javelins. The second rank was already starting their run when the first volley of javelins was still in flight. By the time the second rank hurled their weapons, the legionaries in the first rank had already drawn their swords in preparation for close-in fighting. Unfortunately, as soon as one warrior fell, another leaped forward to take his place.

By the time the rear ranks hurled their spears, the Tungrian and Novanti front ranks collided with the loud hollow sound of shield hitting shield accompanied by the roar of hoarse battle cries. The momentum of the heavier and larger auxilia shields pushed the Novanti line back several paces. The familiar and frightful din of battle reverberated in the valley, a cacophony of metal blade against metal blade, the thunk of battle axes striking shields, the cries of wounded and dying men.

It was too early to assess the battle results; however, his initial impression was the Tungrians were holding their own. The Novanti assault was undisciplined with the rear ranks pressing too closely and hindering the movement of the forward ranks.

Arrius saw Flavius stumble and threw his spear at the warrior who stood over the centurion with an upraised sword. The pilum caught the man full in the chest causing the warrior to fall back impeding the efforts of another tribesman intent on reaching the prone centurion. Arrius drew his gladius and reached Flavius in time to smash his shield into another warrior running toward him, pushing him to his knees then dispatching him with a quick thrust of his blade. He turned to meet the assault from two other warriors who began to press in on him from either side. One of the tribesmen stumbled forward pushed from behind, and Arrius brought the sharp edge of his shield down on the back of the man's unprotected neck with a sickening crunch. From the corner of his eye, he saw a flash of movement and realized Flavius had regained his feet and was once again actively engaged.

Making his way back toward the rear to better assess the progress of the battle, Arrius found he was badly winded. The heavy shield seemed to have gained more weight over the last several minutes. He thought it was possible he was getting a bit old for the rigors of pitched battle. So far, the results were far better than he dared to hope. The Novanti attack was blunted and the Tungrian front rank was being replaced by the second rank as quickly and disciplined as any seasoned century assigned to a Roman legion.

He saw a small group of tribesmen working their way around to attack the Tungrian flank. He pointed them out to Decrius who immediately alerted several legionaries in the third rank waiting with drawn swords to take their place forward. Spontaneously, Arrius joined them as they moved to stop the fresh assault. Soon he was back in the familiar rhythm of shove and thrust. Once he felt a sharp pain high on his sword arm then quickly forgot it in the press of battle.

The first indication the Novanti had enough was the sight of several enemy warriors toward the rear beginning to fall back. Gradually, the trickle became a flood. Becoming aware of what was happening behind them, the forward ranks abruptly disengaged and fled with the rest. For a few more minutes, the Tungrians held position to see if the Novanti would rally. It was soon evident the battle was over, at least for the time being. The ground between their present position and the knoll was littered with bodies. He was gratified to see the number of those in animal skins considerably outnumbered the Tungrians. Even so, Arrius estimated they had lost a quarter of their fighting strength.

Arrius ordered Flavius to take his century back to the knoll and finish preparing the ditch and earthen wall. He noticed Flavius was limping badly from a sword cut across the thigh. The Tungrian dead and wounded were picked up by the survivors on the way back to the defensive line. Legionaries not helping the wounded were busy dispatching any Novanti warriors still alive or relieving the dead of any rings, necklaces and arm bands they happened to see. Other legionaries were methodically decapitating the dead and gathering as many heads as they could carry.

Except for the backs of the retreating Novanti now at some distance down the valley, no other warriors were in sight. The occasional arrow shot from inside the tree line was the only sign they were still close by. Too far away to be accurate, the shafts were more of an irritant than a threat, and the legionaries generally ignored them. With the Novanti drums now silent, the only sounds were the moans of the wounded, the chunking sound of dolubrae sinking into the soft earth and the crash of felled trees to reinforce the earthen wall.

Arrius headed for one of the carts where additional water skins were carried after feeling the usual dry mouth and raging thirst common in the aftermath of battle. He saw Decrius finish wrapping a bandage around Flavius's thigh. From the centurion's white face, he had lost a lot of blood and was on the verge of fainting.

"Decrius, until Flavius is able to resume his duties, take command of the century. Find Plautus and the senior optio from the second century and return here as quickly as possible."

While waiting for the men to assemble, Arrius assessed their situation. So far, they had managed to acquit themselves well. The sobering reality was they wouldn't be able to withstand many more engagements such as the one just fought. If the Novanti persisted, they might yet prevail from sheer numbers alone. Remaining here for the present represented their best option pending the arrival of reinforcements. Arrius looked up at the cloudy sky and estimated only about three more hours of daylight left. Assuming the first messenger he sent reached Villaunus and Querinius, it might be another hour before any relief appeared. If the first messenger somehow did not make it through, Domitius would soon be making contact. He estimated it would be at least two or more hours until the reinforcements arrived about nightfall.

When Plautus and the senior optiones were gathered, Arrius took off his helmet. "Tell your men they fought well. They know it already, but tell them anyway. I don't know if the Novanti will keep on fighting, but I can only assume they will. We must prepare accordingly. I want improvements in our defenses to continue. Leave gaps in the ditch with log barricades forward of the gap to allow maneuver outside the perimeter. I intend to carry the fight to them whenever possible. I want the teamsters to position the wagons in the center of the perimeter in two parallel lines facing back the way we came; put the mules in between the wagons to give them some protection. Consolidate all food and water on one wagon and offload everything else to make room for the dead and wounded. When we leave, I want no legionary left behind alive or dead. Set up two of the tents for the *medicus* to tend the wounded. I plan to pull back from here at first light. I think it reasonable to assume Carbalo's column will be re-directed to provide additional reinforcements once Tribune Querinius realizes we are probably facing the main Novanti force." When he finished, Arrius responded to a few questions then released them to follow his orders.

Arrius heard hoof beats coming from the direction they entered the valley. For a moment, he thought it was the reinforcements from Villaunus; yet, unless somehow Villaunus had been much closer than he thought, he didn't see how he was capable of getting here so quickly. He saw a horse emerge from the trees, and Arrius recognized the horseman was Domitius. From the decurion's jerky movements something was wrong. Domitius managed to slow the horse enough to allow a legionary to step forward and grasp the reins. Arrius hurried over in time to catch the badly wounded officer as he toppled from the saddle. The decurion was still alive, but from the severity of his wounds including the loss of both hands, he wouldn't be for long. It was obvious there would be no immediate reinforcements.

Chapter 11

Sitting astride their horses outside arrow range, Beldorach and Bothan observed the unfolding battle. Beldorach was enjoying himself. No matter what the outcome, his objective had already been achieved. He frankly didn't care who won the battle and would have counted himself even more fortunate if by some stroke both sides fought on until no one was left. He gave only passing thought to the reality some of the dead and dying tribesmen were Selgovan. He regarded them as no more than a necessary investment to achieve his ends. Someday the Novanti survivors now fighting so vigorously would either become Selgovan or remain a Novanti tribe living under the dictates of the Selgovi; either result was acceptable.

In marked contrast to Beldorach, Bothan was livid with rage filling the air with a stream of colorful invectives over the limited success of the ambush.

"I thought you said the Romans would be destroyed." Beldorach knew there was nothing wrong with the location of the ambush. If it hadn't been for the sharp eye of one of the Roman scouts, Roman bodies, minus their heads, would be littering the valley floor.

"It would seem I was wrong, but then again I expected your men to conceal themselves better so the Roman scouts wouldn't see them. I believe I did mention when it happened, it might be better to call off the ambush and wait for another opportunity." He said something at the time to that effect, although he said it in such way to make it sound cowardly if they did withdraw. Bothan took the bait and after a moment of indecision opted to press on, a choice already proven to be a bad mistake.

Beldorach was as impressed with the legionary defense as he was critical of the tribal assault. He recognized the huge Roman riding the black horse days ago and was becoming more confident circumstances might allow him to claim the horse.

"I've a notion to leave the field before the other Romans get here," Bothan said.

"As far away as the other Romans are, they can't get here before tomorrow even if they knew what's happening here. A night attack might be the turning point."

Bothan regarded the other man. "Easy for you to say when it will be the Novanti who will continue bearing the brunt. I think not. Better to leave now before the other Romans arrive and fight them again on a more auspicious occasion." Beldorach for once silently agreed with the sensible appraisal. As he started to make a counter argument, he heard horses approaching from behind. Beldorach saw Tearlach coming toward him carefully threading his way through the trees. To his amazement, the warrior was leading the Roman commander's black horse.

"Beldorach, I've brought you a gift. I think it's the same horse you described when you returned from the south."

Beldorach dismounted and approached the stallion. Unbidden, the horse moved toward him and stopped as Beldorach reached up with one hand to stroke the stallion's neck while grasping the bridle in the other. As he murmured soothing words, he looked questioningly at Tearlach.

"It was as you thought. The Romans tried to send for help, and we were there to intercept them. I sent one of them back to the Romans alive to tell them what happened. I thought it might discourage them." As usual, the small, wily man had been busy and productive.

"Whose horse is that?" Bothan asked.

Beldorach replied without looking at the Novantean as he continued to stroke the horse. "A horse I've coveted since the first time I saw him; however, at the time, the Roman officer, who happens to be over there," gesturing toward the knoll, "was not exactly willing to part with him." The Selgovan finally looked at Bothan. "I left Tearlach behind in case the Romans sent for help. They did and Tearlach was there waiting. Bothan, I now have a new horse, and you have options you didn't have a short time ago."

Bothan looked thoughtful. "You may have the right of it, Beldorach. I'll think more on the matter."

Not very confident in Bothan's mental capacity to think up a reasonable plan other than to run back into the woods like a wounded animal to lick his wounds, Beldorach sighed and took matters in hand. "While you're thinking over the merits of a night attack," once again planting the thought, "I believe I'll have a word with the Roman commander."

Bothan stared at him and laughed in disbelief. "And the Selgovi will be looking for a new High Chieftain before you get half way to them. What do you expect to gain?"

"Possibly nothing, perhaps everything. If I tell them they are hopelessly outnumbered, exaggerating slightly to make the point, it is conceivable they will see how futile it is to keep fighting."

"I intend to take no prisoners back to the villages, only heads."

"As you wish, Bothan, but I have a more practical interest in keeping alive my share of any Roman prisoners."

"I think you risk your life on a fool's errand. But if you're successful, you may have one-third of the captives."

"If I'm successful, I'll take half. If I don't return alive, you may have all the Roman heads you want. Now, if I may trouble you for the loan of one of your drummers, I believe this is as good a time as any to try my little stratagem." Beldorach leaped up on Ferox and guided the horse with his knees out of the tree line. Accompanied by the slow beat of a solitary drum, Beldorach moved forward at a slow walk toward the Roman position, arms extended outward, his palms facing forward.

Domitius breathed his last soon after they laid him on the ground. Unable to speak, he responded to Arrius's question whether any of the cavalrymen survived to carry the message back to Villaunus with a nearly imperceptible shake of the head. Still kneeling, Arrius regarded the numerous and painful wounds visible on the decurion's body. The wounds were inflicted to exact the maximum pain without causing immediate death. He concealed his dismay as he thought over the implications of this latest development. He hadn't realized until now how much he depended on the decurion reaching Villaunus. It was still possible Villaunus would wonder why there was no recent contact with the eastern column and try to learn the reason. Given the extended distances separating the two main infantry columns, it was not unusual for gaps of several hours to occur in between reports. Remote as it was, it was still possible Villaunus would realize something was wrong and send a patrol to find out where the Banna contingent was. He regretted losing Ferox, but this was not the time to dwell on personal loss.

His thoughts were interrupted by the ominous sound of a single drum beating a slow steady beat. Arrius stood up and looked in the direction of the drumming. Although he was unable to make out the features of the single horseman coming slowly toward them, he saw the rider was mounted on Ferox. At least the horse survived, and he thought he would rather the enemy have him alive than see him dead on the battlefield. He noticed some of the archers nocking arrows and held up a restraining hand. "Hold, let's see what develops. I think he wants to talk."

Even with the blue paint on his face, Arrius recognized Beldorach.

Arrius walked through one of the gaps in the defensive line, stopped a short distance from the wall and waited for the Selgovan chief to close the distance. Except for a sleeveless vest made from animal skin, Beldorach's chest was bare and tanned. His unpainted upper arms were adorned with wide, intricately-designed gold bands. He wore leather breeches and calf-length boots. A long straight sword not unlike a Roman spatha hung from a baldric across his left shoulder. Arrius saw from the position of the sword, Beldorach was left-handed. He was struck again by the commanding presence the tribesman projected. Beldorach was the first to speak in his heavily-accented Latin.

"Well, Roman, we meet again under different circumstances. As I told you when we last saw each other, the horse is now mine. I've always thought things have a way of working out for the best."

Arrius was not in the mood to listen to Beldorach's gloating or to engage in small talk. "What is it you want, Beldorach? You didn't come out here to tell me you took my horse."

"You're correct, Roman, I did not. Even though I congratulate you on your impressive stand so far, it is inevitable you will be unable to resist much longer. You've also concluded by now your efforts to seek reinforcements were unsuccessful. In short, your options have become very limited. I deplore needless bloodshed; therefore, I'm here to offer you terms as I feel I am under some obligation to you for escorting me safely from Eboracum."

"You need not feel any obligation for I was only doing what I was ordered to do. I doubt any terms you're prepared to give will be acceptable, but I'll listen."

"Lay down your arms and assemble outside your fort. Half will be prisoners of the Novanti, and half will belong to me. Speaking for the

Selgovi, I will be happy to consider ransoming any or all my prisoners for an appropriate amount we can discuss later. You, of course, will be included in the number I select."

"You insult me and Rome. The circumstances will never occur when I'll surrender. You may kill us all, but you'll lose far more men in the process than you have already."

"I confess, I'm disappointed but not surprised at your answer. I hope you survive what is to come, although I think it unlikely you will, considering how badly outnumbered you are." Arrius was almost persuaded Beldorach spoke with genuine regret.

"Numbers alone aren't everything. You may have noticed," gesturing to the numerous dead warriors lying about headless, "your warriors have already paid a high price, and the cost is not yet finished."

"You have a point although I would call your gods to aid you for there will be no more offers of terms when I leave. Bothan was right. He didn't think you would accept my proposal, but I thought it was worth the attempt. I want you to know I intend to take very good care of the horse. Farewell, Roman. It's doubtful we shall meet again." Beldorach laughed, his eyes shining with amusement. "Who knows, Roman, perhaps we'll meet as something more than enemies in the next life."

Beldorach was still chuckling as he mounted, turned the horse around and leisurely walked Ferox back the way he came.

"We'll attack tonight," Bothan announced dramatically sounding as if he thought of the idea himself.

Beldorach said, "A brilliant decision. The gods will praise you for it."

Bothan was oblivious to the mockery in the Selgovan's words. "We'll attack from all sides at one time and defeat them before they even know what's happening." Beldorach remained silent. He was assured the destruction of the Romans might be inevitable, but it would not be achieved as easily as Bothan believed. The last thing he would do is to launch a night attack against a well-disciplined and fortified enemy prepared to be attacked. The Novanti were about to pay a heavy price for their victory in the unlikely event they achieved it.

Arrius made a last circuit of the perimeter defense in the last of the evening twilight. Soon it would be pitch dark with only the stars and a sliver of moon providing any illumination at all. He looked up and saw clouds forming making the prospect of rain almost a certainty before the night was over.

He was satisfied everything needing to be done was accomplished. It was the waiting that was the most difficult to tolerate. Even though he thought a night attack wouldn't happen, it was better to be ready than take a chance and be caught unprepared. He tried to put himself in the place of Beldorach or whoever else was in command of the tribesmen facing them. He still didn't know the enemy well enough to predict their next move.

So far, the Tungrian response was impressive. Their performance justified his defense of their ability to fight when Sextus Trebius disparaged them at Eboracum. He paused frequently in his rounds to say something to the legionaries as he slowly walked among them. From their amused smiles, they still found his accent and misuse of the guttural language humorous, but it was also apparent they appreciated his comments.

He rounded the first row of wagons and saw a *medicus* attending a line of wounded legionaries, some stretched out on the ground, others sitting with their backs to the wagons. These were the most severely wounded. Those who suffered the usual minor slashes were already treated and returned to their optiones. The pungent smell of blood was strong. The medical orderly glanced up when he saw Arrius but did not interrupt his attention to staunch the bleeding of a severely wounded legionary whose survival was questionable. Their losses were greater than he first estimated. He stopped a moment to speak to several bandaged legionaries conversing in low tones. They looked at him nervously half expecting him to tell them to return to perimeter duty. They began to relax when they understood he would not and was merely looking to their welfare. He saw Flavius sitting on a wagon tongue talking to Decrius, pain etched on his drawn face. Flavius was one of the few centurions who was never a staunch supporter of Betto.

"How is it with you, Flavius?"

"I fear the wound went to the bone. It may be a time before I can walk again. I was reviewing a few things with Decrius."

"Flavius, the century is in good hands and will be waiting for your return. Have you had a chance to tell Decrius what the plan is if there's a night attack?"

"No, Praefectus."

"Decrius, as soon as it's dark enough, every other legionary will move a few yards forward of the perimeter and form a defensive line between the main defensive ditch and the pickets. The pickets will provide early and silent warning of an impending attack. The forward defense line will blunt the assault and confuse the attackers by making them believe they've reached the main defense. When the cornicine blows the signal to withdraw, the legionaries will fall back past a staggered row of imbedded pila and on through the perimeter gaps. The spears may serve as an additional means to disrupt and delay the attack. The archers, armed with swords, will reinforce any part of the perimeter that looks to be in danger of being overrun. If the attack is pressed, we will rely on sword and shield. There will be no surrender. We will defeat them or they will kill us. Do you understand?"

"Yes, Praefectus!"

"Good. It must go as planned, or things will be difficult for us by morning." He exchanged a few more words with the two men before moving on encouraged by the optio's calm demeanor.

He came upon Rufus kneeling with his back to him and in the act of throwing dice with two other legionaries, a minor offense Arrius chose to ignore. When the two legionaries saw who was standing above them, they hurriedly came to rigid attention. Rufus rose to his feet more slowly and turned to face him with his gap-toothed smile showing not a bit of guilt or remorse for having been caught.

"Rufus, it looks as if you and I are fated again to be outnumbered and waiting for an attack. It seems like Sorek all over again."

"We survived in Sorek, and the Jews did not capture the eagle."

"To be sure, Rufus, I've not forgotten. Your men fought hard today. Are they ready to fight in case we're attacked tonight?"

"Aye, they are, and you'll not be disappointed in them, or they'll have more to fear from me than them." He waved a hand toward the distant tree line now barely visible.

"What do you give for our chances tonight?"

"Much better than Sorek, Praefectus. We have a chance — not a very good one, but at least here we do. In Judaea, I thought the gods were about to shit on us for certain." Rufus paused and looked up at the cloudy sky. "It's going to rain. Better have the archers trade their bows for a sword."

"I've already given the order. Did you think I'd not consider that?"

"Officers don't always think of everything or get it right. Fortunately for the cohort most of the time you do well enough."

"I'm glad you've been satisfied with my leadership *most of the time*. In the future, will you tell me on the occasions I don't?"

"You can depend on it."

"Then, Rufus, with you at my side, I hardly need help from the gods."

"Praefectus, for an officer you'll do. Maybe you don't need help from the gods, but I intend to call upon them to do more than permit me to win at dice as I was doing before you interrupted."

The prediction for rain proved correct. During the second watch, a light drizzle began to fall with increasing intensity without sign of letting up. The darkness was almost impenetrable handicapping even the sharpest eyes. The rain and gusting wind further reduced the pickets' opportunity to provide early warning.

A muffled cry on the south side of the perimeter was the first indication the attack had started. Whether the cry came from a picket or a tribesman was impossible to determine. He heard the muted rustling and hushed murmuring as the legionaries on guard woke up the few who were able to sleep in the wet conditions. Then except for the wind and rain, they heard nothing for a few minutes more. With loud cries and the shriek of bone whistles, the attack abruptly began across the entire forward defense line.

With the cornicine standing at his side, Arrius began to count silently. If he gave the signal too soon, the attack would not be sufficiently blunted; given too late, the legionaries now engaged would be overwhelmed. He imagined what it was like out there coping with the difficulty of sensory deprivation, praying for the signal to be given before courage gave way to fear and bowels began to loosen.

Arrius touched the cornicine on the shoulder. "Sound the signal now." The trumpeter blew a sustained blast. He heard triumphant shouts from the attackers as the legionaries began falling back. In the process of withdrawing, Arrius hoped the legionaries wouldn't become disoriented and unable to find their way past the imbedded spears and through the gaps to the main perimeter. There was a slight lull in the battle noise as the legionaries withdrew leaving the attackers momentarily uncertain why the enemy was disengaging so quickly.

The battle tempo became more intense as the attack closed in on the main perimeter. Arrius strained to tell which section of the perimeter might be in danger of being overrun. He heard Decrius's voice calling for his reserve and judged the north end was being pressed the hardest. He ran over to the archers and alerted the optio in charge to be ready to reinforce the north side. He sensed the legionaries elsewhere were holding their positions. The mournful sound of cattle horns and bone whistles signaled a change in the attack, and he braced for the worst. To his relief, the clamor around him gradually diminished as the tribesmen began falling back. Soon there was only the murmuring of low conversations and the cries of the wounded.

As relative silence descended upon the knoll, Arrius speculated on what the Novanti and Selgovi would do next. So far, the attack had not been pressed with great vigor. Although it was impossible to tell at this point what casualties were inflicted on either side, he had reason to think they were better off than he expected to be before the battle began. Perhaps the first assault was merely a probe intended to demoralize their defense. If so, the main, and presumably more aggressive, assault would come any time.

He noticed the rain slackening. The clouds thinned, and stars began to appear. Finally, a crescent moon broke through permitting the first dim view of the immediate area. He sheathed his sword and began making the rounds of the perimeter assessing the extent of their casualties and dispensing words of encouragement. He was thoroughly puzzled by the time he circled the knoll, and there was still no indication of another assault. He called for Plautus and Decrius to report. When the two men arrived, he instructed them to send the pickets back out.

Beldorach smiled in the darkness as the noise of battle began to diminish. As he thought, the Roman defense was proving as formidable as the Novanti resolve was not.

He took the precaution of instructing the Selgovan contingent to refrain from joining the initial attack. Tearlach was angry at the directive arguing Selgovan honor was at stake if they were perceived to be skulking in the background while the Novanti claimed the honors and collected trophies. It was a shame the Novanti did not have Tearlach's bloodlust, or the attack might have been prosecuted more vigorously.

Before the assault lines were in position, he sensed Bothan's enthusiasm for the impending battle was on the wane. He listened in disgust at Bothan's petulant complaints over the rain seeing only another obstacle where he considered the weather conditions favorable. He wasn't pleased when Bothan ordered the signal to withdraw.

"It's time I returned to my lands," Beldorach said. "I believe we're done here."

Bothan grunted, and Beldorach interpreted it as either agreement or the prelude to an argument for the Selgovi to remain. When no other comment was forthcoming, he asked, "Will you continue to fight the Romans or withdraw?"

"We will go north. If the Romans pursue, we will harry them, wearing them down until they have little choice but to go back behind their cursed wall." Beldorach weighed Bothan's answer and concluded it measured the difference between Bothan's defeatist philosophy and his own more aggressive nature. Then again, Bothan was unaware how he was using the Romans to wear down the Novanti Tribe enough where they would be ripe for the plucking. He believed it was unlikely the Romans would ever be defeated unless by some miracle the tribes united in common cause. The ferocity of the Romans here in the valley was further proof. The only chance for defeating them was if a single High Chieftain controlled the separate tribes. In the meantime, while the Novanti incurred Roman anger, he would cultivate a different relationship, biding his time until the day when his power was consolidated enough to bring down the Roman Wall under single leadership — his leadership.

The pickets returned one by one before dawn and reported the same thing. The enemy was carrying off their dead and wounded and giving no sign they were preparing for another attack. Before the first rays of the rising sun cleared the eastern tree tops, it was obvious the tribesmen were gone. Arrius stood on one of the earthen berms and surveyed the battlefield. The only reminder of the conflict was the detritus of battle consisting of shields, helmets and weapons strewn about. Already details from the centuries were searching for any Roman wounded or dead found missing during the night. He saw many of the dead Tungrians were headless.

For whatever reason, the attack was called off early. He didn't believe it was Beldorach's doing; rather, he conjectured the Selgovan's participation had been token.

The jubilant shouts from the legionaries manning the southern perimeter were followed by the blast of a trumpet. Arrius turned and was relieved to see Villaunus leading a column of cavalry emerging from the trees. Querinius was riding beside the cavalry commander.

Villaunus was the first to speak while Querinius maintained a tight-lipped silence. "Hail, Arrius, it looks as if you've had a busy time of it."

"I admit it's been eventful and a near thing. I feared none of my messengers got through to report what we were facing."

"None did. We found what was left of them on the way here. When there was no contact from you by late afternoon, the tribune and I were concerned." From Querinius's silence, Arrius surmised it was Villaunus who finally persuaded Querinius to investigate.

He proceeded to give a cryptic account of the engagement the previous afternoon and the attack earlier that morning. He concluded with a casualty report.

As he listened, Querinius took in the details of the makeshift fort and was impressed despite an inclination to find fault. When Arrius finished talking, he said, "Your losses are excessive considering I see few enemy dead. Possibly you've exaggerated the size of the enemy force."

"They carried off most of their dead during the night. If you need proof, you'll find it over there." Arrius waved in the general direction where the legionaries had arranged the heads taken in a gruesome pyramid to the height of a tall man.

Mollified, Querinius asked in a more conciliatory manner, "Are you able to continue on, or do you think we should turn back?"

"I have no cavalry left. Over a third of my command is either dead or too severely wounded to march. I'll have to send the dead and wounded back to Blatobulgium under escort. In so doing, my strength will be further reduced. I'm willing to go on, but I see no point unless we reorganize and make better use of the cavalry. This time we were fortunate. The ambush was sprung prematurely, and their attack was measured. Tomorrow we may not be so lucky. Under the present circumstances, it would be sensible to end the campaign here."

Querinius's face was expressionless. "It seems I have little choice to do otherwise. How soon will you be ready to leave?"

"It will not take long. We only have to harness the wagons and load the dead and wounded."

For a moment, Arrius and Querinius made eye contact. It was Querinius who looked away first. "Very well, then get on with it. Villaunus, send word to Carbalo to return to Blatobulgium." Querinius watched Arrius walk away and felt vaguely defeated. He knew before the consilium at Blatobulgium ended Arrius was right. If he had followed his advice, the outcome here might have been different with the Novanti destroyed instead of merely bloodied. His hatred of Arrius was blinding him, causing him to say and do irrational things. As long as Arrius lived, he was afraid the pattern would continue. Perhaps Betto's solution was right. The centurion can take care of Arrius some dark night as he hinted at, and he would be rid of the praefectus once and for all.

The return to Banna required two days less as the only halts made, apart from the nightly encampment, were brief and called only to rest the men and mules. The most severely wounded were left at Blatobulgium to recover. They buried the dead following the proper sacrifices to Mars and Jupiter Optimus Maximus and to several other Tungrian gods Arrius had never heard of. The wounded fit enough to travel on remained with the column.

Before leaving Castra Exploratorium where the Uxellodunum and Banna contingents would separate to return to their respective forts, Arrius queried Villaunus concerning the cavalry's belated arrival. Villaunus rolled his eyes in disgust.

"Arrius, Querinius completely ignored the first messenger reporting enemy sighting along with your recommendation to reinforce your cavalry screen. He thought you were being an alarmist. When no other messengers arrived and my right flank screen lost contact with your outriders, I became concerned and convinced Querinius we should investigate. By then, the day was nearly ended, and Querinius refused to move at night; consequently, we didn't start until first light."

"I thought it was something like that. Querinius was right not to move at night. I would have ordered the same. A night move would have been risky, and cavalry would have done me no good at all until daylight. His final mistake, after so many, was ignoring the messenger I sent while there was still enough daylight to get here and make the difference between a decisive defeat for the Novanti and defensive battle for us in which nothing was gained but survival."

"You're too charitable. Even more unfortunate was his refusal to consider moving the columns closer together as you tried to get him to do. It's possible had he done so, the Novanti would no longer be a threat."

"What's done is done. Let's put the matter behind us. Next time, Querinius may be more agreeable to recommendations anyone makes, even if that doesn't include anything I say or recommend."

"Why does Querinius dislike you so much?"

"It seems we were destined in Judaea to become enemies for reasons I'm not entirely sure I'll ever know. When I left Judaea, I thought we would never see each other again, but Fortuna seemed to have other ideas and brought us together, a fate I suspect is as distasteful to Querinius as for me. But we'll speak no more of it. My advice to you is to do what you can to avoid his displeasure as I seem unable to do."

By tacit agreement, Arrius and Querinius avoided each other's company during the return trip and brief halt at Castra Exploratorum except where official duties required them to interact. Before he left for Banna, Querinius asked Arrius if he was going to prepare a report to General Arvinnius, When Arrius affirmed his intention to do so along with a request for replacements, the tribune requested a copy to send in with his as part of the official record of the brief campaign. Arrius wondered how Querinius would be able to describe a generally unrewarding campaign in words to satisfy Arvinnius. He expected Querinius would find a way.

Chapter 12

With a combination of pride and fond amusement, Ilya watched Joric
and Rialus with undivided attention while Arrius and Decrius
patiently demonstrated once again the attack and defense maneuver.
At first when Arrius showed up with the wooden practice swords and
wicker shields, she wasn't pleased, but after Joric's pleadings and
Arrius's entreaties on his behalf, she had little choice but to give in. It
wasn't long after Rialus begged Decrius for a similar opportunity to
learn the basics of sword fighting. When duties prevented either
Arrius or Decrius from participating, Rufus became a willing and
eager replacement. After watching the three men, Ilya concluded
Rufus and Arrius were evenly matched. Decrius was good, but his
gigantic bulk reduced his agility. She was amazed at Arrius's
quickness and strength. He never told her how old he was, nor had she
asked. She no longer noticed the prominent scar on his face that
repelled her the first time she saw it. For someone so formidable in
appearance, she marveled at his tenderness demonstrated more in the
way he made love to her than in the soft words he seldom spoke.

She was still unsure of how she felt about Arrius. Part of her
wanted to spend both days and nights with him; however, he was still
a Roman representing everything she hated over the years. It wasn't
easy to resolve the conflict of becoming the mistress of a Roman
officer and her own Selgovan heritage. She gradually accepted she
had become as much Roman as Selgovan living in a Roman-style
villa, wearing gowns more Roman than Selgovan and speaking their
language during her daily routine.

Arrius and Decrius stepped back and lowered their shields
signaling the two boys to take position in front of them. "Remember, a
shield is an offensive weapon, too, and every bit as lethal as the
gladius. Step forward and put your weight behind the shield. Use it to
knock your adversary down if you can or at least to push him off
balance. When he's unprepared, that's the time to move forward and
strike a crippling blow. If you wound him and he falls, never step over
him or else you may find his sword point tickling your balls."

For the next several minutes, the two men made the boys slow down their natural tendency to rush their movements thereby losing rhythm and exposing them to punishing blows that left them on the ground gasping for air. After Rialus made the mistake of lifting his sword to hack downward, Decrius showed no hesitation and quickly thrust the point of the wooden gladius into his son's stomach. The force of the blow was sufficient to double the boy up, retching and gasping for breath.

"When you lift your sword the way you did, you're exposed, and the outcome is fatal."

A moment later, to Ilya's alarm, Joric made the same mistake, and Arrius delivered a similar blow leaving Joric writhing on the ground. Ilya started to move toward her son, but Arrius silently stopped her with an upraised hand.

"What say you, Decrius, have these young legionaries learned enough for one day?"

Decrius laughed. "Aye, Praefectus, I believe the fight along with the wind has gone out of them."

Arrius tossed aside the wooden sword and shield and headed for the pitcher of wine sitting on the table next to where Ilya stood, lips tightly compressed in anger.

"That was uncalled for; there was no need for you and Decrius to treat them so ill."

"On the contrary, they must learn not to make mistakes. One day their lives may depend on what they've learned, or else they will forfeit them for what they did not." Arrius spoke more sharply than he intended. Relenting, he said, "The boys do well, and because of it, Decrius and I demand much of them. It would do them no good if we spared them the consequences of their mistakes. You think it brutal, but I assure you what they learn will eventually become second nature to them. In the meantime, there will be more such occasions when they will puke their guts until the day comes when it will no longer happen after they know what we learned through hard experience. Joric has the makings of a warrior, and I would do him a disservice if I held back."

She knew what he said was true, but her motherly concerns did not keep her from feeling defensive. "He's not a warrior yet, and it's possible he never will be. He's still only a boy."

"Ilya, look at him. He nearly has his growth, and if you've noticed, his voice has deepened since I came to Banna. He's on the threshold of manhood and deserves to be treated accordingly. As to his being a warrior, he'll decide for himself one day. If he chooses not to be, then he will still have the skills to defend himself should circumstances demand."

Ilya sighed. "I suppose you're right. But it's difficult for a mother to stand by and see her child hurt."

"Then you must not watch the training, and if you do, steel yourself to whatever happens."

Their attention was diverted when the sweat-streaked boys stumbled over to the table. Arrius and Decrius watched with amusement as they drained cups of water Mirah, Ilya's personal servant, poured for them. Arrius and Decrius exchanged looks, and Ilya saw Arrius give a slight nod to the other man. Decrius walked over to where the two men tied their horses and retrieved a bundle of rolled cloth tied to one of the saddles. Returning to the table, Decrius unrolled the bundle, and Ilya was horrified to see two sheathed swords. With a broad smile, Arrius picked up one of the swords and handed it to Joric while Decrius followed by giving the other to Rialus. At first the boys were too wide-eyed and stunned to say anything then they erupted with shouts of joy.

Forcing a stern look, Arrius admonished them, "When you practice together, you will use only the wooden swords. If I find out differently, I'll take them back. Understood?" After the boys chorused a "Yes, sir" in unison, Arrius nodded in satisfaction and turned to Ilya whose face again showed disapproval.

"Ilya, they deserve a reward for their efforts."

"Those are dangerous playthings!"

"They are not given as toys to play with. They're weapons, and both lads are old enough to understand the difference. I'm confident they'll use them responsibly."

Ilya knew she was being unreasonable. Arrius only satisfied what any young man would have coveted, and he and Decrius had gone to great effort to prepare the boys for the gift. Well, the deed was done. It was too late to reverse it, but she resented the fact he hadn't taken her wishes into consideration before making the gesture.

"We shall see," she said in a cool voice. "Joric, you have studies to do, and the tutor will soon be here. Go and prepare for your lessons."

Before taking his leave, a crestfallen Joric directed his attention to Arrius. "Thank you, Arrius, for the gladius and for teaching me how to use it."

Arrius smiled and reached over to ruffle the boy's hair. "It was my pleasure, Joric. You've made excellent progress and are now trained and equipped to protect your mother. You need only practice, and you will soon become as proficient as any legionary. Next time we'll include the use of the pugio in your training."

Sensing the growing tension between Ilya and Arrius, Decrius made his excuses and followed Rialus out of the courtyard to return to his own house. Moments later, Ilya and Arrius were alone.

"What troubles you, Ilya?" Arrius asked. "I think there is more to this than the matter of a sword."

Ilya deliberated if this was the time to tell him who she really was. She had deferred until now in the belief it might mean the end of their relationship. He no longer asked her about the tattoo above her breast. At one point, she'd been ready to tell him of its significance. At the last minute, she decided against it believing she was still not ready.

"It's nothing, Arrius," She felt a wave of nausea passing through her for the second time that day. She forced a wan smile and added, "It's as I said before. It's hard to see your child becoming a man who will soon be beyond my ability to protect and care for. You're right, I must learn to let go." Her eyes glistened with unshed tears at the prospect she not only would lose Joric but possibly Arrius as well.

Betto regarded the naked prostitute lying on the narrow bed with contemptuous anger. "When I pay for a woman, I expect her to at least act as if she enjoys it and not lie there without so much as moving."

The prostitute regarded the centurion with growing fear. Despite his accusation, she had summoned all her skills in an effort to satisfy him but to no avail. Finally, he gave up and rolled off her in frustration. It was always a danger in her profession a client's failure to perform could be taken out in unpleasant ways. Only a few days before, one of the other women was unable to satisfy him, and he had beaten her savagely along with Popillius, the ex-gladiator hired to discourage unruly clients. Even if Popillius was able to leave his bed, it was unlikely he would intervene in her behalf. Because of his reputation for brutality, the centurion was now being charged two denarii for any services, more than four times the rate ordinarily demanded. Trembling in fear, she now expected the worst.

"Come back and try again. This time I'm sure you'll be satisfied and reach the clouds. I'll please you any way you desire, and it will cost you no more than you've already paid." She was desperate enough to forfeit her cut to avoid what she feared was about to occur.

Betto moved toward her eyeing her ample breasts and splayed body clinically. He realized he had already forgotten her name, but what did it matter if he did? The sight of her naked body failed to arouse him as it once would have. He recalled the whore he flogged the previous week and felt himself stirring. Seeing his erection, the prostitute began to relax. Now she was reassured she would be once again in control; that is until she saw him reaching for his heavy balteus.

Arrius no longer ignored Betto's increasingly recalcitrant behavior. Ever since returning from the disastrous field campaign, the incidents involving Betto's heavy-handed approach to discipline escalated until the marks from his vitis were a common sight on the faces and legs of the legionaries. While he was gone, Betto routinely resorted to floggings to punish comparatively minor offenses usually reserved for serious infractions. His appearance deteriorated at the same time his visits to the local brothels increased. If Arrius was to believe the owner of one of the brothels now standing before him, the latest incident was not the first.

"First it was Molina then Popillius and now Vestina. It will be weeks before Vestina can work again; Popillius is leaving, and as soon as Vestina recovers, I expect she will go as well. She may as well, for she'll be permanently scarred from the beating she received at the hand of your centurion."

"What restitution are you asking?"

"First, I want the centurion to stay away from my establishment. I want no more trouble from the likes of him. Second, I demand 75 denarii for the two whores and another 50 to hire a replacement for Popillius."

Arrius realized the latest incident was open to question, but it was pointless to ignore the claim or propose a nominal resolution. It was also important to underscore the new commander's intent to protect even the seamier side of the local population. "You'll take fifty denarii to divide up as you see fit, and I'll see to it Centurion Betto troubles you no more."

"But—," The fat, porcine-faced brothel owner started to say only to be interrupted.

"Take it or leave it. I'll not waste my time haggling with you. Next time hire someone who can do a better job of protecting your wares. I'll send someone to you with the payment before the day is out. Now, be off with you before I decide to lower the offer."

Arrius sent his orderly to find Antius Durio. When the slender cornicularius appeared, Arrius instructed him to deduct fifty denarii from Betto's pay and send a like amount to the brothel keeper. In addition, the centurion was to report to the praefectus without delay.

While waiting for Betto, Arrius reviewed his options. He demurred in his resolve to ask General Arvinnius or Querinius to transfer Betto. He supposed part of the reason was pride on his part. He felt he'd made good progress in winning the loyalty of the other centurions. When occasion demanded, Betto was undeniably a competent officer. Arrius was certain he would neither overcome his dislike of the man nor trust him. Still, he needed all the experienced men he could get including not losing any of those he now had. Perhaps the solution was to take Betto along on the next campaign he was beginning to plan for the area north of Fanum Cocidii. At least that would keep him under his thumb and spare the legionaries left behind including the whores.

He heard a commotion in the outer room and recognized the gruff voice of Matius Betto. A moment later, the centurion stomped in and gave a perfunctory salute.

"You may have passed the individual who just left. He's the owner of one of the local brothels. A brothel, I might add, you recently visited much to the misfortune of some of those who work there." Arrius saw Betto's eyes flicker; otherwise, he displayed no interest or concern. "Your last visit to the establishment has cost you 50 denarii, an amount I've already instructed the cornicularius to deduct from your pay account."

"You've done what? Fifty denarii for having my way with a whore! For 50 denarii, I can buy the place."

"Well, it was the *way* you satisfied yourself is the issue. The original claim was for much more in case you're interested. You can thank me later. You're ordered to stay away from that particular establishment as long as you remain here at Banna."

"You go too far, Arrius. You've no right to interfere in my private affairs."

"You're wrong. I not only have the right, I have a duty to protect the interests of Rome which includes preventing one of my centurions from creating unwelcome disturbances in the local vicus even if it is only a brothel. I warn you, Betto, any similar complaints, and I'll confine you to the fort and the immediate proximity of the Wall. A final comment. In the future, you will address me as *sir* or *Praefectus*. Is that understood?"

"Aye, Praefectus, I understand."

"Betto, in most respects you're a competent centurion. You would do well to curb your temper and moderate your behavior both in the vicus and here in the fort. My preference is for you to do things my way and conduct yourself befitting a Roman officer. If you cannot do this, I'll have no choice but to relieve you of your duties and send you to Eboracum. It isn't necessary for you to like the orders I give you, but it is a requirement you obey them."

"Is that all, Praefectus?" Betto emphasized the title.

"One other matter then you may go. Except for minor offenses requiring similarly minor punishment, all other punishment will be administered on my order only. Any offense meriting flogging, extra duty exceeding a week or worse will be personally approved by me."

"You undermine my authority and degrade my rank. Why not send me to Eboracum now and have done with it?"

"Quite frankly, I've thought about it. My problem is I need all the officers and legionaries now assigned including you. If you want a transfer, I'll see what I can arrange when we return from the next patrol."

"What do you mean when *we* return from the next patrol?"

"It's my intention in a few days' time to conduct an extended patrol north of Fanum Cocidii to find and capture Beldorach, the Selgovan tribal leader. You'll accompany me as the commander of the first century in place of Flavius whose leg will require additional time to heal. Flavius will command Banna in my absence. The reason you're going is so I can keep a close eye on you."

"Praefectus, I will submit a request for transfer before we depart and make sacrifice to Jupiter Optimus Maximus that General Arvinnius will approve it."

"Centurion, I'll be pleased to include my recommendation for approval to General Arvinnius."

Ilya made her way to the table and sat down with a sigh, resting her chin on her folded hands to wait for the nausea to pass. She hadn't slept very well in several days since the bouts of nausea and dizziness caused her to run to the latrine and empty her stomach. She tried some porridge for supper and ate a small portion, but didn't think it would stay down for long.

Mirah peered sleepily around the corner. "Is there anything you wish, Mistress?"

"No, go back to sleep. I'll stay here a bit longer and see if my stomach will settle down." The young woman nodded and disappeared.

Ilya felt a draft, and the lamp flame wavered casting dancing shadows on the wall. Without turning, she said quietly, "Go to bed, Mirah, I'll be all right."

"Ilya, I hope I'm not disturbing you."

Ilya stiffened as she recognized Beldorach's voice. The odor of damp animal skins filled the room. When he sat down at the table, she saw his clothing was soaking wet.

"What are you doing here?" The last person she expected or wanted to see right now was Beldorach.

"I'm on my way south to try once again to encourage the Briganti to fulfill their destiny."

'Do you expect them to change their minds since your last attempt?"

"Not really, but it's always possible. I want to tell them of our latest victory against the Romans."

"That's not what I've heard. I understand many warriors were killed."

"To be sure, the Novanti lost many but so did the Romans; however, the Selgovi suffered few casualties. It really depends on how you interpret what happened. The Romans probably believed themselves the victor, yet it was the Romans who turned back without ever finding the Novanti stronghold. I suppose it was your Roman officer who told you what happened."

"How do you know who told me?"

"I know much what happens on this side of the wall including the truth my cousin has become a whore of a Roman officer."

"It isn't like that at all. We have feelings for each other." She wondered as she spoke why she felt compelled to explain herself.

"Well, it may be as it is, but I admit when I first heard about it, I didn't believe it. After all, the last man I ever thought you'd bed willingly would be a Roman."

"He's a decent and honorable man."

"I suspect you may be right," he replied without a trace of sarcasm. "You probably know I have his horse, and a fine animal he is."

"He told me. He also tells me he will get it back."

Beldorach laughed. "He may try one day, but he won't succeed."

"It may be sooner than you think. He intends to go after you and will leave within a few days." As soon as she said it, she regretted having revealed Arrius's plans. But then she was hardly pleased at the prospect of a major offensive against her tribe even though she felt no longer a part of it.

Beldorach saw the conflict in her face. He also saw something else. The flush on her cheeks, the look about her. He always thought she was beautiful and secretly deplored she was too closely related, or he would have gladly taken her to wife. Tonight, her beauty was radiant. "Have you told him?"

"Told him what? That you are my cousin? The answer is no."

"It's not what I ask, Ilya. Have you told him you're with child?" She was startled. "How did you know?"

"You have a look about you pregnant women seem to have."

"He doesn't know. I only realized when I missed my bleeding."

"What are you going to do? Are you too far along to get rid of it?"

"I will keep the baby."

"Then you will tell him?"

"He has a right to know."

"So the Selgovi will once again be blessed with a Roman bastard."

"It is of no concern to you or the Selgovi."

"What about Joric? How will he react when your belly begins to grow?"

"I don't know." Beldorach succinctly asked the question for which she still did not have an answer. Would Joric think her nothing but a whore as Beldorach said? She knew Joric came close to revering Arrius, yet it might not be sufficient to excuse her conduct.

"Perhaps he'll take you to wife." Beldorach stood up and walked to the door where he paused. "You should tell him soon. You're right about this Roman; he has honor — and he fights well. Too bad circumstances aren't different. I might get to like him."

As Beldorach quietly made his way to the bridge, he congratulated himself on the success of his visit. He didn't in the least feel guilty for having told Ilya he was going south to the Briganti capitol when he had no intention of doing so. Nor did his conscience bother him he'd maneuvered Ilya into revealing the Roman plans for another campaign, confirming what he already suspected they would do. Thanks to Ilya, he even knew when. There were only a few days to get ready. The revelation Ilya was with child was unexpected. He knew she and the Roman were spending time together, but didn't realize it had gone so far. He wondered what she was going to do, but then if the truth be told, he really didn't care. If she told the Roman, and he hoped she would, it might be beneficial to the Selgovi. Any distraction on the part of the Roman commander might accrue to his advantage. Strangely, it was Joric who occupied his thoughts as he slipped into the stream and carefully made his way toward the narrow duct.

Chapter 13

Tiberius Querinius tapped the end of the stylus against his teeth and considered what to write to General Arvinnius. Before receiving a copy of Arrius's report to the commander of the Sixth Legion, he expected the worst based on the results of a campaign he had to admit were less than spectacular. Since his return, he managed to convince himself the outcome wasn't nearly as dismal as he believed Arrius would make it out to be. To his relief, Arrius was not as critical as anticipated. There were no accusations of failure on the part of the senior commander. The narrative was a factual account of events and results. He was relieved Arrius's report did not include any reference to their personal conflict and disagreements. If anything, it was more noteworthy for what it didn't say. Arvinnius was no fool. There were things left unsaid allowing room for speculation on the part of a discerning reader. Arvinnius might wonder why Arrius's column was the only one to be decisively engaged, leaving open the question of the whereabouts of the remainder of the force. He felt more relaxed since his return to Uxellodonum and began his report. He picked up the stylus and began to inscribe on the waxed surface of the wooden tablet.

Salve, Gaius Labinius Arvinnius, Legatus Legionis, Legio VI, Victrix

I give you greetings and pray to Jupiter Optimus Maximus you and the legion are in good health.

I anticipate you have received the report by Praefectus Marcus Junius Arrius concerning my recent incursion north against the Novantae and subsequently learned also included elements of the Selgovae Tribe. It is apparent our suspicion at least two of the northern tribes have entered into some sort of alliances is now confirmed.

I will rely on Praefectus Arrius's report to provide the factual results. I believe it accurately describes the events and accomplishments of the expedition. In all respects, I believe the campaign was a successful one, not only because of the specific results achieved but also for the opportunity to exercise the cavalry and infantry of the Western Wall in other than a training environment. There is nothing

119

so much as an engagement with an enemy force to reveal both strengths and weaknesses that permit us to improve where we must.

While I was satisfied with the vigor, enthusiasm and the capabilities of the majority of the participating officers, cavalrymen and infantry legionaries, I must candidly report there is a notable exception. Unfortunately, it is with great regret I refer to Praefectus Arrius who consistently displayed an unwarranted hostility and hesitancy to me throughout the recent campaign. The following summarizes my observations concerning Praefectus Arrius.

He paused, collected his thoughts and resumed. By the time he finished, he was pleased his description of Arrius's conduct contained sufficient praise for his professional skill but also raised subtle questions concerning his suitability for senior command by writing:

It is possible Praefectus Arrius has yet to fully make the transition from centurion to his present rank. I believe with appropriate guidance and supervision from me he will in time improve his shortcomings. Be assured, I will give this matter my most careful attention.

I remain with the divine help of Fortuna your dedicated commander at Uxellodonum and most loyal tribune of the Emperor and of Rome.

Tiberias Querinius

He put the stylus down with a smile of satisfaction. The letter should cause the general to begin wondering about Arrius's suitability, perhaps even raising the possibility he should be relieved without saying it in so many words. He hoped the message would be plain enough for Arvinnius to take immediate action or alternatively and possibly even better, invest him with the authority to do it himself. He was eager to send the letter on and called impatiently for the orderly.

As was his routine since arriving at Banna, Arrius made random checks of the guard, a practice to keep the guard detail alert from legionary to centurion. After the fustuarium administered to the sentry found sleeping on guard, he was reasonably certain he would find nothing amiss.

Because of their departure later in the morning to begin the punitive campaign against the Selgovae Tribe, he limited his inspection to the main Banna garrison. Having completed his rounds after the second watch, he was halfway down the steps from the north rampart when he heard footsteps behind him. He stopped, turned around and saw silhouetted against the night sky a moving shadow swiftly descending toward him. He saw the unmistakable glint of a knife blade. With no time to draw either sword or dagger, he ducked instinctively as his would-be assailant lunged toward him. Caught off balance and unable to stop his momentum, the man went hurtling over Arrius's shoulder and tumbled all the way to the bottom of the steps where he remained motionless.

Cautiously, Arrius stood and drew his sword. A dark shape emerged from the shadows below and moved toward the prone man. He realized the dead legionary had an accomplice. The second assailant sprang to his feet and drew his dagger. Arrius reached the bottom step in time to meet the other man's lunging attack. The assassin's blade slid harmlessly off the side of his cuirass even as his own sword blade sank deep into the other man's chest. With a gasp of pain, the man fell backward near the first assailant. He hoped one of them was still alive to reveal who was involved and why the attempt was made. It took only a cursory examination of the bodies to determine both were dead.

Arrius heard running footsteps on the stone walkway above. An anxious voice called, "Are you all right, Praefectus?"

"Yes, I'm all right, which is more than I can say for two men down here. Call your optio and have him bring a torch." He heard the guard calling out as ordered. Moments later, two members of the guard detail and the duty optio arrived with torches.

The optio saluted and after a brief glance at the bodies of the two men asked, "Sir, what happened?"

"These two men attacked me. Who are they?"

The optio motioned for one of the legionaries to bring the torch over closer to the bodies. With the toe of his boot, he moved the first man's head until his face was revealed in the torchlight. From the way the head rolled, it was obvious his neck was broken. Without saying a word, the optio moved to the next body. "I know both men. They were assigned to the first watch and belong to the third century."

"Wake up Centurion Naevius and inform him what happened. Have him report to me in the principia. Then take these two and hang them by their feet from the west gate for all to see at the morning formation."

The sun was appearing over the horizon when Arrius mounted the tribunal and surveyed the ranks of silent legionaries and cavalrymen.

"If *Fortuna* had not been with me a few hours ago, the two men hanging from the west gate would have succeeded in taking my life as they intended. Why they did this, I do not know. If there are any among you who have similar designs, I give you fair warning what is in store for you. These cowardly assassins will remain where they are until the sun sets tonight. They will be buried without the benefit of any ceremonies or sacrifices to assure they have no favor with the gods. Neither will there be any markers to commemorate their worthless lives. They will remain forever nameless." He paused and slowly looked around. "Within the hour, we and six troops of Dacian cavalry will march against the Selgovi. During the days and weeks to come, there will be opportunities for any who wish to send me to the gods before my time. If there are those who think to try, be sure to succeed. The men who tried last night were fortunate — they died quickly. If there is another attempt on my life or any of my officers, those responsible will not be so fortunate to die quickly."

Chapter 14

Fifty miles north of Fanum Cocidii in a heavy late-morning mist that left them no drier than if it had been raining, Arrius stood on a high hill with Seugethis and surveyed the wide sparsely forested valley below. He decided the valley with a stream flowing through it and ample forage for the horses and mules would do for a temporary camp. Here would be the base to send out foot and mounted patrols to thoroughly search the surrounding area for any Selgovan presence. He knew before leaving Banna it would be difficult to find Beldorach and the main Selgovan settlement. After the last several days traversing the difficult landscape, he concluded it would take a stroke of fortune to find it.

After Arrius outlined his intentions, Seugethis tugged on his beard and nodded in agreement. "Aye, this place is as good as any and better than some we passed."

"While the infantry is building the camp, I want you to send out patrols in all directions to scour the countryside for any sign of the Selgovi. After the camp is constructed, I'll send out foot patrols to cover the local surrounding area more thoroughly. If we fail to locate the Selgovi in four or five days, we'll go farther north. I confess, Seugethis, I'm less confident of finding Beldorach than I was before leaving Fanum Cocidii. I think the best we can hope for is Beldorach will find us."

Beldorach observed the construction of the camp and smiled in satisfaction. From the moment the Romans left Banna, they were under constant surveillance. It was not until the day before Beldorach joined his scouts to see for himself what they reported concerning the ineffectual Roman efforts to find the Selgovi. Truly, at the rate the Romans were going, it would be sheer luck if they stumbled on anything more than isolated settlements. Given the slow and noisy advance the Romans were making, there would be ample time for his people to disappear into the hills and forests.

He watched the speed with which the temporary fort was being erected, marveling at the impressive industry and organization. By contrast, it would have taken the Selgovi several days to accomplish what the Romans did in several hours. He envied Roman industry and their capacity to get things done quickly. It was not uncommon for a tribesman to put aside a common but essential task and decide to go hunting, or even raiding, leaving a dwelling still under construction or requiring repairs. When the Romans started something, they didn't stop until it was finished. The possible exception to Roman efficiency was the time and effort they expended moving about the countryside. Had he been the one doing the searching, he would have dispensed with the wagons and relied only on pack horses and cavalry. As it was, the Romans burdened themselves with the logistics of a baggage train allowing them to occupy an area for some time, but it would gain them nothing.

"When will we attack?" Tearlach stood behind him.

"The Roman commander would like us to, but I intend to disappoint him."

"We can take them by surprise before they finish their fort."

"Tearlach, have you so quickly forgotten what happened to the Novanti when they *surprised* the Romans? I've no intention of repeating the mistake Bothan made."

"But I thought it was your idea for Bothan to attack the Romans."

"So it was; however, I had my reasons, and while the outcome may not have been pleasing for Bothan, I for one gained and learned much from his efforts at little cost to the Selgovi. The main thing I learned is to avoid fighting the Romans on their terms. Since it is yet early in the day to construct their usual night camp, I suspect they intend to remain here for a time and cast about for the elusive Selgovi, who will continue to remain so."

"The warriors won't like skulking in the forests satisfied merely to watch the Romans. They'll want Roman heads to show their wives and the opportunity to brag of their exploits."

"They shall have them, but not the way you want. We will strike quickly and often, but we will not engage them in a major battle for which they are better prepared than we are. We'll ambush their patrols, slay their guards at night and make them believe they are about to be attacked. Soon they'll grow weary of the chase and return to their stone fort to lick their wounds and regret the day they ever left its safety."

Arrius resumed his inspection of the camp with a critical eye. He suspected Beldorach would be neither audacious nor foolish enough to attack the camp. The Selgovan would more likely take advantage of the rugged terrain he knew so well to attack patrols. That's what he would do were their positions reversed. Still, prudence and a healthy respect for the wily Selgovan chief dictated no shortcuts be taken in preparing the camp defenses.

He saw Rufus giving last minute instructions to the men he was about to take out on patrol and reflected on their time together in Judaea. He doubted Rufus would ever achieve higher rank than optio. He was grateful for his loyalty and for helping him survive the battle in the Sorek Valley.

Arrius noted with satisfaction the precision of the camp layout and how quickly the defensive wall and ditches were being constructed. Betto might have his faults, but when it came to such activities, he knew what to do and tolerated no shortcuts.

Wherever he went, Arrius was met with respectful looks. He wondered if any of the men who appeared so deferential harbored secret designs on his life as did the two legionaries who tried to kill him. He would prefer to think not, yet he was realistic about the effect a few denarii can have on a man's loyalty. That or a grudge fostered by a real or perceived injustice he might be unknowingly held accountable for.

He heard a cough behind him and turned to find Betto, expressionless, waiting to be acknowledged. Arrius returned the salute and Betto reported.

"Sir, the camp walls will be completed within the hour, and the principia tent has been erected."

"Very well, I want the cavalry commander, all centurions and all optios to report to the principia at the start of the first watch. I'll give my orders then for the time we will continue to occupy this camp over the next several days."

"How long do you intend to stay here?"

"Possibly three, even four days if necessary. It depends on the Selgovi. We'll leave sooner if we find their main camp. In the meantime, we must find out where they are. It may take time considering the nature of the surrounding terrain, not to mention the Selgovi seem to be avoiding us."

After Betto departed, Arrius finished his camp inspection. He passed by the medical tent and saw the senior medicus already administering to a legionary who was careless in digging the defensive wall as evidenced by a deep gash on his leg. The white-faced legionary stoically endured the orderly's relentless probing of the wound in his efforts to find and extract any foreign debris. Soon after he rounded the tent, he heard angry voices coming from the direction of the injured legionary. He recognized one of the voices as belonging to Longinus, the centurion of the fourth century. He hesitated a moment debating whether to see what the confrontation was about. He heard the unmistakable sound of a vitis hitting bare flesh followed by a cry of pain. Deciding he better investigate, he retraced his steps and found the medicus angry and red-faced standing between his patient, now sprawled on the ground, and the equally angry centurion. From the way the injured legionary clutched the side of his face, it was clear Longinus struck him with his vitis.

"What seems to be the difficulty here?" Arrius's voice was quiet but firm.

The centurion turned quickly, and Arrius saw a flash of irritation cross his face. "Praefectus, it's nothing for you to concern yourself. I was merely admonishing one of my men for his clumsiness."

"Has he not been punished enough? From what I can see, the wound is bad and painful. Very likely he'll be unable to do much for some time."

"And while he rides the sick wagon, the rest of his contubernium will have to do his share of the work. My intent is to ensure he will not be so careless in the future."

"Do you have reason to think he caused the injury on purpose?"

"Well, no, but he should have been more careful."

"I suspect he would agree with you." Arrius spoke with deceptive mildness. "Now, we'll leave Septimus to finish taking care of his patient before he bleeds to death."

The centurion started to say something then thinking better of it, remained silent and stalked off. Arrius watched him go. Although the centurion had never given any specific reason to question his loyalty, Longinus was one of the few officers left who still seemed to have a strong allegiance to Betto. At least, it seemed so from the amount of time they spent together. He understood his misgivings might have more to do with Longinus's friendship with Betto than saying or doing anything to arouse suspicions.

By the time Arrius finished his inspection of the camp, Philos and the slaves were finished erecting his tent. He handed his helmet to Linius while unbuckling the cuirass with a sigh of relief. He accepted a cup of wine from Cito then sat on one of the camp stools facing Philos. After drinking deeply, he looked over at his friend. "It's good to be in the field again, old friend, and for once, the weather seems to be cooperating."

Philos smiled. "If you mean because it isn't raining, I suspect it may only be an unusual and temporary condition."

"You're right. I think it must rain more here in one day than it does in Alexandria during an entire year. I confess, I miss a drier climate, but I'm growing more used to Britannia."

"Is it because of the Lady Ilya?"

"I think that has much to do with it."

"Have you thought about remaining in Britannia when you leave Banna?"

"Why, I haven't given any thought to it. It will depend on my next assignment. Would you have us leave so soon after arriving?"

A thoughtful look came over the older man's face. "I would have you do what you wish."

"Philos, I know you too well. You have something on your mind."

For a moment, Philos remained silent before saying, "I was thinking of the Lady Ilya. Will you take her to wife?"

In the middle of taking a drink, Arrius choked at the unexpected question. Recovering, he regarded Philos closely. "Why, I haven't thought much of it." His response wasn't entirely true as the idea had crossed his mind on occasion only to be dismissed promptly. He saw his friend's skeptical look. "Well, perhaps I have thought of it," he conceded, brushing his close-cropped hair with one hand. "I can't seem to dwell on the matter without becoming conflicted over what I really want. I confess to finding it easier to leave things as they are until the day I'll see things more clearly."

"To have the gods choose for you when you have so little belief in them to begin with? It's not like you, Marcus. Do you remember what you said to me the night before we reached Eboracum?"

"I don't recall, but I suspect you're about to remind me."

127

"You said there was something missing in your life, and when I asked you if it was Min-nefret, you answered it was not so much her you regretted leaving as it was losing what she represented. Marcus, I've said before, it isn't too late, but time is running out for you to have something more than this." He swept his hand around to encompass the Spartan interior of the field tent. "I've seen the way you look at Lady Ilya, and the way she does at you."

Arrius smiled and tried to steer the subject away from a conversation that made him uncomfortable. "Are you so determined to have me domesticated and burdened with the cares and ties of marriage?"

"I would have you know what I once had," Philos was somber, a haunted look in his eyes, "and what I will never have again."

The quiet response sobered him. Arrius never once asked Philos about the family he lost during a Macedonian raid. It was apparent Philos still felt the loss decades later. Apart from knowing his friend once had a family, Arrius realized he knew nothing about them. Philos never brought the subject up other than in fleeting references. He felt guilty he didn't even know the name of his wife or how many children he had. It wasn't that he wasn't interested so much as it was it never occurred to him to ask. Perhaps that alone was a strong indicator he was content with his life as it was without the distractions and responsibilities unrelated to the army. Ilya never tried to influence him into declaring his intentions either by hint or inference. But then she never told him what she wanted or expected from him.

"Philos, you are both my friend and my conscience. I will speak to Ilya when I return to Banna, although I do not know what I will say."

"I'm confident when the time comes, you'll find the right words."

Arrius laughed. "I suspect you've already made up your mind what I should say and do. Are you so ready to bring someone else into our house?" Philos did not respond to the jocular chiding, silently looking away and giving Arrius the impression he was again reminiscing of events and days long past.

Slowly, Philos turned to face Arrius, fixing him with a steady gaze. Arrius's smile disappeared as he noted the intensity of the other man's expression. "Marcus, I must leave you soon."

Shocked, Arrius was speechless and stared in disbelief. "Why and where will you go?" he finally managed to say.

Philos showed the hint of a smile. "I do not leave willingly or by choice." He recalled the bloody sponge after he used it to clean himself earlier that morning. He realized when he saw the amount of blood, the end was drawing near. He hoped in the last few months the physician in Portus Itius had erred in his diagnosis, but when the pain started several days ago, he knew his fate was confirmed. "As for where will I go? I believe the gods will decide. I have a sickness here," pointing to his abdomen. "I fear it has now reached the point a physician I visited in Portus Itius described as the final stage."

Stricken, Arrius looked into Philos's calm face wondering how he failed to see what was so plainly evident, the sallow coloring, the dark shadows under his eyes. "Is there nothing to be done?"

Philos slowly shook his head. "If anything could have been done, I would have seen to it when I first noticed something was wrong. It is far beyond what the medicus can do for me except to ease the pain, and when that is no longer possible, I have a potion the physician gave me to hasten the end."

"How much time do you have?"

"Who knows, a few days, a few weeks? I've already lasted much longer than the physician said I would. What is certain is this will be my last campaign in the field with you."

"Who else knows?"

"Who else is there? The slaves probably suspect something when they noticed the blood after cleaning the latrine."

"What can I do for you?"

"There is nothing you haven't already done for me for so many years. I've prepared a detailed list of the properties you own and where your money has been invested including my own estate you will inherit. I know you've never shown much interest in such things; however, by most standards you are a wealthy man. Even in Rome, you can live very well if it is where you eventually choose to go."

"I have no desire to go to Rome."

"Marcus, you need to think carefully about your own future. Thanks to you, I will not die alone. I would wish the same for you."

Numbed, Arrius looked away unable to put into words what he wanted to say. Finally, he shook his head and said, "I do not have the words to tell you how I feel. When the time comes for you to end the pain, I want to be there with you. Will you promise me?"

'It would be my honor, Marcus. Now, we'll speak no more of this. There is still time to think and talk of other matters, and it is my express wish it be so."

Arrius stood to leave. "Very well, if that's what you wish, but I'm sorry I brought you with me to face the hardships of a field campaign. If I'd—"

"If I had told you at Banna, you would have insisted I remain there. Would I be any more comfortable or free of pain in Banna than here? The answer is no, I'm where I wish to be — with you."

Arrius nodded and left the tent not trusting himself to speak.

Chapter 15

Arrius was impressed with Longinus's caution and tight control of his century. If the centurion bore any resentment from the rebuke in the medical tent the previous day, he concealed it.

Occasionally, Arrius saw signs of human habitation, a camp fire still smoldering, crude lean-to shelters or long abandoned stone houses with the thatch roofs missing or in disrepair. Once on a distant hill, Arrius saw several men on horseback observing them and making no effort to conceal their movements as they kept pace with the column. A few minutes later, they disappeared from view. He was certain unseen eyes monitored their progress.

By early afternoon, they were approaching the point where it would be time to turn around if they were to reach the camp by nightfall. The weather began to take a turn for the worse, and Arrius expected Longinus to recommend turning around, privately hoping he would. He considered ordering it but decided against it in the belief it would be interpreted as usurping the centurion's authority. The temperature plummeted, and by early afternoon, a light drizzle developed into a steady rain. Visibility was limited as the clouds descended even lower, occasionally engulfing them in a swirling mist. At times Arrius was no longer able to see either the advance guard or the column of legionaries marching behind. When the trail became increasingly narrow, the legionaries were forced to walk in files two abreast. The higher they ascended, the more slippery the track became as it curved snake-like below a high-topped ridgeline on their left and a precipitous drop on the right. Above the wind and rain, Arrius heard the faint splashing of a stream cascading over the rocks somewhere in the mist below.

The narrow path forced the two officers into single file with Arrius taking the lead. Concentrating on the trail ahead, Arrius was unaware of movement behind him until Longinus appeared unexpectedly uphill and on his left. Arrius tried to control his skittish mount as the horses collided. Desperately, he pulled back on the reins to allow Longinus to go on past him; however, instead of stopping, the horse sidestepped toward the edge. Arrius felt the horse sliding closer to the edge, and he made ready to jump off. He glanced at Longinus sitting motionless on his mount quietly observing the drama and making no effort to assist. In an instant, Arrius knew the collision was no accident. He tried to leap from the saddle, but by then the angle and momentum of the panic-stricken horse worked against him. Thrown from the saddle, there was a sensation of floating in space. He heard only the rushing wind and the shrill whinnies of the terrified horse as it somersaulted down the steep slope. With a sickening, bone-snapping thud, the horse struck a large boulder jutting out from the hillside, stopping its descent. A moment later, he landed on top of the animal with enough force to knock the wind out of him. He tumbled farther down the rocky slope feeling pain in every part of his body. The last thing he remembered seeing were tree branches rushing up to meet him followed immediately by a black void.

"Are you certain he's dead?" Betto gave Longinus a skeptical look.

The two men stood talking in Betto's tent shortly after a stunned Seugethis dismissed a consilium hastily convened to inform the other officers of Arrius's apparent death. The news quickly circulated and cast a pall on the usual lively mood of the camp. Even those legionaries who saw the strict side of the praefectus were subdued, for if Arrius was not loved by all, he was nonetheless respected and admired. His death represented change, and change was never accepted in any military camp, especially with Centurion Matius Betto again in command of the cohort.

"He was probably dead before he got to the bottom of the ravine."

"Why didn't you make sure?"

Longinus was irritated. "Betto, even if there had been a way down, and there wasn't, it would have been a waste of time. No one can survive such a fall. He's dead all right."

"You're certain no one saw you?"

"I'm sure of it. The rain and poor visibility along with the curving path prevented anyone from seeing what really happened. The legionaries have no reason to believe anything other than what I told them — his horse lost its footing, and he went over with it."

"Still, I wish you'd gone down and made certain."

"Well, I didn't."

Betto glanced sharply at the other man, "I want confirmation. Go back with Seugethis tomorrow and bring back his body. Seugethis will expect it even if he hasn't thought of it yet. After all, you know the way, and it must look as if we care enough for our esteemed commander to at least retrieve his body and arrange the traditional funeral ceremonies. If by any chance you do find Arrius alive, I'll trust you will manage to finish the job before you return."

"The wolves will finish what's left of him. By now, there's only bones to bring back."

"Then bring back the bloody bones, but I want them as proof I'm rid of him!"

"How much longer will we remain out here?"

"No longer than it takes you to get back here, and when you do, we'll return to Banna by the most direct route in the shortest possible time. Unlike Arrius, I've no particular desire to engage the Selgovi. I'm perfectly willing to let them stay out here without any interference from me so long as they stay north of the Wall. If they do, I'm content to stay south of it."

"What about Seugethis? What if he decides to continue the campaign?"

"He can stay out here if he wants to. I command Banna, and I intend to go back there and attend to the primary responsibility of securing the Wall instead of wasting time out here chasing an enemy we'll never find."

Somewhere ahead and above him, Tearlach heard the shrill whinnies of a terrified horse interspersed by the sound of a heavy object crashing through the undergrowth accompanied by the rattle of falling rocks. He held up his hand to signal a halt to the mounted men behind him. There was a loud crash, and the animal's cries stopped abruptly. Tearlach was certain he heard something still falling and the sound of tree branches breaking. A moment later, it was quiet except for the splashing of the stream they were following. If someone fell from the high trail above, whoever it was couldn't have survived such a fall. The Romans were foolish to attempt the trail in such poor weather, and the result was predictable. Had the Romans taken more time to investigate, they would have found the safer route below and possibly discovered the most direct access to the Selgovan capital farther north.

Tearlach gave the signal to move forward, and the horses slowly picked their way through the narrow defile, crossing back and forth through the small stream and occasionally remaining in it when large boulders prevented access to the banks. He passed by the body without seeing it, lying as it was nearly buried in the waist-high bracken. It took the sharp-eyed Catthoir to spot the helmet first then the arm projecting from the dense undergrowth under the spreading branches of a river alder.

While the others remained where they were, Catthoir dismounted and climbed up the slope toward the body struggling to make his way through the tangled undergrowth. After a brief examination, he called down in a low voice, "He's still alive, but from the looks of him, he won't be for long."

Tearlach slid off his horse and joined Catthoir leaning over the motionless form. In spite of the badly scraped face and blood pouring out of his nose, it took only a brief glance to recognize the tall Roman officer. Tearlach drew his knife without consciously thinking of it, prepared to finish what the fall had not. At the last moment and to the amazement of the other man, Tearlach thrust the knife back in its sheath and motioned for several more of the men to join him. "We'll take him to the village."

Led by Catthoir who claimed the right to the Roman's head for a trophy, the clamor for the Roman's death was unanimous. "Why should we bother? It doesn't look like he has much life left in him, not enough to get him there alive. Let's finish him now and have done with it."

"We'll do as I say."

With considerable effort accompanied by much grumbling and cursing, several men dismounted and helped Tearlach extract Arrius from the thick brush. After Catthoir claimed the sword and baldric, they removed his cuirass and left it. At one point as they maneuvered him down the slope toward the horses, the slippery bank caused one then all of them to stumble and slide the rest of the way to the stream in a tangle of arms and legs. Arrius groaned in pain, and his eyelids began to flutter. Tearlach bent down and shook the Roman's shoulder; however, he found the injured man had passed out. With difficulty and none too gently, they succeeded in draping Arrius over the back of one of the spare horses, tying his hands to his ankles to keep him from falling off. In single file, they headed toward the Selgovan settlement.

The first thing he was aware of was a throbbing pain that enveloped him in waves, ebbing briefly only to quickly return with searing agony. He had difficulty breathing and thought each breath he took was going to be his last and hoped it would be.

As black gradually became gray, he heard voices and tried to understand what was being said, but it was a language he didn't know. The voices seemed to fade in and out; he wasn't sure if they were real or imagined. He opened his eyes and saw dim shapes. The images were blurry and required too much effort to focus on what they were. It was easier to close his eyes and continue to float in a dreamlike world of indistinct shadows where nothing was real except the bouts of agonizing pain.

Seugethis dismounted and examined the muddy trail. It was easy to see by the trampled grass and hoof marks where Arrius's horse tried unsuccessfully to maintain its footing. Cautiously, he made his way to the edge of the steep drop-off and peered over. Directly below him on a rocky outcropping, he saw a dead horse. From where the horse lay, the cliff began to extend outward, becoming less precipitous and more vegetated with dense bracken and gorse bushes. He saw in places where some of the vegetation was disturbed marking where Arrius fell. The slope ended in a narrow, tree-filled ravine where he caught an occasional glimpse of a meandering stream through the leafy canopy obscuring a clear view of the bottom. He understood Longinus's description of the area and defense of his inability to retrieve the body was both accurate and justified. If they were to recover the body, the only safe way to do it was to find a way down into the ravine.

Returning to his horse where Longinus waited for him, Seugethis noticed the disturbed earth and hoof marks above the trail where a horse apparently traveled above the path. He stopped and examined the tracks speculating why they were there. The trail was narrow enough without adding to the risk by one attempting to pass the other, although that was what happened. He rode with Arrius enough to know he was a competent horseman who would not have undertaken such a risky maneuver. Until now, there was no reason to question the explanation Longinus gave upon his return to camp, but the hoof marks told another version of what actually happened.

"Longinus, why did you risk passing Arrius?"

"What do you mean? I made no such attempt. He was senior, and it was for him to remain in front."

Seugethis noticed the uneasy look and the centurion's darting eyes and his suspicions were confirmed. "The hoof prints here tell a different story. I think the result was the one intended."

"What are you saying?"

"I asked you a question, and I'm waiting for an answer."

"All right, I did try and pass him, but it was on his order I did. I told him I thought it was unsafe to try it; however, he insisted I take the lead. My horse stumbled against his, and it was enough for the Praefectus to lose control. Before I could do anything, he went over backward."

"Why didn't you describe it that way before?"

"Because I didn't think the truth would be believed."

"You're right, I don't believe you. There's more here than you're saying. I think before the day is out I'll hear the truth, or you'll have the opportunity to find out how we Dacians get someone to tell what they ordinarily do not wish to reveal."

A look of panic swept over the centurion's face. "I swear it was an accident."

Seugethis reached down and drew his spatha. "Longinus, tell me the truth, or I'll send you to your gods."

Without responding, Longinus spurred his horse uphill in an attempt to gain a dominant position. Although Longinus began with a slight advantage, the Dacian cavalryman was twice the horseman on a better mount; Seugethis reached the ridge-top first and turned his mount into the other horse, throwing it off balance. The horse lost its footing and rolled over on Longinus crushing the centurion's chest.

Seugethis dismounted and said, "Before I kill you, tell me why you did it."

Longinus tried to spit on the cavalryman but succeeded only in making the blood flow even harder in a froth of bubbles, indicating broken ribs had pierced his lungs. "I didn't like him, and I'm not the only one who wanted him dead so go ahead and finish it, you Dacian pig. I'm a dead man either way."

"Who else wanted Arrius dead?"

Longinus shook his head. "You'll hear no more from me."

Grimly, Seugethis lifted the heavy blade above his head to deliver the fatal blow. Longinus glared up at the cavalryman without any sign of fear. Seugethis hesitated then thrust the sword back in the scabbard.

"I'll not stain my sword with your blood. I'll let the wolves and ravens finish you." He bent down and removed the centurion's sword and dagger. "If you're fortunate, the wolves will find you before the Selgovi."

Seugethis walked his horse down to the path below where the centurion's horse stood trembling and favoring a broken leg. After quickly cutting the animal's throat, he mounted and headed back down the trail. At first Longinus cursed him, but before he was out of earshot, Longinus started begging to give back his sword.

Seugethis looked around and decided they must be near the approximate location at the bottom of the ravine where they might find Arrius's body. From the hoof prints along the stream bank, the ravine was a well-used trail. He noted the thick undergrowth and trees on either side of the stream and thought the animals would find him before they did.

Farther down the trail, he spotted piles of fresh dung where horses had stopped for some reason. Curious, he held up his hand to halt the men behind him while he slowly scanned the area looking for further signs. His attention was drawn to the disturbed undergrowth on the slope above him. He dismounted and with difficulty climbed the steep embankment by grabbing bushes and pulling himself up the slope. He looked up and saw the legs of a horse extending over a rocky outcropping far above him, providing further confirmation somewhere in this vicinity he would find Arrius's body.

He saw the badly dented and scratched helmet first, the plume entirely gone except for a trace of the red horsehair. He scanned the broken twigs and trampled undergrowth, noting the brownish splotches of dried blood on the leaves, but he still saw no sign of a body. Nor was there a sufficient amount of blood in the immediate vicinity to indicate a violent and bloody act. His foot hit something hard. He bent down to investigate and found the Roman's cuirass. It occurred to him there was only one reason there was no body and discarded armor. Worse than being killed in the fall, Arrius was alive and at the mercy of the Selgovi.

Seugethis returned to the troop and surveyed the narrow ravine, considering the possibility of following the trail farther north in the hope of catching up with Arrius's captors. Reluctantly, he realized doing so was foolish. Wherever the Selgovi took him, they were doubtless already there. He remembered Arrius's account of the attempt on his life the night before he left for Fanum Cocidii. Why Arrius was singled out for assassination was a mystery. There was nothing uncommon about a new commander being the target of a discontented legionary, but it was highly unusual for a centurion to be the perpetrator. Somehow, Matius Betto was behind it. Unfortunately, there was no proof he was involved. Proof or no proof, nothing would give him greater satisfaction than to part Betto's head from his neck.

The return to camp was made without incident or any further sign of the Selgovi. As the troop thundered through the gate, Seugethis saw immediately preparations were underway to move the camp. He saw Betto in front of the headquarters tent and rode toward him.

"I see you weren't able to find the body," Betto said.

"We found where he fell and his armor, but there was no body. There's every indication he's a prisoner of the Selgovi. Too bad Longinus didn't make the attempt to find Arrius after he fell. If he had, it's possible he would be here today, but then I think Longinus really wasn't interested in finding Arrius alive."

"What do you mean, and where's Longinus?"

"He had an accident. He won't be coming back."

"What kind of accident?"

"It was a similar *accident* to the one Arrius apparently had. Now why do you think Longinus wanted Arrius dead? Or was he following the orders someone else gave him? You wouldn't know anything about it would you, Betto?"

Betto's face was expressionless and his voice controlled. "I've no idea what you're talking about. If you're implying I had anything to do with what happened to Arrius, you're wrong, and unless you have proof otherwise, keep your accusations to yourself."

"Accusations? I make no accusations. It's what I saw and what Longinus said before I left him for the wolves and ravens to finish. I wonder if he was acting on his own or if he was part of a plot to replace the commander of Banna. You're fortunate Longinus refused to tell who else was involved."

"I resent your insinuation I was in any way responsible for what happened. Yes, we had our differences, but they were minor and nothing serious."

"That's not what Arrius told me. He didn't trust you any more than I ever did. He planned to have you transferred out of Banna when the campaign was over. I will recommend to General Arvinnius a formal enquiry is warranted to determine what happened to the praefectus and why. I will also tell the general who I believe was behind it."

"You Dacian bastard, how dare you speak to me or any Roman officer like that. I have a mind to teach you here and now—"

Betto stopped abruptly as Seugethis drew his spatha and examined the blade carefully, running his finger down the length in a gentle caress. Without looking at the centurion, he said, "My faithful companion and defender, I believe I heard someone disparage my lineage, a lineage that goes back generations to the time when Zalmoxis created Dacia and the people to live there. Perhaps it was the wind that said thus and not the treacherous dog who is about to lose its head for owning the tongue that spoke so ill. What is it to be, my pointed friend? Shall I wait to see if the wind or the dog wishes to amend the insult to me and my heritage, or does honor demand a reckoning now?"

Red-faced, Betto stepped back and grasped the hilt of his gladius. Seugethis looked at the centurion, cocked his head as if listening and with a benign half-smile asked, "Does the dog wish to speak again?"

Betto hesitated, his expression uncertain as if weighing how serious the cavalryman was. He quickly looked around and suddenly realized he was surrounded by Dacian cavalrymen while the nearest Tungrian legionaries slowly backed away.

"All right, Seugethis—"

"Praefectus Seugethis."

"Praefectus Seugethis, my words were hasty and spoken in anger. I regret they conveyed more than I meant and did not accurately describe my respect and admiration for Dacia or its people."

"In that case, my sharp and shiny friend, I will let you rest." Seugethis eyed the activity around him. "It seems preparations are underway to leave. Do you intend to go farther north as Arrius planned, or are you returning to Banna?"

"As far as I'm concerned, this campaign is over."

"You seemed quite certain Arrius wasn't coming back to make such a decision."

"From Longinus's description of what happened, I saw no reason to wait for you to confirm the obvious."

"What if I say the campaign isn't over," Seugethis replied evenly with an edge to his voice.

"You can do as you wish and keep on looking for the Selgovi, but I'm now in command of the infantry, and I intend to return to Banna."

"I am the senior officer, and I say the campaign is not yet over."

"You have no authority over me or the Banna garrison."

"Very well, then I've little choice but to leave as well."

"Good, then it's decided," Betto said with satisfaction. "We'll leave at first light."

"On the contrary, I see no reason to remain here tonight. My cavalry will leave now."

"But without cavalry, it leaves me vulnerable on the march back."

"Yes, I suppose it does."

Seugethis passed by Arrius's tent and on a whim dismounted. He hadn't spoken with the Greek since Longinus's return with the news of Arrius's probable death. He found Philos and the slaves busy packing Arrius's personal effects.

"Salve, Philos. I have additional news of Arrius."

"Have you recovered his body?"

"No, unfortunately, we did not. I say unfortunately because there's a possibility he's a prisoner of the Selgovi." Seugethis saw the glimmer of sudden hope transforming the older man's face and quickly added, "It might be better had he died in the fall than taken alive. I can only imagine what they will do to him." He saw the hope fade from the other man's eyes. He was moved to soften the somber news by interjecting a note of optimism. He cleared his throat and said unconvincingly, "Who knows, perhaps the Selgovi have other plans for him."

"What do you mean?"

"They may intend to hold him for ransom or hostage for some purpose we yet know nothing about."

Philos looked skeptical. "Why would they do that? What would it gain them?"

"Only the Selgovi can answer those questions. If they intended to kill him, I think it likely it would have happened by now. I also believe if they had, they would not have wasted any time showing us his head."

"Do you really believe so?"

Seugethis saw the glimmer of hope rekindled in the other man's eyes. He felt a vague sense of guilt for having caused it when he personally believed Arrius's fate was sealed. Seugethis lifted his shoulders and tried to assume a positive expression. "It isn't so much what I believe as what the gods intend." He left to avoid further discussion.

For several moments, Philos stared at the closed tent flap torn between elation and despair. Slowly, the dark thoughts threatening to overwhelm him started to be displaced by the conviction Marcus not only still lived but would survive whatever the circumstances. He suspected the Dacian commander only said what he did to comfort him even though there was no logical reason to be optimistic, but he would remain hopeful all the same. Seugethis was right. It wasn't the Selgovi who would determine Arrius's fate. It was the gods who would decide, and he intended sacrifices to ensure a favorable outcome. He reached up and touched the vial around his neck and was glad he hadn't succumbed to the temptation the night before. There was good reason to live a little longer.

Chapter 16

Athdara regarded the unconscious Roman and shook her head dubiously. "I think he's more dead than alive, but I'll do what I can." She looked curiously at Beldorach. "Why did Tearlach bring him here, and why do you care whether he lives or dies?"

"Tearlach has in mind to return his head and other parts of him to the Romans." He ignored her second question because he wasn't sure he knew the answer.

"Then if he's to die anyway, why bother to help him recover?"

Nettled by her perfectly logical and straightforward question, he refrained from answering her by saying as he left, "Do what you can for him."

For a moment longer, she stared at the empty doorway irritated by the frequent illogical behavior of men. She looked at the unconscious Roman lying on a pallet near the hearth, shook her head, walked to the door and called for Cadha and Machara. When they entered the dwelling, she was already in the process of removing his tunic. "Cadha, bring fresh water and bandages. Machara, help me remove the rest of his clothes. I need to see the extent of his wounds."

As the plain-featured Cadha silently departed, Machara, the more attractive of Beldorach's second wives, asked, "Who is he?"

"A Roman our husband seems to want to keep alive, and for what reason I have no idea."

"Shall we remove those as well?" Machara said giggling as she pointed to his linen underclothes, the only remaining item of clothing left on the unconscious man.

"So you can see if his manhood is as large as the rest of him? The only part of any Roman I care to see is his head on a pole."

Cadha returned with a large earthen bowl filled with water and strips of cloth to use for washing and bandaging. With Athdara supervising, the other two women began to carefully wash the various cuts and abrasions. When they were finished, Athdara realized superficially none of the obvious wounds was particularly serious although as she surmised earlier, a few would require Machara's skill with a needle to close them. She began to carefully run her fingers over Arrius's body probing gently for any broken bones. She found two fingers on his left hand were broken and required setting. She also thought one or more ribs were broken from the bruising midway down on his right side. Even more serious, was the discoloration indicating the possibility of internal bleeding. She reached over and lifted first one eye and then the other and saw the pupils were dilated.

She sat back on her haunches, hands resting on her knees. "I think it's his head and internal organs that may have suffered the most, and there is nothing to be done for either except to keep him quiet. We'll know more when he has to urinate and defecate." As if he heard them, the women observed a widening stain appearing on the front of his underclothes accompanied by the acrid smell of urine. "Well, Machara, I believe you may have a chance to see just how large the rest of the Roman is," Athdara said. The other two women snickered with curious anticipation. "At least the stain isn't pink," Athdara added, looking closely at the damp underclothes, "and it's a good sign." She wondered after she said it why it was a good sign. After all, the Roman was going to die anyway.

Beldorach vaulted onto the back of the big black horse and guided the animal with a slight pressure of his knees. It didn't take long before Ferox was responsive to his every command. He was strangely unsettled the Roman whose horse he now rode was alive and in the village. Why the Roman was alive at all was strange enough after having fallen from the high pass as Tearlach reported. What was it about this particular Roman that circumstances should keep bringing them together? By all rights, one of them should have been the reason for the other's death before now. Destiny seemed to have brought them together for a purpose he yet didn't know.

Tearlach unknowingly presented him with a dilemma. It would have been better and simpler if the Roman had died in the fall, or having survived it, Tearlach killed him and brought back his head. He found himself strangely glad Tearlach had spared him; he had no desire to see the Roman's head on a pole for reasons he couldn't understand. If in the end he surrendered the Roman to Tearlach as the sub-chief had every right to expect, then he would incur Ilya's wrath, possibly encouraging her to return and challenge his position as High Chieftain. There was also the obligation of reciprocating the Roman's hospitality extended during the journey from Eboracum to Banna the year before. If he failed to allow Tearlach to have his way, then he risked alienating his staunchest supporter at a critical time when he could least afford it. His leadership of the tribe was precarious enough without eroding it by protecting the Roman, a gesture few would understand. Why should they when he didn't understand it himself?

Perhaps the Roman would not recover. If he didn't, the matter would be resolved. Even as the thought flitted through his mind, it was followed by the hope he would live then wondered why he felt so. Perhaps it was because Ilya was carrying the Roman's child he wished for his recovery? Considering what she suffered at the hands of the Romans years ago, it was difficult to believe Ilya had spread her legs willingly for any Roman.

Recently he thought he was losing control of events. He no longer felt decisive and was prone to delay making decisions. The future seemed cloudy, full of conjecture and uncertainty. He should be making plans to attack the Novanti, yet he hadn't taken the first step to put in motion his master plan. The tribe was focused on attacking the Roman force now threatening their lands, and there were many among the Selgovi who wondered why he delayed. If the Romans advanced any farther, he would have no choice but to fight. He wanted to avoid a battle if possible, and it was time the tribe understood why. This was no time to jeopardize his move against the Novanti by weakening his own strength at the expense of the Romans in a battle that would decide nothing. He needed to take the clan leaders into his confidence regarding the Novanti.

He spurred the black horse to a gallop, glad to feel the wind rushing in his face and the movement of the muscular animal under him. Resolve began to replace the pervasive self-doubt as his blood quickened in time with the pounding hooves. He began to formulate the argument he would use to make the clan chiefs understand the only way to defeat the Romans over the long term was to unite the tribes under one leader. He counted on their willingness to see the Selgovi as the one tribe whose destiny it was to rise above the others. The first step, a peace treaty with the Romans, would be the one most difficult for them to accept. Without such a treaty and Roman willingness to turn a blind eye, it would not be possible to achieve his objective. The thought occurred to him, the Roman might have a role in accomplishing this — if he lived.

He saw several riders approaching and recognized the deeply-lined face of Tuireann in the lead. From the lather on the horses, they had pushed their mounts hard. Beldorach reined in and waited for them to approach. Tuireann's normally inscrutable face was wreathed in a broad smile as he rode up to Beldorach.

"The Romans are turning back."

"Are you certain?"

"I am. We followed them to make certain."

Beldorach barely contained his elation. This was the sign he'd been waiting for. Now was the time to put his plan in motion. Once again all things seemed possible.

The first thing Betto did was to inform Philos he needed to vacate the praetorium and the Banna fort immediately. Betto watched the wagon depart a short time later indifferent to where the Greek would go.

The second thing Betto did upon his return to Banna four days later was to send an official letter to Tiberias Querinius describing the circumstances leading to the death of the Praefectus Marcus Junius Arrius. By separate message, he provided a different and more accurate account of how Arrius met his end. Naturally, he made it appear Longinus's spontaneous action was the direct result of his own planning and direction. The private message also contained the unmistakable expectation his assumption of the Banna command would be more than a temporary arrangement. He intended to see Querinius made good on his promise.

Philos was prepared when Centurion Betto ordered him to vacate the fort. He not only anticipated it, he planned for it. Although Arrius never went into any lengthy explanation of his opinion or specific problems with Matius Betto, it was obvious the centurion had been a thorn in Arrius's side since the day of their arrival. If the specific nature of Arrius's misfortune was other than what was reported, he would've suspected Betto was at the bottom of it.

The past several days since Seugethis talked to him, he convinced himself Arrius was still alive. If Arrius returned to Banna, he wondered what the outcome might be. He supposed it would depend on what Arrius intended. Although of late Arrius talked about wanting change, he wasn't convinced he could. The one factor that might make the difference was Ilya. He would soon see when he told her about Arrius.

Ilya was lying down when Attorix came to tell her Philos was outside and wished to see her. If there was any question she was pregnant, her fits of nausea, tender breasts and fatigue were sufficient indicators. After examining herself early this morning, she fancied her waist was beginning to show the first visible sign of the growing life inside her.

She hoped the meaning of the trumpets blasting earlier proclaimed Arrius's return. She jumped to her feet filled with joy at the prospect Philos was here with an invitation to visit the fort. She had waited long enough to tell him she was pregnant, and today, tonight, would be the time to tell him he was going to be a father. She ran through the corridor and out into the sun-drenched world blinking against the brightness of the afternoon. She saw Philos with a serious expression on his face standing next to a wagon piled high with baggage and various household items. Philos saw her beaming face change from elation to concern.

"What's happened?" A chill swept over her despite the warmth of the late spring day. "Why all this?" She indicated the loaded wagon. "Where's Arrius?"

"It's believed Arrius is a captive of the Selgovi. Centurion Betto has ordered—"

It was as far as Philos got before Ilya felt the world spinning, the bright sunlight turning to gray. She wasn't aware Philos saw what was about to happen and rushed to prevent her from falling. She came to a few minutes later in her bedroom to a sharp, acrid smell and saw the anxious faces of Philos, Attorix and Mirah peering down at her. She saw Philos holding something in his hand that smoldered. She struggled to sit up but found herself pushed back onto the bed.

"Tell me what happened," she finally managed to say.

Briefly, Philos outlined the circumstances of Arrius's disappearance and what Seugethis discovered the next day. White-faced and never taking her eyes off Philos, Ilya listened attentively to what Seugethis told the former slave. When he finished telling what he knew, there was silence in the room. Gradually, the numbness wore off, and she felt her blank mind begin to function. There was a greater probability Arrius was dead than alive; however, the possibility he was not is what demanded her attention.

"Mirah, find Joric and send him to me right away. He's become close to Arrius, and I would not have him hear what has befallen him except from me. Attorix, see to suitable quarters for our guests and the storage of the wagon. Then prepare my cart with an extra horse and enough provisions for three days for I shall be leaving immediately to go north."

Philos regarded Ilya with bewilderment. "North? Why north?"

"There's no time to waste. I have to find Arrius before it's too late."

"But how and where will you find him?" Philos asked in astonishment. "Even if you do, what will it accomplish except to get yourself killed in the process?"

"If he lives, I know where to find him. Yes, there is a possibility the Selgovi may take my life, but I must do what I can. Beldorach owes me, and I intend to collect on the debt."

"Beldorach owes you? How do you know him?" Philos was more confused than ever.

"Beldorach's my cousin. Because of me, he became and remains High Chieftain of the Selgovi. If Arrius is still alive, he'll be with Beldorach."

"Then I will go with you. You can't go alone in your condition."

"What do you know of my condition?"

"I believe you are with child."

"It appears everyone is aware of my *condition* without my saying anything."

"Not everyone. Arrius doesn't know."

"Yes, and I intended to tell him when he returned. If you go with me, I cannot guarantee we will be allowed to return."

"The last thing I value anymore is my life. I've but a short time left to me, and I would spend the time doing more than waiting for the gods to summon me."

Attorix remained silent until now. "I will go as well. You will need more protection than he can provide." He eyed the aging, one-handed man.

"No, Attorix." Ilya patted his arm to take the sting out of her refusal. "I appreciate your offer, but I need you to remain here and look after Joric. If the Selgovi intend to kill me, you and a hundred others couldn't prevent it. Now there will be no further discussion on the matter. I've a long way to go, and there is much to do before I leave." With a resigned look, Attorix left to prepare the cart while Mirah went to find Joric. Two hours later, Ilya and Philos crossed the vallum and passed through the first mile fort west of Banna heading north.

Chapter 17

"Will he live?" Beldorach looked down at Arrius's pale face.

Athdara shrugged. "There's some improvement. At least, he's no worse than before. We were able to get him to drink and eat a little this morning. Sometimes his body moves as if he is dreaming. I think his manhood is recovering faster than the rest of him."

Beldorach glanced sharply at her, and Athdara smiled. "It seems he enjoys it when Cadha and Machara bathe him; he may be better than he appears."

"It's a good sign, but make sure Cadha and Machara don't take equal pleasure in their ministrations."

"He talks occasionally."

"What does he say?"

"How should I know? His speech has no meaning for me. Now and then he seems to speak Ilya's name. Perhaps it is not a name and means something else in his language."

Beldorach made no reply as he looked at the unconscious man. Two days had passed since Tearlach brought him to the Selgovan capitol, and still there was no indication the Roman would recover. He knew Athdara and his other wives had done what they could to nurse him back to health, yet the outcome didn't look promising. Arrius abruptly sat up mumbling something unintelligible. For a moment longer, he remained in a sitting position, arms hanging limply at his side, looking straight ahead.

Beldorach knelt down. "Roman, can you hear me?"

Slowly, Arrius turned his head toward Beldorach fixing him with an unfocused stare. Beldorach repeated himself, but Arrius made no response. A moment later, Beldorach saw the Roman's eyes roll upward, and he started to fall back. Beldorach reached out in time and gently lowered him to the pallet to prevent further harm to the unconscious man.

Athdara crossed to the fire and lit a small twig. Returning to the pallet, she reached down and pried open one of Arrius's eyelids and held the burning ember above the Roman's face. After inspecting the other eye, she stood up and faced Beldorach.

"His eyes respond to the light. I believe he will live."

"You and the others have done well."

Athdara shrugged, indifferent to the compliment. "I did no more than you asked. I would have preferred to see him die. Better for him if he did, for I understand Tearlach already talks of what he will do when the Roman recovers."

"I don't intend to give him to Tearlach."

"Is that wise, my husband? Tearlach and others will not be happy."

"True, however, they will in time accept it when I tell them why I want the Roman to live. I have plans for him."

"Even the High Chieftain has limits to his authority. They can overrule you then it would not bode well for you or the tribe. Better to give up the Roman rather than risk your position."

"You and the others will soon understand why I want him alive. One live Roman may be able to do more for the Selgovi than a hundred or even a thousand dead ones. It wasn't Tearlach who brought this man here to me. It was destiny."

First there were only sounds punctuated by an ever-present pounding in his head that seemed to go on and on, sometimes loud, sometimes barely heard. He drifted in a void on waves of throbbing pain. There were no shapes or form, only a nothingness consisting of shades of gray and black. Occasionally, he heard voices, but he didn't understand what they were saying. They were mostly women's voices fading in and out, muffled and indistinct. Once he thought he heard someone laughing, and the sound of it was soothing, dispelling briefly the agony of his aching head. He wanted to open his eyes, but the thought quickly disappeared as he plummeted down into darkness.

Gradually, colored images appeared slowly replacing the swirling clouds of gray and black. He struggled to focus on what the images were and meant; however, the effort was too much. It was easier to continue floating in a featureless world absent of form and color. Disembodied, blurry faces leaned toward him, and he tried to concentrate on identifying who they might be. Some seemed vaguely familiar while others he knew were strange to him. He was aware of soothing hands on his body washing him. The coolness of the water and the pleasant sensation introduced erotic thoughts. He imagined Philos and Ilya talking to him, but he was unable to understand what they were saying. Gradually, the images became sharper, and little by little, he began to understand them even though trying to speak required more effort than he could muster. Then came the moment when he recognized Ilya anxiously looking down at him, and he understood it was no longer a dream. He saw her smile tenderly. He spoke her name then felt her hair brush his face as she leaned down to kiss him. This time when he drifted off to sleep, it was peaceful and no longer a kaleidoscope of chaotic images making no sense at all.

Ilya looked at Philos. "I think he knew me."

When she first saw him, she was horrified. The extent of his wounds was alarming even as Athdara assured her he would survive but not for long if Tearlach had his way. She went to Beldorach who tried to reassure her there was nothing to worry about, but from experience, she knew his actions were always prompted by expedience and practical necessity. If it was necessary to further his purpose, he wouldn't hesitate to turn Arrius over to the clan chiefs, and if he did, there was nothing she could do to save him.

"Athdara, thank you for all you've done."

Athdara looked at the younger woman acknowledging the thanks with a curt nod. There was no enmity between them, but they were wary of each other.

Philos sensed the tension between the two women soon after their arrival in the Selgovan settlement. From what Ilya told him of her past during their journey here, he knew her return was not only dangerous for her but also strained the normal existence of the Selgovi. It was possible considering the dynamics of her position in the Selgovan hierarchy, Ilya's life was more at risk than Arrius's.

Thinking it was time to leave her alone with Arrius, Philos left the stone house for a stroll through the settlement that until now he had little chance to explore.

The one aspect so far surprising him the most about the Selgovi was their obsession with personal hygiene, exceeding even the most civilized areas of the Roman Empire. Unless circumstances absolutely precluded it, daily ablutions were routinely observed by young and old alike. He was told even on the coldest days it was customary to bathe with minimal regard for modesty. For both sexes, there was an extreme aversion to body hair except for the head and in the case of the men, the long drooping moustaches often extending to the chest.

The comparatively small number of homes in the settlement surprised him. It was difficult to estimate the total population. Ilya told him many of the homes in addition to immediate family members housed aunts, uncles and more distant relatives. When Ilya said they were traveling to the Selgovan capitol, he envisioned a much larger village. He estimated the settlement was about the size of the Banna vicus if both the dwellings east and west of the Roman fort were combined into one. She said it was the custom of all the tribes to dwell in small settlements to prevent depletion of game and natural resources in one region. Periodically, the tribe would come together for celebrations or when summoned by the High Chieftain to consider matters affecting the entire tribe.

Apart from varying in size, each circular home was identical to the others with walls constructed of stone and watttle with steeply-pitched thatched roofs reaching down almost to the ground. Small ventilation slots were used instead of windows for additional protection against the frequent harsh weather and strong winds in the hilly northern regions. Although Beldorach's dwelling was much larger than the others in deference to his position, the interiors of the homes were similar. From a central hearth, the home was divided into separate cubicles affording a modicum of privacy to the inhabitants. Beds consisting of pallets on raised platforms were arranged against the outer wall. The floor of beaten earth was covered with rushes and long-stemmed grasses that from their freshness appeared to be changed on a frequent basis. The open doorway and the small hole in the center of the roof to allow smoke to escape provided the only natural light during daytime. The gloom of the interior was brightened by a number of clay lamps suspended from the ceiling beams. Unlike the stale smell typical of a legionary barracks, the prevailing odor was a combination of wood smoke and cooking Philos found pleasant.

A stone wall approximately five feet high surmounted by a wooden palisade and rampart encircled the village. A number of smaller dwellings were located outside the palisade, and he assumed those who lived in them were of lower social status than those inside the enclosure. Animal pens were maintained inside the settlement and abutted the outer wall. An inner defensive wall encompassed a low, flat hill where a large stone structure with a timber roof dominated the settlement and Beldorach's spacious home located nearby. Several other and slightly smaller houses presumably belonged to the senior tribal members. He learned the large building containing the dais of the High Chieftain was where Beldorach met with the clan chiefs, council members and priests and as occasion and circumstances dictated, the entire adult population of the settlement. In the event of an attack and the outer wall was breached, the survivors would consolidate further defense in the hill-fort above.

Ilya said the Selgovi prided themselves on their equestrian skills, and each warrior counted his wealth by the number of horses he owned. Instead of being gathered in one large herd, the horses were separated into several small herds to reduce the vulnerability to raids from the other tribes, a practice he gathered was common. The pastures were located some miles from the settlement where forage was plentiful. The horses were looked after by young men who had not achieved warrior status.

At the edge of the village, he followed a path into the forest leading to a glade dominated by a huge oak tree in the center. Hanging from the branches were the skulls of horses, some fresh enough to attract a flock of crows perched in the branches raucously fighting over the rotting flesh. He looked more closely and saw human remains interspersed among the horse skulls. At the base of the tree was a large flat stone that appeared to be an altar with stains indicating ritual sacrifice. He was seeing justification of Ilya's reason for going to Banna to save Joric.

He was about to turn around and retrace his steps when an old, stooped man brandishing a large stick shouted at him in a high-pitched, angry voice. Before he could react, the old man began striking him. By the time they reached the settlement, the old man's cries roused other villagers who surged toward him in a threatening manner.

Philos heard hoof beats, and Beldorach rode into view on the large black horse once belonging to Arrius. One look at Beldorach's grim face, and he concluded he would probably not require the vial of poison hanging from his neck.

Beldorach talked with the old man at length while the crowd listened attentively. Whatever Beldorach said, the comments brought smiles to the faces of the villagers. The crowd dispersed with the old man still noticeably angry stalking off in the direction of the sacred glade.

"It was fortunate you didn't touch the altar or the tree," Beldorach said. "If you had, you would now be dead. I told them what you did was done in ignorance without intent to commit sacrilege. Most agreed, but the priest was less convinced. He wanted you ritually sacrificed. I persuaded them the gods would be offended in receiving the life of an incomplete man," pointing to Philos's missing hand, "particularly one who is so old."

"My thanks for your help although it seems I should also be grateful for my age and infirmity. I must confess until you came, I'd resigned myself to departing this life sooner than I'd intended."

"You seemed to have accepted your fate rather calmly. I wondered if you knew the peril you were in. You were lucky none of the other priests was there with the old one, or you would have been killed on the spot."

"At my age, there are worst things than death such as a difficult bowel movement or no bowel movement at all."

Beldorach laughed. "One day I may think and say as much. Now, tell me how your Roman friend is doing."

"This morning there were signs he is much improved. He recognized Ilya." At the mention of Ilya's name, Beldorach nodded but was no longer smiling when he turned the horse and rode away.

Philos was unclear concerning the nature of the relationship between Ilya and her cousin. They were not so much unfriendly to each other as wary, as if each was waiting for the other to say or do something.

Philos saw Ilya standing with her arms folded outside Beldorach's dwelling. The deep lines etched on her face showed how tired she was. She still wore the same plain woolen dress as on their arrival three days ago. She straightened up and absently brushed a lock of hair from her cheek. If he had any question concerning her deep feelings for Arrius, they had been dispelled by her near frantic effort to reach him. If anything, it occurred to him Arrius seemed more uncertain about Ilya.

Beldorach rode through the gate, dismounted and approached Ilya. He spoke to her at length while she listened attentively without comment. Then both engaged in a rapid-fire, occasionally heated exchange. He wondered what they were arguing about but suspected it undoubtedly had something to do with Arrius, possibly him. After Ilya glanced at him with a concerned look, he assumed at least part of the discussion involved his recent encounter with the Selgovan priest. Beldorach tied Ferox to a post by the low palisade wall before ducking under the low doorway and disappearing inside.

"Beldorach thinks it would be better if you remained within the settlement walls unless you are with someone who knows our customs."

"It's good advice I plan to follow. I wonder why he intervened. If he hadn't, I would have suffered the consequences."

"I know Beldorach — he had a reason. He does nothing unless it serves a purpose including allowing Arrius to live."

"When do you think he'll be fit enough to return to Banna?"

Ilya motioned for him to move away from the proximity of the stone dwelling. "Our return has less to do with Arrius's condition than whether Beldorach will let us leave."

"Do you think he won't?"

"I don't know, but it's possible. With Beldorach, you can never be certain what he will do. The only reason Arrius is still alive is because of Beldorach and that includes us. After all, the Romans and Selgovi are hardly allies, and having the man who commands Banna presents a number of options for the Selgovi. They may keep him prisoner against the day he will prove useful. They may also kill him out of revenge for past Roman depredations as I gather most would wish, or they may try to ransom him. I consider the first two options more likely than the last since the Selgovi, unlike the Romans, have no great interest for the kind of wealth Romans value."

"What can you do to make up Beldorach's mind in our favor?"

"I'll bargain with him."

"What do you have to bargain with?"

"I can make his position as High Chieftain more secure than it is by renouncing any claim to the dais."

"I thought you said on our way here by living outside the tribal lands of your own free will, the High Chieftain forfeits any claim and rights to the leadership of the Selgovi."

"I never renounced my claim to leadership of the tribe. I allowed Beldorach to ascend the dais without protest. I intentionally never left the tribal lands, for if I had, it would have negated any future and legitimate claim I might make."

"I don't understand. Are you saying Banna is part of the Selgovan tribal territory?"

With the trace of a smile, she said, "Possibly not in reality any longer since the Roman's built the wall, but by tradition, the land much farther south of Banna is still claimed by the Selgovi. The Selgovi and Briganti have disputed the tribal boundaries for as long as anyone can remember. The reason I did not go farther south than Banna is it would rule out any possibility of a future claim if I decided to pursue it. Until now, I never thought the circumstances would occur when I would assert my rights."

"Then is it your intention to replace Beldorach?" He sounded incredulous.

"Not at all, and yet Arrius's life may depend on Beldorach believing I will."

"I think Beldorach is not the only clever Selgovan here. When will you *bargain*?"

"In a way, I've already started. I must be careful. If I present the conditions in such a manner it sounds like an ultimatum, he will take it as a declaration I intend to depose him, and I'll never see Banna again. He must come to the idea of negotiating an agreement first then he'll believe it's a solution of his own making."

Philos regarded her with unconcealed admiration. "Lady Ilya, I believe you would have made a very able queen, High Chieftain or whatever the Selgovi call their female leader."

"Yes, it's true," she replied without a trace of false modesty. "My father taught me well."

Chapter 18

Five days after receiving word concerning the untimely death of Arrius, Tiberius Querinius rode through the west gate of Banna with a small escort and saw Betto waiting for him outside the entrance to the principia. When he informed General Arvinnius that Arrius was believed dead, he also recommended Matius Betto assume command of Banna. Unfortunately, if Arvinnius failed to accept his recommendation, the centurion would be a problem, convinced he didn't press the general hard enough. He disliked the idea of being indebted to the centurion who would expect further rewards for getting rid of his nemesis. Although Betto could never prove he had any intent or role in Arrius's death, the centurion would be an embarrassment if he ever spoke of their agreement.

Querinius saw two legionaries hanging limply from iron shackles attached to the wall of the building opposite the principia. Drawing closer, he saw with distaste but no sympathy their bodies were a mass of bloody welts. It was mute testimony Betto was wasting no time emphasizing his authority over the Banna garrison.

Querinius dismounted and handed the reins to an orderly, returning Betto's salute with a nod. Was it his imagination, or was there a shade of informality to Betto's salute, a casual manner in his stance? He would have to make certain before he departed Betto understood he was the senior commander. He wasn't about to tolerate any unwelcome familiarity from someone without any important social antecedents or connections.

Much to Querinius's irritation, Betto spoke first. "We have much to talk about, Tribune," as he led the way into the headquarters where the senior staff waited silently in a line within the outer courtyard. Querinius recognized Antius Durio, the cornicularius, and Publius Gheta, the quaestor, acknowledging them by name but did not recall the names of the other officers. The universal sober expressions of those present was an indication the change in command was not popular.

The perfunctory welcome completed, the two officers proceeded alone to the commander's office. Betto closed the door and without preamble sat down behind the desk leaving Querinius standing in a deliberate breach of protocol and confirming his initial impression and fears Betto intended to take advantage of their relationship.

"Do not forget yourself, Betto, or make the mistake of presuming too much."

"In private, I will *presume* all I wish. Out there," waving toward the door, "I'll render all courtesy and respect to keep up appearances, but in here, you and I have much in common and too much at stake to be overly concerned with meaningless courtesies. Now why don't you sit, and let's discuss where we go from here."

"You're insolent, Betto. You try my patience." Querinius assumed an air of haughty superiority. "You're forgetting I can deny ever having talked to you about anything except official business."

Betto smiled without humor. "Tribune, you may deny what you will. But if the subject ever comes up concerning your intentions regarding Arrius, you may find there are others who knew of it besides me."

Querinius felt a chill of uneasiness sweep over him as he quickly thought back to his past conversations with the centurion. Was he careless in giving Betto an opportunity he already regretted? Instinctively, he knew Betto was bluffing with his implication there were unknown witnesses to their one conversation concerning Arrius's fate. He wanted to be cautious until he determined the extent Betto held the upper hand.

"Come, Betto, this is a poor beginning to what should be a happy occasion for us both." Querinius attempted a conciliatory smile as he took a seat opposite the centurion. "As you said, we have things to discuss and agreements to consider."

"I want to be appointed to command Banna, and I don't mean as an interim commander until Arvinnius finds another praefectus to replace me. I deserve it, and I mean to have it."

"I've already taken steps to see it happens. Have I not already on two occasions spoken of your qualifications to General Arvinnius? And the latest was the same day I received your message. What more do you wish from me?"

"I also want the rank that goes with the command."

Querinius anticipated the request and quickly responded. "I don't have the authority."

"True, nor do you have the authority to appoint me commander; however, you do have influence with Arvinnius as the senior commander of the western Wall, and I expect you to use it in my behalf."

"You have my promise to try, but it must only be after you've commanded for at least three months. Then the justification will be based on merit as well as expediency. Naturally, I will recommend such an arrangement to General Arvinnius." By then, Querinius thought, anything was possible including Arvinnius's approval of Betto's promotion, however unlikely given Betto's less than spectacular record and absence of any marketable political or military influence. There was also the possibility Betto may have a mishap of his own. He would have to think on the matter.

As the senior optio of the guard, Decrius was part of the official entourage waiting in the inner courtyard of the principia for Tribune Querinius's arrival.

The mood of the waiting officers was somber, and there was little conversation. The reality of Arrius's apparent death and Betto's assumption of command for the second time left a pall on the Banna garrison affecting all but a few who remained loyal to Betto. Even Decrius was taken aback at the reaction of the Tungrian Cohort when the news spread like wildfire. A steady stream of legionaries visited the Temple of Jupiter on the edge of the vicus to make sacrifices and give prayers on behalf of the praefectus. He realized the positive impact Arrius made in the comparative short time since his arrival at Banna. For those who returned from Judaea and survived the fate of the *Deiotariana*, they took for granted what Arrius accomplished in turning a surly mob into a functioning unit to take pride in; therefore, for them, the effect on morale was particularly acute. For those who remained in Britannia during the Judaean war, the prevailing mood was one of bitter foreboding and resigned acceptance.

Daily floggings were routine. The latest examples were the two unfortunate men still hanging outside the headquarters who were accused of not having shown sufficient courtesy to Matius Betto. One of the first recipients of Betto's harsh treatment was Rufus who although spared the lash was reduced to the ranks for unwisely daring to question one of Betto's favored centurions. It was not unusual for the centurion to administer the lash himself, and this morning was no exception. Rufus was privately glad Betto administered the punishment, or as officer of the guard, he would have had to wield the lash. With Betto doing it, the rancor and bitterness of the harsh punishment would accrue to the centurion alone.

Decrius recalled the impact on Rialus and Ilya's son Joric who was now staying with them. It was evident the shock of the news had yet to wear off, and both boys were still struggling to maintain their composure.

He thought it curious Ilya disappeared soon after the expedition returned to Banna. He heard she was seen passing through one of the gates heading north in the company of Arrius's friend Philos. Why and where she was going was a mystery when he would have expected her to express her loss in a more conventional way than disappearing. He suspected Joric knew where she went, but when he asked, the boy was evasive. From the quizzical look on Rialus's face, it was also apparent Joric had not confided in him.

The outer door opened, and Betto appeared followed by the tribune. In contrast to Tribune Querinius's impassive and inscrutable face, Betto wore a look of smug confidence. Betto provided a cryptic introduction of each officer as the tribune passed down the line. He observed the tribune seemed irritated having to suffer the obligatory reception.

Unlike his private and abiding dislike for Betto, Decrius didn't have a strong opinion of the tribune. He heard rumors Arrius and Querinius had not gotten along in Judaea although he never saw any evidence of it. The ways of senior officers were not for the common knowledge or understanding of those of lesser rank. If the rumors were true, then Querinius must be rejoicing along with Betto. Betto's hatred for Arrius was no secret down to the most junior ranker in the cohort. If Betto had been with Arrius when the accident occurred, he would have been suspicious. The circumstances left no room for speculation. The sad reality was Arrius was unlucky that day. What a waste. It mattered how a man died, and falling off a cliff was not a worthy end to a warrior befitting the stature of Marcus Arrius. He hoped whatever gods Arrius worshipped would not hold the manner of his death against him.

Arrius stood up, weaving back and forth as waves of dizziness threatened to send him toppling backward on the pallet. He would have fallen had it not been for Philos on one side and Ilya supporting him on the other. For a moment, he thought he was going to faint and made as if to sit back down on the pallet. It was Ilya who insisted he stay on his feet. He gritted his teeth and tried to take a step, but his legs began to buckle. Ilya relented and started to push him toward the pallet, but he resisted and focused on the shaft of sunlight from the smoke-hole a few steps away. At the moment, nothing was more important than reaching the sunlight. Ignoring the painful throbbing of his head and the weakness in his limbs, he took a step and then another until he reached the sunlight. Ilya and Philos helped him return to the bed exhausted but triumphant.

Little by little over the next few days, his progress became more obvious. Ilya was relentless in prodding, cajoling and even berating him in her efforts to accelerate his recuperation. He was now able to stand up unassisted and move about for short periods of time within the confines of the dwelling. His chest and ribs were sore and painful to the touch, obliging him to lie only on his back when he slept. His vision gradually cleared, and the accompanying dizziness began to diminish along with the frequent bouts of nausea. His memories were a mosaic of missing and disjointed pieces, each distinct but without clear meaning. He remembered incidents and events from his early childhood, yet couldn't remember how and why he came to be where he was. Ilya was familiar to him and so was Philos, but he wasn't sure of his relationship to them; he felt a sense of well-being when they were near.

Although still weak, Arrius increased the pace of his convalescence by taking longer walks in the settlement. The physical exercise had a positive effect on recovering his strength, and soon he walked about without the assistance of Ilya or Philos. At first when walking about the settlement, he was the subject of glowering looks and open hostility. In contrast, Ilya was greeted enthusiastically and warmly wherever they went. Even though it was evident to him Ilya enjoyed considerable popularity and respect among the Selgovi, he lacked sufficient awareness to ask how and why it was the case. Gradually, his presence in the village ceased to be a novelty or a target for verbal threats he didn't understand even though the meaning and hostility was plain enough. In time, he was ignored if not welcomed, tolerated because of Ilya's company rather than being accepted in his own right.

Initial preoccupation with his own physical discomfort and his inability to concentrate or remember anything dampened his natural curiosity including how he happened to be here in this strange, unfamiliar place. Ilya avoided responding directly to his questions, recognizing he was unable to absorb an answer that needed to be explained in a larger context. She gave partial answers to leading questions, deftly changing the subject when they became too penetrating.

The persistent and painful ache in his head gradually subsided, and one morning he woke and realized his mind was clear. When Ilya went outside with him for their customary early morning walk, the steadiness of his gaze and his subdued manner signaled it was soon time for her to reveal the truth about who she was.

A few days later, she took him to a quiet spot in a clearing outside the settlement where a small stream meandered through the trees. After collecting her thoughts, she began to speak while Arrius studied her face, listening carefully to everything she said. She described her childhood and who and what her father was including her and Joric's hereditary rights to the Selgovan dais. She told how she allowed her cousin Beldorach to assume the leadership of the tribe to prevent Joric from being sacrificed. She didn't tell him she was pregnant, believing it was a subject better postponed for another time. When she was through, he looked away thoughtfully, weighing what she told him without speaking. His calm, expressionless demeanor was unsettling, and she began to feel uneasy.

After a prolonged silence, he turned to her and spoke, his tone of voice and words impersonal and remote confirming her worst fears she'd waited too long.

"It seems I've been ignorant of many things I should have known long before now." He laughed without humor. "Do you not find it strange the commander of Banna has formed an attachment with a prominent member of the Selgovae Tribe, a tribe that is a known and avowed enemy of Rome?"

"You knew I was Selgovan."

"Yes, I do believe you said as much; however, you neglected to tell me a few other important facts about your position in the tribe and notably your relation to the current leader of the Selgovi. To what extent have you been keeping Beldorach informed of what happens on the Roman side of the Wall?" She bristled at the accusation, but before she had a chance to protest, he continued.

"When General Arvinnius learns the truth, I'll not remain a Roman officer for long, much less the commander of Banna. Do you realize I can be accused of treason against the empire? That is, of course, if I'm allowed to leave here alive. I suppose I have you to thank I still live, or are you and Beldorach undecided what purpose I can serve the Selgovi?"

Lips compressed, Ilya bridled over the unfairness of his accusations even as a part of her realized his reaction was a natural one. Although baseless, it never occurred to her until he said it how the Romans might perceive their relationship as treasonous.

"Marcus, I realize I should have told you, but the time never seemed right. When we were together, I thought only of the future and not the past. It was wrong of me, and I'm sorry I did not speak of it."

"It's a bit late for apologies. You and Beldorach must have found the situation humorous to have fooled me so easily and so completely."

Ilya jumped to her feet, eyes stinging with angry tears. "You're a fool if you believe that, and if you truly do, then there's no future for us." He watched her run away, leaving him to wonder why he felt so alone.

Hours later, his anger disappeared and with it a sobering reality he had treated her unfairly. In retrospect, he understood her reluctance to tell him she was more than a member of the Selgovae Tribe and regretted his emotional and unreasonable reaction. He began to walk faster, eager to make amends. She was right, he was a fool to have said and implied the things he did. How could he have overlooked why she came here to help him?

He was covered in sweat from his exertion when he reached Beldorach's dwelling and burst through the door, scanning the interior, impatient to find her. He saw Philos sitting on a stool by the fire staring vacantly at the flickering embers.

"Have you seen Ilya? I must speak with her."

Philos gave him a stony look. "You're too late. She's gone."

"Gone? Gone where?"

"She left for Banna two hours ago. What did you say to her, Marcus?" Philos asked with an unaccustomed edge to his voice.

Arrius made his way to his pallet and sat down, massaging his head that started aching again. Without responding to the question, he said, "I have to go after her. She can't have gotten far."

"And how will you manage that? Even if you could ride, do you think the Selgovi are going to give you a horse or allow you to walk out of here? You forget we are more prisoner here than guest."

The comments jolted him back to reality. "Philos, she called me a fool, and she was right. I'm even worse, I'm an ungrateful fool."

"What did you say to her?" After Arrius summarized the substance of what transpired, the older man shook his head in disbelief. "Why did you say such things when you know them to be untrue?"

"I've no idea what came over me. I was blinded by my own foolish suspicions, and so I became the fool she accused me of being."

"Did she also tell you she's with child, and if so, did you accuse her it was by someone other than you?"

"She said nothing about a child."

"Too bad you were so busy being wrong and treating her as if she were a whore and a spy she had no interest in telling you something so unimportant as carrying your child. No, you were too focused on venting your own unfounded accusations."

"I've got to get out of here and tell her I meant none of it."

"It's a bit late for that. By the way, if we do manage to survive the Selgovi and get back to Banna, it will be because of Ilya."

"What do you mean?"

After Philos relayed what Ilya intended to negotiate with Beldorach, Arrius felt even worse. "I think the deed must have been done for there was a gathering in the council hall. Ilya was there as well. As soon as she came out, she left without saying anything. She was crying, Marcus."

"I must see Beldorach and undo what's been done. If we leave right away, we can easily catch up to her before she reaches Banna." The possibility occurred to him she might not stay in Banna and would be gone before he was able to get there.

"That won't be possible. Beldorach is escorting her back to Banna."

Chapter 19

It was five days before Beldorach returned to the Selgovan capitol. During his absence, Beldorach's wives saw Arrius and Philos were provided with food and ensured the waste jars were emptied; otherwise, they were largely ignored. They were given the use of a small dwelling close by in the lower part of the village. The furnishings were sparse, but the accommodation was adequate if not luxurious. Worn but serviceable tunics were hanging on pegs.

Arrius was disconsolate and profoundly remorseful. He stopped the regimen of physical exercise he had been following. He remained listless and uninterested in his surroundings, preferring to sit for endless hours staring at nothing. He was neglectful in asking how Philos was faring, and his earlier solicitous behavior of the dying man became more infrequent and perfunctory.

Philos worried as Arrius's physical and mental state declined. He redoubled his efforts to goad Arrius into regaining a sense of purpose, prodding him to take an interest in working to hasten recovery. Curiously, his own physical condition, while not improving, was at least not getting any worse. He hadn't seen any evidence of bleeding in many days, and the occasional sharp, stabbing pain in his abdomen subsided to a dull if persistent ache.

Early one morning, Arrius received a visit from one of Beldorach's wives he thought was named Machara. She entered carrying a bowl of water in one hand and a small, single edged knife in the other. After setting the bowl down on the table, she began making motions for him to take off his clothes. Even though Ilya told him during the many days he was unconscious he was bathed many times by Beldorach's wives, he was now entirely unwilling to have the practice repeated. His refusal was adamant and met with complete bewilderment. After a few more unsuccessful attempts to remove his tunic, she gave up and left in disgust.

The next day Athdara arrived and by holding her nose and pantomiming taking a bath, she eloquently conveyed the idea it was time for him to go to the nearby river to accomplish more than the infrequent sponge baths Philos forced on him. She led them to the section of river reserved for men and boys too mature to bathe with the women.

Arrius removed his tunic and put a foot in the cold water and considered going no farther. Then he saw the Selgovan men of various ages sitting or lying naked on the sun-dappled rocks drying off or calmly submerged up to their necks. Conversation died as the dozen or so Selgovan men looked at him expectantly, some with amused smiles. He realized there was no option except to plunge in or risk certain ridicule. Philos was content to stand in a shallow pool and lave handfuls of water over him, his teeth chattering while Arrius immersed himself in deep water created by a rocky dam. The cold water took the breath out of him in a rush, and he surfaced quickly accompanied by the cheers of approval from the watching Selgovans. Once he grew accustomed to the frigid temperature, he found the water invigorating. Thoroughly refreshed and feeling better than he had since Longinus forced him off the cliff, he climbed up on a flat rock to dry off near several of the other men. He found himself being openly stared at by the other men while they conversed in their incomprehensible tongue. He sensed the discussion was about him but from the friendly smiles, there was no hostility. The notable exception was a smaller, dark-complexioned man who did not smile but kept darting baleful looks in his direction. He perceived he was the subject of frank discussion and what clearly was a candid, physical appraisal.

Arrius and Philos became regular visitors to the rocky pools also serving as an informal meeting place to conduct business or share the latest hunting experience. The water was always cold and bracing, requiring sudden and total immersion to tolerate the frigid temperature. The cold baths had a positive effect, and Philos saw steady improvement in Arrius's physical and mental well-being. The daily trip to the river became a ritual Arrius looked forward to with increasing anticipation. Each time he felt better and better, and his recovery began to accelerate accordingly. He felt only an occasional twinge in his right side left to remind him of his injuries. The only somber note was the presence of the small, swarthy warrior who was almost always there and seldom joined in the good-natured banter with the other men. Arrius ignored the tribesman who silently made no secret of his disapproval he shared the river with a Roman. Had he known Tearlach was responsible for saving him, he would have tried to make a friendly overture instead of returning the baleful looks with impassive indifference.

One morning as he lay half-asleep in the warm sunshine listening but still not understanding the conversation around him, he heard a laugh and Beldorach's familiar voice behind him.

"Roman, they think you have the heavy fur coat of a horse in winter and wonder why you do not shave it off." Arrius turned and saw Beldorach removing the last of his clothing a short distance away. "Selgovan women like their men free of body hair, and Selgovan men enjoy it when the women remove it." Arrius now understood why all the men he saw at the river were completely devoid of body hair except for the immediate genital area, their drooping moustaches, and long hair. He finally realized what it was Machara was trying to do. He assumed until now their hairless chests and legs were a product of genetic inheritance rather than cosmetic preference.

"They also wonder why you have no long hair on your head or on your upper lip, the signs of a warrior. They see your many scars and believe you are no stranger to battle. They admire the long scar on your face and think you are lucky to have survived. You are a puzzle to them."

"I am happy to be of such interest to your people. I'm certain they," gesturing to the other men lounging about, "would be of similar interest in a Roman bath."

Beldorach chuckled as he waded into the water. "We Selgovi find even the ways of the other tribes strange, although you Romans are the most curious of all."

Beldorach made his way toward Arrius and took a seat on a nearby rock facing him. Arrius noticed the spiral tattoo on Beldorach's chest and saw it was a larger version of the same design Ilya wore. He remembered asking her what it signified, but she never answered his question. In retrospect, perhaps it would have been better for both of them if she had.

"What does the tattoo on your chest signify?"

The note of pride was obvious in Beldorach's voice. "It signifies I am highborn, and its size proclaims me High Chieftain of the Selgovae."

He recalled the first night with Ilya when he asked her about the tattoo. She didn't answer his question, and their lovemaking distracted him from asking again.

"What do you intend to do with me?"

"I don't know, and I'm in no great hurry to decide."

"Why did you bring me back here?"

"It wasn't my idea. It was his." He pointed to the swarthy man whose hatred was undisguised. "It was Tearlach who found you and brought you here. He wanted to bring you back to health so he can kill you. He hates Romans. He would have done so where he found you except you might not have known what was happening."

Tearlach spoke in heavily accented but understandable Latin. "One day I will kill you, Roman."

"Perhaps I'll kill you first, and use your hair for a plume to wear on my helmet."

For a moment, Tearlach made no reply as the two men stared at each other apparently ready to settle the matter on the spot. Tearlach stood up and threw back his head laughing with genuine humor and spoke in his native tongue. The men around him, including Beldorach, laughed uproariously.

"What did he say?" Arrius felt somewhat nettled at the amused reaction to his challenge.

"He said your balls are as big as the rest of you, and he thinks they would look fine hanging from his saddle. He wants to know if you will fight him with bow and arrow."

Arrius smiled. "Tell him he would then have the advantage." He held up his left hand displaying the broken fingers splinted and bandaged.

Tearlach said something over his shoulder as he turned to leave. Smiling with amusement, Beldorach said, "That is why he suggested it."

One of the other men spoke up directing his words to Beldorach who listened attentively while glancing sharply at Arrius. When the man was through, Beldorach translated. "Eudeyrn wants to know why one of your men tried to kill you. He says he was watching from above when the other man on a horse pushed you over the cliff. He thinks the gods must favor you to have survived the fall."

"I wish I knew, but it isn't the first time it's happened. As for the gods favoring me, I do not agree else the other man would have fallen from the cliff, and I would not be sitting here."

"Roman, you have enemies enough without having more among your own men. It would seem you are no safer on your side of the wall than ours."

"When you lead men, there will always be a few who dislike what you say and do."

"True, but with the Selgovi, our disagreements are settled face to face. I fought many times with warriors who challenged my orders. I've always prevailed." Beldorach's response was more a statement than a boast.

The man called Eudeyrn spoke again, and Beldorach's face reflected growing interest as he listened. After a few moments, he directed his attention back to Arrius. "He says the next day the man who pushed you off the cliff fought with another man with a light beard near where you fell. The bearded one rode very well, almost as good as the Selgovi. He caused the horse the man without the beard was riding to fall and roll over on him. But it did not kill him, nor could he move because of his injuries. The bearded horseman started to stab him with his sword but changed his mind and left the man to die. Eudeyrn said he was happy to finish what the bearded man did not and took the injured man's head soon after the horseman left."

The Selgovan had to be describing Seugethis. Arrius regretted Seugethis deprived him of the satisfaction of taking care of Longinus himself. The thought of the denied opportunity for revenge was immediately replaced with the cold reality it wasn't certain he would be allowed to leave.

Another man more liberally covered in tattoos than the others spoke up and a look of irritation flashed across Beldorach's face. His reply was terse. Abruptly, the other tribesmen began putting on their clothes to leave. Arrius gathered Beldorach ordered them to leave. When it was apparent Beldorach didn't intend translating the warrior's question, Arrius asked, "What did he say?"

It appeared at first Beldorach was going to ignore the question as he maintained a stony silence staring vacantly at nothing in particular. About the time Arrius thought he wasn't going to get an answer, Beldorach said, "He asked me what I intended to do with you. I told him the same thing I said to you. I haven't decided yet, but I think I may not kill you if you give me your word you will not try to escape."

"Then I am a prisoner?"

"Prisoner? Guest? What does it matter? You've been treated much better than I was at Eboracum."

"You would take the word of a Roman I will not escape?" Arrius paraphrased the question Beldorach asked after leaving Eboracum when he extended the offer to Beldorach.

"I can afford to make an exception with you, for I think you are still in no condition to go very far even if you knew where to go." Beldorach abruptly changed the subject. "You told me your name when we traveled to Banna from Eboracum, but I've forgotten it. Tell me again."

"Marcus Junius Arrius."

"Why do Romans have so many names? We find one name is enough."

Reminded of a similar question Joric asked, Arrius started to give the same explanation then decided it wasn't worth the effort. "It is our custom."

"Then I will call you Arrius. Why was my cousin angry with you?"

Arrius hesitated before answering, ready to tell Beldorach it was none of his business. Deciding her departure and his relationship with Ilya, if there still was one, was very much at the center of his predicament, he said, "I said some things I didn't mean, and she took offense. She was right to do so."

"Did she tell you she bears your child?"

"No. We argued, and she left. I learned of it after she left."

"You're a fool, Arrius."

"You're not the first to say it. All the same, I'm tired of people telling me."

"If you act the fool, you will be called one. I have three wives but no children, and you with no wives have sired a child. Perhaps your gods favor you better than you know or deserve." Arrius detected a note of bitterness in the comment.

"I was also told she intended to forego any rights she may have to leadership of the Selgovi in return for my life. If true, I refuse to accept the terms."

"It is not for you to say anything. You have no rights here. What has been done is in accordance with tribal law and cannot now be set aside. She was foolish to do so, but it was her choice."

"Does that mean you intend to let me return to Banna?"

"It means only for now you live. Do not press me, or I may change my mind and give you to Tearlach."

"If you break your word, you have no honor."

"I did not give my word. I said I would take it into consideration. If she took it to mean I would not have you killed, it was her mistake not mine. Be careful, Roman, men have died for less than challenging my honor."

"Beldorach, you are more clever than honest."

"As High Chieftain of the Selgovi, it is necessary to be clever above all other things as long as the welfare of my people is my objective. If it is in the interest of the Selgovi you die, you will be killed, and the only thing I will promise is it will be done quickly and not slowly the way Tearlach would like."

"When will you decide my fate?"

"Are you in a hurry to die?"

"No, but I have no fear of it. What will make you decide if I live or die?"

"It depends on you."

"You want something from me."

Beldorach hesitated considering how much he wanted to say, or if it would be better to wait.

"You're perceptive, Arrius, but this is not the time."

"When is a better time than this? Will we trust each other more tomorrow or the next than we do today?"

"Do not rush me. There are things I must do first. In the meantime, consider yourself a guest and enjoy Selgovan hospitality. If you wish, I will find you a woman to attend to your private needs. I have in mind a young widow who might find your hairy body not too repulsive."

"I do not wish to have a woman."

"If it is a young boy you want, I cannot help you. Unlike you Romans, we do not have such tastes."

"I most certainly do not wish it. Neither do most Romans."

"I'm relieved to hear it. I did not think I'd misjudged you, but if you change your mind about a woman, you must say so."

"Thank you for your offer, but I prefer to look after such things myself."

"Suit yourself but be careful where you go to find relief. We are a tolerant people except for our young unmarried women. Widows are much safer and grateful for the attention. Enough of serious matters." Beldorach stood up and slicked the residue of water from his thighs and legs with his hands. "The day grows late, and it is time for drinking and feasting. You look as if you need both."

Chapter 20

The non-descript, heavy straight-backed chair itself was only a chair with intricate but worn carvings which no longer held meaning for those who even noticed them. Its significance arose from where it was placed on a circular slab of polished stone. There it became the tangible focal point of Selgovan authority and power. The slab was high enough to place the chair's occupant slightly above any who stood before the platform. It was on this chair and platform Beldorach now sat watching expressionless as the large council chamber began to fill.

There was no extensive protocol involved in convening an open council. The clan chiefs were expected to attend for they knew it was in their best interests and their clans to do so. It was common practice to allow any Selgovan male who wished to observe to stand or sit on the flagstone floor in the back. Observers were discouraged from speaking but not necessarily restricted from doing so if for any reason they felt their clan chief was not representing their interests well enough. Since most clan chiefs held the position largely because of their fighting capability, the likelihood of spontaneous expression from anyone but a clan chief was rare. Frequently when tempers flared, councils were adjourned until matters were settled extemporaneously outside the chamber.

Women were not allowed even when the High Chieftain was a woman; no one recalled the last time a woman held the position. This was not because of any particular bias against women for Selgovan society accorded women virtually the same rights as men. Rather, it was based on a concerted effort to ensure there was always a male heir to the dais. The belief was a pragmatic acceptance a man was better suited to maintain the interest and security of the tribe and to take up arms either in defense or during periodic attempts to expand tribal boundaries. The occasional warfare over boundaries and constant raiding of the neighboring tribes, including the Caledonian tribes farther north, was an accepted way of life for as long as anyone remembered.

There was less good-natured bantering among the dozen clan chiefs or boisterous behavior in the rear of the hall as if there was general recognition the council was about to weigh more serious matters than usual. All knew Beldorach and his temperament well enough by now to anticipate that for whatever reason he convened the unexpected council, it was not to resolve individual or petty clan disputes or to debate which clan would host the annual gathering. Since it had been several years since the Selgovi heard war drums, there was speculation and even anticipation the High Chieftain would make the case for war. It mattered less who they fought than the opportunity of winning battle honors followed closely by the prospect of expanding horse herds or land.

Gradually the noise in the hall died down as individual conversations stopped and attention was directed toward the dais. Beldorach stood up and slowly scanned the assemblage, meeting the eyes of each clan chief briefly to acknowledge his presence. He had given careful thought to how he would present his case. He knew there would be initial resistance to his proposal based on the perception it was defeatist and too long-term to satisfy tribal expectations.

Oratorical skill was prized almost as much as individual courage and battlefield success. Long after what a High Chieftain may have said at council was forgotten, his eloquence, or lack thereof, would be remembered and the subject of debate. Beldorach did not disappoint. He started by recounting how the Selgovi came to be. The tribal origins, more myth than factual, were well-known, and every man present knew it by rote; yet, it was expected he speak of it — not to would be considered an unpardonable break with tradition. He spoke of each clan and its contributions, praising the virtues of past clan members who had distinguished themselves but careful to give equal measure to each clan. After considerable time interrupted only by frequent guttural cries of approbation over his narrative skills, Beldorach broached the reason the council was convened. The crowd sensed the transition from entertaining oration to purpose and leaned forward in anticipation.

"And so we have come to a turning point to decide if the Selgovi will continue to be just one more tribe among many or fulfill the destiny that is ours by right." He paused for dramatic effect to allow the words to sink in, to give them time to accept the idea there was an alternative to the status quo, whatever it might be. "As great and noble as we believe the Selgovi are, our belief in the greatness of our tribe is no different than what the Briganti, the Votadini or the Novanti think about their own. They are just as convinced in their belief as we are. What is also true is the Romans are greater than any individual tribe." He waited for the growls and fist-shaking to subside. He knew they expected him to propose the latest campaign against the hated Roman occupation, and for a little longer, he would let them continue to think so.

"The Romans came among us many years ago and with rapacious greed subjugated the tribes one by one. The southern tribes were the first to feel the Roman lash, the boot upon their necks and the slow strangulation of their freedom and culture. In time, the Roman general they called Agricola humiliated the Caledonians in a major defeat and scattered the Selgovi and our neighboring tribes like chaff in the wind during their progress north. Since then, they constructed a great wall separating us from the Briganti and the other tribes farther south. They prevent us from trading with the southern tribes as we have done since time began unless we first obtain their permission. Even then, we are taxed to pass through their stone barrier. When we return, we are taxed again, and the profit of our efforts goes mainly to the Romans. They would argue the wall has stopped the traditional warfare between us and the Briganti, and it maintains the peace and security for all tribes. I say the wall is an intrusion and an abomination to our rights to trade and, yes, to fight as we have always done."

The hall was filled with a deafening clamor of angry voices shouting agreement. Beldorach thought if the Roman wall was nearby, he would have only to remind them, and an attack would have been launched without hesitation.

He held up his hands to quiet them. When silence again prevailed, he said, "By now you think I advocate attacking the Romans. It would please me greatly to tell you we will. I wish it were so, but I cannot." He paused to allow the howls of protest to die down. He finally raised his hands to quell the protest that gave no appearance of stopping. Once quiet was restored, he continued. "If we attack the Romans, we will fail." The predicted uproar of disbelief and disappointment was even louder than the outburst of a moment ago. Impatiently he called for silence. "The truth is we are too few to succeed. Even if our numbers were greater, we would still lose. They are better organized than we are, and they have mighty weapons we do not. They fight as one while we fight as individuals for personal glory."

"We are better horsemen than the Romans." The shout came from the rear.

"Unfortunately, our horsemanship is not enough to breach their wall." Beldorach held up his hands to forestall further comment. "Not long ago, I saw one of the Roman machines hurl a small spear three times the distance of one of our arrows and with accuracy nearly as great. Before we can defeat the Romans, we must know what they know, we must learn to fight better than they do and even more important, the tribes must come together as one."

Eldorn, one of the border clan chiefs, interrupted. "But you failed to convince the Briganti to join us." Beldorach eyed the somewhat younger man without giving any sign he resented the comment. He didn't get along with the powerfully-built clan chief with the flaming red hair; Eldorn was always the first to voice opposition during clan assemblies and council meetings. However challenging the comment might be, Beldorach was grateful to him for raising the issue as it allowed him to reinforce his point.

"You're right, Eldorn. The Briganti refused because they weren't convinced the northern tribes were committed, and they had more to lose. They also believed the Selgovi, Novanti and the Votadini were incapable of getting along to fight the Romans together. In that, they were justified in their concerns. Bothan of the Novanti wanted no part of an alliance unless he was accepted as the leader."

There were jeers and catcalls following the last comment. Beldorach observed the calls were loudest from those who had aided the Novanti during the recent Roman incursion near the outpost they called Blatobulgium. Bothan had more than proved himself to be incompetent in their endeavor to defeat the Romans although he had to admit his own efforts were of some assistance in eroding the Novantean's effectiveness.

"Then there are the Votadini led by Darach. His name means *mighty oak*." He waited a moment longer before asking, "Do you not think it is a strange name for a sapling?" Predictably, the gathering erupted in laughter at the reference to the small and lean stature of the Votadini's High Chieftain. He finished the analogy by adding, "Darach is a tame sapling who is content to grow in the comfort and safety of the Roman forest. No, the Briganti are right to mistrust the tribes north of the Roman wall. I would, too, if I were a Briganti."

He saw the puzzled looks on the faces of the clan chiefs nearest him who were talking in low tones, undoubtedly conferring with each other to understand where this was leading. Only Briag, the taciturn clan chief of the northernmost Selgovi, wore a slight smile. Of all of the clan chiefs, Beldorach speculated it would be Briag who would be the first to perceive his intent. Briag was quick-witted and able to pinpoint the strength or weakness of whatever was being proposed. Just as important, Briag was popular and influential. If he could win Briag over, he was confident the others would follow.

"Then what is it we must do to restore the pride of the northern tribes and convince the Briganti to join us in turning back the Romans? First, we must fulfill the destiny of the Selgovi to unite the northern tribes to demonstrate our capability and willingness to begin a general uprising. With the tribes joined together in common purpose, we can and will defeat the cursed Romans and destroy the wall dividing our land." He paused to allow the words to sink in before asking rhetorically, "How can this be accomplished? It will not be done easily, nor will it be achieved quickly. I propose the only way it can be done is for the northern tribes to be brought under one leader, united as one with a single purpose, a single resolve. And who should that leader be? Should it be Bothan?"

A thunderous "No!" reverberated in the hall.

"Should it be Darach?"

"No!" came the response shouted even louder than before.

"Who then should it be?"

With a single voice, the clan chiefs and their warriors began to chant "Beldorach! Beldorach!"

For a moment longer, Beldorach allowed the enthusiastic outburst to continue unchecked as he stood impassively, arms folded across his chest. When the clamor finally subsided, he said, "You know I've tried before to form an alliance with the Votadini and the Novanti. You also know my efforts were met with failure. The other tribal chiefs do not see the future the way I do. They argue the Romans cannot be defeated; therefore, we must make peace not war for fear they will come even farther north. I am tired of having my words blow away in the wind trying to convince them to come together while the Romans grow stronger, and we grow weaker. I say to you it is time to replace Bothan and Darach. The Votadini and the Novanti will become Selgovi, and this," drawing his sword and holding the naked blade up for all to see, "is what will be used to persuade them."

Again, the crowded hall erupted in a near universal outburst of approval at the declaration of war. The one exception as he observed the noisy throng was Eldorn whose thoughtful expression and muted response was in marked contrast to the boisterous enthusiasm around him. Beldorach was satisfied with the outcome. It only remained to define how and when they would carry out the plan. First, he must talk with the Roman called Arrius. The Roman must be persuaded to assist without ever realizing until it was too late he helped to bring about the eventual destruction of the Romans.

Now and then Arrius and Philos took long walks in the woods and fields surrounding the settlement taking pains to avoid the stretch of forest where the center of Selgovan worship seemed to be focused and where Philos had gotten into trouble. Despite his pledge to Beldorach, Arrius noticed whenever they got out of sight of the settlement, a Selgovan warrior seemed to be lurking nearby.

Day by day Arrius felt better, and he gathered strength. The soreness in his ribs still made him uncomfortable in taking a deep breath made more difficult by his tightly-wrapped chest.

For several days, Arrius and Philos observed the settlement becoming crowded as a steady stream of tribesmen made camp outside the walls. Beldorach was cryptic in responding to questions concerning the influx of visitors. Arrius assumed from their similarity in dress and habit the visitors were most certainly representing the various Selgovan enclaves Ilya described. Beldorach later confirmed as much.

At first from the feasting and rowdy behavior of the newcomers, he assumed the purpose of the gathering was nothing more than social. When he noticed there were few women and no children, he began to speculate there was another reason. He surmised it more than likely involved another assault on one of the Roman outposts, possibly even Fanum Cocidii. It was more imperative than ever he get back to Banna; however, he couldn't abandon Philos. Nor was there any way Philos would be able to withstand the rigors of a desperate horseback ride all the way back to the fort. More to the point, he didn't think he was physically able to make the journey, not yet anyway.

He and Philos went to the river to bathe as the Selgovi began arriving in small groups. By now they'd become quite comfortable in the presence of the other local Selgovan men who generally tolerated their presence. Even Tearlach no longer cast menacing looks at them. Now, however, their presence at the river drew increasingly hostile words and threatening gestures from the recent arrivals. The local Selgovans did not intervene, allowing the Romans to suffer the abuse which hardly required fluency in the Selgovan language to understand what was being said.

One morning the belligerent behavior gradually threatened to become less verbal and more physical. Fortunately, when things began to get out of hand, Beldorach arrived and with a few brief comments delivered quietly but firmly, the harassment thereafter was limited to low-voiced muttering. Arrius was certain the High Chieftain's arrival that morning was not coincidental; rather, it was intended to make a point for reasons he could only speculate. Beldorach always had a reason for whatever he did or said. On this occasion, it may have been to reaffirm his authority over his tribesmen and a reminder to his Roman guest of the implacable hatred for Rome.

Arrius and Philos sat inside their small quarters and listened to the shouting coming from the large, rectangular building above them. They wondered again why the Selgovan clans gathered.

"Do you think they're deciding what to do with us?" Philos asked.

"I don't believe we're the reason. Beldorach hardly requires a consensus concerning what do with us. If he planned on killing us, he wouldn't have bothered to wait this long. What I find curious is he's kept us alive. It may be he's trying to rally his men to attack one of our outposts. I don't believe Beldorach has enough warriors for a major assault on the Wall. He knows he wouldn't succeed and risks annihilation of the Selgovi if he does. He's up to something, and I wish I knew what it was."

From the sounds of revelry heard that night, they thought whatever the purpose of the gathering, the outcome must have been met with widespread approval. Except for a brief visit from Cadha and Machara bearing a platter of cooked meat and a pitcher of the bitter brew the Selgovans seemed to drink in large quantities, they were left alone. The celebrations continued unabated late into the night and made sleep all but impossible. Dawn was nearly breaking before the noise finally died down, and those still conscious if not sober sought their beds.

Beldorach woke Arrius roughly soon after the sun cleared the distant mountains. Clear-eyed and bare-chested, he carried a long hunting bow and a quiver of arrows hanging at his side from a strap across his shoulder.

"Arrius, we will go hunting." Beldorach's tone was less an invitation than a command. He waited impatiently as Arrius slipped on his sandals and gingerly donned a woolen tunic,

"I don't believe I can yet pull a bow string."

"It is no matter. Perhaps we will hunt something other than game." Arrius was instantly alert. The two men walked through the sleeping settlement in silence with only the half-hearted barking of a dog to disturb the stillness. At the gate, Beldorach spoke to the guard who removed the bolt securing the heavy wooden gate and swung it open only enough to allow them to pass through before securing it behind them. For an hour, Beldorach moved along at a brisk pace without speaking, slowing down now and then to allow Arrius to catch up when he fell behind. Arrius was hard pressed to keep up, and it wasn't long before he felt the perspiration streaming down his face. He desperately wanted Beldorach to stop or at least slow down, but he refused to give in, gritting his teeth against the discomfort. He began to suspect Beldorach might be testing the extent of his recovery.

Whatever the purpose for the early morning trek, it was not hunting. Beldorach ignored the occasional deer bolting through the trees spooked by their fast-paced, noisy progress along the faint game trail they followed. Whatever their destination might be, Beldorach chose to keep it to himself. The Selgovan's silence was beginning to annoy him. He was about to protest when Beldorach stopped in a clearing overlooking a steep precipice. A small stream below flowed over a rocky shelf and plunged in a fine spray into a shallow pool. The sun had already crested the trees bathing the shadowed valley with soft tones of pink and gold when Beldorach sat down on a rock overlooking the tiny, cascading waterfall. Grateful for the chance to rest, Arrius was less interested in the bucolic scene than he was in the Selgovan's thoughtful silence.

At length, Beldorach finally spoke. "Arrius, soon I will have you and your friend escorted as far as the fort you call Fanum Cocidii.

You must be able to ride for it is a long walk. I do not believe you are yet recovered sufficiently to make the trip, but it will be for you to say when the time has come to leave."

Intuitively, Arrius knew Beldorach did not bring him to this place only to tell him this. "So, I will not be handed over to Tearlach?"

"No, but it cost me many horses before Tearlach would release his claim on you."

"You never planned to kill us at all, did you?"

Beldorach regarded Arrius with amusement. "No, did you think I did?"

"It crossed my mind at first. Then I thought you might have a better reason not to."

"For a Roman, you are perceptive. No, it was never my intention to kill you. I felt I owed you a debt for your fair treatment of me between Eboracum and Banna. I could do no less for you."

"Did Ilya have anything to do with your decision?"

"Not as much as she thinks; however, it took much to persuade Tearlach. There was another and more important reason. I want to make a treaty with the Romans. I no longer wish to fight them, and I want you to arrange it."

"If that's your reason for letting me live, you've wasted your time. I have no authority to speak of a treaty or an alliance with the Selgovi."

"I know, but you can talk to those who do. They will listen to you. I trust you to make them understand and believe what I say is true."

"Why?"

"Because I cannot defeat you, and it is useless to try."

"I don't believe you."

"Be careful, Roman, you are not back at Banna yet."

Undeterred, Arrius pressed the point. "I think there is more to it than that. I think the Selgovi alone are not strong enough to fight us; therefore, you need more time to create alliances. Sextus Trebius told me at Eboracum he thought you were trying to get the Briganti to join you. I think you failed, and you don't have the strength to fight us without them."

"What you say may be true. I don't deny you Romans have done your job well. Unlike the Selgovi, the Briganti are becoming very content to be the servants of Rome as the Votadini have become. Your wall has succeeded in accomplishing that, at least for now."

"I do not think you want peace with Rome. The first opportunity you have to attack us and believe you can succeed, you will."

"Perhaps one day, but it does not suit my purpose to antagonize Rome."

"Then why did the Selgovi attack my signal tower?"

"I was told it was the Novanti who attacked the tower."

"It was made to look like the Novanti did it."

"Why would anyone do that?"

"Perhaps it was because you wanted me to think it was the Novanti."

Beldorach smiled but did not reply.

"You were willing enough to help the Novanti in the assault on Blatobulgium."

"The Novanti asked for my help. I had no choice."

"Beldorach, you talk of peace with Rome, but your actions show otherwise. I'll not be used to further a purpose I do not yet understand."

"Then I may have to reconsider your return to Banna."

"It is for you to decide. I'll not bargain for my life by doing or saying anything not in the interest of Rome."

"You talk as if you are the one who decides what's best for Rome. You're only the commander of a small, insignificant fort in your empire while I speak for the Selgovae Tribe. I only ask you to carry my words back to those who are able to decide such things. Roman, who are you to refuse my request?"

Arrius rubbed his temple and studied the Selgovan. "You have a point. If I say your words, and afterward I also say I don't believe you, what then do you think will happen? You must do a better job of convincing me you're sincere."

Abruptly, Beldorach's anger disappeared. "You're right; I'll tell you my reasons. It's true what I said before. I can fight you Romans, but I cannot win. That is not to say one day the Selgovi will not fight when there is a chance to defeat you. It may not come in my lifetime, but it's not important. I'm willing enough to leave it to whoever succeeds me. In the meantime, I want you Romans to leave me alone north of your wall. I will not attack your forts if you do not attack my people. Is that not a reasonable outcome that will benefit both you Romans and my tribe?"

"It would seem so on the surface, but I think there is more to your request than you're saying."

"You are clever. I think you would have made an able tribal High Chieftain, for you are able to see into the darker corners of an issue. Very well, I'll tell you. I intend to make war on the Novanti and the Votadini, and I wish to be left alone to do this."

"I thought the Selgovi were allies of the Novanti and Votadini."

"It is true we have been allies. Almost as many times as we've been enemies. I think it's time for the Selgovi to resolve the relationship in a more permanent way."

"Then one day the Selgovi will be strong enough to fight Rome with you as their leader?"

"Perhaps."

"Very well, I'll tell General Arvinnius what you've said. He will question the motive of the Selgovi as I have. He may also say Rome is better off with three separate and weaker tribes in the north than it would be with one strong tribe."

Beldorach shrugged. "There is nothing more I can say."

"You should know something else. Rome will not sit by idly and allow the Selgovi to grow stronger than they are now. Also, it is not in the interests of Rome to tolerate unrest on its borders. It causes disruption to peaceful trade and encourages others to take up the sword and threaten the empire."

"I'll take my chances Rome will not intervene. I must do what I think is right for the Selgovi. Failure is less objectionable than never making the attempt." Beldorach paused then abruptly changed the subject. "What will you do about Ilya?"

"I don't know. I'm sorry for what has happened between us. It's possible she may not forgive what I said, and I may not be able to forgive her for not trusting me with the truth."

"What about the child she bears? What of it?"

Arrius shook his head. "It will be more her decision than mine."

"It would be easy to dislike you, Roman. I have three wives and many concubines, yet none bears my child. You seem willing to walk away from yours for no good reason." Beldorach stood up. "Come, it's time we returned."

Chapter 21

It was late afternoon on the fourth day since leaving the Selgovan capitol when Ilya wearily guided the horse into the courtyard of the tavern. Beldorach had maintained a brisk pace all the way to where he left her a few miles north of Fanum Cocidii thereafter to make her own way to Banna.

During the journey, she and Beldorach talked little, each distracted and preoccupied by individual thoughts. If Beldorach was curious about her sudden departure and angry demeanor, he chose not to pursue it. She correctly surmised the major reason for their fast pace was her cousin's haste to take her from the Selgovan capitol. She was aware her decision to renounce her claim to the dais was not universally popular. It logically followed Beldorach wanted to preclude any clan chief from actively challenging the deed. Removing her from the center of controversy would reduce the likelihood of anyone using her decision as a pretext to displace Beldorach as the High Chieftain.

There was no sense of loss or regret for the bargain she made with Beldorach since she never seriously considered claiming the Selgovan dais. Nor did she care Arrius would neither understand nor appreciate her gesture. Her anger and bitterness centered on his implication she used him as a source of information to benefit the Selgovae. Long before they reached Fanum Cocidii, she was reconciled to the idea whatever feelings they shared for each other had turned to ashes.

She climbed down from the pony-cart with difficulty due as much to her swelling belly as the fatigue of the journey. She heard excited voices, the clang of metal on metal and the hollow sound of swords hitting wooden shields and quickly concluded Joric and Rialus were busily engaged in their favorite pastime. She realized she was the only one at Banna who knew Arrius was alive, and if Beldorach held true to his word, he would soon return. She knew Joric would be overjoyed Arrius lived. She also knew it would disappoint and confuse him when he learned she and Arrius would not be seeing each other as before. It was obvious to her, as it must have been to Arrius, Joric worshiped the Roman officer. She resolved not to say or do anything to show any anger or bitterness toward Arrius. It would be better for Joric to come to the realization on his own she and Arrius no longer considered a life together. Better that than for her to say anything outright and prompt questions for which she neither did not have nor want to answer.

Leaving the equally tired horse standing with drooping head, she walked to the rear of the tavern to find Attorix and Joric. As she expected, her son was sparring with Rialus, a look of fierce concentration on his face. She found both Decrius and Attorix watching the two perspiring boys as they parried and thrust with grim determination.

Joric was the first to notice her presence. Distracted, he was slow in responding to his opponent's thrust and received a painful blow to his stomach with the unsharpened blade. Joric fell to the ground gasping for breath much to the amusement of the onlookers except for her. Concerned, she hurried toward him, but by the time she reached him, Joric had already regained his feet and greeted her with a weak smile.

"Mother, did you find Arrius?"

Ilya nodded, slightly discomfited his first thought was for Arrius and not for her welfare. "He's hurt, but he mends. I expect he'll soon return to Banna." She glanced at Decrius and saw his startled expression. She turned away from Joric and said to Decrius. "I've told no one at the fort he lives."

Smiling broadly, Decrius inclined his head. "I'll return and inform the senior centurion who will be less than pleased to hear it." With that, he clapped his son on the shoulder and departed for the fort.

Decrius wanted to see Betto's reaction when he learned Arrius was not only alive but returning soon. He anticipated the positive reaction on the part of the garrison and the opposite effect it would have on the unpopular centurion. If there were those who were unhappy with Arrius, they were unpleasantly reminded of how much worse it was to have Matius Betto in command.

Morale had since plummeted and punishment formations were a near daily occurrence. Only that morning there were two desertions reported. He suspected where one of them was, but he felt no obligation to report the information.

Decrius entered the principia and strode toward the office of Antius Durio where he found the cornicularius and quaestor in the process of being subjected to one of Betto's frequent tirades. Whatever the subject, from the grim faces of Durio and Publius Gheta, it probably translated to one more unpleasant irritant for the garrison to endure. Decrius waited patiently to be recognized, careful to keep his face expressionless. It would do him no good to appear satisfied with the news he was bringing. The senior centurion's reputation for taking exception for any slight, real or perceived, was too well known. Betto would see any gloating over his sudden reversal was paid back in subtle ways Arrius would never know about.

Finally noticing the optio, Betto asked with annoyance, "Well, what do you want?"

"I've learned Praefectus Arrius is alive and will soon return to Banna."

For a moment, there was stunned silence in the large room broken first by Publius Gheta. "Well, it would seem it will be necessary for you to vacate the praetorium again."

"Shut your mouth!" Betto didn't bother to look at Publius. He stared at Decrius. "Who told you this?"

"The woman called Ilya who owns the tavern in the east vicus."

"How would she know this?"

"She tended to him after he was injured from a fall off a cliff."

"The Selgovi allowed her to do that? Why would they?" Betto's surprised expression was mirrored on the faces of Antius Durio and Publius Gheta.

"Because she's Selgovan." Decrius immediately regretted his reply at Betto's reaction.

"She's Selgovan?" With a mocking smile, Betto turned to the other two officers. "Do you hear that? It seems our commander is not only alive but has been in bed with the enemy of Rome. Now I ask you, what should we make of this? I'm beginning to understand now why the Selgovi are sending Arrius back to us. I believe I may have a word with the Selgovan wench to learn more of this."

Decrius's moment of triumph was replaced by concern. He never considered the significance of Ilya's tribal identity since she'd been living at Banna for so long. He nearly forgot she was a Selgovan and so had the rest of the local Briganti living in the vicus. Her tribal identity was known from the day she arrived, but it ceased to be of any significance. Even the faces of the other officers reflected concern over the revelation Ilya was Selgovan. Now he thought about it, he could understand how damning the circumstances appeared. It never occurred to him to doubt Ilya or to ask why she lived in Banna and not with her tribe. It wasn't that unusual for members of one tribe to live within the boundaries of another tribe especially along the tribal borders. Regardless of how it may seem on the surface, he was certain Ilya's attachment to Arrius was nothing more than what it appeared to be.

Betto regarded Decrius. "You've done well, Optio, and now you may return to your duties." Then he faced Durio and Gheta. "Assuming his return is imminent, we will have to begin preparing for our commander's arrival although it's possible his return will be somewhat different than he expects." He thought to himself how pleased and appreciative Querinius would be concerning the Selgovan woman.

Told by Mirah a Roman officer was waiting to see her, Ilya felt momentary anticipation it was Arrius returning sooner than expected. She quickly decided that was impossible. His condition would prevent his return for many more days, possibly even weeks. But what if it was Arrius, and did it matter now? Whatever existed between them was now gone except for the life stirring within her. She put her sewing aside and followed Mirah into the courtyard where she saw a stocky Roman officer impatiently tapping a twisted stick against his leg Arrius once told her, along with the transverse crest, signified a centurion. She recalled seeing him from a distance from time to time but didn't know his name. Whoever he was and whatever the reason for coming, she didn't like the look of him. His coarse-featured face and the cold look in his eye sent a chill through her, and she unconsciously placed a protective hand on the swell of her belly. He was a menacing presence, and she wished Attorix were here and not in the village tending to the errands she sent him on. Nor did she like the way he regarded her with a bold, appreciative look making her feel naked. She saw a flicker of comprehension in his eyes when he looked at her belly.

Without preamble, Betto spoke first, his voice assured, imperious. "I'm told Arrius lives and will return soon, and you were the one who brought the glad news. Is it true?" The way he asked the question made it obvious, he was anything but glad.

She inclined her head in a brief nod and remained silent.

"Well, what of his condition, and when do you expect him?"

"I don't know exactly when he will return. He suffered a head injury, and it will take time to heal. There is also still the possibility the Selgovi may not let him return."

"You seem unconcerned. The knowledge is common enough Arrius was a frequent visitor here, almost as often you have been to the *praetorium*. I think the visits have not always been purely social from the looks of you."

"That is none of your business. Now, Centurion, if you've concluded your business, I want you to leave."

"Not so fast. There is more I want to know. Why would the Selgovi allow him to remain alive? Do they intend asking for ransom?"

She lifted one shoulder in a non-committal response. "I don't know. Beldorach will do as he wishes when he wishes without consulting me."

"I understand you are Selgovan."

Ilya was taken aback, acknowledging his statement with an inconsequential lift of her shoulders. How did he know? It must have been Decrius who said as much. Decrius must have known all along from her accent or from having overheard her and Joric speaking the Selgovan language. She was uneasy, wondering what he intended to do with the information. It didn't take long for her to get a glimmer of understanding.

"I'll take your silence as an admission you're Selgovan. I also assume Arrius knew you were; therefore, I wonder what benefit Beldorach may have gained from such a thing."

"I don't know what you mean."

"I think you know what I mean. It's no real wonder now why our recent campaign against Beldorach was so unsuccessful. I think Arrius had no wish to find the Selgovi."

She shook her head in denial. "You imply something untrue."

"What am I implying?"

"You seem to think either Arrius or I helped the Selgovi. You've no proof and no justification for such an accusation even if it were possible for me or Arrius to find or send word to the Selgovi." She feared her words sounded too defensive.

"You must have found the Selgovi easily enough when you went to see him, and they allowed you to come back here." His logic was disturbing.

Ilya felt helpless to keep her answers from reinforcing his opinions. She remembered Arrius once saying soon after he became a frequent presence at the tavern one of his biggest problems at Banna was the attitude and lack of support from some of the officers. She suspected the centurion was one of those officers.

The outer door of the courtyard opened, and Joric walked in. Urgently wanting him away from here, Ilya spoke to him more sharply than she intended. "Joric, please find Attorix and send him to me."

"He hasn't returned yet, Mother."

With a sinking heart, she remembered where she sent him, and it might be hours before he returned. It was obvious the Roman officer intended to pursue the matter. She was equally certain he was capable of employing methods to learn what he wanted including using Joric.

"This is your son?" His question confirmed her worst fears.

"Yes." She returned his gaze with a defiant look.

Betto looked at Joric. "That's good to know." Then to her relief, he said, "Run along then, boy, your mother and I have unfinished business here."

Joric hesitated, uncertain what to make of the situation as he looked from one to the other. "Mother, who is this man and what does he want?"

"Do as you're told, boy!" Betto ordered pointing his vitis at Joric in a threatening manner.

"Please, Joric, do as you're told. Everything's all right. It is as the officer has said, we have things to discuss." She hoped her smile was one of reassurance.

Reluctantly, Joric turned and left with a hurt look on his face. Relieved, Ilya said, "I want you to leave now. I think you and I have nothing more to say to each other."

"On the contrary, I believe the conversation has barely started, and there is much more we have to discuss. I do agree with you though, it is time to leave." Betto walked the few steps to the outer door of the courtyard, opened it and ordered loudly, "Guards!" He turned and faced her, stepping aside to allow four legionaries to file in past him. "You will be my guest at the fort where we will continue our conversation. I'll give you a few minutes to collect some things. Cooperate and my legionaries won't harm you." Realizing she had no choice, she called for Mirah.

Querinius read the latest message from Matius Betto with growing elation. The news Arrius was alive was sweeter by far than the report of his death. He studied the centurion's remarks concerning the Selgovan woman and concluded Betto discovered something only the gods could have arranged for him. If Arrius did return from captivity, it would be as Betto maintained; Arrius was guilty of conspiring with the Selgovae Tribe. Even if he wasn't, the circumstances alone would be sufficient to convict him of treason. He imagined the shocked look on Arrius's face when he found himself arrested for treason instead of being welcomed back as he expected to be.

He considered the best way to proceed. It would not do to publicly accuse him before his return, or conceivably he would hear of it and choose not to come back at all, opting instead to remain with the Selgovi. When he does come back, Betto must make it appear as if there is nothing wrong until he can get there to arrest Arrius. Anything less than his personal involvement would be insufficient to satisfy his obsession for ruining Arrius. After he was in custody, he would inform General Arvinnius. Unfortunately, he didn't have the authority on his own to execute Arrius without the legion commander's personal approval.

After thinking more about the circumstances of the woman's detention, he concluded the centurion made a mistake. There existed the possibility Arrius would learn of it and be forewarned. The only way to mitigate the damage was to make certain Betto did nothing to her to arouse any suspicions. It would be better if he released her, telling her it was an unfortunate mistake; he resolved to order her release immediately. There would be time later for Betto to deal with her in whatever way he wanted.

Betto cursed after reading Querinius's message directing him to let the woman go.

When he brought her to the fort, he placed her in one of the rooms in the praetorium with a guard on the only door. There were other locations inside the fort where he could have put her, but her proximity to his own quarters was not only a matter of convenience, it was also a question of privacy. He was already considering the things he wanted to do to her. Determining whether she was or wasn't involved in a treasonous association with Arrius was almost incidental to what he really wanted from her.

He visited her briefly later that night to describe what was in store for her if she refused to cooperate. He hardly cared whether she cooperated or not. He would use her even if she did confess to any guilt. He would give her the rest of the night to think about it before the interrogation began the next day.

Her calm demeanor never left her as she regarded him with icy contempt. Her composure both angered and aroused him. He restrained himself from ripping off her clothes and whipping her with the vitis. That she was pregnant with Arrius's brat only intensified his desire for both physical gratification and, more importantly, revenge against the man for whom he harbored a burning hatred. He started to imagine what the twisted vine stick would do to her soft, white flesh. It was then with great will power he left her, resisting the urge to remain and take his satisfaction now. To take his mind off her, he forced himself to concentrate on his duties, spending much of the night inspecting the sentries along the Wall.

He was in the process of completing his inspection of the last watch, and his anger over Querinius's criticism still rankled. Feeling cheated, he considered his options. He couldn't ignore the tribune's order, for he still needed and depended on Querinius's patronage to risk angering him. He reread the message and it occurred to him Querinius hadn't specified when to release the woman, which left him free to interpret the order as he saw fit. There was yet time to deal with her. The thought quickened his physical desire and prompted a smile of anticipation.

The officer of the guard, seeing Betto's smile by the light of a nearby torch, relaxed in the belief the centurion was pleased with his inspection. Suddenly, the centurion administered a stinging blow to his upper arm and said, "The next time I find one of your guards missing a neck scarf or anything else, I'll break you to ranker." As Betto walked to the praetorium, he thought the inconsequential blow to the officer was nothing more than a reminder of what the Selgovan woman was about to receive.

Ilya was apprehensive after the centurion left her. She knew Betto was telling the truth about what to expect. She was at the mercy of a man who seemed capable of anything. Even the legionaries who raped her weren't interested in doing anything more than using her to satisfy a basic urge. In comparison, the centurion showed a dimension of sadistic brutality she never experienced or imagined.

There was no question of sleep. His graphic descriptions of what he planned to do were even more horrific for the obvious reason he was aroused in the telling of it. After he left her alone, she vomited into the waste bucket. She knew there would be no mercy from him.

His preoccupation with her not only being Selgovan but also linked to Arrius made it clear what his objective was. She was reminded of Arrius's reaction and understood more fully the jeopardy in which she unknowingly placed him, including the looming threat to the safety of Joric and her unborn child. Once Betto learned she was related to Beldorach, there would be no expectation of any leniency because she was pregnant or innocent of intentionally assisting Beldorach. Her innocence couldn't be proved any more than her guilt, but it in the end, it wouldn't matter.

She was torn between the idea of wishing Arrius was here and dreading the thought he would be. The situation may be so far out of control he was powerless to do anything to save himself let alone her. Although she no longer envisioned a life with him, neither did she want him sacrificed because of her own failure to tell him who she was and her ties to Selgovan leadership.

She heard the rattle of the outside bolt and sprang to her feet edging as far from the bed as the small room would allow. Placing her arms around the swell of her belly in an unconscious effort to protect the life growing within her, she assumed an expression she hoped would mask her abject fear. Instinctively, she was positive any sign of terror would only make it worse. Rape was the least of her concerns — she was already resigned to the inevitable.

Betto closed the door behind him and slowly walked toward her. He was dressed only in a woolen tunic. In his right hand, he carried a vitis.

Distracted by her own random thoughts, she didn't see the first blow coming until the vine stick struck her across the side of her face. The pain was excruciating, and tears stung her eyes. She was only partly successful in stifling the involuntary cry of pain. She reached up and felt the welt on her cheek; her ear felt numb, and she heard a loud ringing. Reeling across the room, she lost her balance and sprawled on the floor next to the bed. Before she stood up, he was striking her across the back and shoulders, each blow more painful than the last. When he stopped at last, she was at first unaware of it as by then the pain reached a threshold where she no longer distinguished individual blows. The room was gray and swirling as she teetered on the edge of consciousness.

Dimly, Ilya heard him order her to stand. With great effort, she grasped the side of the bed and pulled herself to her feet. She stood weaving back and forth attempting to focus on what he was saying while trying to maintain her balance. It was much worse than she expected. From the wolfish smile on his face, it was also increasingly apparent the centurion was enjoying himself immensely. She no longer placed any hope she and the baby could survive the ordeal if what she'd already suffered was only a prelude of what was to come.

"Remove your clothes!" His order seemed to come from a long way off, and she was slow to comply. Impatiently, he grabbed the neckline of her gown and pulled it down forcefully causing her to lurch toward him as the garment ripped to her waist. She started to cover her bare breasts then realizing the futility of it, she allowed her arms to drop to her sides. She tried not to look at him as she focused on the wall behind him. He stared at her slowly tapping the palm of his hand with the vitis, desire plainly written on his face. She forced her mind to think of other things to free herself from the shame and horror of the moment.

"What's that above your breast?"

"What?" she responded dully, distracted, at first not understanding what it was he was asking her.

"The markings, what do they mean?"

She realized he was referring to the blue and green spiral tattoo above her right breast. If she answered truthfully, it might save her while potentially offering further circumstantial proof of Arrius's alleged treason. She started to say it was merely a decoration then she thought of Joric and the baby. "It means I am highborn." She lifted her head proudly, staring disdainfully at Betto.

She saw a flicker of interest cross his face. "What do you mean?"

"Before he was killed by the Romans, my father was High Chieftain of the Selgovae Tribe."

Betto's eyes widened. "Are you some kind of princess?"

"My people do not recognize such a title. I was only the daughter of Bhatar."

"Then you know Beldorach, the current leader of the Selgovae?"

She didn't hesitate to say. "He's my cousin."

For a moment, Betto remained speechless over the admission. His expression reflected a mixture of disbelief, elation and finally cunning. By the gods, he thought, this will finish Arrius once and for all. Querinius will have his wish fulfilled. Standing before him was the means to humiliate and ruin the bastard as the tribune wanted from the start. Querinius would change his mind about releasing her as soon as he knew who she was, but for now, he could take his time with her.

Chapter 22

Each passing day Arrius knew he was gaining both strength and stamina. He was given a docile horse with an easy gait to ride, one that wouldn't tax his weakened and still sore body. At first even with assistance, it was difficult and painful to mount. When he wasn't riding, he took long walks, gradually increasing his pace and distance in an effort to accelerate his progress and his departure. This was not the case for Philos whose health steadily declined. Philos was no longer able to make the journey to the river to bathe; consequently, Arrius began assisting him to bathe in the hut. Both knew his time was fast approaching, and they no longer talked of his return to Banna. Although he didn't show it, the pain was growing worse with more frequent evidence in the nightjar he was passing blood. Arrius told Beldorach, and from the solicitous behavior of Athdara and the other wives, it was apparent Beldorach told them.

Instead of talking of the future, they spent long hours discussing their past, laughing easily as they recalled the lighter moments of their time together. There were moments of silence when one or the other remembered a particularly poignant memory underscoring their deep and mutual friendship.

Arrius returned from riding one afternoon and found Philos unconscious and collapsed on the floor, his underclothing and tunic red from his hemorrhaging bowels, his hand clutching a glass vial; with a sinking heart, Arrius saw it was empty.

Even though still weak from his own ordeal, Arrius picked Philos up and carried him to a pallet. After removing his clothing and washing his near skeletal frame, Arrius covered Philos with blankets and sat beside him waiting for any sign he might yet regain consciousness. It wasn't long before he saw his eyes flutter open. Philos managed a wan smile before his face twisted in agony as another wave of pain swept over him. His breathing was shallow and labored. Arrius saw the dying man's lips move and bent down straining to hear what he was trying to say, but he heard nothing. Gradually, the pain seemed to subside, and his face relaxed.

After a few moments, Philos said in a faint but clear voice, "Marcus, there's little I have to say in the time I have left. You've been like a son to me, and no man has ever had or been a better friend."

"And you were the father I never knew and the friend I will miss until we meet again in the next life."

"If the gods see fit to reunite us in a better world, I will ask you what you did about Ilya and your child. The Macedonians took my family. Do not throw away your chance to know what I once had and still miss. Ilya never betrayed your trust."

"I know that now, but it may be too late. I wronged her, and I don't know if she will ever forgive the words I spoke."

"She loves you, Marcus. Be patient and give her time. One day she'll realize your words were spoken in haste." Philos experienced another spasm. When he continued, his voice was barely above a whisper. "I can see the shadows approaching." After a slight pause, he spoke his last words in Greek. Arrius knew enough of the language to understand Philos was speaking to his family. The words became fainter and fainter until at last with a serene smile, he breathed his last.

Arrius pulled the blanket over his friend's face and sat silently staring off into space. He never felt more alone. Losing Philos, although expected, was more painful than anything he'd ever experienced or could have imagined. He felt his eyes burning and was glad no one was there to see it. To regain control of his emotions, he considered what Philos said about Ilya. He wasn't confident she would or could ever forget his ill-chosen words. He resolved whatever it took, he intended to try and make amends not just for his sake, but more importantly, Philos expected it.

After Arrius raised the subject of funeral rites several days before, Philos dismissed the matter with a shrug and smile telling him to do what he will for he didn't intend to be there to witness it.

He watched the flames as they curled upward through the bier of stacked wood and reached the shrouded body resting on top. He tried to think of the proper words to say, wishing there were mourners present to override the sound of the flames with their lamentations. The Selgovan who helped him prepare the pyre stood by silently observing the ceremony with respectful curiosity.

When Arrius asked Beldorach for assistance in preparing a funeral pyre, the tribal chief assured him even though it was not their habit to cremate their dead, he would see Arrius received whatever help he required. He planned to take Philos's ashes to Banna for interment where he would erect a monument accompanied by proper burial services to compensate for the abbreviated ceremony now taking place.

His mind drifted to his impending departure. With Philos gone, there was no longer any reason to delay his return to Banna. After almost two weeks since Ilya left, his wounds had healed sufficiently he felt he was able to make the trip. He wondered what he would find upon his return to Banna. He suspected they knew he was alive; however, after such a lengthy absence, it was not beyond the realm of possibility General Arvinnius had already replaced him. He was startled to find he was no longer concerned one way or another.

"Tearlach will escort you as far as Fanum Cocidii," Beldorach said as the tribal chief jumped effortlessly off the back of the big black horse Arrius once claimed as his own. He'd grown used to seeing the Selgovan on the back of Ferox, accepting without resentment the outcome of any battle was always accompanied by losses on both sides. "I have much to do and do not have time to take you myself."

Arrius was taken aback at Beldorach's announcement concerning Tearlach. "Are you certain I'll make it to Fanum Cocidii?"

"Do not worry, Roman, Tearlach respects you, and although he doesn't like you, he no longer wishes to kill you unless you have a sword in your hand. He would rather wait and take your head in battle; there is more honor in that. Until you are within a day's ride of Fanum Cocidii, I regret you must remain blindfolded. It is better for us if you do not know where our principal settlement is located. I advise you not to remove it. If you do without Tearlach's permission, he has orders to kill you. He would be happy to carry out those orders."

Changing the subject, Beldorach said, "Arrius, I have a gift for you," handing him the reins of the black horse.

Stunned, Arrius replied with unconcealed pleasure and some suspicion, "Why do you do this?"

Beldorach's face showed the hint of a smile. "Because I can, Roman, and the horse will remind you of what we have talked about."

"Remember what I said. I can promise nothing except to make your proposal known to the senior commander. I'm not confident you will ever secure a treaty with Rome. If by any chance you do, I would be careful not to trust it too much."

"It's enough you ask them for it. As for trusting a Roman treaty, I will to the extent you Romans will trust me. Any treaty lasts only as long as it suits those who agree to it."

"I give you my thanks for the horse. I confess I've missed its size; the stallion's more to my liking than what I've been forced to ride since I lost him."

Beldorach smiled. "Soon I expect we'll have many more like him. He's covered many of my mares in the time he's been here." Momentarily, Beldorach's features took on a thoughtful look. "It's strange, I thought once you and I would meet on a battlefield, and only one of us would have lived to tell of it. Now I no longer believe this will happen, nor do I wish it. It is unfortunate you were not born a Selgovan, for I believe you and I might have been friends."

"It's still possible."

"Perhaps, but I don't think so. Time and opportunity are not on our side, and nothing can change that you are Roman and I am Selgovan. But who knows in the end, you Romans may be right when you say we are all at the mercy of destiny, and who but the gods will determine what they will do?"

In the time Beldorach had the horse, the Selgovan had worked hard to overcome the animal's erratic behavior. Thankfully, Arrius was deriving the benefit. The horse was no longer startled at the least noise or rustling leaves that made him perpetually skittish and difficult to control. Ferox responded instantly to the slightest pressure of a knee or touch of the reins. In spite of the animal's improved temperament, the ride to Fanum Cocidii was nerve-wracking. Without being able to see and not having the benefit of the more secure Roman-style saddle, Arrius maintained a precarious balance by clutching the horse's mane to keep from falling off. The challenge increased when they crossed open country presumed by the breakneck pace maintained at such times. He gripped Ferox's belly with his knees and hung on giving thanks for the sure-footed horse under him.

Now and then, he was lashed across the face or chest by low-hanging branches with enough force to leave scratches and occasionally risk unseating him. Such occurrences never failed to evoke laughter from his escort, particularly from Tearlach. Arrius suspected because of the frequency of the incidents, they were not always accidental.

He was certain their route was anything but direct. He sensed from the way the sun's heat kept shifting on his face, they frequently changed direction to further prevent any chance he might later determine where they'd been. The second night out, he was positive the campsite was near to the one the night before based on the surrounding terrain features that even in the shadows of a setting sun seemed familiar.

Only when they stopped to camp was his blindfold removed. The first thing he did was to make sure the leather bag containing Philos's ashes remained securely lashed to one of the pack horses. In accordance with Roman custom, he wanted to ensure at least a portion of his friend's ashes was interred properly.

He was not ill-treated and was given the same food and in equal amounts as the others. On the occasion when he left the camp to relieve himself, he was never followed. Invariably, the campsites were always close to a stream to water the horses and, possibly of equal importance, for bathing. After spending weeks with the Selgovi, Arrius was no longer put off by their dogmatic insistence on cleanliness and careful attention to personal hygiene surpassing even Roman practice that placed a high premium on such habits. The chilly nights never dissuaded the Selgovans from faithfully performing their ablutions, although the colder the evening, the less time was spent in the daily ritual. By now, Arrius had grown accustomed to the habit and no longer hesitated to join them.

He constantly thought of Ilya. He deeply regretted their estrangement, but he also realized he was unable to completely forgive her for not telling him more about her origin. He knew it would be no less easy for her to overlook his accusations. Nevertheless, he intended to try if only for the sake of the child.

The prospect of fathering a child caught him completely unaware and unprepared. It was more years than he remembered since he last thought of becoming a father, and then he had never dwelled on it. Over the years, what was only marginally important became less so over time, representing as it did the kind of distraction and stability incompatible with serving the legions. He suspected his attitude was based principally on his own father whom he knew only by what his mother told him. He had still been prepared to take Min-nefret to wife even after she told him she was barren — a condition which by then was unimportant. Of late, he enjoyed his time with Joric and as a result, thought he understood a little better what Philos tried to tell him about the joy of being a father. He hoped the boy, if the child was indeed a boy, would turn out like Joric. If it was a girl-child — she would do well to look or be like Ilya.

On the afternoon of the fourth day, Tearlach removed the blindfold and Arrius concluded they were nearing their destination. Soon he recognized familiar terrain features confirming his assumption they were near Fanum Cocidii.

Tearlach quickly reined in at the edge of a clearing and silently motioned the others to do as well. Arrius heard the drumming of hooves and saw a Roman patrol emerge from the other side of the clearing with the unmistakable figure of Seugethis in the lead. The Dacian commander's shouts signaled Seugethis's intention to engage. The Selgovi remained motionless calmly observing the charging horsemen. Hands upraised, Arrius kneed Ferox forward, stopping a few paces in front of Tearlach. Arrius saw a look of disbelief replace Seugethis's grim expression when he recognized who it was.

The war cries began to taper off in confusion when Seugethis held up a hand and reined his mount to a walk. "Salve, Seugethis," Arrius called out.

Omitting any greeting, Seugethis said, "You keep strange company, Arrius. Stand aside and I'll make short work of these bastards."

"No, they're my escort, and I've given my word no harm would come to them."

"You gave them your word? Now here's a tale worth the telling."

Arrius heard movement behind him and turned to see the Selgovi riding away. He faced Seugethis and saw the cavalryman's grim expression was not quite the reception he expected.

"I see you also have your horse again." Seugethis said, a note of accusation in his voice. "It was very generous of the Selgovi to treat you so well. I think you have much to explain."

Irritated at the Dacian's cool manner, Arrius replied with an edge to his voice, "I did not think it would be necessary to explain anything. I grant there's much to tell, and it can wait until we reach the fort."

The two officers maintained an uncomfortable silence all the way to Fanum Cocidii. When they arrived, Arrius saw no obvious changes although the hexagonal fort itself was a beehive of activity. From the number of cavalrymen and wagons present and their activities, Arrius surmised Seugethis was getting ready for an extended campaign.

Arrius grew increasingly irritated with the hostile reaction to his arrival. By the time they surrendered their mounts to an orderly and entered the small headquarters, Arrius was ready to respond in kind to the Dacian's taciturn behavior.

"I suspected there might be some who would not be eager to welcome me back, but I did not think the commander of Fanum Cocidii would be among them."

"Nor did I expect to see you arrive with a Selgovan escort and on the horse the Selgovi captured from you no less. I think others, as I do, will question why you're even alive."

With those words, it dawned on Arrius why Seugethis was treating him the way he was. "I understand. I didn't consider the circumstances of my return and what might be assumed. You're right, an explanation is due."

For the next hour, Arrius detailed his recovery with the Selgovi and how they helped to heal his injuries, concluding with Beldorach's request for him to intercede in his behalf. Throughout the account, Seugethis remained silent and interested. When Arrius was finished, Seugethis had thawed considerably. Any lingering question in the Dacian commander's mind about collusion with the Selgovi was overcome by Arrius's explanation of his captivity and what Beldorach expected to gain with his release. For his part, Seugethis related what happened to Longinus.

"Aye, it was plain as the nose on your face what he did. He tried the same with me, but no Roman is a better horseman than a Dacian. I left him for the wolves."

"That may be, but his head decorates a Selgovan trophy pole. They were curious why Longinus was trying to kill me. I suspected it was you who fought Longinus from their description of you. You might be interested to know they thought you were as good a horseman as the Selgovi."

Although Seugethis pretended otherwise, Arrius knew the compliment pleased him.

"Why was Longinus trying to kill you?"

"I have an idea who might have been behind it but no proof."

"Querinius or Betto?"

"Maybe both for different reasons."

When Arrius said no more, Seugethis surmised the praefectus did not intend to elaborate and returned to the subject of Beldorach's motives. "So, the Selgovan bastard thinks he can buy off Rome with a promise to behave so we'll leave him alone to defeat the Novanti and Votadini. Does he really think Arvinnius will agree to this?"

"I told him as much. I think he believes he has nothing to lose in trying and everything to gain if he succeeds. But that's for Arvinnius to decide."

"Aye, but I'm willing to bet my best horse, Arvinnius will not go along with it. Why should he allow Beldorach the time for the Selgovi to become the dominant tribe in the north when it suits Rome's purpose to keep the tribes divided and consequently much weaker?"

"Most likely, Beldorach has thought of it as we have. If Beldorach achieves control of the other tribes, he may be willing to be a peaceful client state of Rome for the few years it will take to establish his leadership and rebuild tribal strength. The presence of the Wall is proof of Rome's unwillingness to move farther into his domain; however, he wants assurance."

"Arvinnius would be a fool to allow Beldorach to get stronger than he is now."

"I agree, but then what does it cost him to try but some time? One Roman captive and a stallion is a cheap price to pay."

"Although you were blindfolded, can you find Beldorach's village?"

"We changed direction too frequently. I'm certain the camp is less than the four days it took to get here."

"It doesn't matter. We'll find him anyway."

"I don't intend to try until General Arvinnius has the opportunity to hear Beldorach's proposal. If he orders me to go after him, then I will. In the meantime, we will keep our patrols close-in for defensive purposes."

"Arrius, you disappoint me. Zalmoxis grows impatient for the Dacians to honor him."

"Enough of Beldorach. What news of Banna? I assume I've not been replaced."

"Betto commands, but he has the good sense to stay away from here, and I've no desire to go to Banna. The rumor is Querinius wants Arvinnius to appoint Betto commander of Banna. I warn you, Arrius, your reception may not be a cordial one. Whatever Arvinnius chooses to do may depend as much on Querinius as what you have to say. Whatever lies between you and Querinius, it's obvious to a blind man you have no friend and ally there. Do not turn your back on Betto or Querinius."

Seugethis then summarized what occurred after Arrius's disappearance and the following day when he confronted Longinus.

"Longinus must have thought you were dead, or he and Betto would have finished the job. If I hadn't insisted on trying to find your body and discovered the Selgovi got there first, Longinus would have gotten away with the deed with none the wiser. When I found where you fell and the Selgovi had been there, I assumed you were alive and taken captive. I thought you would have been better off dead. Until a short time ago, I and everyone else thought by now you were."

"It grows late in the day. Send a messenger to Betto I'll stay the night and return to Banna tomorrow. I'll also need the loan of a fresh tunic and a gladius."

Tribune Sextus Trebius silently considered with his one good eye the gleeful look on Querinius's face. In the two days since his arrival at Uxellodonum, he conceived a hearty dislike of the tribune bordering on contempt. In his forty years of service, he'd seen too many officers like Querinius — marginally qualified, and entirely self-serving. He wondered what circumstances caused Turbo to recommend this feckless creature for an independent command. Too bad Turbo was dead. He would have liked to hear what his former protégé had to say about Tiberius Querinius.

Querinius went to great lengths to make the case for Arrius's treason based on his relationship with the Selgovan woman who as it turns out, happens to be related to Beldorach. The circumstances of Arrius's return after being gone so long were odd and required an explanation. What was equally curious was Querinius's reaction when the messenger from Fanum Cocidii informed him Arrius would arrive at Banna the next day. Why Querinius appeared to take such delight at

202

the prospect of accusing Arrius of treason was strange and even suspicious. He had the impression if left to Querinius, there would be no inquiry and no trial for Arrius, only an execution.

Arvinnius was convinced there was something between the two men beyond personal dislike. He recalled Arrius's reaction at Eboracum when told Querinius was going to be given command of Uxellodonum. Arrius would not comment, but his silence on the matter spoke loudly and conveyed the impression there was something between them. In discussing it with Arvinnius, both agreed whatever it was, it was something to do with their service together in Judaea.

Still, he wasn't inclined to jump to any unwarranted conclusions especially when they were proposed by Querinius. He and Arvinnius had different opinions of the tribune. He didn't think Querinius had the leadership qualities required of a Roman officer. Arvinnius tended to measure according to a broader scale that included having political influence and agreement with his own personal view on the importance of ambition. With Turbo dead and his patronage gone, Trebius wondered how much longer Arvinnius was going to tolerate him. While they got along, it was apparent Arvinnius would have preferred someone else as his second in command, someone more malleable with political influence in Rome.

"Querinius, we will not go to Banna tonight. I've no intention of standing at the gate waiting for Arrius to arrive so I can arrest him for treason, at least based upon what you've told me thus far. If he's guilty of what you accuse him of, then I'll consider an arrest followed by a formal inquiry. Do I make myself clear, Tribune?" Privately, he thought if Arvinnius was here instead of in Rome seeing to his political future, the legion commander would have expected him to do what Querinius proposed.

Querinius suppressed his disappointment. "Of course, Tribune, it shall be as you say, but I do not wish to give him the opportunity of escaping should he learn of what he's suspected."

"Escape, where do you think he can go? Where would he want to go, back to the Selgovi? If he liked the Selgovi so much, why would he come back here to this dung heap?"

"Possibly as an agent for the Selgovi."

"Querinius, you seem convinced of his guilt and even obsessed in holding him accountable for actions you have yet to prove or convince me. I ask myself, why is this the case? Can it be you have your own reasons for seeing Arrius brought down?"

"Not at all, I only want to be certain there are no doubts about his loyalties. Rome cannot afford a commander on the frontier whose motivations are not entirely vested in Rome's interests."

"Spare me, Querinius. I've served the empire too long and in too many places to be lectured by the likes of you how the frontiers need to be safeguarded."

Querinius's face turned red at the sharp rebuke. "I only meant to emphasize the risks involved if Arrius is guilty."

"Well, at least now you're ready to wait until he's proven guilty before you condemn him. Perhaps you'll even be willing to hear what he has to say before you call for his execution."

"You judge me harshly, Tribune."

"And I think you judge too quickly. Unless I see the proof, Arrius is one of the last men I would believe guilty of treason. I think you have other reasons for your accusations of Arrius that have nothing to do with safeguarding the frontier of Rome. When I told Arrius at Eboracum you would command at Uxellodonum, he was less than enthusiastic; however, he would say nothing of the reason. Arvinnius also believes there is something between the two of you. I'll have the truth of it before I return to Eboracum, you can be sure."

"I will report the substance of this conversation to General Arvinnius. You have misjudged my character and called to question my motives when I was only doing my duty."

Trebius threw back his head and laughed. "Well, why don't you do just that? It will save me the trouble of doing it myself. Who knows, Arvinnius may even take you seriously, and that's more than I can do. For the life of me, I cannot understand what Lucius Turbo saw in you to recommend you for the command you have."

"I've suffered enough of your abuse, and I won't listen to anymore of it."

Querinius walked stiffly to the door. Before he got there, he heard Trebius say in a mild voice, "Well, Querinius, you might have balls between your legs after all." He paused and amended, "Although I suspect they're small."

Chapter 23

Ilya lost all concept of time as each day merged into the next. She remained closely confined except for the brief periods when he allowed her a quick bath across the courtyard in the room set aside for the purpose. Even more than the physical abuse, she hated the feeling of being unclean. No matter how hard she scrubbed in the brief time he gave her to bathe, she didn't feel clean.

She saw no one except when a legionary brought her food and water once a day and emptied the waste bucket. She thought about refusing to eat, but the thought of the baby growing inside her stiffened her resolve to live.

She dreaded the night when Betto was most apt to visit her. To her surprise, he stopped the beatings after a few nights, and she felt the welts beginning to heal on her back. She knew without looking in a mirror the first blow across her face would leave a lasting reminder of her ordeal. When he wasn't sexually abusing her, he seemed content in reviling Arrius for whom it appeared he had a deep, irrational hatred. She thought her captivity and debasement was less to do with physical gratification than a desire to strike back at Arrius. He no longer questioned her about being a Selgovan spy either because he was satisfied there was nothing more to make of her ties to Arrius, or it was no longer the main reason for holding her captive.

She worried constantly about Joric and the thought it might occur to Betto to use him to satisfy his rage against Arrius. Since he hadn't done that must be due to Betto's ignorance of Arrius's attachment for Joric and not because of any reluctance to spare the boy. After his treatment of her, she knew the depraved centurion was capable of any act of cruelty.

She fantasized about the various ways she would kill Betto. In vain, she searched the room for anything to use as a weapon. Although she was nearly as tall as he was, his powerful build made any attempt on her part futile to contemplate. She had no choice but to endure and survive for the sake of the baby. She wondered why no one came to her assistance. Surely Decrius or Rufus knew she was here. Decrius would have been the first person Joric would have gone to when she failed to return. She concluded Betto's absolute power made it impossible for anyone to intervene in her behalf.

Her first glimmer of hope came when the door opened one morning to reveal the familiar and concerned face of Rufus carrying a fresh bucket and a tray of food. The legionary placed the tray on the table and immediately held a finger to his lips, cautioning her to silence as he closed the door behind him. She tried ineffectively to arrange her torn dress to better cover her nakedness as tears began to sting her eyes.

Rufus took in her condition at a glance, his face registering his shock at what he saw. Ilya spoke first. "Have you come to take me away?"

Shaking his head, Rufus replied, "No, it cannot be done, Lady. Betto has given strict orders. He means to keep you here until Praefectus Arrius returns then he intends to accuse him of treason with you as proof. Decrius arranged to have me assigned to bring you food."

Her shoulders sagged, his words confirming her worst fears. "Is there any news of his return?"

"There's a rumor he's at Fanum Cocidii now, and he'll return tomorrow. The fort has been alerted the senior commander from Uxellodunum and another officer from the Sixth Legion will arrive tomorrow to arrest the praefectus for treason."

"Do you believe the accusation?"

"No, but Betto has convinced many he's guilty."

"What about Joric? Is he safe?"

"He is. Don't worry, he's staying with Decrius. He only knows you are being detained as we all thought. No one knew how it really was with you until one of the guards told me. Betto told everyone you were being well-treated."

She sat down on the bed with tears of frustration and anger flowing down her cheeks. "Rufus, give me your dagger. If Betto and I are dead then Arrius will have a better chance of proving his innocence."

Rufus shook his head. "Decrius said you would ask that. He said to tell you not to give up hope. There are many who are faithful to Arrius and even more who hate Betto enough to prevent any harm coming to Arrius. You must wait until tomorrow. I must go now before the guard becomes suspicious." Rufus collected the waste bucket and slipped out the door.

Long after he was gone, she wished the night would be over but also dreaded the outcome, reluctant to build up her hopes for nothing. She heard the rattle of the bolt and tasted bile. She didn't need to look up to know Betto was back.

Ignoring Arrius's protests, Seugethis decided to escort him with a troop to Banna. Arrius didn't tell the Dacian he would have preferred a quieter arrival without fanfare; however, Seugethis insisted seeing the look on Betto's face alone would be worth the effort. He also made the point that his presence with men to back him up would offer a better chance for a fair hearing.

Trumpets and beating drums signaled their arrival at the north gate. Arrius cursed under his breath. It was precisely the kind of welcome and attention he wanted to avoid.

They clattered through the north gate leading directly to the principia. Lounging on the covered porches of the barracks on either side of the narrow street, off-duty legionaries regarded them curiously as they rode by. Arrius saw three ranks of legionaries drawn up in front of the headquarters and the familiar figure of Matius Betto standing to one side of the formation. Seeing the formation blocking the narrow confines of the street ahead, Seugethis led the escort to the left between one of the infantry barracks and the combined storage and workshop building facing the east side of the headquarters and the praetorium. Arrius correctly assumed the Dacian's intent was to avoid the congestion of infantry in front of the headquarters by circling around to gain access to the main street connecting the east and west gates.

If Betto was unhappy or disappointed to see him, the centurion's impassive face did not reflect it. Concealing his dislike of the officer, Arrius reined in Ferox and dismounted, returning Betto's salute without comment.

With a sardonic smile, Betto said, "So our wandering Praefectus has finally decided to return."

"Hold your tongue, Betto. Before this day's out, I'll have you on your way to Eboracum."

"On the contrary, Arrius, if you're fortunate enough to see the sun rise tomorrow, it will be you who will be on the way to Eboracum — in chains, I might add. Guards, seize him by order of Tribune

Querinius. Marcus Arrius, I place you under arrest for treason for conspiring against the empire of Rome."

Stunned, Arrius felt his arms pinned to his side as Seugethis with the cavalry troop behind him rode up from the left. "What's the meaning of this, Betto?"

"It means he's under arrest for treason." Arrius saw Tiberius Querinius emerge from the doorway of the headquarters with the hulking form of the one-eyed Sextus Trebius walking behind him.

"Stand aside, Seugethis, and do not interfere, or you'll face the consequences," Querinius said.

"I prefer the word detained for the time being," Trebius amended. "Come, Arrius, we have much to discuss. Whether the centurion's threat of having you off to Eboracum in chains will occur is yet to be determined much less ordered. Seugethis, you Dacian son of a pig, it is good to see you again. I'm happy to see Zalmoxis has yet to claim you. Step down and join us."

Seugethis, dismounting, replied in kind. "If the pig was my mother, you must be my father," eliciting a hearty laugh from Trebius.

"Well, she was the best-looking Dacian bitch I ever had."

The ribald exchange eased the tension, and Arrius saw a look of uncertainty appear on Querinius's face. He didn't need a detailed explanation to know who was behind the reception Betto must have been more than pleased to organize. He should have known and anticipated Querinius would somehow find out about Ilya and use the information against him. He wondered how he learned of it so quickly unless somehow Ilya was the source. He felt a chill travel up his spine as he resisted the thoughts beginning to crowd his mind. Was this further evidence of betrayal? If so, why would she risk placing herself and Joric in jeopardy unless he was the one required to pay the price for her and Joric's freedom?

Arrius saw a look of disappointment on Querinius's face as Trebius ordered the guards to release him and return the gladius and pugio Seugethis gave him before leaving Fanum Cocidii.

"Arrius," Trebius said in a quiet voice that did not lessen the firmness of the invitation, "we'll adjourn to the headquarters and see to this business before things go too far."

Arrius and Seugethis followed Trebius inside the courtyard where under the colonnaded porches on either side stood most of the cohort's centurions, senior optiones and the headquarters staff including Antius

Durio silently observing the unfolding events with growing curiosity. The cornicularius was pale, a worried frown on his face. Publius Gheta conveyed silent support with a nod as he passed by the quaestor. Out of the corner of his eye, he glimpsed Decrius.

A small table and chair was positioned at the opposite end of the courtyard. Another larger table was located to one side with two of the headquarters clerks sitting behind it. It appeared the inquiry was going to be something more than a few informal questions.

Trebius proceeded directly to the small table and removed his helmet. Turning to face the four officers who now stood before him, he spoke in a voice loud enough to ensure everyone in the courtyard could hear. "I, Sextus Trebius, Tribune and acting commander of Legion VI, *Victrix*, will conduct an inquiry into the charge of treason against Praefectus Marcus Junius Arrius, commander of the Second Cohort, Tungrian, and First Ala, Dacian. A record of the proceeding will be maintained and provided to General Arvinnius. Tribune Tiberias Querinius, since you are the officer who has made the charge, you will now state the justification and present any proofs to support the accusation." After motioning Querinius to step forward, Trebius sat down, resting his forearms on the table and eyed the tribune with a steady look.

Querinius's manner and voice was smooth and unruffled. It was evident he was well-prepared to state his case. "I was alerted several weeks ago Praefectus Arrius, supposedly killed while on campaign, was reported to be alive and in the hands of the Selgovi. It was also reported he would return to Banna at some future date. Naturally, when I first received the news, I was pleased an experienced officer such as Arrius would be returning to resume his duties. Soon after, I was informed Praefectus Arrius had formed an attachment of long standing to a Selgovan woman residing in the vicus adjacent to Banna. Of greater significance, she was known to be a blood relative of Beldorach, the Selgovan High Chieftain."

"Who was the source of your information?" Trebius asked.

"It was Centurion Matius Betto, the acting commander of Banna in the absence of Praefectus Arrius."

"How did he learn of the woman's identity?"

"I do not know."

"Then in time I shall ask Centurion Betto. Continue."

"When I learned of the woman's presumed relationship to the Selgovan leader, I became increasingly suspicious of the praefectus. My suspicion began to grow when I considered the poor results of the recent campaigns against the Novanti and Selgovi along with Arrius's extended absence while a prisoner — or a guest of the Selgovi."

"Did you believe the poor results of the campaign may have been attributed to Praefectus Arrius somehow keeping the Selgovi informed?"

"I did."

"By what manner or means do you think he was informing the Selgovi?"

Looking somewhat uncomfortable at the pointed question, Querinius shifted his weight from one foot to the other. "I really don't know. I merely pose it's a strong possibility."

"I see," Trebius said in neutral voice. "What other proof do you have to offer, Tribune?"

"I see he arrived on the horse the Selgovi captured from him during the campaign. It is a fine animal, and I wonder how and under what circumstances did the Selgovi see fit to return the horse when anyone would have been pleased to own it. I myself offered to buy the horse from him, but he refused to part with it."

Trebius leaned forward with an interested look. "I recall the horse in question and agree it is a remarkable animal. In due course, I'll ask Praefectus Arrius the very question you raise. What else do you have to offer to substantiate your accusation?"

"I believe I've adequately justified my concerns."

"Very well. I would like to question Centurion Matius Betto."

The centurion stepped forward and waited for Trebius to speak. Trebius gave Betto a hard look, pausing a moment before asking the first question in the same neutral tone.

"How did you find out the woman Praefectus Arrius was seeing was Selgovan?"

"One of the optiones who first told me Arrius was alive happened to mention it."

"How did this optio know she was?"

"I did not think to ask although in this region it is not uncommon for members of one tribe to live near or within the boundaries of a neighboring tribe particularly here at Banna where the Wall divides the traditional tribal lands."

"Then the fact she was a member, or former member, of the Selgovae Tribe was not particularly significant by itself?"

Betto hesitated before replying. "That is correct, sir."

"It became significant then only because Praefectus Arrius was known to be frequently in her company?"

"Sir, it was common knowledge she and Praefectus Arrius spent time together."

"Did you consider if their friendship for each other was so widely known it would seem needlessly reckless for Praefectus Arrius to use the woman as a conduit for the Selgovi as you seem to think?"

"It occurred to me perhaps something so obvious might be intentional to conceal the purpose of their frequent time together." The smooth answer indicated Betto anticipated such a question.

"What would be the motive for him to pass information to the Selgovi?"

"I've no idea what his purpose was or what he hoped to gain. Possibly the woman was able to persuade him, or he was being paid."

"How did you find out she was related to the Selgovan leader?"

"She volunteered it."

Arrius clenched his fist in anger. Until now, he thought Trebius's questions and the responses given did not represent a credible case for treason. If Ilya had been providing information to Beldorach without his knowledge, his guilt would be no less than if he had been the one committing treason.

"Why did she acknowledge her relationship to Beldorach?"

"I have no idea, Tribune."

"Did you believe her?"

"I had no reason not to. She has markings above her right breast, and when I asked her what they meant, she told me they meant she was highborn and related to Beldorach."

"The woman willingly removed her clothes to prove she was of Selgovan nobility?" Trebius asked in astonishment. "Why would she admit to this when it might cast suspicion on her and Praefectus Arrius?"

Betto hesitated long enough in answering for Trebius to say, "I see. You arrested and interrogated her; therefore, she may not have been so willing to volunteer the information."

Betto began to cast nervous looks at Querinius and remained silent only nodding to acknowledge the answer. Arrius took a step toward

Betto, his hand on his sword. "If you've harmed her, Betto, by the gods, I'll kill you if it's the last thing I ever do."

Trebius's voice rang like steel. "Have done, Praefectus! This is an inquiry and not a place to settle personal scores. If you can't control yourself, I'll have guards in here who will. How he obtained the information is of no interest to me. The only relevance is the information itself and whether it's true or not." Trebius turned to Betto. "Did she admit to passing information to the Selgovi?"

"She did not."

"Is the woman available now for questioning?"

"She's here at the fort and being detained in the praetorium."

"Very well, bring her here. I want to question her myself." Betto saluted and immediately left the courtyard. "In the meantime, I believe it's about time to hear from you, Praefectus Arrius."

Trebius watched closely as Arrius silently took the position in front of the table.

"On the surface, Arrius, I find your association with the Selgovan woman, shall we say at the very least, unfortunate. Did you know she was related to Beldorach?"

"I did not, only that she was Selgovan."

"Did you not find it strange a Selgovan woman was living on this side of the Wall?"

"Not necessarily. While rare, there are instances of intermarriage between the various tribes, and I attached no importance to it."

"Was it because of a marriage arrangement she came to live here?"

Arrius hesitated before replying concerned the circumstances might add to the suspicion she was hostile to Rome. "No, she was forced to flee the Selgovi to save her child from sacrifice."

"I assume the child was to be killed in support of some barbaric rite?"

"Yes, I believe it was something like that."

"When did you learn she was related to Beldorach?"

"She told me when I was with the Selgovi."

"What was her reason for telling you, and why did she wait so long?"

"I don't know, perhaps because she was about to tell me she was pregnant with our child."

"What were the circumstances you were captured by the Selgovi?"

"One of my centurions forced me off a cliff. When I came to, I found I was badly injured and being looked after by the Selgovi."

"One of your own centurions caused this to happen?" Trebius sounded skeptical. "Where is this centurion now?"

Seugethis spoke up. "He's dead, and I'm pleased to say I had something to do with it. I can vouch for what the Praefectus has said concerning how he happened to fall into the hands of the Selgovi."

Trebius acknowledged the Dacian's testimony without comment.

"I should imagine the key question for this inquiry is why did the Selgovi heal your injuries, give back your horse and allow you to return to your post unharmed?"

"Beldorach wanted me to offer a proposal to General Arvinnius, specifically a treaty of peace between the Selgovi and Rome."

"Am I to believe your life was somehow spared as a gesture of Selgovan goodwill?"

"Not at all. Beldorach needed someone, preferably a senior Roman, to bring back his proposal and avoid risking his life or the life of one of his clan chiefs."

"What is Beldorach's proposal?"

"It would be better to reveal the details of his proposal in a less public manner."

"Very well, we'll deal with—"

The tribune was interrupted by screams of agony piercing the relative quiet of the fort. A moment later, a wide-eyed optio ran into the courtyard. Trebius stood up, annoyed at the interruption.

"Tribune, Centurion Betto has been stabbed!" the optio exclaimed.

Chapter 24

Trebius glanced at Arrius. "Do you have a medicus?"

Arrius spotted the cohort's senior medical officer. "Velius, come with me," Arrius said as he followed the optio with Trebius and Querinius close behind. Walking quickly, the four officers left the principia and traveled the short distance to the adjacent commander's quarters. By the time they entered the praetorium, the screams tapered off to a series of mewling cries. Arrius saw Betto lying on his back in a pool of blood, knees slightly bent, face contorted in pain. A bloody trail led from one of the slave's rooms to where Betto lay. A short distance away, he saw Rufus supporting a disheveled Ilya from behind. Her ashen face was a mask of hate, eyes fixated on the prostrate centurion.

Velius hurried over to the centurion and knelt to examine him while Arrius went to Ilya. At a glance, her appearance gave ample testament of how badly Betto treated her. He noted her hands and the front of her filthy, torn dress soaked in blood and her left breast exposed, revealing the blue-green spiral tattoo now streaked with red. There was a purplish welt across the side of her face and bruises around her neck. He vowed, no matter the consequences, if Betto somehow survived his present wound, he would kill him.

He called her name, but she did not respond and continued to stare at the blood-soaked centurion writhing in agony. Arrius took Ilya by the shoulders shaking her gently until he saw a flicker of recognition in her eyes. She started to say something then her eyes rolled up, and he felt her rigid body began to sag. Arrius caught her before she fainted. He looked at Rufus and said, "Take her to my quarters."

As Rufus reached for Ilya, Arrius's eyes were drawn to the hilt of the legionary's dagger, elaborate enough to have graced a centurion's balteus rather than the typical pugio carried by a legionary. Without thinking more about it, he turned to the knot of men surrounding the prone centurion.

Arrius looked down at the wounded centurion's groin and saw a knobbed dagger handle looking much like a rampant phallus replacing the centurion's missing penis. Even inured as he was to the awful and

214

common sight of battlefield carnage, he was startled at the nature of Betto's wound.

Velius, who had been crouching down examining the wound, stood up silently shaking his head. "There's nothing to be done, the wound is mortal. If I remove the blade, he will only die more quickly." The medicus hesitated. "Do not ask me to remove it. He deserves to die this way."

"Then leave the blade where it is and see to the woman."

Arrius turned to the optio who summoned them. "What happened?"

"I went into the room with Centurion Betto where she was being held. She was lying down. He pulled her upright, and when he did she reached out and withdrew the centurion's pugio and cut him several times between the legs. I called for Rufus to come and watch her while I went to the principia."

Arrius glanced up and saw Trebius's puzzled expression. After a moment of silence, the senior tribune was the first to speak. "Well, we can't tolerate a local woman castrating and killing one of our centurions even if the man's conduct has been particularly brutish."

"I'll see she pays for this with her life," Querinius said.

"I don't think so, Querinius," Arrius said, his voice cold. "Betto's not yet dead by her hand."

"I think it is a fine point you draw, Arrius. It's unlikely the centurion is going to get up and walk out of this courtyard, and even if he was able to, I doubt he would want to, given what damage the dagger has caused."

"I agree, Tribune." Arrius drew his sword and placed the point on Betto's throat, pausing only a moment until the centurion's eyes realized what was about to happen. Betto's mouth opened wide in a silent scream as Arrius thrust downward. Betto's sightless eyes remained half open.

"Arrius, it seems you've answered the question who killed the centurion while raising the question of how to resolve this. We can't tolerate killing off our centurions because they act like brutes. After all, we train and expect our centurions to act like brutes, else how are they to keep the optiones and legionaries in line? Now I have the commander of a cohort dispatching one of his centurions. I believe even a praefectus has limitations to his authority, and running a sword through a centurion's throat certainly must be one of them.

Unfortunately, I'm left with the dilemma of determining what should be done. What would you do, Querinius?"

"I would charge both the woman and Arrius with murder and add the charge of treason. Murder is customarily punished by strangulation and treason by crucifixion."

"Then how do you propose we should kill them, Querinius, assuming I determine both are guilty of treason? Strangle them first then crucify them or the reverse?"

Irritated by Trebius's sarcastic questioning, Querinius replied stiffly, "I defer the details to you, Tribune, so long as the end result is the same."

Trebius looked at Arrius and thoughtfully scratched his jaw with the three fingers of his left hand.

"Arrius, you must have an opinion about this, and since you seem to be at the center of the matter, I would like to hear what you have to say."

Querinius protested. "I hardly think the accused has any right—"

Trebius silenced him with a peremptory command. "Tribune, allow me to finish my inquiry." Querinius froze realizing he'd gone too far. Trebius resumed. "Arrius, you were about to comment?"

"Assuming the matter of treason is determined to be nothing more than a figment of Querinius's wishful imagination, as it increasingly appears evident, that leaves the matter of Centurion Betto's death unresolved. If there was no treason then she was imprisoned and ill-treated without provocation. That she was severely abused while detained is also obvious. By Roman law, she and I would be considered husband and wife, and I reacted as any husband would when I saw the battered condition of my wife."

"Your explanation seems reasonable enough for the time being," Trebius said, ignoring Querinius's sudden protest to the contrary. "Since we are in less public surroundings here, what I'm interested in most is not the matter of Centurion Betto's death but rather what Beldorach said."

Arrius briefly summarized Beldorach's proposal omitting any of his own conclusions while Trebius listened carefully without interruption. When Arrius was finished, Trebius remained silent for several minutes deep in thought before asking, "What's your opinion? Do you think he'll do what he says?"

"Beldorach's an opportunist. He will do whatever he thinks he must to further his own ambition and the welfare of the Selgovae Tribe. If he believes peace with Rome is to his advantage, he will observe it but only as long as it serves his interests. I believe he was truthful when he said he has no desire to fight Rome, at least for now. He knows he cannot win, but he will change his mind as soon as he thinks the Selgovi are strong enough and he's able to convince the northern tribes to join him."

"I agree with you. General Arvinnius must be the one to decide what will be done. If the tribes are warring, it serves Rome's interest to allow it until the Wall is threatened. The natural conflict existing among the tribes has served Rome in the past and will likely do so in the future. But if the tribes are able to come together under one strong leader then it's another matter. We'll speak no more of this to anyone until I've had a chance to inform General Arvinnius."

"I think Beldorach's offer is mostly a product of Arrius's intrigues," Querinius said.

"You may have a point, Querinius. Perhaps it's time we returned to the headquarters to complete my inquiry." Before they left, Arrius directed the other guard to get assistance in removing the centurion's body.

The return to the principia was made in silence with Arrius and Querinius studiously ignoring each other's presence. As the three men entered the courtyard of the principia, the low hum of conversation tapered into silence. Arrius caught Decrius's eye and motioned him forward. When the optio drew close enough, Arrius told him to send Rufus to inform Joric his mother would be all right.

Trebius resumed his seat and announced in masterful understatement, "It seems the centurion Matius Betto has met with unfortunate circumstances with or without the satisfaction of the gods and is no longer a member of the First Tungrian Cohort. May he serve in whatever afterlife the gods consider is appropriate for him. Now it's time to conclude my inquiry into whether the charge of treason is warranted concerning Praefectus Arrius. After listening to the allegations made by Tribune Querinius and the former centurion Matius Betto, I have concluded these two men are deserving of praise for their dedication and zeal in looking after the interests of Rome."

Arrius listened in disbelief and observed the triumphant expression sweeping over Querinius's face.

"However, after weighing the statements made against Praefectus Arrius and his explanation of events, I believe he's been accused based on a series of circumstances over which he had no control or intent to create. Such circumstances, while understandably sufficient for Tribune Querinius and the late Centurion Betto to initially believe treason was committed, do not in my opinion constitute any proof treason was committed. This inquiry concludes with my recommendation to General Arvinnius that Praefectus Marcus Junius Arrius be exonerated of all suspicion in the charges against him."

The courtyard erupted in cheers of approval. Querinius was stunned. Standing, Trebius turned to Arrius and Querinius and said in a quiet voice, "There is more I have to say, but I will do so in private," gesturing to the doorway leading into the headquarters.

Once inside Arrius's office, Trebius stood behind the desk and regarded the two men sternly. Querinius stood stiffly, his lips compressed in a thin line showing his displeasure at the outcome of the proceedings.

"What is to be done in the matter of the woman and Betto's murder?" Querinius asked.

"Why, I should think it's time for the burial ceremonies befitting a centurion to be carried out. I believe the garrison at Banna can manage it. As for the woman, it appears the Praefectus has matters in hand. I gather you would have wished otherwise, Querinius, but the matter is closed, and we'll waste no more time debating it." The tone of voice was enough to emphasize the issue was not open to further discussion.

"But I protest most strongly, a centurion has been murdered, and—"

"Silence!" Trebius said, a vein in his forehead pulsing with anger. "I have more than enough reason to believe Centurion Betto created the events leading to his own demise. I stop short of saying he deserved his fate. In any case, I'm no longer interested in pursuing the matter and advise you not to bring it up again."

Throughout the exchange, Arrius ignored Querinius, keeping his attention focused on Trebius. Privately, as preposterous as the charges were, he didn't expect to be completely vindicated. The question of Betto's death was completely sidestepped leaving him to wonder why.

Trebius's attention focused on Arrius. "It's apparent from the reaction of your officers my conclusion was as popular with them as it was not with Tribune Querinius. I want you to understand you've acted unwisely in forming a liaison with the Selgovan woman. From the damage it has already caused, I fear little good will come of it in the end. While you may not be guilty of treasonous intent, your behavior has created a perception you may be. Unlike Querinius, I don't believe you're guilty.

"I confess I am less bothered about the charge of treason than I am concerning the motive behind the charge Tribune Querinius made. I suspect, as did General Arvinnius, there is something more behind this than either one of you has seen fit to divulge. Querinius, General Arvinnius is of the opinion you may be unduly committed to the prosecution of Praefectus Arrius. He has gained this perception from your correspondence to him. Your unfounded accusations against the praefectus today causes me to share that perception. It is time for General Arvinnius and me to understand the conflict between the two of you. I might add, it's the main reason I came here and not to inquire into any dubious charges of treason. Now, who wishes to speak first?" Trebius seated himself and stared grimly at the two men standing before him.

"In deference to his rank, I'll allow Tribune Querinius to speak first."

"Tribune, I protest the outcome of the proceedings and the inference I am somehow to blame. Furthermore—"

Trebius stood up and said through gritted teeth, "Enough! If you do not wish to answer my question directly, you may leave, and I'll accept whatever Arrius tells me without question or reservation. Don't try my patience again."

Querinius struggled to regain his composure. After several moments, he began in a halting voice. "For reasons unknown to me, as primus pilus of the *Deiotariana* Legion, Arrius showed nothing but disrespect to my position and to me personally. He took every opportunity to ridicule and demean me in the presence of other officers, a practice he has continued during our service in Britannia. It is clear to me Arrius has wished my downfall and will do anything to ensure it. I believe he is envious he wasn't recognized by the emperor following the final battle of the *Deiotariana* as I was."

Trebius looked sharply at Arrius. "Turbo said in his letter to me he personally presented the emperor's award to you while you were recuperating, although I've not seen you wear it."

"I threw it in the sea when I left Judaea."

"Why?" Trebius asked in astonishment while Querinius, equally dumbfounded, remained silent.

"I didn't wish to be reminded of Judaea. There was no honor in what was done there."

Trebius looked perplexed, staring hard at Arrius. For a moment, Arrius thought he was going to pursue the reason for his last comment. He was relieved when the tribune shifted his attention back to Querinius. "Well, do you intend to enlighten me further, Tribune?"

Querinius, obviously discomfited by Arrius's remarks, lifted his shoulders. "What more is there to say?"

"I have a feeling there's much more although if that is all you have to offer, let's hear what you have to say, Arrius."

"Much of what Tribune Querinius says is true, but the Tribune neglects to say why I disliked him and why I did not respect him."

When it appeared Arrius was not going to elaborate further, Trebius asked, "Do you intend to explain the reasons for your opinion of the tribune, or am I to be left guessing? So far, I've learned nothing except what I already knew — you don't like each other. Usually when two men dislike each other, there's a reason or reasons. Arrius, I believe you need to enlighten me, or my report to Arvinnius will include a recommendation both of you should be replaced."

"Very well," Arrius paused briefly. "I believe the tribune was behind an attempt on my life during our service in Judaea." Arrius briefly summarized the circumstances leading to what Aculineous said during their fight before it ended with the centurion's death.

Trebius made no visible sign of accepting or rejecting what Arrius said. "You seem to have a habit of killing centurions. We lose enough centurions in battle without your contributing further to Rome's losses. Did he name Querinius as the one who paid him?"

"He did not."

"Then you only suspect it was Querinius who arranged the assassination attempt, but you've no proof?"

"That is correct."

"Arrius, why by Jupiter would Querinius want you dead?"

"I think it was to curry favor with General Gallius."

Trebius looked incredulous. "I find it somewhat unusual a legion commander would wish harm to his primus pilus. Do you have some explanation why you think there was some sort of conspiracy against you by the legion's two senior officers?"

"I do not suspect General Gallius at all. It is true, General Gallius and I did not get along well. We had our differences and not unknown to other officers in the *Deiotariana* including Tribune Querinius. I believe the Tribune anticipated the general would be pleased if I was removed. I've come to believe I was more to blame for our differences than General Gallius."

"Arrius, you seem to have a knack for attracting enemies. What have you to say, Querinius?"

"I agree with what Arrius said about General Gallius and their relationship. Arrius was disrespectful and argumentative during council meetings causing General Gallius to lose his temper on many such occasions. I vigorously deny I had anything to do with encouraging or paying Aculineous to kill him. He is ready to tell lies about me during the legion's final battle in the Sorek Valley." Querinius immediately looked as if he regretted introducing the subject.

"What lies? Trebius asked shifting his gaze back and forth between Arrius and Querinius. "Would one of you like to comment further?"

When Arrius remained silent, Querinius swallowed audibly and finally spoke. "He would claim I spent part of the battle in the medical tent when I only stopped in to see if the wounded were being looked after. As a result of my diligence, he as much as accused me of cowardice."

Trebius's expression was contemptuous. "Given the eventual fate of the *Deiotariana*, I, too, would have found it strange even cowardly for the senior tribune to be visiting the wounded during the height of a battle. Under the circumstances, I can easily see why Arrius may have reached such a conclusion. A conclusion, had I been there, would have been similar to mine."

Querinius's face was crimson with anger. "I wasn't afraid. I did my duty and the emperor rewarded me with this." He touched the gold torque around his neck.

No longer able to restrain himself, Arrius stepped toward Querinius and yanked the torque from the tribune's neck and hurled it across the room. "By wearing it, you insult and mock all those who died bravely in the Sorek Valley."

Noting the haunted look on the tribune's face, Trebius knew the truth of what really happened in Judaea.

"Well, I believe I have a sense of it all now," Trebius said. "Tribune, there's no way to prove or disprove the accusations you and Arrius lodge against one another. If I were to choose which of you to believe, the ring of truth lies more with Arrius than you. I intend to advise General Arvinnius you should be replaced at Uxellodonum. If I had the authority to do it, I'd relieve you now, but unfortunately, I do not. Under the circumstances, it will save a great deal of trouble if you were to accompany me when I leave tomorrow for Eboracum. I advise you both to say nothing of the reason. Querinius, I'll put it about you're leaving to assume your duties as a senator to avoid any speculation reflecting adversely on the army and give the emperor just cause to regret his unwarranted recognition of you."

Querinius, now pale and trembling, said through clenched teeth, "If it's the last thing I ever do, Arrius, I'll see you dead for what you've done to me."

"On the contrary, Tribune, I think Arrius has done very little to you. It is you who have done it to yourself. If it were not for the reputation of the army, I would bring charges against you myself. It is too much to hope you provide the solution to the problem with your own sword; however, it takes a certain amount of courage to stick a sword in your own belly, and somehow, I don't believe you have the mettle."

Wordlessly, Querinius walked across the room to retrieve the neck device. Trebius said harshly, "Leave it where it is, Tribune, or I swear I'll spill your guts on your boots myself."

Querinius hesitated for only a moment, turned on his heel and walked stiffly out of the room.

Trebius bent down and retrieved Querinius's torque and tossed it on the desk. "How did Turbo err so badly in rewarding a man so undeserving?" The grizzled tribune's question was rhetorical. "And why did you remain silent?"

"I was unconscious when Turbo arrived at the battle site. I suspect he found Querinius and assumed he did his duty when all he did was survive. Who knows, perhaps he did rise to the occasion after I fell. Gallius was already dead so when Turbo found Querinius, he made the logical assumption the tribune acquitted himself honorably. When I learned Querinius was to be recognized by the emperor during Turbo's last visit to me, I chose not to say anything to him. I would do the same again."

"Why did you throw away an award coveted by so many and earned by so few?"

"Part of it was because it was the same award Querinius received. Mainly, it was because I no longer believed in the war, and I wanted no reminder of it."

Trebius looked doubtful. "I don't understand. What was so different about Judaea? War is war. Legionaries and civilians die, and now and then even a legion or two suffers in the bargain. The campaigns in Parthia and Dacia, not to mention the constant uprisings in Gaul, all resulted in severe measures taken by Rome."

"You may be right, but it was somehow different in Judaea. Hadrian wasn't content to subjugate the Jews; he wanted them annihilated. I understood his reason for taking stern measures considering the Jews rebelled earlier; however, it went too far, and I grew sick of it. When we stopped killing Jewish warriors, we started killing the civilians sparing only those who were commercially valuable as slaves. That is until the markets became saturated with too many Jews. Then we killed them all."

Trebius gave Arrius a steady look. "Best not say such things to Arvinnius if you wish to remain in command here. He wouldn't understand what you're saying, and frankly, neither do I."

Arrius laughed humorlessly. "I'm not sure I do either except I want no more part in wholesale slaughter."

"What if the tribes rebel in force? What will you do?"

"I'll fight the battles, but I'll not do again what we did in Judaea."

"What if you're ordered to do so?"

"Then it may be time for me to put down my sword."

"Arrius, you think too much. Such thinking leads to a conscience. Rome doesn't want its officers to have a conscience or think on such matters. Thoughts like that lead to questions Rome doesn't expect to hear much less wish to answer."

"You're right, Tribune," Arrius said with a wry smile.

"What about the woman? Arvinnius will not be happy to hear about her. From the looks of her, she's with child I assume is yours."

"There's no question the child is mine, but it's a complicated matter. I think we will go our separate ways in spite of what I said earlier. More by her wish, I think, than mine."

"I advise you to find comfort with a whore instead of a wife. A wife asks too much of a man and more than the army can or should tolerate. You and I are much alike. We've spent too much time with legionaries to think we can ever be content with anything else. I've sired brats in Gaul, Dacia and, yes, even Parthia where it was difficult to pry a woman's legs apart long enough to get between them. I took pleasure in the act at the time and took even greater pleasure when I left them. A wife makes demands on a man, makes him soft, and the next thing is you're sitting in the sun with brats climbing all over you. After a while, you're no longer interested in the things keeping a man's blood going and his prick hard."

Arrius smiled at the older man's blunt and dismal description of domestic life, nodding in half-agreement. "I suppose there's more truth in what you say than I'm willing to admit, but unlike you, now and then, I think there may be more to living than whores and legionaries."

Trebius picked up his helmet and placed it on his head adjusting the cheek guards as he did so. "Then you and I will disagree on the point. Well, I'm off to Eboracum to attend to Querinius's departure. Until Arvinnius can find another tribune to replace him, I'm placing you in command of Uxellodonum and Banna. Who knows, Arvinnius may see fit to promote you, but frankly, I doubt it. You should know, Arvinnius has concerns about you. You are the one, not Querinius, he expected to eventually relieve. He thinks you may not be tough enough when it comes to fighting the tribes. After listening to what you said about Judaea, his concerns may be well-founded. You're a good soldier, Arrius, and I'll do you a favor and not relay your opinions to Arvinnius. When and if the general comes out here again, I'd advise you to keep such thoughts to yourself."

"Is Arvinnius planning a major campaign in the north?"

"Arvinnius wants to be appointed governor of Britannia. He thinks a successful war against the tribes will bring him more recognition than keeping the border peaceful."

Arrius had the impression Trebius knew more than he was willing to say. "Then Arvinnius will probably not look with favor on any peaceful overtures from Beldorach."

"He will not. Oh, he'll go along with it for a time, but then he'll use Beldorach's success as a reason to further his own plan to invade."

"I warned Beldorach it would be unlikely for Rome to tolerate a single strong tribe. I thought it was Hadrian's purpose only to

224

maintain the border. Whatever trouble happened north was no affair of Rome so long as it did not cross into the south."

"It depends on the extent you believe there is a threat in the north. There's always the risk of allowing trouble there to grow until it begins to stir unrest south of the Wall. Can we afford to take the chance it will not? I believe General Arvinnius may be right in thinking to solve a small problem before it grows into a larger one. Besides, Hadrian is old and, I'm told, no longer the man he used to be. He won't be around much longer. Who knows what the next emperor will or will not do after the Senate proclaims Hadrian a god?"

"Has Hadrian announced who will be the next emperor?"

"No, but there's talk he plans to adopt Antoninus Pius as his son, and if he does, it will be confirmation Hadrian intends him as his successor. That's what happened when Trajan adopted Hadrian."

"Who's Antoninus Pius?" Arrius asked.

"He's no soldier for certain. Didn't even do token service before becoming a senator. I'm told he's never been out of Italy except for the one time he served as a provincial governor. He's one of Hadrian's councilors. Well, whoever he is, it probably won't change things this far away from Rome."

Neither man was to know for many months how wrong Trebius was.

Chapter 25

Shortly after Trebius departed for Eboracum, Arrius met first with Antius Durio to learn what transpired during his absence. With typical efficiency, the cornicularius reviewed the strength, medical and disciplinary reports; identified the changes Matius Betto made; and approved the latest promotions and reductions recommended by the centurions. Arrius immediately reinstated Rufus's rank of optio. In place of Betto as second in command of the cohort, he appointed Flavius who was still recovering from his severe leg wound. He appointed Decrius as acting centurion in place of Flavius resolving to do everything possible to see Decrius's new status would eventually become a permanent promotion.

Almost all changes Betto inaugurated had one thing in common — a senseless and tyrannical effort to further restrict the lives of the legionaries. Arrius did not need to be told the attendant effect the changes had on morale. He quickly rescinded nearly all Betto's changes. He was especially outraged over the harsh punishments administered during the weeks he was gone. Grimly, he realized his first priority was to undo the damage caused by Betto.

He gave instructions to Antius Durio for Betto's funeral arrangements. He rejected his recommendation to throw the body on the vicus refuse pile for the pigs and carrion birds. The centurion would be accorded only the bare minimum attention without the elaborate ceremonies and sacrifices normally accorded an officer of high rank. The cornicularius was further discomfited when Arrius placed him in charge of the arrangements, such as they were.

Publius Gheta summarized the results of the latest equipment repairs, status of the requisitions sent to the legion's quaestor and ration and forage inventories. The quaestor reported the local grain crop, now halfway through the growing season, promised to be a bumper crop at harvest time, thus assuring full granaries with enough left over to provide the Sixth Legion with an impressive surplus.

After making arrangements to assemble the garrison in the basilica to reassert command of the cohort, Arrius started to leave the headquarters to see how Ilya was doing when Velius entered the courtyard.

"How is she?" Arrius asked the medicus.

"Her physical injuries are less than the damage to her mind. She will have some permanent scarring on her back and cheek, but I fear they are minor to what she has suffered mentally. Betto treated her badly in every way."

"What of the child, will it be all right?"

"Who can tell? Pregnant women are hardly my specialty. She's not lost it yet in spite of all she has gone through, and that's encouraging."

"Thank you for your help, Velius. I would appreciate it if you would continue to look in on her over the next few days."

"Praefectus, she's no longer here. She asked Decrius to take her home right after I finished administering to her wounds. She was insistent and refused to consider remaining even though Decrius and I urged her not to leave."

Arrius understood she wouldn't want to stay where she'd been subjected to such brutality. He was even slightly relieved she was gone. He dreaded the awkwardness of their first meeting since her departure from the Selgovan settlement. He realized he was intentionally prolonging his meetings in the headquarters to avoid seeing her, leaving him to wonder, if other than the child, there was enough left between them to salvage.

Preoccupied with his own thoughts, Arrius hardly noticed when Velius saluted and left to resume his duties. He concentrated on what he would say to the legionaries later in the day but found he was distracted by thoughts of Ilya. He tried to resist the obscene images of Betto and Ilya together that kept flashing through his mind and wondered if either one of them could ever forget what happened to her. She overcame her earlier and bitter experience resulting in Joric's birth, but could she do it again? Except for him and their brief time together, Ilya had even less reason to accept or tolerate anything Roman than before. After what he said to her and what she experienced with Betto, he was doubtful there was any future together. He questioned if either one of them even wanted to try.

He left the headquarters and led Ferox toward his quarters. He heard the clatter of wagon wheels on the cobblestones and saw Decrius preceding a wagon through the east gate. Rufus was driving the wagon and behind him sitting on top of the wagon's cargo were his four slaves. The solemn expressions on their faces indicated they knew Philos was dead. A feeling of overwhelming loss engulfed him like a dark cloud. Since his friend's death, his occupation with other matters, particularly those marking his return to Banna, had blunted his grief. Now it even crowded out thoughts of Ilya. He knew he needed to make suitable funeral arrangements for Philos including commissioning a suitable stone marker.

As Rufus guided the wagon through the praetorium entrance, Decrius dismounted. "Salve, Praefectus," the optio said quietly after saluting. "The Lady Ilya is back at the tavern. She would not stay here."

"I know, Velius told me. Thank you for taking her." Then gesturing to the wagon, Arrius asked, "What's all this?"

"Betto made Philos remove all your things after returning to Banna from the campaign. Philos didn't know where else to go so he took everything including your slaves to the tavern."

The two men walked the horses into the courtyard and watched silently as the wagon was unloaded. Finally, Arrius turned to Decrius. "I've appointed Flavius as second in command of the cohort. You are now acting centurion of the first century. I'll do what I can to make it permanent."

"I'm honored, Praefectus. I never expected to achieve such rank."

"Because you're not Roman?"

Decrius lifted a shoulder and said without bitterness, "It has not been exactly an advantage to be a Britannian here at Banna."

"Well, you deserve it. I can only promise to try and get General Arvinnius to make it permanent."

"It's enough you make the attempt, and for that I will always be in your debt."

Arrius nodded then called for Rufus.

Rufus, noting Arrius's hard-eyed, grim expression, was apprehensive as he nervously came to attention in front of Arrius and Decrius. After a moment of ominous silence, Arrius spoke. "Rufus, tell me what really happened here."

Rufus shifted his feet uncomfortably and avoided looking Arrius in the eye. "I don't understand what the Praefectus means." Decrius observed the exchange with a puzzled expression.

"Since when have you taken to wearing a centurion's pugio?" Arrius pointed to the elaborate dagger in Rufus's belt. "Unless I'm mistaken, that dagger belonged to Betto."

Rufus took a deep breath. "It was the Lady Ilya's idea. She wanted me to give her my dagger several days ago to kill Betto. I refused and told her it wasn't safe for her to try anything. I was afraid she wouldn't succeed, or she might try to kill herself. This morning she asked me again, and I couldn't refuse her any longer."

"In her condition, she was able to cut off his penis?"

"She asked me to help. I promised Silaxtus, the other guard, five denarii if he would help me. When Betto came to take her away, we followed him into the room. We grabbed him from behind and held him across the table. She was supposed to cut his throat, but instead, she pulled down his small clothes and cut off his cock and balls. Then she stabbed him several times between the legs before burying the blade to the hilt in his crotch. Silaxtus became frightened when the centurion screamed. I told her to finish him. She refused. I took the centurion's pugio and was going to cut his throat; however, the Lady Ilya would not allow it — she said he deserved to die slowly for what he did. She also said it must not look as if we helped her. It was her idea to replace my dagger with his. When Betto no longer had the strength to resist, I sent Silaxtus for help. I thought he would be dead before anyone came." Rufus raised his hands in supplication. "What else could I do?"

Except for the specific details, the legionary's account confirmed his suspicion Ilya did not act alone.

"It appears I must do something, Rufus. I can't overlook your role in this matter; therefore, I will have to promote you to optio again. I've already informed the cornicularius." Arrius heard Decrius chuckle as the two men saw the look of disbelief replacing the legionary's worried expression. "It would be better if the details of what happened here did not become the subject of barracks rumors. See that Silaxtus gets his five denarii and keeps his mouth shut in the bargain. Now then, optio, I believe you have other duties to attend to." Rufus saluted and started to walk away. Arrius called after him, "Rufus, you have my thanks for what you did."

After addressing the assembled cohort in the basilica as the last act of the duty day, Arrius returned to his quarters and removed his helmet and cuirass in preparation to visiting Ilya. He determined the last thing she needed to see was the usual trappings of a Roman, an unwelcome reminder of what she'd gone through.

He had finally run out of reasons to postpone facing her. Throughout the day, he tried to think of what to say to her and was no closer to finding the words. He felt somehow responsible for her ordeal. If he hadn't accused her of dissembling, in all probability, she would have remained in the Selgovan capitol and returned to Banna with him thus avoiding Betto's notice. Garbed only in tunic and cloak, he mounted Ferox and reluctantly headed in the direction of the tavern.

This time of day, the tavern should have been filled with off-duty legionaries thirsty after a long day and eager for a more relaxed atmosphere. Instead, the establishment was quiet. The outer door to the courtyard, usually wide open, was closed and locked. Arrius walked Ferox around to the rear of the building where Ilya's private rooms were located. There he found Joric sitting disconsolately by the well.

Arrius was struck by how much the boy seemed to have grown in the interval since he saw him last. At the sound of the horse's hooves crunching on the gravel, Joric looked up and saw Arrius, but instead of the usual smile of welcome transforming his face, his expression remained guarded as he silently watched the horse and rider approach.

Dismounting, Arrius called out a greeting. "Joric. I've come to see how it is with your mother."

"She's not well. She said you would come, but I was told to tell you she will not see you now."

"I know. She's been sorely used. I've come to do what I can."

"I think your offer is too late. Why were you not there to prevent what happened?" Joric's anger was plainly visible on his drawn face.

"I wish I'd been there more than you can ever know. I did not know she was taken prisoner. The man who did it is dead, and there are no others like him at Banna."

Ferox whickered softly and began to prod Joric with his muzzle looking for the treat the boy always had for him. Joric stood up and put his arms around the horse's neck pressing his forehead against the animal's sleek coat. When the boy finally looked up, Arrius saw his eyes were wet with unshed tears.

"She sits staring at the wall and won't talk to anyone, even me. I don't know what to do for her."

Arrius placed a hand on his shoulder and squeezed. "I don't know either, Joric. We must be patient and allow her to heal in her own way and in her own time. She's a strong woman and will recover, but I fear it will take time."

"Is the baby yours?" Joric abruptly shifted the subject.

"Yes, I'm the father. I did not learn of her condition until after she returned to Banna."

"Why did you not come back with her?"

"Beldorach would not allow me to leave, and I was still recovering from injuries."

"Will you marry her?"

Arrius hesitated before responding. "If she will have me, in truth I would do so. According to Roman law, we already are even though the proper ceremonies have not been conducted. My public acknowledgement the child is mine is sufficient to make it so. Unfortunately, I do not believe your mother agrees."

"Then my brother or sister will not be a bastard like me." The boy spoke without bitterness.

Arrius was stunned. While Ilya told him how Joric was conceived, she said Joric believed his father was killed in battle before he was born. How did he learn the truth?

"Why do you say that, Joric?"

"Beldorach told me I was. Mother thinks I don't know. It doesn't matter. I'm still Joric, and one day my name will be famous for who I am and not because of the father I never knew."

Arrius was impressed with the boy's maturity beyond his years. He wondered what Beldorach's purpose was in telling the boy. He was certain Beldorach had a reason.

"I once wanted to be like you, a Roman officer, but I no longer wish it. Except for you, Romans have not been good to my mother. I expect one day I will fight them when I become a Selgovan warrior although I would not want to meet you in battle."

Arrius was taken aback at the prospect of being on the opposite side of a battlefield. Surely the gods would never be so unkind. He made an attempt to brush off Joric's doleful view of the future.

"I will never allow that to happen. I would walk away before I would ever lift my sword against you."

For a moment, man and boy stared at each other, both realizing more than simple words had passed between them. For the first time in his life, Arrius realized what it must be like to be a father. He wondered if his own father ever felt this way and was saddened to think from his recollection of the brief and indifferent relationship they'd shared it was unlikely he ever did.

Arrius mounted Ferox and turned the horse toward the road. Behind him, he heard Joric say, "Arrius, you must come back again." Then with unusual perception for a youth of his age, he said, "She needs you more than she does me."

For the next two weeks, Arrius was consumed with his duties including several extended visits to Uxellodonum where he found a warm reception following the unpopular tenure of Tiberias Querinius. He considered moving there and turning Banna over to Flavius, but after weighing the merits, he concluded splitting his time at both locations allowed him to maintain better control over both garrisons.

Thus far there was no communication from General Arvinnius to give him a sense of how the legion commander felt about what happened at Banna. The legion commander's silence was enough to conclude, at least for the time being, Arvinnius intended to support the one-eyed tribune's decisions. He received only one cryptic message from Trebius ten days ago informing him Querinius had left Eboracum to assume a post with the XX Legion, *Valeria Victrix* at Deva. He felt sorry for whoever the general of the twentieth legion happened to be. Upon further reflection, he decided it was the legion's centurions and below for whom he felt more sympathy.

From the increase in refugees fleeing the north through the wall gates, it was evident Beldorach's campaign against the Novantae Tribe was beginning. Most of the travelers came from isolated border settlements neither Selgovan nor Novantean but unfortunate victims caught in the middle of a tribal war. Battle reports and progress concerning which tribe might be gaining the upper hand were both sporadic and conflicting. Arrius gathered Bothan must be acquitting himself better than Beldorach expected, and indications were no quick resolution to the conflict would be reached.

When his duties allowed, he tried to see Ilya, but his attempts were rebuffed. She remained secluded seeing no one except Mirah and Joric. The tavern remained closed. Joric was cordial enough, but his demeanor was more reserved. Arrius was at least satisfied Joric seemed able to make an exception in his case for his growing dislike of Romans in general. Arrius noticed he no longer saw Joric and Rialus practicing their swordsmanship. When he asked about it, he received a non-committal shrug.

The only time Arrius saw Joric become animated was when he rode Ferox, proving he had the natural ease of a born rider. Although the stallion was still spirited, the time spent under Beldorach's care had completely transformed the animal's previous unpredictable behavior into a responsive, dependable mount. Observing the boy's equestrian skills and comparing them to Beldorach's exceptional horsemanship, he was convinced there must be something about the Selgovan heritage that created a special bond between man and horse much as he'd observed with the Dacian cavalrymen.

Arrius noticed when Joric talked to the horse, it was always in Selgovan and Ferox seemed to respond to it as quickly as Latin. At first without any conscious intent, Arrius began to expand his limited capability to use the Selgovan language by conversing with Joric. The boy proved to be a patient and interested teacher, and Arrius was a willing student. Apart from considerably improving his understanding and use of the language, the impromptu language lessons had another salient benefit by providing the means to gradually bring the two of them back together in a semblance of their past relationship.

The waning days of summer were fast approaching when late one day Arrius rode up to the tavern and found Ilya sitting by the well, her hands folded almost as if she was expecting him. In contrast to his confusion and feeling of awkwardness, she seemed composed, almost serene. There was a scar on her cheek where Betto struck her. Her hair no longer hanging loose was braided in the Selgovan style. Arrius thought she had never been more beautiful.

She was the first to speak. "Thank you for helping Joric. The last few months have not been easy for him."

"They've been even more difficult for you, Ilya. We've been worried." She nodded in wordless acknowledgement. "I'm sorry for what I said to you the last time we were together. I was blinded by my own anger and didn't see the truth even though it was plain enough to see."

"We both made mistakes. I should have told you who I was. Decrius told me you were accused of treason and placed on trial because of me. I'm sorry for being the cause."

Arrius shook his head. "They were my enemies. If it hadn't been you, they would have found another means to try and finish me. Betto's dead and the other officer is no longer here. Beldorach told me you renounced your claim to leadership of the Selgovae. I wish you hadn't done that."

"I believe Beldorach intended to let you go anyway. He has great respect for you even though he's not known for his love and admiration of Romans."

"Then why did you do it if you thought he would release me?"

"There was more to the bargain I made with Beldorach than your freedom."

When it was evident she didn't intend to elaborate further, Arrius changed the subject. "How are you now?"

"If you mean my physical health, I am well. My body has healed, and the baby thrives." She winced and touched her belly. "It must be a boy to kick so hard. It will not be long before it comes. How is Philos? Does he fare well?"

A shadow crossed his face, and he looked away swallowing hard without answering.

"Then he's gone from this life."

Arrius nodded. "He died a few days after you left."

"I knew he wasn't well, but he never spoke of it. He loved you, Marcus. He saw in you the son he lost long ago. He lost more than any man or woman should in this life. You gave him a reason to live as long as he did. I'm sorry for your loss."

"My loss extends beyond the death of Philos. I fear I've said things you will never forget or forgive."

When she was slow to reply, Arrius felt a hollow emptiness inside. He dreaded she was about to confirm what he was afraid of hearing.

"Marcus, it may be our time has come and gone. It isn't because of what we said to each other. Given time, we might reconcile words said in the anger of the moment. It's what happened to me since I'm unable to forget. While I do not hold you at all to blame for what was done to me, it has changed me, possibly forever. My body may have survived the ordeal, but something else died inside me." She wrapped her arms tightly around herself and shivered in spite of the warm evening. "I don't believe I can ever suffer the touch of a man again. Can you understand?"

"Does it mean I'll not be welcome here to see the child?"

"The child is ours, and nothing will change that. I want him or her to know you as a father. But I don't want you to expect anything more from me I'm unable to give." She rose and walked quickly toward the tavern, head bent so he wouldn't see the tears streaming down her cheeks.

"It could be you will change," he called after her.

She hesitated at the open door and without turning said, "Perhaps, but I can give you little hope I will."

Chapter 26
137 CE

The winter months were especially harsh, and keeping essential roads open to the signal towers in the south and along the vallum between the Wall garrisons became a herculean effort. Contact with the northern outposts was virtually nonexistent for extended periods when deep snow frustrated even the most determined efforts with travel by horse and wheeled cart virtually impossible. Slow as they were, ox-drawn sleds offered the sole means for transporting supplies and conveying dispatches between the headquarters located along the Wall and the legion headquarters at Eboracum. Those who lived in the region the longest told Arrius this was the worst winter in memory.

Morale plummeted as the men endured the tedium of guard duty and constant drills conducted in the basilica or on snow-covered training fields. The legionaries spent countless hours maintaining equipment that didn't really require it. The centurions bore down on the optiones, and the optiones dispensed punishment in a concerted effort to keep the lid tightened down on hot tempers and raw nerves. Arrius imposed harsher punishments than he wanted fearing lenient treatment would encourage further infractions and disobedience.

Some of the men resorted to self-injury to avoid guard duty on the Wall ramparts where the frigid temperatures and howling wind quickly produced painful sores on any exposed skin. Several legionaries were severely injured, and one was killed when he slipped off the ice-covered ramparts. Assuming the harsh conditions were causing equal difficulties for the native tribes, Arrius reduced the number of sentinels and the amount of time for each guard relief, thereby minimizing time a legionary would have to endure the misery and peril of the biting cold.

The deep winter snows virtually isolated the fort from frequent contact with the Sixth Legion headquarters. A month after Trebius returned to Eboracum, Arrius received a cryptic, impersonal message from General Arvinnius prolonging his temporary appointment as acting commander of Banna and Uxellodonum. The word temporary confirmed his private suspicion Arvinnius had no intention of making the appointment a permanent one. He surmised his command of Banna was in jeopardy based on his association with Ilya and concern for his reaction to the Judaean rebellion.

Arrius divided his time equally between the two garrisons. He made a concerted effort to visit the northern outposts as often as the weather would permit. With patrols at Blatobulgium and Fanum Cocidii now limited to the close-in areas surrounding the garrisons, little was known of tribal activity in the north. Except for the scraps of intelligence gleaned from occasional refugees transiting the Wall gates, there was little to indicate the extent of Beldorach's success, or lack thereof, in achieving dominance of the other tribes.

The stone carver he commissioned to prepare the grave marker for Philos completed his task, and Arrius was satisfied with the result. He hoped Philos would be pleased with the location in the cemetery a short distance from the edge of the bluff providing a panoramic view of the river and valley beyond.

The snow made transporting the tall, rectangular monument to the cemetery easy and fast; however, the ground was so frozen it required several hours for the stone carver's assistants to excavate deep enough to secure the stone. By the time it was finally in position, Arrius was as eager to escape the bitter cold as the laborers. Before leaving for the relative warmth of the fort, he took one last look at the marker and experienced a hollow feeling inside. He never realized how much he'd taken Philos for granted. He missed their conversations and the easy companionship they'd shared, particularly since he and Ilya seemed as estranged as ever.

He tried to see Ilya and Joric as often as his duties would permit. More often than not, Ilya remained closeted in her private apartments leaving him alone with Joric. Ilya was remote but not hostile to him. On rare occasions, she would share a cup of wine or a modest supper with him. She gave no indication of resuming a close relationship, nor did he make any overtures suggesting it.

If anything, her advancing pregnancy seemed to enhance her beauty. Her temperament was subdued, even serene with no hint of the physical and emotional trauma she endured. While he missed the intimacy they once shared, he regretted more her apparent indifference to the world about her. Gone was the passionate and vibrant inner spirit that first attracted him. In her place was merely an image of someone he once knew. Out of curiosity, he asked her if she planned to reopen the tavern. Her answer was vague, and he had the impression she'd given no thought to it one way or the other.

Even as she withdrew from him, his friendship with Joric became closer. Joric proved to be a patient and persistent teacher in helping him to learn the Selgovan language. As his vocabulary expanded, Arrius was conversing easily if not eloquently in the native language.

Arrius enjoyed the boy's company, marveling at his intelligence and rapidly developing maturity. Physically, Joric was almost as tall as he and as agile and quick of mind as he was in body. He was impressed with how quickly Joric distilled the salient points of a debate to reach a conclusion more mature than others his age. Whatever his future destiny might be, Arrius was convinced Joric had the potential for leadership. If Joric changed his mind and chose the Roman Army for his future, he had both the aptitude and qualities to go far despite the prejudice he would experience because of his non-Latin birth. Philos reminded him not long before his death that he was a rich man; he resolved to use that wealth to help Joric and Ilya any way he could. The path to becoming a Roman officer could be less difficult to travel with denarii to ease the journey, assuming the other prerequisites were met; he had no doubt Joric would meet them easily.

The first indication the worst of the winter was over was an early spring day when a warm sun and a cloudless sky began turning the roads and vicus streets into slush. The streams and rivers rapidly swelled with melting snow making fords impassable. The eastern hillsides showed the first signs of life as the tips of the spring grass emerged to give sheep and horses something other than the diet of winter forage and the close confines of stable stalls. It was on such a day on the way back to Uxellodonum from Blatobulgium when the messenger from Decrius intercepted Arrius with the news Ilya was in labor.

He departed for Banna as quickly as he was able to break away, stopping briefly at Uxellodonum to satisfy his conscience he was not completely abandoning his duties for personal and private considerations. Arriving at Banna early in the evening, he went to the principia to learn if anything required his immediate attention and to inform the duty centurion where he was. He stopped at his quarters only long enough to remove his armor before mounting Ferox and spurring the horse through the east gate toward the tavern.

Attorix evidently was on the lookout for him and took charge of the tired horse. His growing premonition something was wrong was confirmed when Attorix failed to respond when he asked how the baby fared. Instead, the hulking servant gave a non-committal grunt and abruptly turned away, leading Ferox toward the stable in back. He burst through the door, and his worst fears were confirmed when he saw Joric's white face and Decrius's grave expression. It was the stillness that filled him with sudden dread.

Correctly interpreting Arrius's drawn face, Decrius said, "She lives, but the birth does not go well."

"And the child?"

Decrius shook his head. "The baby is positioned the wrong way. Iseult, my wife, says it is unlikely it will survive unless the birth comes soon. Ilya is also growing weaker and cannot last much longer. When I sent you the message, everything seemed to be progressing as it should be. It wasn't until much later when Iseult realized how serious her condition is."

"What about Velius? Can he help?"

"He's already seen her. He wanted to cut her belly to spare her life at the cost of the child." Decrius paused and lifted a shoulder apologetically. "Iseult would not permit it. She believes she can save them both."

Arrius crossed the room and gripped Joric's shoulder to reassure him all would be well while trying not to give in to the clammy feeling of despair sweeping over him. He regretted not having stopped at one of the roadside shrines on the outskirts of the vicus to make suitable offerings for the safety of Ilya and the child. He wondered if he was about to pay for years of religious indifference.

Mirah appeared with a pitcher of wine and left it on the table then took a seat near the closed door behind which the drama of life and death was unfolding. Arrius poured himself a cup to quench the dryness in his mouth and throat. He was refilling the cup when Iseult, her forehead wet with perspiration, opened the door and ignoring the men, beckoned for Mirah. The two women quickly disappeared inside and closed the door.

For what seemed an eternity, the three of them sat without speaking, listening to the faint murmur of voices in the adjacent room, straining to hear and understand what was being said. A series of muffled screams punctuated the silence bringing Arrius to his feet and heading for the bedroom door. It was Decrius who stepped forward and placed a restraining hand on Arrius's arm. "You cannot help in there. With the help of the gods, Iseult and Mirah will do what is necessary." He pulled Arrius gently but firmly away from the door.

Moments later, the screams tapered off, and a brief silence descended followed soon after by the unmistakable squalling of a baby.

Grinning, Decrius said, "With a voice like that, it can only be a boy."

The door opened, and Iseult emerged. She walked directly to Arrius carrying a cloth-wrapped bundle from which came lusty cries. "Praefectus, praise to the gods and the strength of his mother, you have a son." Then in the Roman fashion, she laid the bundle at his feet.

Arrius bent down and took up the infant, holding it cautiously and reverently. He looked down in awe upon the tiny puckered face vigorously protesting the difficult entry into the world. He was overcome by an indescribable happiness and contentment. Up to this point, nothing in his life had prepared him for this precise moment. Ilya's swelling belly, natural as it may have been at the time, did not give him the sense of reality as cradling the small life now in his arms. It took a moment longer for him to find his voice. Lifting the child up, he announced formally the essential words required to confirm the child's patrimony.

"Before the gods and the emperor and in accordance with the laws of Rome, I acknowledge this child as mine." Immediately he turned to Iseult. "Will Ilya live?"

She glanced at Joric before answering. "I cannot say. She is very weak, and she was not as strong as I would have liked when her time came. If the bleeding stops and she is able to see the dawn tomorrow, there is a chance. More I cannot say. You must ask the gods to intervene for it's beyond mortal hands to help her now. This I know for certain. If she does recover, she will not bear another child."

"Can I see her?"

Iseult hesitated, and Arrius thought she was about to refuse when she evidently changed her mind. "It can probably do no harm, but if she sleeps, don't wake her."

Arrius passed the infant to Joric. "You may greet your brother, Joric. I hope you will always look after him when I'm no longer able." An uncertain look on his face, Joric awkwardly took the infant.

"What should we call him? Will he have as many names as you, Marcus Arrius?"

The question hadn't occurred to him. Until asked, he'd given no thought to it at all. "I'll have to think hard on the matter. By Roman custom, his name day will be nine days from now."

"What will you name him?" Before Arrius responded, Joric said, "I think you should call him Esugenius."

"Does the name have a meaning here?"

Joric looked up and replied with no hint of bitterness in his voice. "It means well-born." In a flash, Arrius realized how Joric must have felt when he claimed the baby as his son, only emphasizing to the boy he was bastard born.

"I think it's a fine name and has a similar meaning for the Roman name Eugenius. So be it."

Arrius entered the room where Ilya lay and where the strong and familiar odor of blood filled the room. Still as death on the narrow bed, she was as pale as the snow outside.

Mirah finished gathering up the soiled linens and started toward the door; Arrius was shocked to see how blood-soaked they were. Iseult had not exaggerated Ilya's condition. He wondered if he had been here when Velius examined her, whether or not he would have made the same decision Iseult did. Or would he have decided in favor of one over the other? He didn't know the answer only that he was grateful he arrived too late to make the choice.

He knelt beside the bed and took her hand. He was alarmed at how cold her fingers were. He squeezed her hand but felt no response. There was so much he wanted to tell her, and yet he couldn't find the words. He felt her slipping away and was desperate to tell her how much he loved her, regretting his unfounded accusations that drove them apart.

Iseult entered the room. "Praefectus, you must leave her. Whatever happens, she is at peace."

He stood conscious of how tired he was. "Does she know the boy is all right?"

"She knows and is grateful for the gift she has given you." The woman regarded Arrius with sympathy. "She loves you and spoke your name many times. She wasn't afraid of dying, only you wouldn't know the love she has for you."

Not trusting himself to speak, Arrius delayed responding. "I'm glad you told me. It gives me hope. If she lives, perhaps one day I'll have the chance to make amends. Whatever is required for her and the boy, I would be grateful if you would see to it. If she—," he was unable to complete the thought.

"If she dies," Iseult finished for him, "there's time to find a wet nurse for the child. But we'll not speak further of death until we must lest we wake *Cyhiraeth* who will alert the underworld with her screams. It is to *Brigit*, our goddess of the Briganti, who watches over childbirth, I will give thanks to her for helping this night."

Arrius nodded slowly and made no response as he walked to the door. Iseult called after him, using his name for the first time since he had known her. "Do you wish to stay the night, Marcus Arrius?"

"Yes, but there is something I must attend to first." He saw her puzzled face and said, "It's been a long time since I spoke to the gods. I hope they still remember me after such a long silence."

Over the next few days, Ilya seemed on the verge of recovery several times only to fall back into a state of near death as her fever-ravaged body fought to maintain a tenuous hold on life. During one of her brief lucid moments, she recognized Arrius and gave him a wan smile. Unable to speak, it wasn't long before she lapsed into a nether world somewhere between life and death. Iseult remained at her side maintaining a constant vigilance and leaving only long enough to locate a wet nurse when it was obvious Ilya was unable to nurse the baby.

Distracted as he was, Arrius turned over much of his duties to Flavius to spend additional time at Ilya's side. He never stopped marveling over the small form he helped create. Becoming a father was not something he'd ever thought much about or particularly cared to experience although Joric did much to awaken his paternal interests during the past year. Now he was a father, and he didn't understand his previous indifference.

By the fifth day, Iseult assured him Ilya had survived the worst, and her recovery was no longer uncertain. Although still weak, she steadily began to gain strength through Iseult's attentive care. Eugenius, as all now referred to the infant, thrived. The wet nurse, a broad-faced stocky woman who lost both her baby and her husband within days of each other, was dutiful and unobtrusive in keeping the boy well-fed. When told the woman's name was Ulla and it meant *to fill*, Arrius thought she was well-named. He was beginning to believe the gods forgave his long inattention of them and interceded in helping Iseult find the woman. He resolved in the future to do better in paying homage to the deities. It would not do to risk offending them again.

Arrius was amazed to see the changes in the infant as he seemed to grow by the day becoming less wrinkled each time he saw him. Ilya was strong enough to take an interest in the infant's welfare, but her attempts to nurse still proved futile. Gratefully, she accepted the life-giving nourishment Ulla provided.

Ilya was friendly enough when Arrius came to see her; however, her remote behavior remained unchanged. Reluctantly, Arrius accepted the reality her feelings toward him stemmed from the lingering effects of Betto's brutality and had nothing to do with him. He continued to hope she might one day change.

On the ninth day, he informed Ilya he registered the infant's name as Eugenius Lucius Arrius in recognition of both his Britannian and Roman heritage, only Latinizing the praenomen. Ilya was pleased.

The tavern was re-opened briefly to give Arrius the opportunity to host the naming feast. Ilya put in a brief appearance at the predominantly male gathering comprised of the fort's officers and optiones. By all accounts, it was an unqualified success and when over, Rufus along with several other attendees had to be carried back to the fort. Throughout the revelry, except for brief periods when Ulla offered a nipple, Eugenius remained indifferent to the raucous attention. Arrius thought afterward the occasion would have offered the perfect opportunity to be attacked with most of the garrison's officers in less than fighting trim.

In addition to formally registering the infant as his child and heir with the local magistrate, he also formally acknowledged Ilya as his wife to further clarify her legal status although she seemed generally indifferent enough to the legal aspects of their union. He wanted to go farther and adopt Joric as his son but was disappointed when Ilya refused even if she was appreciative of the gesture. When he pressed her for a reason, she gave a vague answer having something to do with allowing him to choose who and what he was when he came of age, leaving him to speculate if Eugenius's birth unfairly affected Joric. If Joric believed so, he carefully concealed any evidence of it. He was always eager to see Arrius, and their time together, whether involved in weapons training or language lessons, remained important to both of them.

Months later, Arrius remembered it was some time since he had made an offering in the name of Philos. On a whim, he mounted Ferox and set off for the cemetery. He stopped at one of the shrines long enough to have a goat slaughtered to the delight of the priests more accustomed to having to make due with a diet of chicken or pigeon.

At the cemetery, Attorix was standing next to a pony-cart. As Arrius drew closer, he saw Ilya standing by Philos's marker, radiating health and vitality he hadn't seen since she left the Selgovan settlement.

"Salve, Ilya, I didn't expect to see you." He noted the fresh-cut flowers she placed below the marker and realized who was leaving the flowers he found on previous visits to the grave. "So it's been you leaving the flowers."

She nodded. "I miss him still. He was the kindest, gentlest man I ever knew. He found no fault with anyone."

"Except me — and with good cause."

She glanced at him. "I would have thought you least of all."

"It was because of what I said to you before you left to come back here. He thought I treated you unfairly, and he spoke the truth. He only forgave me when I told him he was right, and I was wrong. I suspect his only disappointment in me was I remained unmarried and did not have children. As I look back, I know he never stopped missing his family, and unfortunately for him until I met you, I was the only family he had."

"What do the words on the stone mean?" She motioned to the rectangular written words on the shaft.

Hic iacet
PanPhilos
Amicus ad vitam aeternam
Sit tibi terra levis

Arrius translated. "Here lies Panphilos, friend forever, may the earth be light upon you."

"He was a good friend to me as well. He told me once if his daughter had lived, he would have wished her to be like me. Philos told me he wanted you to have what he lost."

"I'm not certain I have it yet. In the eyes of Rome, you are my wife, and yet we do not live as husband and wife."

Ilya's face colored, and she replied in a low voice, "I know, Marcus. I think you should divorce me and find a woman who can give you what I'm no longer able. I do not want to make promises I cannot fulfill on the possibility I may change in time. It would be better to accept me as I am or leave me, and I will understand."

"You're forgetting Eugenius," Arrius said, his voice flat. "He's the only son I'm likely to ever have since you are unwilling to allow me to adopt Joric. You realize according to Roman law, if I do decide to divorce you, I have the right to take Eugenius from you."

Ilya looked at him in wide-eyed shock. "You wouldn't."

"I've no wish to unless I'm given no other alternative. I'll not be parted from my son."

She drew herself up, the color draining from her face. "Then if it's the price I must pay, I'll submit to you."

"It isn't your submission I want."

"Marcus, I do not believe I can ever be the woman I was for you or any man. If you're waiting for that to happen then you may be waiting in vain. My love is still yours, but I'm not able to give more even though I know it is your right to expect it. If we are to remain married, I advise you to find a concubine who can give you what I cannot."

With an equal measure of anger and disappointment, Arrius turned away and mounted Ferox. He reined the horse around until he was facing Ilya. "I'll not force myself on you, nor do I propose taking the boy from you. Either resolution is as unwelcome to me as it is for you. For now, we'll leave things as they are." Without giving her a chance to reply, he spurred Ferox in the direction of the fort.

Disconsolate, she walked toward the cart where Attorix waited patiently. She hadn't known of the Roman law that accorded such rights to the husband, nor did she question its existence. She despised Betto even more for having been the cause of her physical estrangement with Arrius. Even dead, the centurion tormented her for she felt like a prisoner all over again. She didn't blame Arrius for feeling the way he did although she also knew while she lived there was no way she would risk being parted from her son. She would do whatever was necessary to prevent such an outcome even if it meant returning to her homeland now there was no longer any risk to Joric or the future he may yet have.

Chapter 27

Beldorach winced as he vaulted into the saddle. The spring grasses were already fetlock deep, and he still felt the lingering effects of a long winter and the illness that kept him on his back far too long. He fought off a momentary wave of dizziness from the sudden exertion. His leather breeches and tunic hung loose on his gaunt frame. He feared he would never regain the strength and robust form he once took for granted.

He hated the reality he was too weak to lead the initial post-winter attacks against the Novanti. From all reports, little progress had been made thus far. He attributed the latter to his absence and a waning enthusiasm for the effort on the part of his clan chiefs. He resisted Athdara's strong pleas to remain and allow more time for his recovery. Privately, he knew she was right, but he also recognized if he didn't take an active part now, the campaign was destined to fail.

Fortunately, the Votadini had not taken advantage of his illness, evidently content to let the Novanti take the brunt in the tribal warfare. At present, it was enough for the Selgovi to deal with Bothan who was proving to be more resourceful and dangerous than he would have credited. He suspected Bothan was being advised by someone outside his own council. The latter gave credence to intelligence reports one of the tribes located north of the Novanti was ready to assist Bothan if they weren't already. The thought was sobering and argued in favor of quickly defeating the Novanti before the Selgovi became hopelessly outnumbered. The one favorable sign so far was the inactivity on the part of the Romans making him believe Arrius must have been successful in convincing his general to remain on the sidelines, at least for the time being.

To break the stalemate, he devised an audacious plan to press the Novanti from the east while striking simultaneously from the north. The objective was to force Bothan to withdraw southward against the Roman outposts possibly as far back as the stone wall itself. He assumed the Romans would not sit idly by and tolerate the Novanti moving in on them and the hopeful result for the Selgovae Tribe was Bothan would face Roman spears and suffer calamitous casualties. He intended to personally lead the attack from the north. By the time the summer was over, *Cernunnos* would decide whether he or Bothan would be the one to live.

The consilium General Arvinnius convened was not unexpected. Arrius anticipated the legion commander would lose no time following Hadrian's death to announce any changes affecting the Britannian frontier. When an emperor died, some degree of change was inevitable; however, Arrius didn't believe there would be any major changes planned for the northwest frontier.

Arrius found little changed when he arrived at Eboracum several days later. The fort seemed even larger after the relative small size of the Banna and Uxellodonum forts he was used to. Apart from a few other centurions and tribunes stationed near Banna, he didn't know most of the other twenty-odd commanders stationed on or north of the Wall.

Except for Sextus Trebius and General Arvinnius, he was unquestionably the oldest officer even though he was junior to most of the other commanders. In subtle ways, it was made obvious from the aloof manner he was treated, he was regarded as someone without political influence or prospects. This was further emphasized by General Arvinnius's cryptic announcement he was replaced as commander of the Uxellodonum garrison. The directive was not unexpected considering the importance of that particular command in the overall Wall defense. Publicly, the legion commander accorded Arrius little recognition for his time spent as temporary commander. In contrast, the general lavished praise for the new commander, Tribune Gaius Cornelius.

Tall and spare, physically the tribune might have been a younger version of General Arvinnius. His Hadrianic beard was a notable difference in comparison with the legion commander's clean-shaven face. Arrius was prepared to dislike him out of principle, and yet he found Gaius Cornelius affable and genuine enough. His Cornelian name underscored both his aristocratic heritage and political importance. That alone was sufficient to explain why the legion commander was going out of his way to recognize the new officer.

Arrius knew the meeting was not going to be pleasant when the stern-faced, thin-lipped general did not give him permission to sit. He didn't have long to wait to have his premonition confirmed.

"Arrius, against my better judgment, I was forced to accept Trebius's recommendation to appoint you temporary commander of Uxellodonum. Had I gone to Banna instead of Trebius, it would have been you instead of Querinius I would have relieved."

"Why didn't you?"

"Unfortunately, Trebius gave me no choice — I was away in Rome at the time." Seeing the look on Arrius's face, Arvinnius added, "My absence was not made public to avoid giving the native tribes an excuse to make trouble. Arrius, I suppose I owe you some explanation for my doubts about you particularly when Trebius says Banna is much improved since you arrived. Querinius had faults, but I at least understood him. You, on the other hand, are a puzzle."

"What have I said or done to give you reason to mistrust me?"

"I was not at all satisfied with your comments when I talked about bearing down on the native tribes soon after your arrival. You seemed to be overly preoccupied with your own ideas concerning their welfare rather than what Rome thinks. In comparison to you, Querinius's opinions and comments seemed more in line with my own views, and I might add, those of Rome. Under normal circumstances, I would overlook our difference of opinion. The current circumstances are no longer normal as you will soon appreciate before the consilium is over. We are about to begin an enterprise where I cannot afford to have concern for the loyalty and resolve of one of my field commanders. I suspect you were different before going to Palaestina. Before then I would not have the doubts about you I do now. I don't know what happened to you in the Jewish war, and frankly, I do not care; but I think you've changed and not for the better. In spite of Turbo's high praise of you and your long record of service, my trust and confidence in you has eroded."

Arrius started to interject a comment; however, the general impatiently cut him off. "Furthermore, there is the matter of you taking a native woman for a wife and by Jupiter's balls, not just any woman. I understand she's the blood relative of the very man who is now stirring up trouble all along the Wall. Is it true you've a brat by this woman?"

"I have a son I've formally acknowledged."

Arvinnius shook his head in disbelief. "You astonish me. Since the early days of the Republic, the Roman Army has been improving the bloodlines of local populations with its bastards. Why couldn't you be like everyone else and be content to do the same?"

This time Arrius refused to be silenced. "General, my private life is my own. My rank gives me the privilege to marry whomever I want, when I want with or without Rome's or your approval."

Arvinnius sat back, his face showing a mix of disbelief and anger at the sharp response. "Praefectus, be careful in the manner you address me. You already have enough against you without adding insolence and disrespect."

Arrius had a flashback to some of his past confrontational encounters with Gallius. He wondered if he was doomed never to get along with legion commanders. He tried to contain his anger knowing an argument with Arvinnius would not end well for him. Even as he tried, he was unable to keep from saying what was on his mind.

"General, I've served under the eagle for nearly 28 years and not once during that time has there been an occasion or reason for any man to question my loyalty or dedication to Rome. Even when I didn't think some of those I served were worth the lives of the legionaries I led or the blood I lost, I obeyed without reservation. Now you question my personal affairs may interfere with my ability to do my duty. I resent and reject your right to pass judgment on my private life."

Arvinnius slowly stood up. "I'll overlook your outburst this once. I confess I gave you provocation, although I don't apologize for it. You're wrong if you think I do not have the right to take into consideration the personal lives of my officers if there is a possibility the legion may suffer as a result. I think you're a dangerous man. Trebius told me something of what you said about your service in Palaestina and your refusal on principle to wear the award Turbo gave you. Rome cannot risk having its officers believe and think independently as you do, particularly its heroes. Arrius, you have a conscience, and such a thing weakens a man. Belief in the destiny of Rome to rule the world must be absolute no matter the cost."

Arvinnius looked away, absently rubbing his forehead. "Arrius, you don't understand how precarious the empire is, how close we are to losing it all. Palaestina cost us dearly and much more than a legion. What we nearly lost was greater than what the Jews suffered. They lost a country; we are on the brink of losing an empire. The only way for Rome to continue to exist is through unquestioned obedience, ruthless strength and the will to exercise it without hesitation or remorse. It is the gladius and the pilum that created the empire; it will be those same weapons to keep it intact. I want you to reflect on what I've said for the extent you agree or disagree with me will depend on whether you continue to command on the frontier. Now go before you say anything more we'll both regret."

Two orderlies carried in a large wooden screen and unfolded it to reveal a geographical depiction of the areas immediately to the north and south of the Wall with the notional tribal boundaries outlined. The Wall was also shown as a heavy dark line with each principal fort and mile fort indicated by small squares. One of Arvinnius's staff officers stepped forward and proceeded to give an assessment of the native tribes throughout Britannia. The officer reported the tribes under control of the Twentieth Legion at Deva in the western and southwestern regions of Britannia were generally pacified and posed little or no threat of insurrection. The assessment was less optimistic for the tribes under control of the Sixth Legion. The Brigantae Tribe remained a potential threat by virtue of being the largest tribe in Britannia. Because the Briganti rebelled before was sufficient to predict they were likely one day to try again. The tribe's occupation of an extensive area immediately south of the Wall made it essential to keep them firmly under control. The briefer then focused exclusively on the northern tribes and the perception Beldorach intended to dominate the region.

When the briefing ended, General Arvinnius stood up. "As you may know, of all the tribes north of the Wall, the Votadini have always been the most loyal and trustworthy; it is the only tribe to maintain friendly trade relations with Rome. Darach has proven his loyalty by being the source for most of our recent information concerning Beldorach's current efforts to subjugate the Votadini and Novantae Tribes. According to Darach, Beldorach has achieved mixed success so far. He's been forced to concentrate exclusively on defeating the Novanti, presumably leaving the Votadini alone for now until he consolidates his gains in the west. He also undoubtedly realizes if he were to give serious threat to the Votadini, we would have no choice but to launch a full-scale attack north to defend them.

Thanks in part to Praefectus Arrius, we know much about Beldorach's long-range objectives. You may not know for a time the Praefectus was a captive, or was it a guest, of Beldorach?" Arvinnius gave Arrius a pointed look. "Therefore, I call on Arrius to give us a firsthand account of the tribal chief's intent."

Arrius stood and referred to Arvinnius's veiled insinuation saying, "General, I think it's material to understand the circumstances in which Beldorach revealed his plans to me." Arrius saw the legion commander frown. "I was captured after being badly injured while on campaign against the Selgovae. It was soon apparent Beldorach kept me alive for a reason. At first, I thought it might be for ransom, but then I realized he wanted me to convey a message to General Arvinnius. He thought that if Rome knew he was attempting to unite the tribes by war, he would be left to accomplish that objective in the belief his success would be in Rome's interest. His rationale was Rome would only have to deal with one tribal leader in the north. He would then be willing to consider a treaty with Rome."

"Do you believe he intends peace with Rome if he defeats the Novanti and Votadini?" Arvinnius asked.

"I do not. I believe Beldorach thinks once he controls the north, he can convince the Briganti to join him in fighting Rome. Without the Briganti, he knows he has no chance to achieve that objective."

"Do you think he can succeed if he is able to enlist the support of the Briganti?"

"General, I don't know the answer. I think his chances are certainly improved, but I don't have sufficient knowledge of the Briganti to make an assessment one way or the other."

"I accept your answer, Praefectus. If Beldorach were to succeed in consolidating the north and then enlist the support of the Briganti, it could lead to a general uprising of the Iceni and the other southern tribes. With Rome's interests threatened already in multiple locations throughout the Empire, we would be hard pressed to hold on to Britannia; that fact brings me to the purpose of this consilium.

"Recently, I went to Rome with the governor of Britannia to discuss the military situation facing us. My specific concern is a border region becoming increasingly volatile. I am happy to report our illustrious Emperor Antoninus Pius shares my concerns and has approved my plan for pacifying the north once and for all. Next spring as soon as the weather permits, all auxilia forces now positioned on the Wall and under control of the Sixth Legion will join in a general offensive against the northern tribes. The legionary forces here at Eboracum will join in the offensive by initially replacing the auxilia units along the Wall. As the auxilia units move north, the Sixth Legion will abandon the Wall and proceed north. The function of the Wall will continue to be used for customs control with select forts retained for use as supply depots. A new Wall will be constructed farther north to define the frontier at a location," Arvinnius faced the map, tracing a line approximately 100 miles north of the present Wall, "here and considerably more narrow than where the border is now located."

Silence reflecting the astonished reaction of the officers followed as General Arvinnius resumed his chair. Arrius was no exception. Although he warned Beldorach it was highly unlikely Rome would ignore unrest along the frontier, he believed it would consist of no more than a punitive campaign, never thinking it would include shifting the border north. He conceded the practicality of the plan. It was bold and if successful, would eliminate the risk of a more unified and stronger north. He understood now why Arvinnius questioned his attitude concerning Judaea in addition to his relationship with Ilya. It was also apparent Sextus Trebius knew about the plan and tried indirectly to warn him.

Arvinnius looked around the room with a calculating, almost predatory look in his eyes as if waiting for someone to have the temerity to disagree with him. He fixed Arrius with a cold stare while addressing them all. "I've decided I've been too forbearing with the northern tribes. I intend before this campaign is over they will neither have the will nor the capability to cause trouble again. As the Jews came to understand the meaning of *pax Romana,* so will Beldorach and the other tribal leaders. If any man here hesitates or fails to take any and every means at his disposal to achieve my purpose, I will consider him derelict in his duty to me and to Rome." Arrius knew General Arvinnius was talking specifically to him.

The remainder of the day was spent in examining and discussing the myriad administrative and operational details essential to translate the legion commander's vision into a workable plan. During the ensuing discussions, Uxellodonum's new commander interjected sufficient comments attesting to his military experience. Arrius was impressed with the tribune's frequent and astute questions concerning the fighting habits of the Britannian Tribes. Tribune Gaius Cornelius appeared to be everything his predecessor was not.

During the two days at Eboracum, Arrius saw Sextus Trebius only in passing, exchanging no more than a few brief words and those in the company of other officers. Arrius almost had the impression the grizzled tribune was going out of his way to avoid him. He was therefore pleased when an orderly found him before leaving for Banna and informed him Trebius wanted to see him. The orderly escorted him to the same office where he first met the tribune. Arrius found him hunched over a stack of waxed tablets frowning in irritation. The tribune glanced up as Arrius entered the room and pushed aside the tablet he was reading with obvious relief.

"I've only one eye left, and the other grows dim from spending too much time reading these." He gestured in disgust at the stack of tablets. "I don't know what the army and its legions would do if we ran out of wax and wood. It will be no different when I get to Germania."

"You're going to Germania?"

"It seems I'm to join the First legion, *Flavia Minerva* as senior tribune without delay — I believe General Arvinnius emphasized the words *without delay.*"

"I don't understand. I'd heard nothing, nor was anything said about your departure."

Trebius leaned back and regarded Arrius with a grim smile. "I'm certain Arvinnius wanted little said about it. I thought it might benefit you to know why. In a way, I suppose you're the final reason I've incurred Arvinnius's displeasure although I suppose I said enough to encourage it myself. Hadrian's and Turbo's departure for more ethereal pleasures removed any reluctance to rid himself of an outspoken subordinate. The general was less than pleased with how I settled things at Banna and the reason I transferred Tiberias Querinius to the Twentieth Legion. While you and I may not hold Querinius in high regard, the same cannot be said for General Arvinnius.

"Arvinnius is more comfortable with those he can control. He's a capable general, but he prefers subordinates who do not make a habit of questioning his decisions or opinions. It did not help matters when I disagreed with his latest plans to shift the border north. I should have realized the idea originated with him. In hindsight, to disagree was, shall we say, unwise."

"What did you tell Arvinnius about his plan to push the border north?"

"I told him it would stir up the Caledonian Tribes, and if that happened, we wouldn't have enough legions in Britannia to prevent a general uprising. Going after Beldorach is one thing, but to give the Caledonians a reason to make up for Agricola's victory at Mons Graupius is taking too big a risk. One way or the other, Beldorach must be eliminated before he gets any stronger than he is now. He may be the first tribal leader in many years to have both the will and the ability to unite the northern tribes."

"So you don't believe Beldorach when he says he will become a client of Rome if we leave him alone to finish consolidating the tribes under the Selgovi?"

"Not for a moment, and I don't think you do either."

"I said as much during the consilium."

Trebius stood up and came around the table reaching out his arm to grasp Arrius's forearm in farewell. "I've a feeling we'll not meet again unless it's at a campfire at the feet of the gods or under their asses, a most likely fate for a former primus pilus." Arrius smiled at the reference to their previous positions as senior centurions.

"Who will replace you here as senior tribune?"

Trebius regarded Arrius with a sardonic look. "Why, it will be none other than Tiberias Querinius returned to the Sixth Legion by special request of General Arvinnius. Don't tell me the gods do not have a sense of humor."

Chapter 28

The last vestige of a long summer disappeared, and the fall harvest was underway when Beldorach began to think the defeat of the Novanti was almost within his grasp. Not that there was much of a harvest for either the Selgovi or the Novanti consumed as they were in a desperate struggle for tribal supremacy. There was grave concern by both tribes the supply of grain harvested was barely adequate to see them through the winter months ahead.

The Selgovan attack from the north with simultaneous pressure from the east had generally been successful although it progressed more slowly than Beldorach wished. The offensive forced Bothan farther and farther west, and Beldorach was convinced the Novantae tribal chief would not have the capability to resist much longer.

With Beldorach in the lead, the small reconnaissance patrol threaded its way through the trees ducking under the low hanging branches and stopping frequently to listen for any noise different from the usual sounds of the forest. He would have preferred leaving the horses behind to move more quietly on foot, and he suspected the men behind him probably thought the same. The horses were an accommodation to him. Reluctantly, he became reconciled to the certainty he would never again have the strength and stamina he once had. It was requiring more effort of late to conceal his fatigue. There was a physical price to pay, but he didn't want to remain in camp and rely exclusively on what others told him of Bothan's latest dispositions.

He was convinced the Novanti would not be much farther ahead as he skirted a small clearing to remain in the cover of the trees. Something ahead caused the horse's ears to twitch forward. He reined to a stop and held up a cautionary hand to stop the other riders behind him.

At first, he wasn't conscious of any pain, only a sharp, sudden pressure on his chest. Instinctively, he grabbed the horse's mane and the saddle pommel to keep from falling. Then he felt a sharp, stabbing pain. He looked down in detached wonder at the feathered shaft protruding from his chest. Dimly, he heard triumphant yells ahead mixed with warning shouts from behind. He felt more tired than he'd ever been as the strength drained from his body while he slowly slipped to the ground. He heard a snap as the arrow broke off during his fall. The pain increased as the wooden shaft was driven farther into his chest. He fought the urge to close his eyes fearing if he did, he would never open them again. The sound of receding hoof beats told him he was alone. He knew he had to get on his feet and unsheathe his sword or the Novanti would butcher him where he lay. He struggled to get up and found he was unable to. He always imagined a more spectacular departure with the bodies of his adversaries strewn about him in costly payment for taking his life. He felt vaguely cheated to die by a sliver of wood rather than a sword blade. More than anything, he resented the idea his head would be on top of a Novantean spear before long, his power lost to him forever when *Cernunnos* came to collect his spirit.

He heard voices becoming louder and turned his head. Several men approached cautiously, two with swords drawn; the third man armed with a bow stopped and nocked an arrow drawing the string back to his cheek. He braced himself for the arrow's impact for he knew there was nothing he could do to avoid it. A voice from the opposite direction gave an order. He saw the bowman allow the string to relax before lowering the shaft until it pointed to the ground. He felt a spasm deep in his chest followed by a shooting pain that nearly took his breath away. For a moment, the leaves on the branches above him became blurry, and he was overcome by a feeling of lassitude dulling the pain in his chest. A familiar voice spoke his name.

"Beldorach, your time has come."

With great effort, Beldorach turned to face the direction of the speaker. Gradually, he made out the features of Crixtacus, one of Bothan's clan chiefs kneeling above him.

Beldorach started to reply and found he was having difficulty trying to speak. He heard Crixtacus again. "Even if I were inclined to spare you, you'll not live to see the sun go down. I advise you to take the short time you have left to make yourself ready to meet the Hunter."

Beldorach heard what Crixtacus said but no longer had the strength to respond. He felt nothing, only regret for what little he accomplished. He hoped his successor would be able to do more. His last thought was that Tearlach and the clan chiefs would carry out his wishes as instructed and tradition demanded.

"Crixtacus, it was my arrow that took him. I claim the right to take his head," the bowman said.

Slowly, Crixtacus shook his head. "You will not. Beldorach will meet the Hunter with his head on his shoulders."

The other men clustered around the body regarded Crixtacus curiously. One of them said, "Bothan will only expect to see his head. Why bother to take the rest of him back?"

"I don't intend to take him to Bothan. I will give him to the Selgovi. Get his horse and tie him on it then bring mine here."

The men stared at Crixtacus with incredulous expressions. The bowman spoke what the others were thinking. "Bothan will not be pleased." The others muttered in sullen agreement.

"Bothan will be happy enough. Without Beldorach, the Selgovi will turn back. It's time now for the Novanti to do to the Selgovi what they've done to us."

Tearlach observed the single rider coming toward them holding his sheathed sword aloft in the accepted signal for a truce. He motioned for the men around him to put down their weapons. As the horseman drew closer, he recognized Crixtacus even as he identified the horse the clan chief led was the one Beldorach was riding that morning. The body across the back of the horse was Beldorach, dashing any lingering hope the scouts were wrong when they reported Beldorach's certain death.

Crixtacus calmly reined in and lowered his sword regarding the large band of Selgovan warriors before him without the least sign of fear.

"I know you, Crixtacus," Tearlach said.

"And I recognize you, Tearlach. Against the wishes of my men, I've brought Beldorach to you for proper funeral rites and burial."

"I think you will have a lot of explaining to Bothan why you've done this."

"That may be as it will, but a man must do what his conscience tells him."

Tearlach acknowledged the comment with a slight nod. "I would not do as much for Bothan."

"I think Bothan will not lose sleep worrying about it." Crixtacus casually turned his horse and walked his horse away in a display of personal bravery that drew admiring looks from the Selgovan warriors.

Tearlach thoughtfully watched Crixtacus until he disappeared into the trees. He hadn't expected the High Chieftain to die on this day, but from his recent comments and physical condition, Beldorach believed his time was running out. It was strange the premonitions a man would get about the future, almost as if the gods were allowing you a little time to prepare yourself before summoning you to the other world. He'd known others before a battle who predicted their deaths, and without exception, they died. Neither he nor the clan chiefs questioned or protested when Beldorach drew them aside a few nights ago and predicted his life had but a short time to run. His instructions were very specific, and whatever the consequences, his wishes would be followed. It only remained now to carry them out.

It was a long ride south, and Tearlach was feeling the effects when he passed through the Roman gate west of Banna. The guards did not give him a second glance assuming he was another local tribesman going to the vicus to barter the goat carcass he shouldered. He felt naked without his sword and missed it even more than he did his horse. He knew if the guards discovered who and what he was, the sword would have done him little good.

A short time later, he skirted the rear gate of the main fort and made his way directly to the tavern where he hoped to find Ilya. He dumped the carcass on the ground and quietly slipped through the door heading down a hallway in the direction where he heard voices. He heard a baby's cry abruptly stop, replaced by a woman's laugh. Tearlach entered the room and saw Ilya sewing while another woman suckled a baby. Both women looked up with startled looks when they saw him standing in the doorway.

Ilya knew before Tearlach spoke why he was there, and she gave a sigh of resignation. She'd hoped this day would still be a long time coming.

"Beldorach's dead," Tearlach announced without preamble confirming what she already knew in her heart and dreaded to hear. "You know why I am here."

Ilya nodded and stood up suddenly feeling empty and tired.

"We must go now," Tearlach said. "There's no time to lose — the Novanti are going on the offensive."

Joric burst through the door on the opposite side of the room. When he saw Tearlach, he was momentarily startled to see the swarthy man dressed in rough peasant clothing.

"Joric," Ilya said, "we must leave immediately. Beldorach is dead. Before he died, he named you High Chieftain of the Selgovi."

Ilya was proud Joric showed no emotion, accepting the announcement with a calm demeanor belying his youth. She anguished over her reluctance to tell him of the bargain she'd made with Beldorach. It wasn't only for Arrius she agreed to give up her rights to the dais. She wanted what Joric deserved to have. She was pleased but skeptical when Beldorach quickly acquiesced without argument, relieved at the prospect tribal leadership would remain in male hands. She wondered if Beldorach would have been so willing to agree if he had known the arrangement would be implemented so soon and before Joric reached full manhood.

Joric's claim to tribal leader made it impossible for her to agree to Arrius's wish to adopt him, a step that would have caused Beldorach to repudiate the agreement. For Joric's sake, even at the risk of further widening the chasm between her and Arrius, she needed to preserve his right to fulfill his destiny.

To Ilya's relief, it required little persuasion to induce Ulla to come along. If she hadn't, there would have been little choice except to send Joric on alone with Tearlach. She needed time to prepare her son for the demands soon to be made of him. It was always difficult for the new High Chieftain before and immediately after when the clan chiefs would be competing to increase their influence and their boundaries at the expense of another clan. With the Novanti determined to reverse their losses, Joric would need advice he was too young to even realize he needed. As Bathar's daughter, she felt well-qualified to advise him without hidden bias or personal gain except to ensure he succeeded and the tribe prospered.

She instructed Joric and a tearful Mirah to pack the few things they would take with them. It was not lost on Ilya when she saw the first thing Joric packed was the gladius Arrius gave him.

While the pony cart was being loaded, Ilya sat down and hurriedly wrote a brief message to Arrius. Before she was done, her eyes were smarting with tears she tried not to shed. Although she had long since given up hope, she harbored a lingering wish, unrealistic as it was, they would one day recapture a semblance of what they once enjoyed. She felt a pang of guilt in taking Eugenius with her. It was easy to imagine how he would feel when she thought of the devastation she would experience if their roles were reversed. She knew the act would finish any chance they might have to reconcile their differences. It was a consequence she was forced to accept faced with the impossibility of parting from the infant.

When she was through, she gave the tablet to Mirah with instructions to give it to Decrius late tomorrow afternoon. By then, she and Joric would be away from Banna.

It was late in the day by the time Arrius and his escort crested the hill and saw the walls of Banna. A part of him marveled each time he saw the Wall extending to either side of the fort and on across the rolling hills. It was difficult to get used to the idea Hadrian's monolithic creation was soon to be abandoned. It took only the imperious order of one emperor to build such a thing and the order of another to leave it. It was a colossal stone barrier no longer serving Rome's purpose, but it still remained to divide a country. Perhaps the very idea it could be abandoned was symbolic of the power of Rome. He recalled past comments both Beldorach and Ilya made to him underscoring their hatred of the thing. At the time, he wasn't certain he understood or appreciated their resentment particularly when, from his perspective, the Wall stabilized the region by physically separating the warring tribes. He was starting to understand their passionate objection and suspected if he'd been a Britannian or a Selgovan, he probably would have voiced the same sentiments. It wasn't long ago such a thought wouldn't have occurred to him.

He urged Ferox to a faster gait, pulling his light linen cloak around him. He regretted not bringing his heavier woolen sagum against the chill evening breeze indicating winter was close at hand. Since he was no longer the commander of Uxellodonum, he would be spending fewer cold days and nights away from Banna. The prospect of seeing more of Ilya and his son outweighed the initial disappointment he felt when Arvinnius replaced him with Gaius Cornelius. Military competence in the eyes of Arvinnius apparently was less important than unquestioned obedience to his authority and agreement with his views. Querinius had obviously convinced Arvinnius in a way he hadn't the tribune was prepared to do whatever he was ordered to do. But then he'd done much the same while serving the legions, including his time in Judaea, no matter how unpleasant the task. What he didn't yet understand is when he began to change and why. Until recently, the thought he could or would change was something that wouldn't have occurred to him. His obedience was assumed by the legion commanders to the same degree it was by him. The more he reflected on what Arvinnius said to him at the consilium, he was surprised to still be in command of Banna. As they clattered across the bridge, he briefly considered stopping at the tavern but quickly dismissed the idea. There would be time tomorrow to see Eugenius.

Arrius no sooner entered the headquarters courtyard when he saw Flavius coming toward him. "From the look on your face, all is not well here at Banna," Arrius said.

"I fear I have grave news for you. Your wife and son are gone."

"What do you mean gone?"

"She was last seen five days ago in a cart being driven north through one of the western gates by her older son. There was a plain-faced woman with her." From the cryptic description, Arrius knew the other woman must have been Ulla, the wet nurse and not the pleasant-featured Mirah.

"How do you know she isn't coming back?"

Flavius handed a waxed tablet to Arrius that Decrius brought him the day after Ilya was sighted. Arrius read the brief message with growing anger and disbelief. His initial reaction was to mount Ferox and go after Ilya and Eugenius. The blindfold he wore until Tearlach removed it near Fanum Cocidii had not prevented him from having a general idea where the settlement was located. It didn't take him long to dismiss the idea of going after them for practical reasons. By himself, the Selgovi would hardly allow him to bring back Ilya and the infant if she did not wish to return, assuming they would even allow him to get there. It was also beyond consideration to muster a force from Banna and Fanum Cocidii large enough to find and bring back Eugenius without endangering the security of the Wall.

For weeks, Arrius went about his duties grimly determined to put the past behind him and concentrate on what he knew best. His stern face and hard eyes discouraged any conversation except what was necessary to run the fort. By virtue of their duties Flavius, Antius Durio and Publius Gheta received the brunt of Arrius's ill-temper. The three men did their utmost to avoid their commander, but the comparatively small confines of the fort and the requirements of attending to their responsibilities made it virtually impossible. While there was no return to the mindless discipline and cruelty displayed by Betto, Arrius did not overlook the least infraction, and those who were derelict in their duties were punished accordingly.

In time, Arrius came to realize his morose behavior and self-imposed isolation was the main cause for the slipping morale only made worse by another winter already promising to be as severe as the last one. Gradually, he began to let up and allow the centurions and optiones the freedom to deal with disciplinary matters better left to them in the first place. As the months wore on and Arrius became more reconciled to what happened, life at the fort began to resume a more normal pace.

Mindful of the legion commander's plan for a spring offensive, Arrius quietly began to make preparations. By direction of General Arvinnius, the officers and optiones were deliberately not told of the offensive to preclude any chance the tribes would learn of it. The pace of training increased. With Publius Gheta, Arrius inventoried all supplies and equipment, requisitioning additional stores and equipment beyond the normal levels usually maintained. When he ordered the construction of extra supply carts, it didn't take long for rampant speculation to focus on the probability of another advance against the northern tribes; however, even the wildest rumor did not consider the scope of General Arvinnius's intent.

The prospect of a diversion from the dull routine of guard duty elevated morale, and the incidence of disciplinary action declined along with it. Arrius was aware of the excitement building within the garrison and appreciated the positive effect it had on reducing the number of punishment formations.

What was missing was the anticipation he normally would have felt before a campaign. He knew why. He tried not to dwell on the stark possibility the cohorts he commanded might be the very instruments responsible for taking the lives of Eugenius and Ilya. He started losing sleep, and when sleep did come, the nightmares started with little variation. There were recurrent images of the frightened

Jewish children he discovered hiding behind the bushes. He was haunted with images of Joric lying on a bloody battlefield. The longer the winter wore on, the more the stark reality of his predicament preyed on his mind and undermined his will to carry on as if nothing was the matter.

He didn't know the precise moment when he decided he would not go north with the legion. Perhaps subconsciously he made it the day he learned Ilya was gone. The alternatives were to seek an assignment away from Britannia, possibly Germania, anywhere or — leave the army. By any standard, thanks mainly to Philos, he was a wealthy man and could afford to go where he pleased. Either alternative was preferable, if not desirable, to blindly accepting the inevitable and unacceptable consequences of the forthcoming campaign. He was sure Arvinnius would be happy with either choice he made.

Fanum Cocidii was little changed since his last visit the month before apart from the effects of the melting snows turning the surrounding fields and the inner fort into a muddy quagmire. On the surface, his visit to the outpost was another routine inspection. His real purpose was to bid a quiet farewell to Seugethis. A few days before without informing anyone except Flavius, he wrote to General Arvinnius of his intent to leave the army as soon as his request was approved. The Dacian was one of the few men with whom he'd formed a close attachment based on the similarity of their views and their mutual admiration for each other.

He found the usually boisterous and blunt-speaking Seugethis strangely subdued and distracted, and when Arrius pressed for an explanation, the Dacian commander was evasive. It was only when Arrius confided his imminent departure and his reasons for it Seugethis became more interested and attentive to his visitor.

Seugethis was more understanding than he expected him to be. "Strangely for different reasons, I'm faced with a similar dilemma. It seems there is unrest in my homeland, and Dacia is again on the verge of rebellion. If there is a rebellion, I cannot remain here and continue to serve Rome. Unlike many of my men who have been away from Dacia long enough they are more Roman than Dacian, I still have family and ties to my country. I may have to leave soon after you." Seugethis gave Arrius a hard look. "I trust you'll say nothing of this. General Arvinnius will not be pleased if he learns of any of this."

"You may depend on that. If he learns of it, it won't be from me." Arrius gave Seugethis a searching look. "How will you be able to leave Britannia without being stopped?"

"It is easier than you imagine. How do you think I know what is happening in my homeland? But it's better for both of us if you do not know." Then changing the subject, Seugethis asked curiously, "Where will you go?"

"Back to Italia, I suppose. Far away from here."

Seugethis regarded Arrius with a questioning look before saying quietly, "I wonder if you will find what you are looking for in Italia. I think it will not be easy for you to leave the legions. You will find it difficult not to have a sword at your side and legionaries to command."

"What you say is true. It is all I've ever known or wanted." Arrius paused and then said as much to himself as to the Dacian, "I can no longer do things I once would never have questioned. Judaea was the cause."

It was now Arrius who appeared distracted, and Seugethis was the one trying to understand his visitor's reserved manner. Arrius stood up and abruptly announced it was time he returned to Banna.

The two men left the headquarters and walked slowly toward where the escort stood waiting for the order to mount saying little, both aware their paths were unlikely to cross again.

"I hope you find what you are looking for, Marcus Arrius."

"I wish the same for you, Seugethis."

Arrius vaulted into the saddle and without looking back, spurred Ferox in the direction of the Wall.

As he rode toward Banna, he recalled what Beldorach said to him during one of their conversations after leaving Eboracum. *"You think you have everything, and yet you have nothing but the responsibility to defend what others own. You have no home but a stone fortress in a foreign land while I at least have fields and forests I can lay claim to."* At the time, he rejected Beldorach's words for they held no meaning for him. That he remembered them at all was telling and a tacit admission the Selgovan was right. What once satisfied him and seemed enough was nothing more than a fading past. He'd given unquestioned allegiance to Rome and everything it stood for. He had been well-rewarded for his service with rank and wealth. But he also knew there was nothing to look forward to but an empty future.

It required only a few days after returning to Banna to quietly attend to the few things left to do before departing. Then it was merely waiting for the formality of Arvinnius's approval to leave the army. A week later, quicker than he expected, Antius Durio handed him the document authorizing his separation. The speed permission was granted was testament to the legion commander's eagerness to see the last of him,

He paid a final visit to the cemetery and made the appropriate offerings to the gods in Philos's name. He didn't believe it was a final farewell for while there was no way to know when he might return, he believed one day he would. He gave each of his four slaves enough denarii to purchase a small piece of land somewhere and a horse to carry their few belongings. It wasn't surprising when Cito and Linius told him their plan was to remain together and buy a farm in Italia. Menga and Sartos said they intended to remain in Britannia. The last he saw of them was when they disappeared through the east gate to begin their new lives.

He thought it was better to leave late at night without the usual formal ceremonies to mark the occasion. To further ensure his departure was accorded minimum attention, Arrius arranged with Flavius to have Decrius and Rufus in charge of the guard force the night he planned to leave. He left his armor and most of his other military-related accouterments behind taking only personal clothing, his balteus and his sword. At the last minute, he impulsively picked up the vitis, the twisted vine stick Trevinius Lavinnius, primus pilus of the VI Legion, *Victrix*, had given him and added it to the small bundle he fastened to the pack horse.

He led Ferox and the packhorse out of the praetorium courtyard and turned right toward the north gate. In the dim torches flanking the gate ahead, he saw a small knot of men and cursed when he saw it was more than the few guards he expected to see. His instructions were explicit. Apart from Decrius, Rufus and the two guards, properly bribed, of course, he expected no one else.

One of the men stepped forward from the shadows and stood next to Decrius. It was Flavius. "Salve, Marcus Arrius, it's late to be traveling the roads."

"Flavius, I did not expect to see you here — trouble sleeping?" Arrius looked into the shadows at two other men standing a few paces behind Flavius. "It seems Antius Durio and Publius Gheta are also up early to greet the day. Perhaps it would have been better for all of us had you remained abed."

"It occurred to me to do that," Flavius said, "but then I would miss the opportunity to bid you farewell or perhaps to convince you to change your destination."

"Save your words for a more likely cause and a decision made as much by the gods as me. I hope you don't intend to change my mind with more than words."

"No man here will draw his sword to stop you — at least while you are on this side of the Wall. General Arvinnius will have a price on your head worth the risk of taking it even though we know your capability to defend it with a gladius."

"I'll count on that, but I'll not draw my sword against any man here or Rome except to defend what is close to me."

"Then farewell, Marcus Arrius. I pray Jupiter will give you what you seek."

Rufus was the last to come forward to grip his arm. In the dim light, Arrius saw the optio was having difficulty controlling his emotions. In many ways, the optio represented every legionary he ever served with — coarse, brutal, incorrigible and yet fiercely loyal when it mattered most. It was Rufus and all the others like him he would miss most of all.

Arrius mounted Ferox and waited as the gate swung open. With nothing left to say, he spurred the black stallion north into the darkness.

Epilogue

Arrius looked back only once at the outline of the fort and the Wall looming dark against the starlit sky. He felt freer than he'd ever been. He tried to remember what Trevinius Lavinnius told him in the valley below Banna. He couldn't remember the exact words nor did he understand what the primus pilus was telling him. It was something about symbols like the legions' eagle were only symbols. He also said generals and Rome would use you, and when all was said and done, the only thing left were memories, some good and others best forgotten. He finally understood what Lavinnius meant. It was late, but he still hoped it wasn't too late to believe in something more than symbols.

He wondered if Banna and the Wall had somehow become his prison holding him captive to a past no longer relevant and a future without promise. At one time, he might have blamed Judaea exclusively for changing him, causing him to question who he was and what he really wanted. It took the birth of Eugenius and Ilya's departure to complete whatever started in Judaea. The thought of what would happen to them when the spring offensive began was enough to threaten his sanity. He knew he couldn't prevent what was about to happen to the northern tribes, but at least he might be able to keep it from becoming another Judaean bloodbath. And it was the only way to try and hold on to the only legacy that mattered to him.

Arrius had a prickly sensation he was being watched long before he detected the actual proof of it. The stillness of the forest warned him first. Two days north of Fanum Cocidii, there was reason to expect they would find him. Indeed, he made every effort to ensure they did. His fire the night before was larger than necessary, and he took pains to cross clearings and bare hillsides without seeking the comparative concealment of the tree lines.

A slight-built man in leather tunic and leggings emerged from the trees ahead and sat motionless on his horse and waited as Arrius walked Ferox toward him. Arrius heard rustling behind him and on either side; he was surrounded. Tearlach was not a promising omen for his first encounter with the Selgovi.

"Why are you here, Roman?" Tearlach asked without preamble.

Struggling to remember what Joric taught him, Arrius replied haltingly in the Selgovan tongue. "I seek Ilya and my son."

Tearlach's eyes widened, and he responded in Selgovan. "I think perhaps it will only be your head Ilya will see. The rest I will leave for the wolves and crows."

"Perhaps, but I doubt it will be you who will do it. My sword will be in your belly, and your balls will be on the ground before your men can save you."

"Ah, you remember me, Roman."

"I remember you, Tearlach. I think my head and sword will remain where they are. If you intended to kill me, you would have done so already."

"You're right, I'll take you. This time it won't be necessary to blindfold you because once I take you to the settlement, you will not be allowed to leave."

"I've no intention of leaving. I've come to stay."

As they passed by the dwellings outside the lower enclosure, the villagers stopped whatever they were doing to stare curiously after him. He heard a joyous yell and his name shouted out from the fort above. He recognized Joric's voice before he saw the young man running toward him. Arrius dismounted and braced himself in time to keep from being bowled over by the enthusiastic welcome.

"Arrius, why are you here?"

"I came to serve the High Chieftain of the Selgovi, and I wanted to be with Eugenius, of course. Perhaps your mother may even be willing to see me."

He wasn't aware Ilya was behind him until he heard her soft voice. "I think it's quite possible she will."

He turned and saw her standing a few paces away looking more beautiful than ever. The smile on her face looked promising.

"I bid you welcome, Marcus Arrius."

For the first time since Ilya left Banna, he felt at peace. He considered the possibility it was the first time he ever had.

Glossary of Terms and Place Names

Terms

Ala (ah la; al aye — pl): Wing; refers to Roman cavalry. During the time of Julius Caesar and the Republic, the Roman Army depended on foreign cavalry placing its emphasis more on heavy and light infantry to win battles. Caesar's battle experience in Gaul taught him the importance of cavalry, and gradually the Romans began to place more importance in cavalry capabilities for reconnaissance patrols, skirmishing and flanking maneuvers. By the second and third centuries, the Roman army completely embraced the use of cavalry and had become proficient in its use. The cavalry *alae* were the highest paid in comparison to the infantry units attesting to their increased value.

Auxilia (owks ilia): Auxiliary refers to the non-Roman forces that frequently manned the frontiers.

Ballistae (ball is tray): Catapults of one form or another. The large *ballista* or *onager* (mule) launched stones while the smaller *scorpiones* (scorpions) shot arrow-bolts.

Balteus (bal tay oose): The Roman military belt more than any other item distinguished the legionary. Divestiture of the belt was considered a severe punishment and a disgrace.

Bracae (brack-eye): Leather trousers worn to just below the knee.

Bucellata (boo si lahta): The hard-baked biscuit, much like hardtack, made from ground wheat mixed with water then baked.

Caliga (ae): (cah leg a; cah lee gye): The hobnailed boot-sandal all Roman officers and legionaries wore. They varied in thickness if not in basic design according to the weather and terrain. Somewhat open around the upper foot they were laced to mid-calf or higher, depending on the weather. In winter and cold regions, legionaries wore socks and wrapped their legs in felt or wool cloth for additional warmth. The Emperor Caligula derived his name from the time he was a small boy and spent much of his time around legionary barracks. Because of that, he was given the nickname "Little Boots."

Castigato (cah sti gahto): Corporal punishment as when a centurion would strike a legionary with his vine (vitis) stick.

Century: A unit of 80 men commanded by a centurion; 60 centuries to a legion. The century was divided into ten *contubernia* with eight men assigned to each *contubernium*. Each *contubernium* shared a mule to carry their baggage, a tent in the field, a room or rooms in garrison and was allocated rations as a small unified mess

Centurion: The imperial legion in the second century C.E. had an assigned strength of 5000 legionaries organized in ten cohorts. The first cohort consisted of five centuries with each century having an assigned strength of 160 legionaries. The first cohort with 800 legionaries was nearly double in size to the combined strength of the other nine cohorts. The first cohort was commanded by the *primus pilus* (first file), the senior centurion and fourth in command of a legion. The five centurions of the first cohort were called the *primi ordines* and enjoyed great prestige and privilege; an assignment to the first cohort was coveted and a sign of advancement. The other nine cohorts with a total of 480 legionaries were organized into six 80-man centuries with each also commanded by a centurion. The basic unit of a century was the 8-man *contubernium* in which the legionaries shared a tent, shared rations and represented a close-knit bond considered to be the cohesive backbone of the legion.

The centurions were expected to be at the cutting edge of the battle leading by example and frequently stepping forward to personally engage an enemy in individual combat. For that reason, the casualty rate among centurions was incredibly high; consequently, the prestige and financial incentives were commensurate with the risk. The duties and responsibilities of the primus pilus were considerably greater than that of the other centurions. By tradition the position was held for only one year after which transfer as primus pilus to another legion was possible. Just as likely, it was a significant step to assuming the position of *praefectus castrorum* (third in command of the legion ranking below the senior tribune), promotion to praefectus and independent command below a legion (as in the case of Arrius), or procurator in the civil service. After leaving the position of primus pilus, a centurion would be customarily addressed as *primi pilatus* in recognition of his previous position.

The rank of senior centurion elevated the beneficiary to equestrian status, which equated to the upper middle class in Roman society. The term equestrian was figurative rather than literal and connoted sufficient wealth to be able to afford a horse, an important distinction in a class-oriented society. Once a primus pilus completed his tour, he could be reappointed to the position, be reassigned to another legion in a similar position, leave for duties outside the legion in a civil post or simply retire.

Cornicine (cor nee seens pl): Horn blower.

Cornicularius (corn e cue lahr ius): Senior administrator of a military headquarters.

Decurion (decuriones pl) (day cur e on): An officer commanding a *turma* or cavalry troop.

Denarius, denarii (pl): The largest Roman coinage denomination. It is estimated the legionary foot soldier was paid about 180 denarii a year with the combined infantry and cavalry legionaries earning more. The cavalryman was the highest paid legionary. The centurions were at the top of the army pay-scale and, depending on seniority, earned as much as five times the amount of an ordinary legionary. Legionary pay was withheld to pay for rations, equipment and fodder; therefore, it is impossible to say with any certitude precisely what the legionary had left for discretionary spending, but it is safe to assume it wasn't very much. Withholdings were even made for burial. In the event the legionary died, he would be assured of appropriate ceremonials and offerings in his behalf.

Dolubra(e) (doe loo bra — doe loo bray pl): Combined pick and axe

Ferrata (feh rahta): Legion name meaning Iron.

Fustuarium (foos twar e oom): A harsh sentence reserved for particularly serious offenses such as sleeping on guard or cowardice. The condemned man was set upon with cudgels by members of the individual's own unit, probably his century. The punishment was occasionally administered to an entire unit including a legion when the charge was cowardice. In such cases, lots were drawn and every tenth man was condemned. The term decimated refers to this practice. In most cases, the individual or individuals died from the brutal beating. If an individual somehow managed to survive (probably rare), he was summarily dismissed from the army in disgrace.

Gladius (glah dee oose): The short sword carried by officers and legionaries.

Medicus (medi coose): Medical officer.

Optio (optiones pl): A rank below centurion. The optio carried a knobbed staff and was generally positioned in the rear to prod legionaries who appeared to be ready to break ranks. Most likely they were equivalent to senior sergeants.

Phelorae (fay lor eye): Military decorations worn on the cuirass or on a leather strap across a segmented corselet

Pilum (pee loom), pee la (pl): Although one generally thinks of the short sword, or gladius, as the weapon most characterizing the Roman legionary, it was the heavy javelin that defined the Roman Army even more. Slightly over six feet in length, it had a long pyramidal shaped point that took up almost a third of the total length of the weapon. The Roman Army depended on volleys of pila to deliver a punishing barrage before the front ranks charged. The metal shafts of each pilum were not tempered and bent easily on contact. The latter was an intended consequence and resulted in weighing down the shields of the opposing ranks allowing more lethal opportunity to wield the gladius at short range.

Praetorium (pray tor ium): The commander's quarters in a Roman fort.

Principia (prin sip ee ah): The headquarters building in a Roman fort.

Primi pilatus (pree me pee la toose): Former primus pilus-senior centurion.

Primus pilus (pree moos pee loose): It literally means first file and was the form of address and title of the senior centurion commanding the first cohort (about 800 men) in a Roman Legion. In seniority, the primus pilus ranked only below the legion commander, the six tribunes and the *praefectus castrorum* (see above). The position was prestigious and the apex of a centurion's career.

Pugio (poo gee oh): The dagger each legionary wore on the *balteus* on the opposite side from the *gladius.* Centurions wore the dagger on the right side while the legionary wore his on the left.

Quaestor (kway eh stohr): Quartermaster in charge of stores and supplies for a legion or other military unit.

Sacellum (sahc el loom): The sacred shrine where the legion standards are stored.

Sacramentum (sahc rah men toom): The oath each legionary took to the emperor after recruitment and later during the empire to the legion commander he served to assure personal loyalty

Scutum (skoo toom): Shield (plural — **Scuta**)

Sesterce (ses ter see, sestercii -pl): A coin worth approximately a quarter of a denarius

Testudo (teh stu doh): A tight defensive formation named for the tortoise was used extensively and was formed when the inside ranks placed their shields over their heads while the outside ranks kept their shield facing outward. The formation provided protection from arrows and other missiles from above and the flanks.

Torque (tor kwee): Military decoration worn around the neck

Tribunus Laticlavius (tree bun oos lah tee clah vee oose): Senior tribune in the legion. He wore a cloak with a wide purple strip differentiating himself from the narrow stripe of worn by the junior tribunes. He was second in command to the legion commander.

Valera (way ler ah): Valorous.

Vexillation (vex eel lat shun): A term used to describe a detachment to or from a legion. Typically, the Roman legions lost or received vexillations from other legions according to tactical or strategic requirements. The vexillation concept was more likely to have been exercised at the cohort level to maintain unit cohesion.

Via Principalis (wee ah prin se pahlis): One of the two main streets of a Roman fortress bisecting the *via praetoria*. Near the intersection of these two roads is where the headquarters or principia would be located.

Victrix (wik triks): Legion name meaning Victorius.

Vitis (wee tis): The distinctive twisted vine stick a centurion carried symbolizing his rank. It was also frequently used as an instrument for administering corporal punishment.

Place Names

Banna (Bah na): Birdoswald, England. In Latin, Banna means tongue or spur and refers to the geography of its location at a sharp bend of the River Irthing.

Belgica (Bel ghee ka): Generally modern day Belgium and part of northern Germany.

Blatobulgium: Birrens, Dumfrieshire, Scotland

Britannia (Bree tah nee ah): England, Wales and Scotland.

Bravoniacum (Brah voh nah ki oom): Kirkby Thore, England, approximately 25 miles south of Birdoswald.

Burrium: Usk, Monmouthshire, Wales; the Roman name may mean "Place of the knobs" because of the small hills surrounding the fortress

Camboglanna: Castlesteads, Northumbria

Castra Exploratorum: Netherby, Scotland

Dacia (Datiae or Datia — Da-chee-ia): Extended over what is now the Carpathian-Danube region consisting roughly of Romania, parts of Hungary, Bulgaria, Yugoslavia and Moldavia.

Deva (Dew wah): Chester, England.

Durovernum (Duroh vehr noom): Canterbury, England.

Eboracum (Eh bor ah coom): York, England. The ruins of the headquarters of the former ninth and sixth legions lie under York Minister Cathedral and were discovered in the last century when the cathedral foundations were being repaired. They can be seen today via a self-guided tour of the crypt.

Fanum Cocidii (Fah num ko cee dee): Bewcastle, England, located 7-8 miles northwest of Birdoswald (Banna). The Latin name Shrine of Cocidius probably derives from the local Britannic god Cocidius who was variously associated with the forest and hunters but was also depicted in statues and stone etchings as a warrior. Fanum Cocidii was the only known Roman fortress named after a deity. It is possible Fanum Cocidii was a fortress used by local British tribes before the Romans arrived, and the Romans either adopted the existing name or coined it out of respect for the deity. The worship of Cocidius was widespread in Britannia and bore similarities to the

Roman god Sylvanus. The similarity may have accounted for the Roman inclination to honor and worship the deity.

Gaul: Generally encompassing modern day France including Belgium and Luxembourg.

Parthian Empire: Encompassed the area generally including what is present day Iran and Iraq

Portus Itius (Por tus Ee tee oose): Boulogne, France.

Rutupiae (Rhu too pee-aye): Richborough, England, ten miles or so north of the town of Dover and about five miles south of Ramsgate.

Uxellodunum (Ux el lo doo noom): Stanwix, England, a suburb of Carlisle in northwest England. It is thought this was the probable location for the command headquarters for the entire wall defense. For command and control, this far western location may have been favored over a more central site based on the greater threat posed by the Novantae and Selgovae Tribes populating the west and central sections respectively. Positioning the largest cavalry unit on the wall at this particular location would have provided a rapid response in the event the far northern outposts were attacked. It also makes strategic sense for the Romans to locate a large body of cavalry here as a cavalry *ala* (wing) was traditionally used to screen the flanks of an attacking legion. Should the Romans launch an attack north of the wall, the cavalry wing would likely have been used to screen the western flank.

Bibliography:

Blair, PH. *Roman Britain and Early England 55 B.C. — A.D. 871*, W.W. Norton & Company, New York, London, 1966.

Bowman, A.K. *Life and Letters On the Roman Frontier*, first published by the British Museum Press, London, 1994; subsequently by Routledge in the U.S. and Canada, 1998.

Burke, J. *Roman England*, W.W. Norton & Company, New York, London, 1983.

Caesar, Julius, *The Gallic War*, translated by H. J. Edwards, Loeb Classical Library, Harvard University Press, Cambridge Massachusetts, 2004.

Cowan, R. *Roman Legionary 58 B.C. — A.D.* illustrated by A. McBride, Osprey Publishing, Botley, Oxford, UK, 2003.

Eban, Abba *Heritage, Civilization and the Jews*, Summit Books, Simon & Schuster, New York, 1984.

Goldsworthy, A.K *The Roman Army At War, 100 BC- AD 200*, Oxford University Press, 1996.

Harris, S., *Richborough and Reculver*, English Heritage, London, 2001.

Josephus, *The Jewish War*, translated by G.A. Williamson, with introduction, notes, and appendices by M. Smallwood, Penguin Books, Ltd, London, 1981.

Luttwak, E. N. *The Grand Strategy of the Roman Empire From the First Century A.D to the Third*, The Johns Hopkins University Press, Baltimore and London, 1979.

Renatus, FlaviusVegetius *Roman Military*, translated by John Clarke 1767, Pavillion Press, Inc, Philadelphia, 2004.

Speller, E. *Following Hadrian*, Oxford University Press, Oxford, U.K. 2004

Tacitus, *The Agricola*, translated with an introduction by H. Mattingly (1948) and revised by S. A. Handford (1970), Penguin Books, London England, 1970.

Webster. G. *The Roman Imperial Army, of the First and Second Centuries A.D.*, University of Oklahoma Press, Norman Oklahoma, 1998.

Wilmott, T. *Birdoswald Roman Fort*, English Heritage, London 2005.

Don't Miss the Final Chapter in the Arrius Saga.

Arrius Volume III Enemy of Rome

Coming from Moonshine Cove in early 2019

Read the first chapter beginning on the next page

"Somehow I knew I would see you again, Marcus Arrius but I never thought it would be here," Joric said before asking. "But how can it be when you command the fort at Banna?"

"I am no longer a Roman officer and in command of anything except Ferox here, and I wonder sometimes at that." When Marcus saw Joric was framing another question, he forestalled it by holding up a hand and adding, "There's time enough to say more of this later. He turned to Ilya and was suddenly tongue-tied. He searched for something to say and managed a banal "How are you?" before belatedly adding, "And Eugenius?"

"We are very well, Marcus, and even better now that you've come."

He stood frozen, speechless, staring silently into her eyes, oblivious of the curious throng gathered around them. He wanted to reach out and take her in his arms but was unsure how she would react. A moment later, she decided the matter when she stepped forward and embraced him, clinging tightly to him. Marcus could feel the swell of her breasts pressing against his chest.

"Marcus, it's been too long. Forgive me for what I've done," she said her voice husky with emotion.

"There's nothing to forgive, only a past to forget. What was done and said doesn't belong here. It's only the future that matters now," Marcus said in response, certain he never believed more strongly about anything.

Their reunion was interrupted by Tearlach's surly voice, "Roman, your future here has yet to be decided. It remains for the High Chieftain and the clan chiefs to determine what will become of you."

"You forget, Tearlach, I'm now High Chieftain of the Selgovi, and the clan chiefs will provide advice and counsel only when I seek it."

Marcus was not the only one surprised by the sharply worded comment. Surprisingly, far from showing any hostility at the rebuke, Tearlach looked more pleased than angered. After giving a brief nod in silent acknowledgement, the Selgovan abruptly turned his horse around and rode back toward the gate without so much as a backward glance.

Joric calmly watched Tearlach depart, his face expressionless. Marcus saw the resolute thrust of his jaw and realized there was nothing left of the youth he once knew. Joric had always seemed to him more mature and confident beyond his years, and it was even more evident now. Marcus believed it was mainly circumstance that tested a man's mettle and contributed the most in developing character. He thought Joric's assumption of tribal leadership had surfaced inbred qualities that boded well for the Selgovi.

Marcus took a step back to look at Ilya. If anything, she was more beautiful than ever. Her green eyes were shining and told him more than words she was happy to see him. She was dressed in a simple but elegant shift gathered at the waist that emphasized her lithe and becoming figure. It was apparent she had gained back the weight she had lost as a result of Betto's cruel treatment followed by Eugenius's difficult birth which almost claimed her life. Except for a small braid on either side of her face, her honey-colored hair hung loosely down her back to her waist. The once livid welt across her cheek caused when Betto struck her with his *vitis* was now only a faint white line. He suspected it was a mark she would bear the rest of her life.

Ilya thrust her arm through Marcus's and urged him through the inner gate leading to the upper level of the fort. As they walked along, Ilya spoke happily of the events that had occurred since her and Joric's arrival in the village. Joric led Ferox and the pack horse, interjecting only brief comments while Ilya described the ceremonies elevating Joric to the tribal dais. It was evident from her somewhat and uncharacteristic emotional description, she was both pleased to be back with her tribe and proud her son was its rightful leader.

Interested though he was, Marcus wanted to interrupt to ask of Eugenius but chose instead to let her chatter on until finally she stopped in mid-sentence and said in exclamation, "But I haven't said a word about Eugenius!"

From that point on, she spoke of nothing else. "Marcus, your son is perfect in every way. I'm certain he will have your size, and he will be handsome—that is if he can avoid scars to his face," referring to the prominent scar caused by a Parthian cavalry sword extending from the hairline on the right cheek and down to the chin. He was used to people staring at the wide scar. However terrible as the wound appeared, it was no more than most legionaries wore, seen or unseen, from having engaged in a lifetime of battles and campaigning. Even without the scar, his square-jawed face and the deep lines on either side of a prominent, hooked nose had prompted some to say his face was more intimidating than handsome. In any event, he was satisfied that with his large size and Ilya's height the odds favored Eugenius would be sizable when fully grown. Marcus also hoped for his sake he might bear the more regular and pleasing features of his Selgovan mother than his own Roman heritage.

While Joric tied Ferox to a post outside, Marcus and Ilya entered the low doorway of the large, circular dwelling. Apart from the open door, the only natural light came from four narrow windows and the opening in the thatch roof allowing the smoke to escape from a raised and centrally-located hearth. After his eyes grew accustomed to the gloom after the comparatively bright afternoon sun outside, he saw the room had been rearranged somewhat since Ilya and Athdara had brought him back from the brink of death. The room was now separated into several compartments by cloth screens providing a modicum of privacy for the occupants.

When he began to distinguish form from shadow, he recognized Ulla sitting close to the doorway weaving. Ilya had been forced to rely on the passive, heavy-set Brigantian woman as a wet nurse for Eugenius when she was unable to provide milk for the infant. Ulla paused in her task long enough to look up briefly with disinterest before continuing her work, her fingers a blur as she expertly wove the threads into an intricate design.

Athdara sat in profile on a stool near the fire holding an infant that he presumed was Eugenius. Older than Ilya, Athdara was still striking with aquiline features and high cheekbones not unlike Ilya and typical of Selgovan women in general. Had her hair not been streaked with gray, she would have looked much younger than she was. Her presence was somewhat surprising. Until now, he had not given thought to what may have become of her and Beldorach's other two wives following the tribal leader's death.

From the happy gurgles and toothless smile on Eugenius's face and Athdara's contented expression, it was clear to Marcus she was an accepted feature in the infant's life. Athadara looked in his direction. If she was pleased or displeased to see him, she gave no indication, nor did she make any comment. Silently she stood up and walked toward Marcus holding Eugenius in her outstretched arms. When Marcus took the baby, he saw a look of regret in her eyes that made him realize the infant was a constant reminder of what Beldorach had been unable to give her and why Joric had become the tribal leader of the Selgovi. He supposed she and Ilya had reached some kind of accommodation. During his recuperation when Ilya had come from Banna to nurse him, he recalled the relations between the two women had been strained.

Eugenius was everything Marcus hoped he would be. His eyes were neither blue nor gray but somewhere in between. Fixating on Marcus's nose, the infant's small fingers managed to find their target, and the prominent appendage received a vigorous squeeze that made his eyes water. Laughing at his distress, Ilya took the baby in her arms only to surrender him to Joric who had entered the dwelling. While Ilya and Athdara watched calmly and Marcus did so with concern, Joric tossed the baby into the air several times in quick succession. From Eugenius's pleased reaction, it was evident he was accustomed to such treatment. It pleased Marcus to see the bond developing between the two of them, and he hoped it would continue during their lifetimes.

While Ilya poured cups of wine, Athdara served wooden platters on which she had ladled generous portions of some sort of stew from a pot hanging from an iron tripod positioned over the fire. Marcus didn't realize how hungry he was until he'd tasted the delicious food. For the time being, conversation tapered off as they devoted their attention to the meal. Even Eugenius remained relatively quiet as he suckled greedily at one of Ulla's breasts. As appetites were satisfied, Ilya asked how it was Marcus came to leave Banna, and when he intended to return.

"I've left the Roman Army for good and have no intention of returning to Banna. It's my hope you and Eugenius will come away with me when I leave Britannia."

He saw a cloud come over Ilya's face, and she glanced quickly at Joric. In an instant, he knew if he left Britannia, he would travel alone.

Joric quickly responded by saying, "Marcus Arrius, while I lead the Selgovi, you will have a place with us for as long you wish. Let us have no more talk of departing when I have so much need of both of you here."

"Tell me, Marcus, was it my departure that caused you to decide to leave the army?" Ilya asked with an anxious expression.

"I'll not deny it, but in truth, I think I would have left anyway."

Joric's face registered surprise and he asked, "But why?"

"I think it was Beldorach who finally caused me to think about what I had become, although I realize now, Philos was the first to try when I think back to some of our past conversations." Marcus was still adjusting to the reality his former slave who eventually became his closest friend had died in this very settlement.

"Beldorach?" Ilya questioned.

"When I escorted him to Banna from Eboracum shortly after my arrival in Britannia, we argued about many things, usually over Roman intentions and tribal rights. He accused me of having nothing and said I defended what others own while he had fields and forests to claim. Ilya, I didn't understand him or how right he was until I met you. It's ironic that it was someone Rome considered an enemy who eventually made clear to me what Philos had been saying for years. After you left, I realized there was nothing left for me at Banna. I could no longer carry out orders in which I no longer believed."

"What orders?" Joric asked quickly, seeming to perceive there was more to Marcus's words than professing a desire for a new life and a place to live it.

"Several months ago, I attended a *consilium* convened by General Arvinnius, commander of the Sixth Legion. During the council, Arvinnius outlined Rome's plan to abandon the Wall and move north into Caledonia where a new wall will be constructed. The site for it is considerably farther north than where we are now. In the process, the tribes in the immediate proximity of the Wall are to be completely subjugated or driven farther north. Arvinnius doesn't care if the Selgovi and the other two tribes remain where they are or go north; however, if they remain where they are, they will be subject to the full measure of Roman authority."

"But why is such a thing being done now?" Joric asked without any sign of alarm. "It makes no sense to leave behind something that took so long to build," he added thoughtfully before Marcus could reply.

"Arvinnius never explained why, and there was no reason to ask. It is not the province of Roman officers to question orders. But I suspect it has to do with ambition. General Arvinnius wants advancement, and the new emperor wants to establish his imperial reputation. Antoninus Pius has never served in the Roman Army. It's possible he seeks an easy military victory abroad to obtain it. And the northern tribes, including the Selgovi, continue to threaten *pax Romana*."

"You said an easy military victory. Does the Roman emperor expect the tribes to simply accept Roman occupation without a fight?" Joric asked. "If so he underestimates us. We will defend our lands."

"Then the Selgovi and the other tribes that resist will be annihilated. You will die fighting a war you can't possibly win. The alternative is to submit and avoid death or slavery."

"We have no choice but to fight!" Joric retorted without any bluster. "Do you think so little of our fighting abilities we will be defeated so easily?"

"You forget, Joric, I've fought for Rome for over thirty years in five different legions. I've fought both the Novanti and Selgovi. Believe what I say. You have no chance against the most disciplined army in the world. Even if the tribes were to join together and numbered many more times than I believe they do, you still can't win. In the end, you will be fortunate merely to survive."

Until then Ilya had remained silent. Now she spoke dispassionately. "I've no doubt everything you say concerning the might of the legions is true; however, you misunderstand what Joric is saying. Our situation has little to do with pointless resolve and everything to do with practical necessity. The Selgovi simply have nowhere else to go. We either fight, or we make peace with Rome."

"Will the Selgovan clans consider an overture of peace? If so, I'll return to Banna and intercede on the tribe's behalf."

When Joric responded, his comments impressed Marcus by being devoid of the false bravado he might have expected from a young and inexperienced leader.

"There may be one or two clan chiefs who might consider a truce, but the rest will not. The clan chiefs think and act as warriors first, each concerned more with his clan than with the tribe in general. Talk of peace before fighting first would be interpreted as a sign of weakness."

"Why can't you go north?" Marcus asked logically.

"The northern tribes would prevent us from entering their territory," Ilya said. "The Epidii and Venicones have reason to hate us possibly more than the Romans. They stay in their hills, and we have always remained in the lowlands. It has always been so. There are many more tribes farther north than the Epidii and Venicones that we've never seen. The

Caledonian tribes can be depended on to resist any encroachment from the south, tribal or Roman."

Marcus was fast becoming exasperated at Joric and Ilya's fatalistic acceptance of what to him was an untenable position. "Seventy years ago the tribes united against the Roman general, Agricola. Is it not possible to do so again?"

"I recall my father telling of this," Ilya commented. "Bathar was there and saw how badly the tribes were defeated even though they outnumbered the Romans by many times. The defeat had as much to do with tribal rivalry and failure to cooperate as it did with Roman fighting ability. I've no doubt the memory of that defeat still lives on as do the reasons for it."

"Then would it not be plain enough in the recollection of such a defeat to consider peace with Rome?"

"Marcus, you still have much to learn about us. We are a proud people and will not submit without attempting to defend what is our right to hold."

Marcus could think of nothing more to say, and a gloomy silence prevailed until Joric asked, "How much time do we have before the Romans begin their advance?"

"Preparations for the invasion began weeks ago. While no exact date has been set, I should think you have perhaps sixty days when the weather is better. The *auxilia* forces now positioned on the wall are ready now, but it will take time for the Sixth and Twentieth Legions to move forward from Eboracum and Deva. The legions will not be in the initial wave. The auxilia legionaries now stationed on the wall will be in the lead with the legions following close behind."

"Then it is likely your Tungrian and Dacian legionaries will be the first to fight us?" Ilya said, less a question than a statement of fact. "It's difficult to imagine Decrius and Rufus would fight us."

Marcus nodded and responded with a bleak expression, "Yes, it's true. They will do what they have to. Decrius must serve his twenty-five years to become a Roman citizen, and the only home and life Rufus knows is that of a Roman legionary."

"Were you involved in the planning?" Ilya asked. Marcus could only nod his head in grim silence. "And you were allowed to leave Banna to come here knowing you might likely reveal their plans?"

"I left at night in secret, and only a few I trusted knew where I was going. General Arvinnius will eventually learn of it."

"If he should learn of it sooner, will he advance the date of the attack?" Once again Marcus was impressed with Joric's logical question.

"It's possible; however, it will still require time for the legions to complete their preparations for the campaign. Arvinnius will not move until he's ready. Surprise is less important to the Roman Army than being prepared. He also knows as well as I do, if the tribes had advance warning and another year to get ready, the outcome will still be the same. If the tribes resist, it will be like Judaea, and northern Britannia will be destroyed. Rome cannot afford to be defeated. Arvinnius plans for and expects only success. It will not end any other way."

"It seems you've made a poor bargain by coming here," Ilya said without any hint of bitterness.

"I had no choice. Whatever happens, the gods have decided for me, and for once I do not question their wisdom as I once did."

"Well, whatever happens, I'm glad you're here," Ilya said.

"And I say the same Marcus Arrius," Joric added. "Do not give up on us yet. We may yet find a way out of this dilemma, but I think the solution is not here with us tonight."

Marcus did not realize until Joric spoke how late the hour had grown. He had also failed to notice that Athdara and Ulla had disappeared during the discussion, taking Eugenius with them. Joric stood up and announced, "There is much to think about, and I've found I do my best thinking alone and on the back of a horse. I'll return when *Vindonnus* conquers the night sky," referring to the Selgovan sun god. His intent to leave Ilya and Marcus alone was transparent.

After Joric disappeared into the night, Marcus was grateful for his tactful declaration while filled with doubt concerning what to do now he was alone with Ilya. Their estrangement since Eugenius's birth made him feel awkward. He was afraid to say or do anything that would make things worse than they were already. Even dead, Betto remained a barrier between them. Ilya sat quietly staring into the fire, and Marcus knew her thoughts were similar to his. After a few moments passed, she looked at him and spoke.

"I know our separation has been as difficult for you as it has for me. I've tried to forget what happened to me, and I fear I never will. But I've also decided if I can remember something so horrible, I should be able to call to mind our time together with equal clarity. I think that will be much easier to do now that you've come here if you will only be patient with me."

"Ilya, I want you and Eugenius to leave here with me."

"Leave? But where would we go?"

"Anywhere you want as long as it's away from here. Perhaps to the far south where there is no threat of war."

"Marcus, I can't leave here. Joric needs me, and this is my home."

Her response was not unexpected. Marcus nodded his acceptance and saw the relief on her face as she stood up and came toward him. For a moment, they stood slightly apart gazing wordlessly at each other as if waiting for the other to say or do something to overcome their hesitation. Finally with a sigh, she stepped into his arms and embraced him, holding him tightly. He breathed the scent of her hair and felt her warm breath on his neck, but the closeness of her did not arouse him as it once had. It was still too soon for her. Marcus thought it was also true for him as well. They did not make love that night or many nights thereafter. For the time being, they were content simply to be together again.

CPSIA information can be obtained
at www.ICGtesting.com
Printed in the USA
BVHW031454180819
556130BV00004B/359/P